To the Morenos,

Thanks for being super cool from day one. I am glad to know both of you and thanks for supporting my 1st novel.

Your Friend & Librarian,

Through You

Jaime Perez

AuthorHouse™
1663 Liberty Drive
Bloomington, IN 47403
www.authorhouse.com
Phone: 1-800-839-8640

© 2011 Jaime Perez. All rights reserved.

No part of this book may be reproduced, stored in a retrieval system, or
transmitted by any means without the written permission of the author.

First published by AuthorHouse 10/12/2011

ISBN: 978-1-4634-6793-7 (e)
ISBN: 978-1-4634-6794-4 (hc)
ISBN: 978-1-4634-6795-1 (sc)

Library of Congress Control Number: 2011915366

Printed in the United States of America

Any people depicted in stock imagery provided by Thinkstock are models,
and such images are being used for illustrative purposes only.
Certain stock imagery © Thinkstock.

This book is printed on acid-free paper.

Because of the dynamic nature of the Internet, any web addresses or links contained in
this book may have changed since publication and may no longer be valid. The views
expressed in this work are solely those of the author and do not necessarily reflect the
views of the publisher, and the publisher hereby disclaims any responsibility for them.

Thanks Mom and Dad.
This was all possible
Through You.

Chapter 1

"Breathe! Come on Baby breathe! Stay with me!"

I honestly didn't know what I was doing, or if I was making any significant difference. I don't recall ever trying so hard at anything and simultaneously feeling so useless and ineffectual. Sweat was dripping from my face and onto my wife's belly profusely. What more could I really do? The doctors and nurses seemed calm and unworried, but I was pretty sure they were mentally trained to maintain such impartiality. Either this, or their countless previous experiences with misfortune had rendered them numb to other's pain and suffering.

Regardless, they weren't the ones holding my wife's hand and noticing her progressively weakening grip. I felt that her grip would strengthen only whenever mine did. If I loosened my grip, she would loosen hers. I didn't exactly know if this was a particularly good sign or a bad one. This scared me. After all, I was only 20 years old, and she was 17. In seven days she would turn 18. Neither of us had ever been through anything as traumatic as this. I was actually naïve and ignorant enough to think that we were both too young to die, or shall I rephrase this to state that "she" was too young to die. After all, I was just an onlooker offering futile guidance to the woman I love.

"Does everything look alright Doc?" I asked partially optimistically.

I must have been speaking to myself, or maybe my voice wasn't projecting beyond my wife's screams of anguish. Whatever the reason, I wasn't sinking in to any of them. All I could think of was that they were ignoring my constant, permeating questions because they were prolonging having to give me any discouraging news. At this point, I not only felt unhelpful but trivial as well--almost invisible.

This time I screamed to the point that tears came out of my exhausted,

1

red eyes. "God damn it. I asked is everything all right Doctor?! Can anyone hear me?!"

Although I was not given a satisfying verbal response, at least I was being acknowledged. One of the nurses got up and took me outside to a dark, long hallway that seemed to have no end. The combination of my moistened skin and the ungodly cold temperature in the hospital gave me the chills. Or maybe my chills were induced by the potentially sour news I was afraid and unwilling to receive.

She sat me in a chair and explained, "Mr. Perez, the current situation was a little challenging, but…"

"What do you mean 'was' challenging?" I rudely interrupted. "Why are you speaking in past tense? Is she going to die?"

The word 'die' seemed to echo throughout the empty, dark and long hallway. Before the echoes seemed to subside, the nurse who failed to comfort me or give me any responses to my questions was ordered back in to my wife's room. This time I decided to stay in the hallway, alone with no one to ignore my concerns or my pains.

I sat in the hospital hallway in Lawton, Oklahoma with my face in my wet and wrinkled hands. The saturation was attributed to a mixture of my tears and my wife's perspiring palms from when I was clutching her seemingly lifeless hands. I began to take comfort in the empty, dark and long hallway that was currently embracing me. For a moment, I mentally interpreted my surroundings to be a premonition of what my life was soon to become without my wife…empty, dark and long, just like this hall.

Although getting sleep was the last thing on my weighted mind, this is exactly what happened; I fell asleep. The combination of inanition and sleep deprivation was too much for me to endure. I realized after reflecting on the day's events that I had not eaten or slept for over a day and a half. While I was asleep, I had a pleasant dream—unlike the unpleasant day I was currently having.

I dreamt that I was at home celebrating my birthday with all my neighborhood friends and my mom. I was at the head at the table about to blow out 8 flaming candles. Everybody was asking me to make a wish, but I was purposely stalling. I wasn't ready to blow out my candles just yet. I looked around the dining room at all the smiling faces staring at me. I couldn't genuinely return the gesture to all those around me because my dad was not present. I wanted him there to share this special moment with me. All I could think about was his absence. I kept asking myself, "Why isn't Daddy here?" I was being selfish, and I realized that I couldn't keep delaying the inevitable.

"O.K., O.K. Here I go." I said in hidden disappointment.

The second that I closed my eyes to make my wish, all my friends cheered me on in relief. My wish took about 10 seconds to make and one second to come true. Upon opening my eyes, my dad walks in the house with the most impressive-looking bicycle I have ever seen. Its glossy chrome was near blinding, and I could actually see my partial reflection on the shined tires as if I were looking into a black mirror. I wasn't aware at the time that my dad's absence was attributed to his having to pick up my bicycle at the local Montgomery Ward.

At the same time that my father opens the door and enters with my bicycle in my dream, the doctor opens the door to my wife's room and calls me to join them. It was as if my dream and my life were momentarily in synch. At exactly 3:23 AM on August 22, 1968, I wiped the sleep from my half-opened eyes and slowly stumbled towards room 221. As I approach the room, my hearing appears to be muffled, as if my ears are covered with fluffy pillows. Suddenly, my hearing appears to resume to normal as I hear the delicate and sweet sound of a baby weeping. My wife's beautiful and breath-taking smile is second only to the miracle she is carefully holding in her arms.

"It's a boy Mr. Perez. You and your wife Veronica are the new parents of a 2 and ½ lb. baby boy!" Doctor Hamilton uttered as he and the nurses removed their blood-soaked gloves.

I felt paralyzed by surprise and elation, yet at the same time I was concerned for my premature son. Before the delivery of my son, I had never seen a baby small enough to fit in a shoebox. I couldn't move and everything seemed surreal and blurry. I precariously attempt to walk towards my wife's bed to hold my precious little boy, but I never get there. I suddenly see a blackness embrace me, then nothing. That's the last that I remember of that particular moment.

Before my blackout, I remembered seeing my wife on her hospital bed. Now I too was on a hospital bed, minus the faded, green scrubs and the concerned doctors and nurses. My vehement vertigo was making it relatively difficult to make sense of anything. I could hear whispering voices outside the doors of my room as if secrets were being kept from me. I couldn't recognize to whom any of the voices belonged, but I could hear someone say, "I think we should wake them up and tell them."

Them? I turned to my left to surprisingly see my wife lying on the very

Jaime Perez

same bed I remembered her in before my momentary lapse of consciousness. I got up to see how she was doing. She was half asleep and half awake, but she looked much more alive than what I remembered from a few moments before. Her normal color was back, and her smile was genuine and comforting.

"I was beginning to wonder if it was you or me who gave birth," said my wife with a subtle chuckle.

"Why do you say that?"

"The minute you saw me holding our son, you collapsed and hit your head pretty hard on the metal bed frame. You have been out cold ever since." My wife giggled slightly as if to subliminally insinuate that I was taking this experience harder than she was. This was comforting to me. Knowing that my wife was slowly returning to normalcy made me warm inside. I couldn't care less about my current state, even though my head was pounding, my empty stomach was growling, and my natural predilection to have answers was not being fulfilled, it didn't matter—as long as V was all right. I was lacking vim and felt enervated from the previous wearying hours.

"That explains my pounding headache then. How are you feeling?"

"Much better than before you fainted." She grabbed my hand and caressed my face as if to telepathically assure me that everything was going to be fine. This moment of sweet, satisfying solace didn't last long enough. Dr. Hamilton walks in our room with a troubled countenance. I was afraid to ask him if anything was wrong, so I didn't. Actually, I didn't have to ask the doctor anything; he empathetically and willingly began to explain what was happening.

As he was speaking, I began to think of all the things that could possibly explain Dr. Hamilton's troubled look. Did our baby not make it? Aside from being born premature, was our baby not normal? Is our baby sick? A thousand questions were springing in my head, and this added to my already pounding headache. I could see Dr. Hamilton's mouth moving, but my thoughts muted his voice and disallowed me from hearing anything he was saying. It wasn't until my wife vehemently grabbed me by the forearm that I returned to my usually acute senses.

"What's going on? I didn't quite hear what you were saying Doc. Sorry." I asked apologetically.

Dr. Hamilton cleared his throat and resumed to speak slowly and clearly so as to insure I would not have to ask him to repeat this again. "We have a complication to confront concerning your son."

"What kind of complication?" I asked with a troubled tone.

V had apparently heard the doctor the first time because she was already in tears. Hearing it for a second made her sobs increase, and her tears seemed to double in number as if I could actually count her flowing droplets of anguish.

"Your son's heart is not completely formed. He has a small hole the size of a BB. He has what we call a congenital heart disease. This is not uncommon in 'preemies'."

The doctor resumes by showing my wife and me x-rays of our son's heart. I didn't care to look. As a matter of fact, I ripped the x-ray photographs off the illuminated section of the wall before he could explain any further and assured the doctor that my wife and me know what a hole looks like.

Although I was hesitant to know the answer, I asked without hesitation and with controlled anger, "So what exactly does this mean? Are we losing our son before we can even get him home?"

"We need to keep him here to continue to monitor the situation Mr. Perez. Taking him home is not the best thing for anybody right now. In addition, hospital policy does not allow us to release premature babies until they reach 5 lbs. It may be several months before you can take him with you."

"Several months?" I asked, thinking that this was some overly inflated and cruel protocol.

"Can my husband see him for the time being?" V asked in a soft yet quivery voice. I had already forgotten that she had already seen the baby upon delivery, before I fainted and collapsed.

"Of course you can, but we have to take you to his room on another floor. I will take you there."

The doctor waited a while until V and me seemed calm and composed. He could obviously see that we were both in shambles from all that we had been through in such a short period of time. Although I know my wife and I were eager to see and hold our son, we both remained stationary and pensive. We held each other's hand for a moment. For that moment, I felt the same way I had when V and me held hands for the first time. Even though moments like this are not usually likely to arouse thoughts of music, my love for V and my passion for music compelled me to think of our favorite song, "You're too Good to Be True" by Franki Valli. Music was how I would often cope with existence and maintain my sanity through the tribulations and challenges that life would throw at me. Nothing had changed. I was still crazy about her, and I could somehow feel that she was

5

Jaime Perez

equally crazy about me. It was time to shut off my mind's music and face reality. It was time to go see our son.

Although the life-changing ordeal in the hospital lasted roughly 3 hours, it seemed to have dragged on for 3 months. Ironically enough, it was 3 months before that I received the news that would eventually change my life more than I could ever imagine. My number had been picked; it was time to become something I had no desire to become.

Chapter 2

Because we were at the Ft. Sill Army Base in Oklahoma and far away from home, V and I didn't have the typical, joyful family and friend visitations that most couples have after the birth of their firstborn. We were a young couple of high school sweethearts displaced on the army base we were forced to inhabit.

A few months after I graduated from high school in 1968 in Pharr, Texas, V and I had decided to get married. V had not yet finished high school, but we were excited about getting married and spending the rest of our lives together; so we did just that. It undoubtedly felt like the right thing to do, and to this day, I have no regrets about how we handled things. Approximately 7 months after our wedding, we had our first child—an army baby. That's what we would refer to babies who were born on army bases—army babies. Four months into our marriage, I received that dreadful letter in the mail—the letter to notify me of my being drafted to fight for my country and serve in the Vietnam War. I remember not being able to open the envelope that contained my notice of service. If it weren't for my trembling hands that eventually tore the envelope, I would have likely held it several more hours. I knew what this meant; I just didn't want to accept my forcibly-bestowed, patriotic fate. I was only 18 years old, fresh out of high school and still a kid, but that would change soon enough. I spent two physically abusive months in basic training in El Paso, Texas at Fort Bliss. I often wondered if the committee or individuals responsible for naming Fort Bliss had a perverse sense of humor because Fort Bliss was everything but blissful. After basic training, I was given notice that I was to go to Fort Sill to begin boot camp. My pregnant wife, my unborn child and I were on our way to unfamiliar Oklahoma.

I, along with many others, had no idea what our country was doing in Vietnam to begin with. Vigilant, violent protests were common in all parts

7

Jaime Perez

of the country. As a matter of fact, many of the soldiers in my company at the Ft. Sill Army Base were against the war but couldn't do much about it. Many of us were forced to take our lives and mold them into the exploitable human chess pieces the United States government wanted us to be. Most of us were useless and blind pawns, and even though they tried to instill a sense of value and merit, we knew we were as replaceable as a burned out light bulb.

I had the option to reside in the barracks with my platoon or to remain with my wife in an off-base duplex we were renting in Lawton, Oklahoma. I naturally chose to stay with my wife at our duplex before the pregnancy as well as after she was released from the hospital. During her time at the hospital, I wasn't too certain if staying alone was a good idea. I wasn't getting any quality sleep, there was a lot on my mind concerning my son's condition, and I wasn't looking forward to leaving my newborn son and my wife alone while I was off to war. To help my uneasiness, I would hang out in the barracks with the other soldiers in my platoon in hopes of getting to know them better and with intentions of establishing some semblance of normalcy. I thought if I got to talk to some of these guys, maybe I could learn a few things or at least take my mind off of the persistent vexations that were present with my every breath. Although I had no desire to be a soldier and fight desultorily, it often brought an unexpected yet much-needed pleasure to get to chit chat with the men who may very well save my life in the weeks to come.

Our barracks had approximately 30 men, and it was safe to say that the majority of those 30 men were not looking forward to our blood-saturated futures. Luckily for me and for a few others who were not combat material in my platoon, there were a few born-to-be soldiers among us. Guys like Private First Class Ivan Capelletti were constantly foaming at the mouth in anticipation when they found out they were going to get the pleasure and privilege to legally take someone's life. Capelletti was an Italian-American from New York. To me, he looked Italian, but sounded totally American. He used to brag about how good he was with a gun, and how he rarely missed any of his targets.

"I can shoot anything, anywhere, anytime. My weapon is an extension of my body, and I can use it with unparalleled precision. The only times I miss are when I want to. Don't force me to prove it, or you'll end up going home in a body bag before we even leave for battle." Capelletti bragged.

I honestly didn't think that Capelletti was as good of a shot as he said he was, but as inquisitive as I am, I wasn't moronic enough to ask him to prove it to me. He looked too young to have any significant experience with a firearm of any type. He also seemed like the kind of alpha-male that wanted respect and attention at all costs, even if it meant having to dishonestly brag about himself to achieve his much-needed accolades. I initially feared Capelleti because he seemed so gung-ho and blood hungry, but ironically it was this particular type of soldier-monster that you wanted on your side and not your enemies. Regardless, I never turned my back to him, even when asleep. I don't think anyone ever did.

Morales was another zealous warmonger. Aside from both being Private First Class, he and Capelletti were so much alike, but so very different as well. They were simultaneously homogenous and dichotomous in character. As a matter of fact, Morales and Capelletti were the only Private First Classes in our platoon. Unlike Capelletti, Morales was the kind of man who liked to speak with his actions and not so much with his mouth. Jonas was Morales' first name, but no one called him that because it was also his father's name, and he loathed his father beyond imagination. Whenever Morales was asked about his old man, he would start to sweat, the veins on his baldhead would surface, and his nostrils would flare. Ironically, he would never answer anyone's pervasive questions about his father; it seemed that his revealing physical reactions were enough to suffice anyone who had the nerve to ask.

Morales would say, "Because we are doing our country a favor by sacrificing our lives as soldiers, or martyrs as I would put it, in a questionable war, we should be allowed to kill one person of our choice who we utterly detest before we go overseas. This way, we can get used to how it feels to kill a person and therefore killing the enemy wouldn't be so traumatic. That seems like the logical thing to do."

Morales always had an interesting yet idiosyncratic way of seeing things. Sometimes, as outrageous as his rants often were, I was able to find some semblance of justification and sense in what he would say. Although no one in our group ever dared to ask Morales who he would like to deprive of life, we all had a feeling who his choice would be. Whenever he wasn't angry, he was rather reserved and pensive. By looking at his face, you could easily discern that there was a lot going on in his mind. I felt comfortable with Morales, partly because I knew he had a good heart underneath all that exasperation and partly because we were the only Mexican-Americans in our troop.

I suppose I was much better off than Joseph Smith. He was the only Black in our barracks, and he always appeared to be watching his back.

Jaime Perez

You can't blame him. His grandparents and parents had all been beaten and/or lynched at one time or another. I had to often remind him that Mexican-Americans had nothing to do with these atrocities, and he would smile and say, "That's right. You and Morales are Brownies. It's the Whities I have to watch. Watch my back Perez, and I'll watch yours." He said with a loud laugh that seemed to resonate deeply throughout Ft. Sill. Smith would refer to Morales and I as Brownies because of our ethnicity. I could tell he didn't mean it in a condescending way because Smith just wasn't that kind of guy. Besides, being called Brownie is nothing compared to the spiteful names he was often called simply for being of a color darker than most; hence, his indignation was warranted. His past was difficult for him to erase, and he was the most vocal in our troop about expressing his anti-war sentiments.

"Personally, I think all Blacks should be exempt from serving in any war because that's all we've been doing since we were dragged to this country—serving. This war is bullshit, and everything about this war reeks of bullshit. You want to hear what I think Perez?" Smith asked.

"I think I already know what you think. Actually, I know that I know what you think Smith. You just told us for about the 400th time." I assured him.

If you were to close your eyes long enough, you could easily forget that Nicholas "Nick" Brown was in the same room as you. He was the mute of our group. He wasn't medically mute, but his laconic personality led us to believe that he might be the type of man to explode at any given minute. He seemed introverted, scared, and disturbed. Because he rarely spoke, we didn't know much about him. We just knew that he was a white boy from Arkansas, and my guess was that he was a serial killer back home. His strange silence was eerie and goose-bump inducing. I didn't see him as a protrusive and conspicuous serial killer, like say Charles Manson with his crazed, guilt-admitting eyes. Nick seemed more of a clandestine and somber serial killer, not the ostentatious, showy type. This was a more dangerous type of killer. Nick was such a human conundrum that we never teased him, not even the valiant Capelletti would give him any shit. Hell, he might wake up one day and kill us all in our sleep. In all honesty, Nick was probably a good guy. His appearance and personality were misinterpreted deterrents. It was just harmless yet unfair personal entertainment to draw these conclusions about our mate because it helped us pass the time.

Second on my list of "people to watch with both eyes" behind the

Through You

testosterone-superfluous Capelletti was Jerry Wilson. I have no idea how he was selected to serve his country. I personally felt the interview process was scrupulous and invasive, but he must have had secret connections with someone in the military and used these connections to somehow allow him to be a soldier. Aside from his looking ecstatically forward to being part of the war, he had a somewhat psychotic personality and an insane look about him. He always had this overly eager facial expression, similar to a child who is impatiently dying to open his Christmas presents on Christmas morning. Also, he would often mix topics of conversation when speaking, and these topics would have nothing to do with each other; this didn't exactly do his already dubious persona any justice. The fact that he liked to sleep completely naked in the company of several strangers didn't make us feel particularly comfortable either. He must have stayed completely silent during his enlisting interview because his schizophrenic, multiple personalities would have easily made their way out of his unofficially disturbed mind. Although come to think of it, maybe the Army preferred disturbed minds that did as they were told without any dissidence. I don't mean to malign Wilson; he wasn't a bad guy. I just think he was too uncomfortably uncanny for all of us. He was definitely the kind of boy that only a mother could love. Oh, I forgot to mention, he was the biggest liar any of us had ever known or will ever know. Everything he said was inflated beyond capacity. If we were balloons, we would have all burst from his hot air. He made car salesmen seem as honest as nuns.

"Back home in Indiana, I have 4 sweeties waiting for me when I get back from 'Nam. Gentlemen, they are the most beautiful specimens you have ever laid your eyes on. We are talking the magazine cover type. Women so perfect, you would have thought you died and went to heaven. Two of them are former Ms. Indianas." Wilson bragged.

"Let me guess. Are the other two former Mr. Indianas?" Capelletti interjected.

"Not that I know of? Wait, are you trying to insult me or question my manhood Capelletti?" Wilson ingenuously asked.

"No Wilson, you do that yourself just fine. Hey Wilson, tell Perez here to whom you are related."

"Have you ever heard of The Beach Boys, Perez? You know, the singing group that has more top 40 hits than The Beatles and Elvis combined?" Wilson rhetorically asked with pure excitement.

Morales spilled and choked on the chilled water he was attempting to drink. What he heard, Wilson's blatant inaccuracy about The Beach

Jaime Perez

Boys having more hit songs than both The Beatles and Elvis combined, made it difficult for Morales to swallow both the water as well as Wilson's comment.

"Yes, I have heard of The Beach Boys. Who hasn't? Let me guess, they are somehow and unfortunately related to you!?!" I teased and went along with his fantasy.

"Yes Sirree! Three of them are my older brothers, Dennis, Carl and Bryan. They used to sing me to sleep when I was younger. It was actually me that convinced them to form a group and sing professionally. Many of my close friends back home actually think that I sound a lot like them. Want me to show you?" Wilson said as he began clearing his throat to display his inherited gift.

"No!!!" We all screamed and pleaded in unison.

"You are going to lead us all into an episode of mass suicide Wilson. If you start singing, I will kill us all, beginning with you. And don't forget, I don't miss." Capelletti joked with a convincing and determined facial expression. At least, I hope he was joking. Something tells me he was, or maybe I was just trying to attest the hard-sought humanity in Capelletti's often inhumane soul.

Wilson kindly insisted. "No really. I don't sing that badly. My brothers would often…"

"O.K. cut the crap!!!!" Morales intervened and exclaimed with a bit of anger, probably due to his choking on his water. "You are not related to three of The Beach Boys, and they probably are not even from Indiana. There is no way they have more top 40 hits than The Beatles and Elvis combined, and you do not have two former Ms. Indianas waiting for you back home. The only part I believe about your delusional, made-up story was Capelletti's contribution—the two former Mr. Indianas who are waiting for you back home. I think I can speak for just about everyone here when I say that we don't want to hear your bullshit stories or your singing. I'm beginning to think that the worst part of this war is your being here with us."

Wilson responded with partially teary and irritated eyes. "I don't need you to believe me for any of this to be true."

"And you also don't need to say it for it to come true, so keep your mouth shut, or I, we, will gladly add another hole in your face—one that doesn't speak." Capelletti expressed with frustration.

"Hey Morales." Capelletti whispered. "Aren't The Beach Boys from the West Coast, like California or somewhere out there?"

"I really don't know, but I know I don't care." Morales answered. "You know what? If The Beach Boys are from California, which I think they are, how can Wilson be from Indiana and his brothers from California?"

"Tell me Morales, wouldn't you abandon your brother in another state if you had a brother like Wilson? I am pretty sure I would leave his ass without hesitation. Regardless, this boy is crazy or full of shit. I lean towards full of shit." Capelletti deduced and explained in a soft voice to Morales who was getting ready for bed in the cot next to Capelletti.

For a moment, everybody was quiet. At times, I felt like we would end up killing each other before being unwillingly and inevitably displaced to the dank lands of Vietnam. Somehow, we miraculously managed to contain the quarrels before they became uncontrollably violent. This was probably one of the few remaining elements of humanity that we still possessed—the ability to refrain from killing each other. Aside from this, we were repressed animals. Some of us were pissed off, some of us excited. Together, we were just men waiting for our inevitable orders to become monstrosities.

In regards to Wilson, he was definitely an aberration from the norm, but then again, in a time of war, what is the norm? In retrospect, we were all slowly and insidiously becoming aberrations from the ordinary. In a time when killing people from other countries who rightfully disagree with you is encouraged, I don't think I really care to know what normal is right now, or maybe I was just reluctant to accept a normalcy with which I couldn't find peace.

There were others in the barracks, like Sergeant Mills who had his own sleeping room and some others whose names I didn't know, but they mostly kept to themselves or formed mini-cliques within our platoon. Many of the others rarely spoke to us, but their silence was not out of conceit or vanity; it was because most of the other guys were always busy writing or getting rest from the tedious days we all shared. I began to feel a little selfish for not writing to Mom and Pop back home. I had V here in Oklahoma with me and could talk to her about my day anytime, but Mom and Pop were probably at home wondering if I was even still alive. As I lay on my bed that very night trying to get some sleep, I realized the next morning at 0430 hours that I had cried myself to unconsciousness. It was nothing new for any of us to be subjected to have to listen to dilapidated soldiers praying or crying themselves to sleep as the rest of us tried to achieve momentary yet welcomed moments of lost consciousness because it happened every night, but I somehow felt uncomfortable about having the men in my platoon

Jaime Perez

hear me cry. I guess realizing that I had not written one damn letter to my parents since I had arrived at Ft. Sill several weeks ago made me feel morose, inconsiderate and cold hearted. I hoped that I was not becoming a robotic soldier with a bloodless heart of metal who hadn't a care in the world. I want to remain human; I want to be vulnerable; I want to care; I want to feel, and most importantly, I want to be me.

Chapter 3

That very same night, I wrote my first letter to Mom and Pop, and I wrote at least two per week in hopes of making up for my thoughtlessness. I apologized to them for not keeping them informed, and I sent them pictures of V, Gilbert and I. I had brought a Polaroid Camera with me to capture my experiences, but I had not really put it to good use. Now I had good reason to take pictures. It was killing my parents to be unable to physically see their grandson, but I assured them that V and Gilbert would be going home as soon as I was given my assignment overseas. I would tell Mom and Pop about my new soldier-brothers and about all the excessive crap they put us through just to get ready for a war. Of course, I wouldn't mention anything that would heighten their already instinctive anxiety. Ironically, this was probably the only time I didn't feel improper about being dishonest. They asked about my daily routine, so I wrote them a considerately condensed tolerable version of life at Ft. Sill. I didn't tell them everything because this would have likely induced fatal strokes on both my parents.

Boot camp at Ft. Sill was degrading and emasculating. We were sent here for OJT, or on-the-job-training. It seemed more like on-the-job-degrading (OJD). Listening to Sergeant Mills and Captain Benson incessantly and unnecessarily bawl out at us wasn't exactly how I intended to spend my first year out of high school. Every morning was the same thing, get up by 0430 hrs, eat breakfast at 0445 hrs, and begin the day at 0500. On the first day alone at boot camp, I had been screamed at and humiliated more than I had ever been in the 18 years leading up to this day, and that's because I was doing exactly as I was told. No one was exempt from the barrage of belittling bellows, so we just tolerated it because we knew things could be far worse than the uttering of a few words that could be ignored and shut out with a little practice.

15

Jaime Perez

The last thing I wanted was to be put in the dreadful stockades. This was where disobedient and insubordinate soldiers were placed for several hours, sometimes even for days depending on the severity of the violation. It was similar to solitary confinement in the public prison system, except worse because the laws of the outside world didn't apply to us. The stockades were the antithesis of heaven; it was safe to say that the stockades were the closest to hell that many of us at Ft. Sill had ever been. You had to pass by the stockades in order to get to the cafeteria from our barracks. If we didn't obstruct our nasal passage, we would, without fail, lose our appetite for the time being, and it was virtually impossible to complete our physical training on an empty stomach. The first day, before I knew anything of the stockades, I, as well as a few others, spewed our previous meals due to the suffocating and nauseating stench. If I would attempt to describe the malodor that hovered stealthily by the entry of the stockades, I would best describe it as a combination of urine, feces, fresh blood and vomit—this concoction of putrescence, without a doubt, was contributed by those unfortunate and recalcitrant enough to be confined within the stockade walls. The unwholesome stench was so foul that some of us could swear that we could actually see it, a visible stink. No one was brazen enough to clean the filthy stockades, and it was an ostensible fact that they had never been cleaned-NEVER. The penetrating stink was notoriously known for saturating one's clothes; if I were more religious, I would perhaps even admit that it had the potential to saturate one's defenseless soul.

Our days would start off with an inhuman amount of running and calisthenics. Capelletti would often say to me through heavy respiration during our jogs, "I am not planning on outrunning these Vietnamese bastards; I plan to kill them with my unmatched marksmanship. This exercising crap is a waste of my time. Don't you agree Perez?"

I rarely ever responded to Capelletti's questions. They seemed more rhetorical in nature, and Capelletti came off as a kind of self-proclaimed omniscient being who never asked a question for need of an answer.

Every once in a while the guys would utter an unexpected but justifiable wise crack that would somehow make me laugh throughout our "torture sessions". One time Morales sarcastically asked Sergeant Mills, "Hey Sarge, are we training for battle or for the fucking Olympic Games?"

I don't know if I laughed because his comment was humorous or if I was laughing from having lost my mind from trying to complete these muscle-numbing cruelties that we did each and every day. Everyone who laughed, which was practically all of us, was ordered to do an extra 5 miles for being, as Mills put it, "pansy smart asses who would not last one night in Vietnam without shitting our pants". Although Morales increased our pain by 5 miles, I actually needed a good laugh. I even thanked him for his comment, and he looked at me with a bewildered look, obviously attempting to calculate whether or not my comment was honest or sarcastic. Between finding out that my son was suffering from a congenital heart disease and the harsh reality that I might not make it back alive to attempt to lead a normal, battle-free life, laughs were few and far between for me. This was one of many times that I had to laugh off excessive physical, mental and verbal abuse in order to keep my composure and not lose the minute traces of sanity left in me.

In between our rigid and barely bearable exercise sessions, I was expected to do my kitchen duty. My duty as a soldier, since I really didn't have the hunger and appetite to kill, was to cook for all officers and satisfy their hungers and appetites. I wasn't exactly a culinary arts student, but it really wasn't too challenging to satisfy a soldier's appetite at boot camp with mediocre cooking.

The little that I knew about cooking I learned back home from my mom. My innate curiosity often led me to our mouth-wateringly perfumed kitchen to see what scrumptious meal Mom was creating for my sisters and me to feast upon. I would pick up a few of her recipes, and she would sometimes let me try to emulate her to see if I had what it takes to survive in the kitchen.

"Cooking isn't easy Beltran. It takes a real man to be able to endure hot stoves, dirty dishes and hungry, demanding mouths to feed. Plus, what are you going to do if I die? I'm not going to be around forever." Mom would say jokingly but with a hint of sardonic truth.

I'm pretty sure my mother wasn't counting on my dying before her, but with my current situation as a soldier, it wasn't difficult for anyone to foresee that that untimely misfortune could definitely manifest itself. I didn't exactly have the luxuries and resources to display my above-average kitchen skills here at Ft. Sill like I could in Mom's kitchen, so I had to make do with the little I was given. Apparently I was doing a good job because some of the soldiers from other platoons and other companies would feel the annoying need to make their childish comments.

"This is some good shit Perez. I wouldn't mind having a girlfriend like you who can cook for me. Are you sure you weren't a woman in a past life?" I understood that any type of distraction was needed for many of us to manage making it to the next day, even if it meant being an asshole

Jaime Perez

to somebody who didn't deserve it. I completely understood the various coping methods being implemented at Ft. Sill; this was just another means of survival.

Actually, my mother's culinary inculcations were not what earned me kitchen duty; it was my work experience back home that got me the often-ridiculed honors of being a food service specialist. I worked as a meat cutter for our neighborhood grocery store. Even though I wasn't going to be doing much meat cutting at Ft. Sill, I didn't really have any other specialty that could be put to use. Soldiers are grouped, assigned duties and given a Military Occupational Specialty (MOS) Code based on their specialty. My meat cutting experience was noted, so my MOS Code was 94B20. All 94B20s were part of the food service specialist group. This is probably one of the least-respected specialties of all because it didn't entail killing or other manly specialties that generated impressive bragging rights. There were MOS Codes for counterintelligence agents, translators/interpreters, heath care administrators, field artillery tactical data systems specialists, psychological operations, field artillery officers, and of course for my under-appreciated, lackluster "specialty", food service specialist. My categorization didn't really exasperate me too much because I actually felt that my chances of survival would be exponentially increased if I were to mind my own business in the kitchen rather than somewhere else I had no business being.

One time, one of the other Wise Ass commanding officers even felt the need to utter, "Damn Perez!!! Where'd you learn to cook, the Girl Scouts??!! We could use a bitch like you in our group."

Morales would jump in, "You wouldn't know what to do with a bitch; that's why your girlfriend is humping somebody else back home!!! Don't worry; I'm sure you will find something to your liking in 'Nam. I picture you with a Weiner dog type or maybe even a Cocker Spaniel." Morales unabashedly said "weiner" and "cock" emphatically.

Morales' physique was enough to quiet most soldiers at Ft. Sill. He was a formidable 6"3', and because he was Mexican-American, everybody felt he was a little crazier than most. They were wrong; Capelletti was the crazy one of our group. The second Capelletti saw the wise-ass commanding soldier getting up to retaliate against Morales, he had the effrontery to get up to defend his military brother with a clenched fist, against a superior officer! Without Capalletiti even saying a word, Mr. Wise Ass sat right back down to avoid getting pulverized and humiliated in front of the entertainment-hungry onlookers. This was fortunate, because just as things were about to get unfavorable, Sergeant Mills struts by and says, "Let's go ladies. It's time to clean up your mess, and bring extra unused tampons because it's going to get bloody dirty out there." I suppose that Capelletti could have gotten in some serious trouble for confronting a superior officer, but something told me that Capelletti would have welcomed the trouble with a smirk.

Wilson almost laughed at Mills' comment, but I think he realized that Mills was insulting everyone, including Wilson. His partial laugh quickly turned into a look of perplexity, which was actually Wilson's usual expression. Nick Brown got up, as expected, without any comment or reaction, while Morales and Capelletti gave each other manly winks that indicated that they had each other's backs, even off the battlefield.

Smith felt the need to offer some advice to Mr. Wise Ass, "Hey man. Why don't you just save your energy for the enemy? I don't want to be here anymore than you do. Just keep it cool, and maybe we'll all make it out of this irrational war alive. You know what I'm saying?"

All kitchen staff, cooks included, was expected to clean up before resuming with the hot day's monotonous events. They didn't give us much time to do this, and they expected immaculate cleanliness. My time in the kitchen was my "thinking time". This is when I was able to clearly think about V and our son, Gilbert. These are probably the only times throughout the day where I can actually bring forth an honest smile to my otherwise stoic face. The day's monotony was to my advantage because I didn't really have to think about what I was doing in the kitchen—it came naturally. This allowed me to drift off mentally into a utopian yet almost forgotten world—a world where my family came first, not a world where one's survival was decided by pure chance. By day's end, I felt torn, battered and defeated—not exactly the way a soldier is supposed to feel before setting off to defeat the enemy.

Chapter 4

With the exception of the year I was drafted, my childhood was pretty basic and practical. I never got in any real trouble, and I kept up with good grades considering I really wasn't enticed by school; this was probably due to the fact that I never truly felt stimulated by my studies. It all came too easy to me that I never really put all my effort into it, but I managed to get by. Even though I felt minimally challenged and often uninterested, I knew that finishing high school was integral to any success I sought, and it was also expected of both my parents. Dad had always instilled in me that hard work is what defines a man; I could see this first hand by the convincing example he set for me. Knowing this about my dad, I wasn't surprised that my parents put me to work as soon as they could.

During my latter high school years was when I got my meat-cutting job at the local grocery store. I would work to help out with some of the living expenses back home; I didn't want to seem like a lethargic freeloader who was parasitically feeding off my parents. I was already dating V, so I was also trying to save up money for my own car, a wedding ring, and a deposit on our own place. In time, I would eventually realize that I was not going to be able to live in that cozy home I had previously hoped for because getting drafted obviated that idea. V and I found a duplex near Fort Sill in Oklahoma, but it was nothing like the home I had hoped for.

Before getting drafted, I expected to find a small, cozy place for us that was close my parents' place so that we could still be there for each other when need be. V's parents conveniently lived down the street, so it seemed like the practical thing to do. Our close proximity to our parents would ease the inevitable yet uncomfortable transition of moving out on our own. I have to admit that the happiest days of my life were the years I was together with V, previous to being drafted. We had all our lives ahead of us; everything seemed like the perfect daydream where nothing could go awry. My naiveté would soon desist with my draft notification. I felt as if some of the best potential years of my life were going to be unfairly, albeit legally, taken from not only me, but also my wife, parents, and now my son. After being drafted, my once optimistic outlook on life became full of despondence and dejection.

"You can do anything you put your mind to Son. Don't let anyone or anything stop you from pursuing your dreams." My parents would tell me more frequently than I would have liked. I had soon come to realize that these little words intended to comfort me were nothing but overly unrealistic adages widely used to give hope to the otherwise hopeless.

I understand that my parents were only trying to give me words of wisdom to help me reach my full potential, words to live by, but I have always felt that being brutally honest is far more beneficial and advantageous than conveying false hopes. Truth can often be cruel, but lying is a far worse cruelty in my opinion.

In this case, there was really nothing I could legally do short of lying to the government to get out of fighting in this war. I was not deemed mentally or physically incapable; I was not flatfooted. Since I had no other brothers, I was not a sole-surviving son, and with a wife, it was a little too late to convince anybody into believing that I was gay—which I wasn't. Because of this I felt I was doomed to be another historical statistic—another fatality in the list of those who had previously fallen and the numerous list of those to soon fall.

I will never forget the day my Mom and Pop found I was drafted to serve in the United Stated Armed Forces. My mother couldn't stop crying. I actually thought she was going to suffer a stroke or from hyperventilation due the odious news we had received. I was the youngest of 3 children, and I was the only boy. My two sisters didn't exactly know what being drafted entailed, but my parents and I surely did. Certain things a person sees, depending on the profundity of the situation, can be very difficult to erase from a person's mind. Seeing my mother drop to the floor as if she was enervated from finding out I was drafted and witnessing my father attempting to appease her anguish is a profound scene that will forever be etched in my mind. I hated seeing my mother cry, and there was really nothing I could do to ease her unsparing pain. Even though I was now several hundred miles from home and being prepared to be thrown into a world that any loving mother would boldly condemn for her son, I can actually still clearly hear my mother's dismal, unyielding weeping every

Jaime Perez

time before I go to bed; that sound still rings in my head like echoing church bells. I'm sorry Mom…

My father on the other hand rarely produced any tears, whether of sadness or happiness, but he undoubtedly had a big, altruistic heart. He was our supplier, our provider; everything we had was because of his hard work. We didn't see much of him because of his long hours on the job, but we knew his family fueled his hard work. He worked for an oilfield services company, so sometimes we wouldn't see him for several weeks straight. His aching bones, his sprained back, and his lack of fulfilling sleep were all daily sacrifices he endured to sustain his family. Mom did her part too; she supplied the love and compassion that was of vital importance to the nurturing and rearing of children. It was a good balance, my mother supplying the abstract and my father supplying the material. My parents were everything I could ask for, and I only hoped that I could prove to be as good of a husband to my wife and as great of a parent to my children.

I know I am not the only soldier at Ft. Sill who has a problem holding and using a gun to ensure our survival by killing another. Although I am unaware of any by name, I know I can't possibly be the only one who hesitates with apprehension every time I pull the sensitive trigger of my weapon. Luckily for Capelletti and Morales, they don't have this problem, but my inability to be as gung-ho and as entertained by violence as those two was brought upon from a childhood experience. At least, this is what I believe has made me wary of firing a weapon.

When I was about 12 years old, my Pop, his brothers and I would go hunting on our family's ranch property. The area was just shy of 100 acres of beautiful, deep green waves of brush that housed wild boar, deer, quail, turkey, and other local game. Whenever hunting season would come around, my Pop and my uncles would make it a point to make our overpowering presence known to all the lesser creatures on our land. One year, Uncle Dan felt that it would be better if we killed our own turkey for Thanksgiving instead of having to purchase one.

"Shit, we probably have enough turkeys in our back yard to feed us for all future Thanksgivings. Why the hell are we spending money to have somebody kill a turkey for us when we are just as, if not more, capable of acquiring our own bird feast. It will be saving us money, and we will be entertained by the thrill of the hunt as well. What do you say?? Who's in???" My Uncle Dan asked in sheer excitement. I actually have never seen anybody's eyes come so close to popping out of their sockets like my Uncle Dan's when he proposed his idea.

22

Everybody looked at each other as we all sat on the unlacquered, wooden front porch of my Uncle Tony's ranch house. Nobody was speaking, but it seemed like a good idea to me. I felt like this would be a good chance for me to become a man, to use this as a rite of passage from childhood to early manhood. I loved hanging out with my uncles and my Pop, it made me feel mature and grown up, like I was worthy of being around grown men. The uncomfortable silence compelled me to speak like I was the leader of some covert military mission about to be deployed to unfriendly and unfavorable hostile terrain.

"Why don't we get up at 5:00AM tomorrow, and get us some birds? I will deplume whatever we kill. We should get all our clothes, weapons and rounds ready today so that we can just wake up and get going first thing tomorrow. It's already going to be 10:00PM, which gives us close to 7 hours of sleep. I think we should also take a few bags of beef jerky, water for hydration, our binoculars, and I still have the bird caller that you got me for my birthday Uncle Raymond. I've gotten pretty good at using it. I am sure I can lure every turkey on our property into coming our way in minutes." I said with unexpected confidence.

I guess I must have sounded a little precocious and silly because my three uncles and my Pop were all laughing their asses off. My Uncle Tony was laughing so hysterically hard that he kicked and spilled his 12-ounce can of Schlitz all over Uncle Dan, who was sitting next to him. I didn't know how to react to my obviously amusing remarks, so I joined them in their merry laughter. After my familial audience regained their composure, wiped away their tears of laughter and recaptured their breath, my Pop said, "Why not? Let's do it."

"If we are going to do this, we need to go to bed now. I'm outta here boys. See you in the morning. If I don't wake up, somebody get me up." My Uncle Raymond said as he got up with his usual over-exaggerated grunts of imagined pain that made him sound much older than he actually was.

Everyone else simultaneously got up, and quickly went to bed. I had a difficult time sleeping that night. I must have tossed and turned for a few hours until I lost consciousness. It wasn't a fear-induced, momentary insomnia, but an excitement-induced one. I was going with my Pop and my 3 uncles on a Thanksgiving turkey hunt. I had only previously gone hunting with them twice before, but this time was significantly different. We were going to bring home a trophy, or trophies, that we were actually going to prepare for our families to enjoy. In addition, I felt that I was the one who motivated and convinced everyone else to embark on this

Jaime Perez

potentially male-bonding event, so I felt like an integral part of something important—my family. Feeling like one is a part of something that means the world to them is all any twelve-year old boy really wants; I was no exception. I must have eventually fallen to sleep with a smile from ear to ear because that's exactly what it felt like.

The next morning was the most anticipated day of my life, even more anticipatory than all Christmases and birthdays combined. My excitement was evident in the fact that I actually woke up at 4:55AM without the buzzing alarm, five minutes before our alarms were set to wake us to begin heading out on our hunting expedition. It didn't take us too long to get all our necessities and belongings packed. By 5:20AM, all of us, with the exception of Uncle Raymond, were ready to head out. Uncle Raymond was one of those people who could sleep through a Category 5 hurricane and not lose a wink of sleep. If insomnia were to have an exact opposite, Uncle Raymond would be diagnosed with it.

"Hurry your ass up Raymond. We want to hunt the bird and eat it for Thanksgiving, not Christmas." Pop said to his youngest brother in a jokingly, yet serious manner.

"Guys, I need to take a shower first, or I won't be fully cognizant out there. You guys go on ahead without me, and I will be right behind you. I'll find you guys. I know the land like the back of my hand." Uncle Raymond assured us.

"Fine, but hurry, or you'll miss all the action." Uncle Tony stated.

By 5:32AM, we were on the outer edge of the game-filled hunting grounds. A few years back, my uncles had created a path through the dense trees and prickly cacti that stretched from one end of the acreage to the other. This was their usual walkway through the unyielding, thick brush. We followed this path and kept our eyes focused to both sides. Everybody had a gun but me; my father felt I was too young to be holding a gun of any kind, so he adamantly refused my use of a firearm. I concurred with Pop. I was actually a little intimidated by guns, which was probably attributed to my lack of using them. I looked at my watch; it was 3 minutes until 6:00AM and still no turkeys in our sight. There was a wild boar that looked at us and fled wildly, but today we were not interested in boar, quail or deer, only turkey.

"Use your bird caller thing-a-ma-jig Beltran." My uncle Dan wisely commanded.

I excitedly reached in my camouflage pant pockets; I searched my jacket pockets. I looked in my backpack. Nothing. I started to sweat

24

because I disappointingly realized that I failed to do my part by bringing the most important tool for our hunt, besides the guns—my bird caller.

"I can't find it…I'm sorry." I said remorsefully searching and re-searching all possibilities.

I almost started to cry out of anger, disappointment, embarrassment and resentment, but my Uncle Tony said something that saved me right before I was about to uncontrollably begin oozing puddles of tears.

"Don't worry about it kid. True hunters like us do not need the help of any gimmicks to succeed with our kill. Let us not depend on trickery and deception, but pure skill."

Just as Uncle Tony unknowingly rescued my manhood, my Uncle Dan unexpectedly shoots without warning to our left and a little behind us. He runs vehemently to the area where he had shot his rifle, about 30 yards away. Whatever he shot hit the ground hard because we heard a thump a few seconds after Uncle Dan shot. We all carelessly ran behind him without any concern for the needle-sharp cacti that pierced our skin and the flexible walls of trees that literally slapped our faces. As we begin to catch up to Uncle Dan we see him fall to the ground on his knees. He has his back to us, so we don't see what he has shot; but for the first time in my life I hear him crying so loud that every bird and animal on our property must have flown or run for safety from hearing his earsplitting screams. As I get a clearer view and approach the blood-saturated soil, I realize Uncle Dan has shot his baby brother, Raymond. The site of a potential dead man, particularly my uncle, made me nauseous and compelled me to puke out some beef jerky I was snacking on just a few minutes before the accident. All my uncles are in overwhelming disbelief, but somehow my Pop spontaneously forces me towards his waist and turns me around to face him, covering my face. I can feel his pounding heartbeat through his jacket. I was in such a state of shock that I was not crying, yet. Just as the unspeakable reality was beginning to set and I was about to cry, my Pop tells me to follow the path back to the house and have somebody call an ambulance.

Without thinking twice, I run as fast as I can to the house and do just as I'm told. I ran back so fast that I could feel the wind hitting my face and shoving the tears away from my eyes, allowing me to see where I was going without having to wipe my face.

"Mom, Dad wants to you call an ambulance because Uncle Raymond has been shot. Hurry because I think he might still have a chance of surviving!!" I somehow managed to utter this in one gasping breath after running non-stop for close to half a mile.

Without hesitation, my mom makes her call as I return to the wooden porch and anxiously await my Pop and my uncles. My aunts follow me outside and obliviously ask me what happened, but I can't manage to say anything. Nothing but weak puffs of air came out of my mouth. My vision is blurred from my sweat and tears. I can't believe this is happening. I begin to feel partly, no totally, responsible for what happened. After all, it was me who persuaded everyone to take part in this turkey hunt turned disaster.

I wipe the blinding tears from my eyes and, in the distance, I see my uncles carrying Uncle Raymond's body towards the house. Pop is carrying a bag, but I have no idea what its contents are. I begin to faintly hear the haunting sirens approaching the house as my Pop and uncles arrive at our doorstep. All my aunts are feverishly questioning my uncles as to what exactly had happened. I begin hearing multiple recollections of the terror that had just occurred. I had just witnessed what happened; I didn't want to have to hear it also. The ambulance quickly pulls in reverse as my uncles carry their baby brother onto the vehicle and aboard the ambulance. Pop looks at me as he hands the bag to Uncle Tony.

"Here. He's not going to make it without these." Pop said as Uncle Tony reached for the bag before closing the ambulance door behind him. I realized the bag's contents were my Uncle Raymond's innards. Pop must have gathered them from the ground and bagged them just in case Uncle Raymond was to somehow pull through this successfully. The ambulance then raced away, and I stood still, staring at it until there was nothing more to look at.

Pop was drenched in his little brother's blood, particularly his hands. I ran up to him and hugged him at waist level. "I'm scared Daddy. I'm really trying not to be scared, but I am." I said as I became slightly hyperventilated.

"It's okay to be scared Son. You just witnessed something that I hope you never have to see again. Your fear is expected." I stood holding him for a few minutes more until my emotions appeared close to normal. I looked up at Pop, and he was looking straight down at me, as if he was watching me the whole time I held him.

"Get washed up." He finally said with a failed and unconvincing 'everything is going to be all right' tone.

I took a shower, and somehow managed to take a brief nap. I felt this was the only way to escape the day's events, even though the day would be waiting for me once I woke up. Pop's opening of the door was what woke me two hours later. I could hear in the background that my uncles were back from the hospital, and my Pop's dismal expression braced me for the grief-filled truth he was about to impose on me.

"We lost your Uncle son. He lost too much blood, and his innards were too damaged and therefore useless. My little brother is dead." My Pop valiantly attempted to say without crying again, but the pain was way too much for him to restrain. I held my Pop tighter than I ever had and cried with him. Mom eventually came in to see how we were holding up, and she joined us to complete our trinity of grief and bereavement. The three of us must have cried for about 20 minutes. Outside my uncles and aunts were doing the same. This was by far the saddest and ugliest day of my life. My Pop had mentioned earlier that dreadful day that he hoped I would never have to witness a similar tragedy like this again. Now that I was drafted, I had a portentous, unsettling feeling that there was a strong likelihood that I was going to vividly witness a few more of these tragedies than I would care to.

My Uncle Raymond's untimely death was more than likely the primary reason I was unable to be a little more daring with a firearm like Morales and Capelletti. I can't say that I was emotionally scarred to the point that I was unable to function normally in society, but if I think about that dreary day, I can recall it all with impeccable detail: the sights, the sounds, the smells, my Pop's heartbeat on my cheek, Uncle Tony's look of utter shock and my Uncle Dan's unwillingness to accept that he had shot and killed his little brother as he constantly nodded his head in negation to what was happening. Some things cling to you until the day you die, regardless of how adamantly you try to shake them off. It's like trying to shake the color off your skin—it's hopeless and impossible.

Chapter 5

V was released from the hospital 6 days after giving birth to Gilbert. Once she was released, I momentarily abandoned the men in my barracks to be with my wife. For the first few weeks, it was just the two of us in our rented duplex. Gilbert was to remain incubated in the hospital while receiving special attention from the hospital staff. Everyday we would visit him and spend a few hours with our fragile son. It was disheartening to see him incubated and plugged to machines with tubes. It just didn't look normal, but V and I knew it was absolutely necessary for the sustenance and viability of our child.

When Gilbert was finally released to us, 6 weeks later, I took advantage of the heartfelt yet abrupt time with my wife and child because I had an ominous feeling that I was soon going to be given orders to leave the country to fulfill my dubious military obligations. Every morning before retuning to Ft. Sill, I would kiss my son and wife goodbye before leaving, and the first thing I would do upon reaching the fort grounds was to apprehensively glance at the bulletin board centrally located at the Ft. Sill headquarters. This is where we got our orders, if any. The situation overseas must have begun to get a little heated because the list of names posted on the bulletin board seemed to get uncomfortably lengthier with every passing day. At first, I remember seeing only one page of names per week; now they were up to four pages of names.

V and I felt that it was time for her and Gilbert to go back home to Pharr, Texas. Our families were eagerly anticipating getting to finally see and hold our son, and our finances were slowly depleting. One would think that serving your country paid relatively well, but this was not the case. My thin income had to support my wife, our fragile, newborn child and me. I couldn't afford plane tickets to Texas for V and Gilbert, so we both decided that they would have to travel by bus. The Greyhound bus ride would take a little over 24 hours, but this did not daunt V. For the first time in my life, I was going to be miles away from my son and wife, and unfortunately, it wouldn't be the last time this would happen. Pretty soon I wouldn't even be on the same continent as my wife and child. Sure enough, nine days after V and Gilbert arrived in Texas, I saw my name on the new list that was thumb tacked to the bulletin board. My orders were posted, and it was official—I was going to South Vietnam for approximately one year—if I survived for that long.

As I entered the barracks, the guys obviously knew by reading my revealing face that my name was on the list. None of them had been by headquarters to see if their names were added to the list of unfortunate souls, and honestly, I hadn't noticed anybody else's name but mine. I was therefore unable to inform them on their statuses.

Immediately, Capelletti, Morales, Smith, Brown, Wilson and most of the other men in our barracks jumped and raced out like a pack of starving, rabid dogs chasing a helpless yet overdue meal. Wilson was so eager to find out if his name was on the list that he ran outside before putting any clothes on. I don't think he realized he was naked until he was about halfway to the headquarter doors. Coming from Wilson, this really didn't surprise anyone in our barracks because they had come to expect such questionable behavior from him, but the other men from the neighboring barracks who unfortunately witnessed Wilson's temporary display of nudity were going to probably be visually scarred by our eccentric barrack brother for the time being.

"What on God's Earth do we have here Private Wilson?" Sergeant Mills rhetorically asked in reaction to Wilson's bare state. "Is this your idea of a 'shock and awe' tactic? The element of surprise is widely recognized as an effective tool in warfare against the enemy in covert operations demanding meticulous precision, but you aren't even on enemy soil yet Wilson! Can your 'shock and awe' practices wait until there is a necessity for them?"

"Sir, yes sir!" Wilson confidently replied even though he didn't appear to be very confident in complete nakedness. "May I be excused sir?" He asked after realizing he wasn't clothed.

"Of course, you are excused Wilson. Keeping you out here exposed would render me in violation of the Eighth Amendment of the United States Constitution which prohibits the infliction of cruel and unusual punishment." Sergeant Mills stated sardonically and with a slight tone of

Jaime Perez

amusement that was rarely exuded by any Sergeant, at least in the presence of inferiors like us.

As Wilson hurriedly scampered to the barracks to get dressed, Smith bravely asked for permission to speak. "Permission to speak Sergeant Mills!"

"What's on your mind Private Smith?" Sergeant Mills authoritatively positioned himself one inch from Smith's recently shaved face, probably in an attempt to flaunt his superior rank.

"Sir, if you would have allowed Wilson to roam the camp grounds naked, would you be in violation of the Eighth Amendment for inflicting cruel and unusual punishment on him or on us for being unwillingly subjected to witness such an offensive act of nature against our will?" Smith said with a subtle smirk on his face.

Everyone within hearing distance stood motionlessly and silently, waiting to hear how Sergeant Mills was going to respond to Smith's smart-ass remark. Mills, still standing one inch from Smith's face, stared at him with a stern look, and within seconds, he broke out in belches of face-reddening laughter before everyone. Realizing that it was all right to breathe easily, the rest of us joined Mills in harmonious laughter.

After Mills was able to control himself and continue to speak normally, he responded to Smith. "I guess it would have been just as cruel to all of you men who witnessed this as it would have been to Wilson. Although I don't think it would have been very unusual to you Smith. I saw the way you were checking out Wilson's hairy crotch and drooling over it. I hope there's nothing improper going on in your barracks at night."

A second roar of laughter just as loud as the first broke out amongst all of us, including Mills and Smith. Somehow, in between laughs and his difficulty of breathing, Smith managed to innocuously utter, "Sergeant Mills, that's not funny sir!!"

"Obviously it is." Sergeant Mills managed to say while laughing and pointing to all the amused soldiers to help prove his point.

"I hear that Wilson is single and looking Smith. You may just be his type." Morales teased even though we knew that Wilson supposedly had a handful of potential soul mates at home.

Capelletti had to contribute to the somewhat friendly yet partially improper slandering. "You better hurry because rumor has it that Wilson has a couple of former Ms. Indianas and former Mr. Indianas waiting for him when he gets back home."

After a while everyone took deep breaths, wiped the tears from their

30

eyes and quickly resumed to the normal, sterile atmosphere of Ft. Sill. Eventually, everyone regained their composure and dispersed to continue their banal routines.

The second I noticed my name on the list I had begun to feel that discomforting ball in my throat that one feels before an emotional episode of profound sorrow or disappointment; except this time, my fusion of emotions included fear. I couldn't help but think that I may go off and die, leaving my family behind to fend for themselves. I wasn't about to begin bawling like a little girl in front of all these overly testosterone-producing bodies. I had originally planned to save my tears for bedtime, when I could wisely disguise my pain and fear in the darkness among the choir of others who were taking this hellish experience as difficult as I was, but I realized that I didn't have to hold back and disguise my pain until then. I took advantage of the previous laughter session that had just transpired right outside of headquarters. While others were crying of laughter and joking about Wilson's hairy balls, I was simultaneously crying about other things, things way dearer to me, things I may lose forever. I was able to camouflage my emotions amongst the amusement of the other soldiers. No one noticed that my tears were attributed to pain and not laughter; at least, I hoped no one had noticed.

As everybody headed back to the barracks, I realized that it was close to 0500 hrs, and we still hadn't had our breakfast. We continued to get dressed to start another day in the monotonous and systematic life of a soldier. While inside, I asked if anybody else besides me was on the lists; everybody nodded 'no'.

"You're a lucky bastard Perez. I honestly wish I were in your shoes Bro. You know if we could switch places, I would do it in half a heartbeat. You'll be fine man; you worry too much." Capelletti tried to comfort me with his manly tap on the back that for some reason, always made me lose my balance. Those were actually the most humane and thoughtful words I had ever heard Capelletti utter since I met him. I didn't think he was capable of such consideration and thoughtfulness; unfortunately, his previously non-existent amiableness did nothing to provide me with solace from knowing I was on my way to hell.

I had to somehow manage to get through this day knowing that I had finally been assigned to do my reluctant part overseas. I guess this was, in a sick and masochistic way, a relief. At least I knew where I was going; most of the others were worrying themselves sick and losing sleep over their uncertain and unassigned futures. I tried to

Jaime Perez

find comfort in my knowing, but it didn't seem to help. Upon day's end, I had planned to call V to tell her of my assignment before going to bed. I promised her that I would let her know the day I found out for myself, and I intended to keep my promise to her. I knew this call would be an emotional one, so I had decided to wait until the lines for the payphones were minimal.

After I had completed my day's obligations, I waited until about 2130 hrs to see about using the phone to call V. By that time, most soldiers were getting ready to hit the sack. I thought about calling Mom and Pop afterwards, but I wasn't too sure that I would be able to endure two emotional phone calls in one night. There were only 5 phones available for our use, and only one of them was unoccupied. I had kept in touch with V at least twice a week since she had returned home to Texas, but tonight's phone call was more challenging to make. I had to hang the phone up twice and dial again because I had noticed that my trembling hands had dialed inaccurately. I unnervingly hung up the phone and contemplated doing this tomorrow. As I slowly got up to return to my bed where I often sought refuge from reality's unkindness, someone's hand firmly grabbed my shoulder from behind—it was silence personified, Nicholas Brown.

"It's not going to get any easier by procrastinating Perez. If you somehow find a convincing excuse to wait until tomorrow, you'll likely find another excuse for the day after, and then another, until you drive yourself crazy. No one, in the history of humanity, has ever conquered an obstacle by running away from it, and I respectfully doubt that you will be the first to achieve this insurmountable yet equally cowardly task. Sit your ass down and make the call." Confidently and commandingly stated the usually reticent Brown.

Although Brown was not a stranger to me, this Brown was completely alien to me. I had never heard him speak like this, or at all for that matter. Even though I was shocked to have actually finally heard what his voice sounded like after several weeks of sleeping in this man's barracks, I was equally shocked by the truthfulness in this man's words. Both his unfamiliar voice and his eye-opening, philosophical remarks took me by surprise.

"Wow! Contrary to popular belief, you actually are capable of communication." I said.

"I like to consider myself more of a listener than a speaker. People who talk too much, often get on other's nerves. Those of us who spend most of our time in observant silence rarely bother those around us. If my opinion

32

is requested, I will gladly give it; if not, then it still exists, but just not as explicitly as that of others. One thing you learn from listening Perez, is that 'Opinions are like assholes. Everybody has one, and they all stink.' So, are you going to regain your courage and make the call?" Brown continued to amaze me.

"Well since you have so selflessly enlightened me with your tidbits of wisdom, I now feel obligated to resume with my original intentions of calling my wife."

Brown began his walk to the barracks, but just before he reached for the exit door, I managed to get his attention. "Hey Brown." I said, and he turned to me, giving me a facial expression as if he were expecting my calling him. "Thanks for talking with me."

Expectedly, with half a nod, half a smirk and no verbal response, he turned and continued his stroll back to our temporary home away from home. I don't know why, but I watched Brown walk to the barracks through the small glass window on the exit door until he stepped inside. As I came back to my senses, I looked around the phone booths and saw that I was alone. I picked up the phone unwaveringly and made my promised call home to V.

As I dialed the number on the rotary phone, a sudden thought brought a much-needed smile to my face. I don't know why I hadn't thought of this earlier. Being that I have now been officially assigned to active duty in South Vietnam, I have the golden opportunity of visiting back home for a week before heading out to war. I started to daydream of how things would be back home and began picturing the things I would likely do on my short yet highly anticipated visit. I became pleasantly lost in a euphoria I hadn't felt for quite a long time. While in my mental paradise, I realized that the phone had been ringing for quite sometime, and there was still no answer. I don't exactly know for how long I was in my reverie, but the phone must have rung at least 20 times. Although it was a little after 2200 hrs, I didn't think V would be asleep, but then again, how does one predict the sleep patterns of a parent with a newborn? I waited for another 7 to 10 rings; then I began to worry. Is everything all right? Is Gilbert's condition worsening? Hundreds of questions entered my mind all at once that I started feeling a slight headache. I couldn't let my worries get the best of me, so I had to call once again. I dialed carefully and slowly this time. As the rotary dial retracts to its original position after having dialed the last number, I hold my breath and await someone, anyone, to answer at the other end.

Jaime Perez

"Hello…hello? HELLO!?" It was V who answered, and for a cloudy moment I was unable to speak. A momentary paralysis from elation kicked in. Gilbert's infant cries could be heard in the background, and all I could do was listen to my child's enthusing bawling and my sorely missed wife's angelic voice. It seemed like forever since I had seen or spoken to either of them, but it had actually only been two days since I last spoke to V.

"Hi V. It's me." I somehow managed to utter before she hung up.

"Damn it. You scared me babe. What, did you forget how to speak or something?" V said with a slight tone of relief.

"No, no. I'm sorry. Hearing your voice and Gilbert's cries in the background was just a little overwhelming that I lost my senses. Plus, I wasn't expecting you to answer."

"Well babe, Gilbert is still a little too young to begin answering the phone. He would probably just put it in his mouth and chew on it without end. Who else would answer the phone here?" V asked jokingly.

"It's just that I had called before, and there was no answer."

"No answer? We've been here all day. Your parents came by earlier to see and take care of Gilbert while I went grocery shopping, but that was earlier this afternoon. The phone hasn't really rung all day." V explained.

I tried to make sense of what had happened with my first call attempt; then it hit me as I laughed. My laugh obviously concerned V. "Are you losing your mind Baby? If so, can they release you and send you back to me where you belong? A soldier can't successfully accomplish his orders if he's crazy; can he?"

My laughter heightened by my idiocy as well as V's rhetorical yet amusing interrogation. "I just realized that the first time I called you I had dialed our number at the duplex. That is probably why the phone continuously rang without answer—the duplex is probably still unoccupied from when we left. I don't know what I was thinking." I foolishly explained.

"Well, it seems like you've just solved the mystery of the unanswered phone Mr. Sherlock Holmes." V said much to my enjoyment. It was comforting to hear that V was back to her witty and funny self. Much of my happiness depended on V's happiness. It's the way things are when soul mates meet and become one.

Just as I was about to explain the reason for my calling later than usual, V asks, "Dialing old phone numbers, becoming temporarily mute and losing your mind, I'm beginning to think that you have something on your mind that is consuming you. This is not just a call to say 'hi', is

Through You

it Beltran?" V asked with a concerned voice. She infrequently called me by my first name unless there was reason for concern, as she clearly and accurately extrapolated. "What is it?"

"I have good news, and I have bad news…" I answered.

Chapter 6

Just as I was about to explain to V my true reason for calling, Brown walks in as if looking for something he had left behind. He approaches the phone booth he was previously using and picks up a paper that I assume was his. As he passes by me to return to the barracks, he briefly and without a word displays the paper he had forgotten; it was a photograph of what appeared to be him with his brother or a good friend. Being that Brown wasn't the most gregarious man I'd ever met, I wasn't too sure who the man with him was in the photo. He looked back at me before leaving the phone station and smirked as if to convey his gratification for taking his advice of not procrastinating my inevitable and promised phone call to V.

"Are you still there? Hello? Why are you torturing me? My curiosity is killing me Babe." V brought me back to my senses with her anticipatory pleading.

"Sorry V. I was distracted by one of my barracks brothers. O.K., the bad news is that I have finally received my orders. Well, I think of it as bad news; others feel that I am fortunate for knowing. I will be leaving to South Vietnam in roughly 4 weeks. I am expected to be there for approximately one year if everything goes as planned." I was going to continue with the good news portion of my call, but I was hindered from proceeding by V's soft and delicate weeping. "Are you O.K. V?" I voiced with slight concern.

"Of course I'm not O.K.? What am I going to do for a whole year without you Beltran? Am I supposed to just pretend you don't exist and try to raise our ill son by myself? I haven't even finished high school yet, and I have no job! What if you don't come back?" V said tremulously in sheer delirium.

"V, you have our families there with you at your disposal in case you need anything. A year will go by faster than you think, and I have every

36

Through You

intention on coming back to be a husband to you and a father to Gilbert. We knew this was going to happen sooner or later V. I need you to be strong with me here because I am scared shitless. I have everything to lose, and the biggest thing I stand to lose is you." I tried to sound stern and composed, but my voice began quivering. I couldn't exude any hint of fear or uncertainty and expect V to remain strong willed.

I quickly began regretting my calling V and taking Brown's advice when V showed some signs of hope and, in turn, instilled some hope in me. "I'm sorry Babe. Really, I am. You have enough going through your head, and you don't need me adding flames to your already scorching hell. I'm going to use every ounce of energy to be strong and get through this because our child will be dependent on my guidance and nurturing for the time being. Again, I'm sorry."

After a few moments of stillness, I continued. "Thanks for understanding V. You make me a stronger man than I could ever be without you. Honestly, you and Gilbert are what keep me focused and strong. It's you two that constantly motivate me to do all I can to come out of this alive. They say that war changes a man, and that is probably partially true. But love keeps a man's heart pumping for more life. It is your love that fuels me, and I have no doubt that it will be your love that brings me back alive. Everything will be all right." I tried to comfort her as well as myself.

"Yes, you're probably right. Well, now that you got the difficult part of this call out of the way, what is the good news?"

"Oh yeah. I almost forgot. The good news is that I will be allowed a L.O.A. before being sent overseas." I said expecting some sort of excitement from V.

After about 5 seconds of silence, V said, "Huh? Can you speak in regular, non-military terms Mr. Soldier so that I can understand you?

"Ha Ha. I'm sorry about that. I guess I sometimes forget how the normal outside world communicates. I have obviously been a soldier for far too long already. I will be granted a L.O.A., leave of absence, which means that I can go spend some time with you, Gilbert and everybody else back home before I am to fly overseas." I explained.

"That's great Babe! So when does this 'L.O.A.' go into effect?"

"I need to find out for sure from my superiors. My plans are to drive out of here in about two weeks and spend another two weeks there. Immediately upon conclusion of my L.O.A., I will probably be expected to fly out of McAllen to connect to Washington before heading out to South Vietnam, so I will be leaving you the car. Hopefully that will simplify

37

Jaime Perez

matters a bit for you there. I will call you at least a day before I plan to leave so that you can plan for my arrival."

"Great, I am looking forward to that day." V said in much better spirits than at the beginning of our conversation.

"I need to wake up in about 5 hours V, so I better get going for now. Give our son a goodnight kiss for me, and we will talk soon."

"I love you Babe, hurry home because everybody misses you, especially me."

"I love you too. Goodnight." I waited to make sure that V had hung up the phone. When she did, I hung up and began mentally envisioning my trip back home. Although I was really looking forward to this trip, I knew it was going to be extremely difficult to leave all my family when my L.O.A. comes to a conclusion, and I thought about how sad my departure from home was going to be. Then I realized that I needed to stop sucking the happiness out of everything delightful and enjoy things for what they are. I felt that I was going to drive myself crazy if I continued unsoundly and unhealthily deforming life's felicities into infelicities.

I got up and pensively walked back to the barracks to get some precious rest. It was close to 2300 hrs now, and some of the men in my barracks were still awake, Nicholas Brown was one of them. Brown and I had never spoken more than two words to each other. As a matter of fact, the pivotal conversation we had at the phone booths was the most I had ever heard him speak. I felt the need to show my appreciation to Brown for instilling some good sense into me concerning my making the phone call to V. I didn't want to force a conversation on an otherwise conversationally-challenged man, so I did the next best thing—I kindly tossed a few pieces of Bazooka brand bubble gum on his bed next to his notebook as a token of my gratitude. I wasn't expecting him to say anything, but as I turned back towards my bed to finally put this day behind me, Brown said softly, "Hey, get back here Perez. I've got to tell you something."

Ironically, now I speechlessly and stupefiedly make my way to Brown's bed as he moves his belongings aside and makes room for me to sit down, so I do just that. "What do YOU want to talk about Brown? You've become rather verbose today all of a sudden."

He smiles and begins the rare act of speaking. "First of all, thanks for the gum. That's the nicest thing anybody has done for me since arriving in this shit hole, but I'm not trying to wastefully deprive you of your sleep with a frivolous conversation to discuss your kindness. I...I want to tell you something because I have to tell somebody. Tell me Perez, have you ever

38

kept a secret for so long that the secret begins eating you from the inside out? I don't mean the kind of secret you promise a good friend to keep, not that kind of secret. I mean the kind that you've faithfully kept to yourself for as long as you can remember, but you suddenly and inexplicably come to a point that you realize you have no intentions of continuing to keep this matter a secret."

I had noticed that Brown had not looked me straight in the eye since he started talking. He would look down as if he was reticently confessing ignominious and unspeakable sins. I understood that speaking to someone else already had him out of his comfort zone, and that this must difficult and unfamiliar to him. I realized that he was waiting for my response to his question. "Yes, I have a feeling I know what you're talking about. Why do you ask? What secret is consuming you so much to the point that you felt the need to engage in a rare conversation with someone you minimally know?"

"The reason I feel comfortable telling you is because you seem like an honest and sound person, and like I mentioned before, I obviously listen and observe more than I speak. I have observed that you are respectable to others, and you don't appear to be unfairly judgmental of other's differences."

For the first time since the beginning of our conversation, Brown looks me in the face, but says nothing. It's almost as if time had stood still for about 5 long seconds, until I put it back in motion with a question. "What do want to tell me Brown? Spill it out."

"I'm gay Perez." He said unashamedly and succinctly.

This was obviously not the kind of confession that one is used to hearing in a place like this. Since I arrived here, I have heard admittances of everything from extra-marital affairs to excessive drug use, but admitting one's homosexuality was definitely a new one I had never heard before nor was I ever expecting to hear. I felt the need to say something, but I was both surprised and therefore at an unexpected loss for words. I couldn't help but think about the stories that I heard from Morales and Capelletti about men who they heard had both dishonestly and honestly stated that they were gay in hopes of being exempt from having to serve in this war, so I naturally used this to break the silence.

"Why didn't you say anything before? I mean, why didn't you use this as an excuse to exonerate you from having to be here?" I asked without the intentions of humiliating Brown.

"I'm here because I want to be here. I signed up for this to prove to my

Jaime Perez

Dad, I mean, to prove to every close-minded and foolish person that being gay doesn't limit a man's potential. A man's potential can only be limited by himself, gay or not. I don't see why my sexual preference should afford me any partiality, especially when I don't think I am less of a man for being the way I am. I can fight for my country as honorably and courageously as any straight man, and I therefore do not use this as an excuse to grant me favors or concessions." Brown stopped and looked at me as if expecting some sort of response.

"You're right Brown. You're absolutely right. I didn't mean to offend you by thoughtlessly recommending that you use your sexuality to your advantage. That was inconsiderate of me, and I meant no offense by it. I guess I was just caught by surprise. I would have never guessed you are gay. I am flattered that you have confided in me with your secret Brown." I said with a tone of shamefulness.

Brown was about to speak when Smith, who sleeps in the bed next to Brown, angrily interrupted with a restive and raspy tone. "Will you faggots stop your annoying whispering and go to fucking sleep already? Damn, you're worse than girls. What's so timely that it can't wait until the morning?" Smith didn't wait for an answer to his rhetorical questions; he just simply covered his whole head with his pillow and tried to get some sleep. I honestly think that Smith was more asleep than awake otherwise he would have likely made a comment at the fact that Brown was actually capable of speaking.

Brown and I couldn't help but quietly laugh at Smith's indignant comments. Smith had no idea what we were talking about, but he was right. It was getting late, and we needed to get some rest before we wake up in sleepless regret.

Brown held out his hand to shake mine. I firmly shook his hand and thanked him for his previous and helpful advice on my procrastination, and he returned the gratitude for my listening to his situation. I slowly got up from Brown's bed and made my way towards mine. As I lay down, I stared at the wooden ceiling and reflected on the day's events. I was sent to Ft. Sill to become an adept soldier and to soon fight a war that was many miles away. The ironic part is that I had come to realize that many of us, like Brown and myself, were fighting our own internal wars here at home, within and against ourselves.

40

Chapter 7

Sleep came relatively easy that night, at least for me it did. Smith wouldn't have agreed with me, as his first words for the day would have proven.

"Perez, I had a dream that you and Brown were chitchatting last night on his bed, and your partially audible voices were disallowing me any sleep. At first I thought it was actually happening, then I realized that if Brown were speaking, it must undoubtedly be a dream because he doesn't speak in real life."

I conveniently went along with his misperception because I was pretty sure that Brown's surprising confession was intended to be kept in secrecy. "You had a dream in which Brown actually uttered syllables!? I would pay for that once-in-a-lifetime experience. Hell, I would pay to hear the bastard cough, sneeze, sigh or anything with an element of sound." I said as those listening, as well as myself, broke out in our first laugh of the day, even Brown displayed a quasi smile.

I got dressed and left a little earlier than most of my barracks brothers so that I could get a head start in the kitchen with breakfast. As I began thawing out slices of frozen bacon in the sink before placing them in the cooking pan, I began to think about what Smith had said a few minutes before, about having heard Brown speaking. I was so awestruck by Brown's words that I wasn't really paying much attention to our surroundings, but it did seem like Brown and I were the only ones awake at that hour. I hoped for Brown's sake that no one else heard the contents of our discussion. With all the alpha-males in our barracks, one's unconventional sexual preference would likely bring forth uneasy tension and unneeded bitterness amongst us.

As the hungry soldiers made their way to the food line before another monotonous and grueling day of on-the-job-training, I could see Capelletti, Morales, Smith, Wilson, Sergeant Mills and a few of the lesser known

41

Jaime Perez

soldiers from our barracks entering the cafeteria. I didn't see Private Brown. Although I was concerned, I didn't ask about him to the others because this would have likely raised some suspicion since I had never before voiced wonder about anybody else in our barracks, so I kept quiet and diligently went on as if I hadn't noticed Brown's absence.

Captain Benson came in briefly and shouted to the men that there were new sheets posted on the bulletin boards. This compelled all those eating to hastily finish their meals so that they could quickly go by the headquarters to see if their names were posted. As the cafeteria was slowly emptying, I still saw no sign of Brown. Finally, as the final minutes of breakfast approached, Private Brown raced in with just enough time to grab a biscuit and some orange juice. He quickly looked at me and nonchalantly without a word began walking outside towards the headquarters like everybody else. Each of us had our own jobs to do in specific areas, so I would likely not get a chance to speak to anyone about their assigned orders, if any, until sundown. Considering last night's conversation with Brown, today ended up being like any other day. Just as I was about to finish up my duties in the cafeteria and resume outside for calisthenics, Captain Benson caught me by surprise

"Perez, why are you still here?" He said is his usual loud, semi-intimidating and always wet holler.

I quickly turned to him and responded, "Sir, where am I supposed to be Sir?"

"Only a madman would prefer to be here with a bunch of animals instead of at home with his family. Don't you want to go home Perez, or have you become an animal like the rest of them? I hear you are a new father Perez. Is that so?"

"Sir, yes sir. My son Gilbert was born on August 22, 1968 right here at Ft. Sill sir."

He lowered his tone from his usual holler to a regular speaking voice that sounded extremely odd for me since I was not accustomed to hearing Captain Benson speak in a tone that was less expressive than a bellow. "Perez, anybody can be a soldier, anybody can be husband, but it takes much more to be a father. Why don't you get your ass home and start working on your fatherhood skills? I'm pretty sure the other 94B20s will survive without you. Go spend as much time as you can with your wife and son, because honestly, we don't really know what the good Lord has in store for you."

"My intentions were to leave next week, but if I can leave earlier, I will

42

gladly do so sir." I said as my heart raced from the excitement of no longer having to painfully wait for my leave of absence to commence.

"Meet me in my office in exactly 10 minutes, and we will get everything ready for your leave of absence. Call your wife and family Perez. You're going home early."

"Thank you Sir." I said trying to avoid foolishly jumping up for joy as I saluted him, hopefully for the last time.

I ran to my currently empty barracks and attempted to let the reality sink in. Everybody was busy training, so I was able to spend a few minutes alone, 10 minutes to be exact. I took a long and absorbed glance at the four walls that had contained my cries, worries, nightmares and fears for the past, displaced months. Although I felt like a part of me was going to be left behind within these barracks' confines, I wasn't going to have a rigorous time or any regrets about leaving Ft. Sill. In a peculiar way, I was going to miss my barracks brothers. You'd have to be heartless and inhuman to not miss this eclectic bunch of men after spending months with them, even if we came dangerously close to killing each other on many occasions. I had roughly 5 minutes before having to meet with Captain Benson, and I did not want to keep him waiting. I realized I needed to stop my heartfelt reminiscing of the past months or else I was going to get emotional, and I did not want Captain Benson to even begin to think that I was crying. I gathered my composure and headed towards Captain Benson's office.

"Permission to enter Sir." I said as I stood by the open door of his office.

"Come in Perez. It looks like your set to go. The information and documents you need to leave the country after the conclusion of your L.O.A. are in this folder. I've gotten approval to relieve you of your food service duties for the rest of the day to allow you ample time to get all your things packed up and for you to do what you have to do. Do you plan to leave tonight or tomorrow morning?" Captain Benson said with a surprisingly interested tone. Previous to today, I never really had any sort of significant conversation with Captain Benson, probably because he was too busy worrying about Captain things, whatever those may be.

"The drive is approximately 10 to 12 hours Sir. I plan to leave first thing in the morning so that I can arrive in McAllen before sundown. I appreciate you expediting my L.O.A. Sir. If I may be so bold Sir as to ask why you did this priceless favor for me?"

Before responding, Captain Benson ordered me to sit down on one of the black leather chairs directly in front of his desk. "Perez, I'm going to tell

43

Jaime Perez

you something personal that I don't share with just anybody." I felt my eyes spontaneously open wide as I wondered what Captain Benson was going to willingly share with me about himself. After last night's conversation with Brown and now Captain Benson's upcoming revelation, I was beginning to feel like a psychiatrist or confessor. I sat down as instructed, not knowing what to expect.

Captain Benson took a long, deep breath that emanated with the subtle aroma of chewing tobacco. "Perez, I am an only child. When I was 5 years old, I lost both my parents in a car accident back home in Kenosha, Wisconsin. I never really had the luxury of getting to truly know my biological parents. Aging has blurred most of what I remembered as a child, and the first 2 to 3 years after I was born were likely beyond recollection. My paternal grandparents graciously and benevolently took on the task of raising me so that I would not have been subjected to the capriciousness of orphanhood. I got married immediately after graduating from high school with the ecstatic hopes of having children. I felt a vexatious void of parentage throughout my childhood, a void that I felt and hoped I could eventually and vicariously fill by being someone's father."

As Captain Benson continued with his story, I was mentally trying to somehow discern what he was trying to communicate to me and why he felt compelled to share a part of himself with someone who was nothing more to him than just another soldier, a distant acquaintance, at best, a distant acquaintance that would likely be forever forgotten and lost with the others who were deployed before me. Then, as he resumed opening up to me, his purpose all of a sudden became clearer.

"Does that make any sense to you Perez? I wanted to be a father because I felt it would remedy the fatherly absence I experienced as a child. I needed to achieve a sense of completeness that I felt this would bring. Unfortunately, I to this day have not accomplished that seemingly simple task. After several years and numerous failed attempts, it was brought to my attention that I was sterile, unable to have kids of my own. Can you believe that Perez? A Captain in the United States Army shoots blanks. How ironic is that? I've looked at your files. You are a newlywed and a new father as well. I can never be what you are Perez, a father. Sure, I suppose my wife and I could have resorted to adoption, but that wouldn't have sufficed. I wanted to procreate with my flesh and blood, my DNA, but it will never happen, at least not in this lifetime. This is why I expedited your L.O.A.. Now that you are a husband and a father, I am ordering you to go home and be a daddy as well. I would literally give my right arm to

44

be able to do what you have done, so I want you to take advantage of the time you've rightfully earned to spend with your family, wife, your son or with whomever else you spend time. I want you to opportunistically treat the next few weeks with your family as if they are the final days you will ever spend with them. Hold them like you mean it; love them like you've never loved before; spend as much time as you possibly can with them. Hell, if you can manage it, don't even sleep while you're there. Just be the best son, brother, husband, father and daddy you are capable of being. You are still very young Perez, but unfortunately death isn't prejudicial. It takes what it wants, when it wants, because it wants. Start packing your shit and prepare to finally begin living your new, government-issued life."

I stood up and saluted Captain Benson for probably the last time. For some odd reason, the Captain's wife crossed my mind. I didn't happen to notice any pictures of her on his desk, so I felt naturally obligated to ask about her. I figured, since the Captain was already sharing his personal life with me, it wouldn't hurt to ask him of his wife at a time like this.

"Sir, if I may ask before leaving, how are things with Mrs. Benson?" I asked hoping to receive a joyful response.

He looked at me as if with indecision and shame but responded to my seemingly pervasive question anyway. "She left me shortly after we were informed of my infertility. She wanted her own children just as badly as I did, so she divorced me and looked for someone who could successfully fulfill her desire to become a mommy. I don't blame her. I've since given up on the overrated institution of marriage and have patriotically decided to fully devote my life to my country. So here I am, a lifer, a man married to his country. That's not exactly what I had in mind, but here I am."

I suddenly felt like a nosy and inconsiderate ass for asking about the Mrs., so I apologized to Captain Benson about his divorce. He wittingly retorted. "Don't be sorry. She was a bitch anyway. She wasn't' worth the sock lint that rests between one's toes."

I left Captain Benson's office before I aggravated matters any more. "Good day Sir."

As I walked out, I heard Captain Benson say, "Don't forget Perez, live life everyday like you're dying. And that is by no means an exaggeration."

I had been so consumed with the day's events that I hadn't called V to let her know of my early dismissal. I made my way to the phone booths to make my call. At this time of day, everyone was outside busy with physical training; so all the phones were conveniently unoccupied. I took advantage of this, making certain that I dialed the right phone number this time.

45

Jaime Perez

The line rang continuously, but before I began to panic, I remembered that V and Gilbert had an appointment with a local pediatrician to monitor our son's congenital heart disease. They wouldn't be home until later that afternoon. This is when I decided to make a surprise visit instead of an announced one.

I returned to my barracks and lay down on my rock-hard cot for a while. It had been a long while since I had been in a room alone with nobody to talk to. Although I was looking forward to going home, I suspected that the two weeks with my family would be the fastest two weeks I've ever witnessed. It was as if I was pessimistically expecting those two weeks to be a presaging prelude to my potential peril. I thought about Captain Benson's pragmatic advice as well as my future in South Vietnam as I began to surrender my cognizance by closing my eyes. A nap wouldn't be a very bad idea right now. I wasn't particularly fatigued or restless from the present day since I had been excused of all my obligations after breakfast, but somehow my cot, the silence, the calmness, the solitude all proved to be a little too tempting for me to fight off. This was a battle that I would unashamedly surrender to willingly and as frequently as allowed.

Chapter 8

An acrid and foul stench furtively made its way through my unprepared nasal passage. This odor was so strong that it almost brought tears to my eyes. Its relentlessly penetrative power became apparent to me when I noticed all the other soldiers covering their noses; a few of them even vomited on themselves.

"God damn it! What is that fucking smell? I've taken shits that smell much better than this." A fellow soldier sitting next to me yelled with his jacket covering his mouth.

"That is the sweet smell of death, ladies." The pilot of the helicopter smiled and stated without any obvious effect from the lingering stink. He appeared to be unaffected and/or miraculously immune to it, whatever the smell was. After a while, I realized his response was not a metaphor as I had previously conjectured, but his reference to the smell of death was meant literally. Although they were slightly camouflaged among the long, green blades of grass, the randomly diffused and numerous crimson blotches made the lifeless and, in some cases, the crawling corpses easier to detect. This is when I realized that the permeating stench I was unsuccessfully trying to avoid smelling was actually the smell of death. Some of the blood-drenched bodies were screaming and reaching up to our helicopter as if begging to a listless God for aid. To be quite honest, I couldn't really distinguish if the woeful souls on the ground were our allies or our enemies.

I looked around and didn't recognize any of the soldiers who were with me aboard the hovering helicopter. I wasn't too sure if my hearing was playing tricks on me, but I could swear that I could hear the unsettling sound of guns being fired along with the earsplitting and irritating jarring of the helicopter. I took a quick glance down through the helicopter's unsafe and wide-open side door to reassure myself that I was only hearing

47

Jaime Perez

things. Much to my dismay, my eyes substantiated what my ears had heard; there were guns being shot, a lot of them, and they appeared to be aimed directly at us.

Just as I was about to suggest that somebody should quickly close the door, the pilot yells, "O.K. ladies, we are here." I didn't exactly know how to react to that unexpected comment, or maybe I was just reluctant to react. Within seconds, another man began tossing us out of the plane, one by one. We weren't too far off the ground; we appeared to be roughly 6 feet in the air. His rhythmic approach to throwing us off afforded me the ability to prepare for my turn. I could sense my body stiffening up to accept the fall. As I was lunged out of the aircraft and into unfamiliar territory, I never seemed to hit the ground. It was as if 6 feet quickly became 60,000 feet. While my body twisted and turned in the deep blue sky from my seemingly perpetual descent, I began to feel dizzy ad nauseam and soon began to witness a shortness of breath. My inability to breath resulted in my seeing several black spots. Just as everything seemed to turn black, I jerked myself awake and began uncontrollably flailing at the air.

Accompanying my flailing was the simultaneous laughter of those I would soon see for the last time. Apparently, Smith had covered my nose and mouth while I was sleeping. My nap-induced vertigo made it challenging for me to focus and return to cognizance. After a few more seconds, I gathered my senses and laughed along with the group of men I had sweat, cried, laughed, tolerated and argued with for the passed months. In some strange way, I was actually going to miss these guys, even the ones who kept to themselves and never spoke a word to anyone, unless you count the often incoherent gibberish that some of these men uttered during a nightmare. They had slowly become like furniture in one's home, often overlooked yet noticeable when missing. Being that everybody was in the barracks, I concluded that training was done for the day; I deduced that I had napped for close to 3 hours.

"What in the hell are you doing here Perez?" Morales asked.

"I was about to jump off an aircraft and probably break my leg on the fall."

"What? Were you dreaming again?" Wilson asked with ecstatic curiosity as if he was deprived of any dreams.

"It was more like a nightmare, or shall I say "daymare" if that even exists. Thanks for saving me Smith, even though you came short of suffocating me to death." I said with slight sarcasm.

"Why in the hell are you in here asleep anyway? Aren't you supposed to be in the kitchen preparing some of your insipid gourmet dinners for us?"

"I am sorry to inform all of you that my culinary magic will no longer be performed here at the Ft. Sill kitchen. I apologize for the unexpected inconvenience gentlemen." I said self-importantly.

"Well, where are you taking your magic now Mr. Houdini?" Smith asked me with a convincing tone of genuine concern as he referred to me as one of the greatest magicians of all time.

"Captain Benson gave me word that I could leave early on my L.O.A. We spoke a little bit after breakfast, and I have been cleared to leave first thing tomorrow morning. I will spend roughly two weeks at home with my family then fly to South Vietnam at the conclusion of my L.O.A. Did anybody else get their names added to the 'lists of death' this morning?"

Smith, Morales, Capelletti and Wilson all simultaneously responded with a disappointing 'no' while Brown silently nodded in negation.

"None of you?" I asked again for reassurance.

Smith responded. "Nope, our futures are at a standstill right now. Are you packed and ready to go?"

"I've got most of it done. I'll finish the rest later tonight. Let's go get our last dinner together, huh?"

"Hell yes. I am starving." Wilson said as he quickly got up and childishly ran towards the cafeteria as if he was being timed.

We all walked out far behind Wilson's lead to grab our last dinner together. I felt a slight ambivalence about everything that had transpired today. I was totally ecstatic about going home, but I felt a biting trepidation about the days that would follow my visit. I mean really, how does one prepare for war? Boot camp and basic training are a nice start, but there is still so much beyond our control that can't be taught. Some things, like dodging live bullets, seeing dead bodies, tolerating the smell of rot, surviving in unfamiliar enemy soil, maintaining one's composure and keeping one's sanity amidst all the insanity, to name a few, are impossible to train and prepare for. These nightmarish realities are beyond the scope of erudition. I suppose it's conveniently advantageous for the military and the government to be unable to accurately reconstruct the horrific scenarios of war; otherwise, the testosterone and confidence levels of many of these gung-ho soldiers would quickly plummet. Although my previous "daymare" from earlier in the day was only a subconscious and grossly diluted depiction of real war, it was vivid enough to open my eyes to the overlooked afflictions that battle so presumptuously imposes. My current

Jaime Perez

thoughts led to an interesting discussion over dinner amongst my barracks brothers and me.

"Hey Perez, so what was your 'daymare' about earlier today? It must have been very graphic because I saw you lightly convulsing in your sleep as I approached your bed." Smith asked.

Wilson obviously felt the need to contribute one of his often offbeat oral offerings to our discussion. "Yeah, I saw you too Perez. It looked like you were having a wet dream of some sort. Don't feel bad. I had one last night, and I owe it all to Marilyn Monroe." He added as he looked up with a disturbed and somewhat distorted smile as if trying to recall his nocturnal emission.

"Wilson, can you keep your unwanted and revolting perversities to yourself? We're about to eat here, and the last thing I need is to hear you talking about creaming your pants at night. Aren't you too old for that kind of shit anyway?" Morales rhetorically asked, but Wilson answered anyway.

"I've been having those types of dreams since I was about 12! It's not my fault; I can't control that shit. It just happens. Sometimes, when I fall asleep during a rainstorm, I…"

"All right Wilson, enough!" Capelletti interrupted with obvious disgust. "Let Perez speak. It's his last night here for God's sake. Can you let this man talk? You can tell Brown about your wet dreams later tonight. Brown's a good listener. Go on Perez. What was your daydream, I mean your 'daymare' about?"

I don't know if the guys were doing this out of sheer curiosity or out of sincere respect since I was soon to leave, but they all looked my way, gave me their undivided attention and awaited the details of my subconscious vision.

"I had a dream that I was being dropped in a very hostile area in what I believed was Vietnam. The first thing I remember was being on a plane with a bunch of unfamiliar soldiers in the back of a helicopter, and just as I'm about to be dropped, Smith's failed attempt at suffocating me wakes me. I've never been in a war, never killed a man, never fought for my life, and I'm pretty certain that I've never experienced anything like I am about experience in the next few weeks. I've been having surprisingly life-like dreams ever since I arrived at Ft. Sill. Although my expectations only go as far as what my subconscious episodes allow me, what I am seeing, feeling, smelling and hearing in my dreams are really daunting me beyond what I used to feel before my dreams began. It's as if my dreams are changing me

50

Through You

or preparing me for the worse. My previous ignorance of war allowed me to live my life with a slight semblance of tolerance and optimism, but the more I am subconsciously exposed to war, the more I feel I am becoming unable to cope with what lies ahead. Do any of you guys understand what I am saying? What I'd like to know from you guys is whether we're better off knowing or not knowing the truth. Is Thomas Gray right, or is Sir Francis Bacon right?"

"Huh? How did you just go from war to bacon Perez? You are losing your mind." Wilson said as Morales nodded his head in repulsion to Wilson's overt stupidity.

"You never cease to amaze and astonish me Wilson. I really don't know how the United States Government would allow a retard to fight in a war. It must be out of sheer pity. Retardation has to be an exclusion from serving, isn't it? I have a retarded cousin back home, and he is nowhere near as idiotic as you." Morales said as he obviously lost his patience with Wilson. He continued, "Thomas Gray is an 18th Century poet who is known for the quote 'Ignorance is bliss.' while Sir Francis Bacon is a Renaissance writer who is known for his words, 'Knowledge is power.' Didn't you learn anything in school Wilson?"

"I didn't learn that shit. It was probably covered one of the days I was absent with the chicken pox." Wilson uttered in audible soliloquy.

Capelletti was unsurprisingly intrigued by my shared query so much that he confidently declared his secular view before the others. "Gentlemen, it is obvious that Sir Francis Bacon was right. The more you know, the stronger you are PERIOD. Ignorance is what we as a species strive to overcome. It's what sets us apart from monkeys, dogs, whales, cows, and every other living thing on the planet. All medical advancements and inventions are a product of knowledge, not ignorance. Ignorance is degenerative, just look at the prime example of religion. Religion transgresses humanity every day; it weakens and debilitates like an incurable and fatal disease that kills everyone it infects. Only in a moronic world should ignorance be deemed as bliss."

"Wait a minute Capelletti." Smith interjected with a noticeable irritation. "I tend to think of myself as a good person, and my family and I are Baptists."

"I never said religious people are bad; I meant that religion is bad because it dispels ignorance. Ignorance is never good." Capelletti defended himself.

"Sometimes I feel happier when I don't know things; therefore, I

51

Jaime Perez

think ignorance can be blissful." Morales bravely challenged Capelletti's postulation.

Capelletti retorted in mild surprise. "What? I'd expect to hear such asinine and ludicrous incongruities from Wilson, but not you Morales."

"Let me give you an example of when ignorance is better than knowledge. Let's say you are somehow absolutely certain of the exact day that you will die. You will live your life so consumed and wretched beyond belief that your life can't even be enjoyed and relished. All you will think about is your last day, totally ignoring and unable to fully and richly live the preceding days. Your ignorance of your final days allows you the peace of mind and bliss that ignorance affords you because you have no knowledge of when you will die. Or, let's say you have a brother or sister who has just died in a car accident. Your mother had just suffered a massive heart attack a few days before, and you know that if you tell your mother about your sibling's death, it will likely cause her to have another heart attack, one that she will not be able to endure. You mother is better off being ignorant of the situation because the knowledge of the accident will kill her." Morales managed to have all of us pondering among ourselves and trying to evaluate the principle of his argument.

"Your first example is simply science fiction. We will never be able to know exactly when we will die because our lives our unfolding as we live them; our lives haven't happened yet, so that can't be determined with absolute certainty. You might want to send your little idea to Rod Serling; I'm sure he would appreciate the submission. Your second example practically suggests that lying is righteous and virtuous. This wouldn't exactly make your God proud would it? If your mother is so weak that the news of her child's death will likely trigger another heart attack, then you need to accept the brutal truth that she is more dead than alive. By lying to her, you are only prolonging the inevitable, and that sounds pretty damn cruel to me. I can't accept either of your examples with any validity for your argument Morales. I still firmly believe that 'Knowledge is power' holds considerably more truth than 'Ignorance is bliss'." Capelletti recanted.

Morales, still unconvinced with Capelletti's heartfelt opinions, broke the pensive atmosphere with his teasing of Wilson and Brown. "Well, Wilson isn't very knowledgeable of anything and therefore unable to fully comprehend the concept associated with 'Knowledge is power', so he is likely to be biased to agree with 'Ignorance is bliss'. This renders his views to be obviously inconclusive. Brown, on the other hand, hasn't spoken a word since his arrival here, so he is likely to side with the notion that

Through You

'Silence is power' or even 'Silence is bliss', so we won't even bother futilely asking Brown." Although somewhat cruel, we all laughed at Morales' premise, even Brown and Wilson.

"I don't know what to tell you Perez. Maybe your dreams are strengthening you or weakening you. One thing is certain, you will find out when you land in Long Binh, Vietnam." Smith assured me.

As our enlightening conversation came to a close, I realized I hadn't even begun to eat any of the cold and often tasteless food on my plate. Even though I hadn't eaten since breakfast, I wasn't really hungry. I guess my eagerness and anticipation to go home must have downplayed my hunger, or maybe the sordid sights and sickening smells from my dream were, in a way, still with me. Whatever the reason, I wastefully tossed my untouched dinner as we all got up to return to the barracks.

We all started to unwind and get comfortable by taking off our boots and lying on our beds. The whole day, for me, had been somewhat hazy and nebulous. It's like I am here physically, but not mentally. My leaving this place and my return home felt surreal as if it still hadn't kicked in completely. It seems hard to believe that my displaced life will ephemerally turn to much-missed normalcy once again, at least for two weeks that is. I remembered that I had not notified V or anybody else back home of my early L.O.A. Imagining the looks on everyone's unexpected faces brought a smile to mine. Then I thought of my son. The last time I saw him, he was small enough to comfortably fit in a women's shoebox. I sincerely hoped that my son had grown enough to physically demand something more spacious, like a crib.

I started gathering a few of my personal belongings to put them in my car. I didn't have much to take, but what I did have was important to me. The letters I had received from home, photographs of me here at Ft. Sill, photographs of V with and without me, a little portable AM radio, a few magazines that helped briefly take my mind off of the horrors of war, some garments of clothing, my dog tags and a black leather Bible that Mom had given me before leaving to become a soldier. I held the Bible in my hand before placing it inside my green Army-issued duffle bag with a black, identifying stamp that read PEREZ. Not once did I open the Bible; in actuality, I forgot I even had it with me. For some reason, nobody was talking or making any noise, and I could see with my peripheral vision that the guys, were looking at me as I packed up my stuff.

"Hey *Hermano*. Do you want some help with that?" Morales cordially offered as he simultaneously broke the peculiar silence that was lurking

53

Jaime Perez

within the barracks. His speaking of Spanish made me smirk with surprise. I knew Morales spoke Spanish; he just rarely resorted to it, so it was a little odd to hear him call me 'brother' in Spanish.

"Thanks Morales, but I'm all right. It's not much." I tossed my bag over my shoulder and headed out towards my car. The evening was serenely calm, and a subtle night breeze presented me with a pleasant whiff of sweet fresh air, much unlike the repulsive stench I had subconsciously been exposed to earlier that day. I tossed my belongings in the back seat and sat down for a while inside my red '65 Corvette Stingray. I thought about taking a little evening cruise through the town of Lawton to reabsorb the area's scenery one last time before leaving; then I thought about the long drive home I had to endure tomorrow. Quickly, this idea was abandoned. I needed to get a good night's rest for tomorrow's commute, so I returned to the barracks. As I slowly near the barracks, I begin to hear music coming from inside. I can't quite establish what artist it is, but my fondness for music lures me to increase the pace of my stride towards the music's source. Usually by this time, the men are mechanically preparing for bed. Tonight though was a little different. Just as I approach the barracks door, I am able to fully recognize the song and the artist; it was The Beatles singing the appropriately titled, "When I Get Home".

Sergeant Mills had allowed Wilson to play some music on his record player for a few minutes before bedtime in honor of my leaving. For a moment, the barracks looked like a dorm full of carefree, college freshmen enjoying the sounds of rebellious rock and roll, well everybody except Smith, who reproved this style of "noise" and preferred the Motown sounds of Stevie Wonder and Marvin Gaye over this rhapsodic ruckus. Smith was being a good sport and was going along with the celebratory and jovial environment.

"How did you know The Beatles are my favorite group Wilson?" I managed to ask with slight difficulty due to my laughing.

"You mentioned it to me a while back. I guess I'm not that retarded after all, huh? How do you like my choice of song? I chose "When I Get Home" because it's probably what you are thinking this very moment. I was going to put some Beach Boys but..."

"Stop it with your Beach Boys bullshit Wilson. Don't ruin the moment." Capelletti authoritatively interrupted as soon as he could.

"Bringing some records and a record player was a good idea Wilson, especially coming from you. You should have chosen "Drive My Car" though; that song would have been just as appropriate, and I like that

54

song a little more." Added one of the other soldiers in our barracks who I didn't know by name.

As Wilson confoundedly perused through the song listing on the record sleeve to see if that song was on this record, I quickly displayed my fanaticism for the band by explicating, "That song is on another album called *Rubber Soul*. This one we are listening to right now is *Hard Day's Night*."

"Holy shit, he really is a big fan." Smith said with slight amazement as his eyes nearly doubled in size at my unexpected knowledge.

For the next few blissful minutes, we all just lay on our beds listening to The Beatles and savoring the sonorous moment at hand. Sergeant Mills was an obvious fan of the band as well because he voluntarily allowed us to listen to one complete side of the record before commanding us to get some shuteye.

That evening at Ft. Sill was, for apparent reasons, one of the most memorable ones I am able to recall. I can't honestly say that there was a plethora of joyfully momentous occasions at Ft. Sill. After all, we were being trained to legally kill others who didn't see things the way our government did, but that night was probably the only night that nobody cried themselves to sleep, nobody had lifelike nightmares that woke up others and nobody seemed to have difficulty sleeping. Even Smith, who was forced to persevere through the aural pandemonium to which we cheerfully subjected him, managed a good night's sleep. It was a peaceful way to close a particularly difficult chapter of my life. It seemed too perfect and almost utopian, and it eventually proved to be too good to be true.

Chapter 9

Although everybody seemed to have slept restfully and without interruption that evening, that didn't apply to me. The temporary ease and comfort I felt that evening before losing consciousness was short-felt and followed by another unpleasant dream. This surreal vision seemed more lifelike and, therefore, a bit more unsettling than others.

After a lengthy, practically non-stop drive from Oklahoma to South Texas, I finally arrived to my sorely missed home. As I reach for my duffle bag, I close the car door behind me to surprise V with my unexpected and early arrival. Everything at our two-story apartment complex looked just as I had remembered, everything except one thing that brought uncertainty and discouragement. From a distance as I walked towards apartment # 17, I noticed a yellow floral bouquet decorated with mini United States flags hanging on the center of a door. I abruptly yet unthinkingly stop as if I had hit an invisible wall. I knew what a yellow bouquet of flowers meant, and the thought of a fellow soldier passing was difficult for me to swallow, especially with my nerve-wracking deployment coming up in two weeks. I didn't recall having a neighbor serving in the United States Armed Forces, but as an active soldier, I knew I had to pay my respects later that day, regardless of whom was suffering the loss.

I reach for my keys and attempt to unlock the door of my apartment. Oddly enough, I have a difficult time because the key does not enter the keyhole. I took a careful glance at my keys to make sure I was using the correct one. I laughed to myself after I realized I was using the ignition key of my Corvette to try to open my apartment door. Once again, this time with the appropriate key, I place the key in the keyhole after a few struggles with nervous trembles. The key goes in without any trouble, but to no avail, the door doesn't open. I tried to remember if V had mentioned changing locks and/or keys in one of her letters, but I couldn't recall her

56

mentioning such a significant detail as this. Just as I had relinquished to my failed efforts and thought about knocking on the door, I noticed I was trying to open the door to apartment # 15; our apartment was the next one down, the one adorned with the yellow bouquet on the door. I hesitantly and apprehensively continued to the next door in sheer bewilderment. I felt my heart stop for a few seconds and began to wonder what was going on.

For a moment, I felt like I was dreaming and not really there. I motionlessly and perplexedly stood in front of the door of apartment #17; I was hindered from reaching to unlock the door by what I had heard behind it, the faint mournful cries of many. I expected to hear my son weeping, but these cries were those of several grieving adults. What I heard insidiously filled me with disquietude. The crying suddenly began to get louder and clearer as if the grieving were approaching the door. Suddenly, before I can open the door myself, the door flutters open from the inside, and I see Mom rush out, covering her tear-soaked face with her trembling hands. Dad, with tears of his own, was following right behind her, obviously concerned for her well-being. Aside from not knowing the cause of sorrow, I was also confused by the fact that Mom and Dad passed me by without acknowledging my presence. Inside, V was in tears as well, as she gently held Gilbert in her warm arms while attempting to speak to someone on the phone. I stood in the middle of our living room without the ability to speak and in utter confusion. V concluded the phone call and sat down on our brown leather couch. She too had failed to acknowledge my presence. I reached down to take Gilbert off her hands and allow her to grieve a little more freely, but I was inexplicably unable to grasp him. I then attempted to empathetically caress V's sorrow-stricken face, but again I was unable to feel anything. Everything appeared to have the substance of an abstract. It was as if everything I saw before me was an illusion, almost like trying to feel your face on a body of water when you realize it is only a mere reflection. It was unusually odd. In addition to being unable to grasp anything solid, I also noticed my emotions were lacking sensitivity. I wasn't bothered by my family's failure to acknowledge me after months of displacement at Ft. Sill; I wasn't even truly concerned with the reason for such obvious grief. I had been in my sullen living room with my lamenting family for several minutes without anyone having said anything to me. Instead of being bothered and concerned like I should be, I felt as if I could only discern and recognize emotions, not actually feel them to the fullest. The only emotion I was fully receptive of was confusion. As all

Jaime Perez

the uncanny idiosyncrasies of this scenario suddenly began to pervade my impassive soul, it was V's next striking comment that further enlightened me on what exactly was currently occurring.

"Whyyyyyy!?!" V fiercely wailed with more agony than I was aware she was capable of exuding as she simultaneously fell to her knees and hit the floor. "It's not fair! I can't accept the fact that my husband is dead!!"

Like an epiphany, it all suddenly became so clear, why I couldn't feel anything or anyone, why everyone was crying, why I couldn't open the door and why my own family wasn't acknowledging me.

"I don't know what to say Veronica. The pain and shock disallow me from being able to even think straight. I never thought I would have to bury my own child. What could be worse than burying your own child?" Dad hugged V as he helped her up to sit her on the couch. Although he tried, he failed to comfort her.

Mom also came to hug V but said nothing. Just as Mom appeared as if she was about to say something, V's parents, Virginia and Al, gloomily walk in. Mournful embraces broke out amongst my in-laws and my parents as well V.

I was so engulfed by V's, my parents' and my in-law's emotions that I had failed to give my son Gilbert much attention, but eerily, he didn't seem to fail to notice me, even though he couldn't have possibly remembered who I was from having seen me for only a few weeks after his birth. Since I had arrived at the apartment, no one had made eye contact with me because I obviously wasn't physically there, only spiritually. Yet, my son on the other hand had been utterly silent and practically motionless the whole time I was there. He wasn't even blinking, but he was looking directly at me. It was as if only he could see me, and his seeing me rendered him completely stationary like a figure at a wax museum or a lifelike mannequin. I stood there lifeless, statuelike and in shock at the fact that he somehow seemed to be able to see me. At first, both of us just looked at each other for several seconds, then the impossible happened—Gilbert began walking towards me even though he had just barely learned to crawl! With an inquisitive and curious look, he, without any signs of difficultly or unsteadiness, began to approach me on the other couch I was sitting on. His ability to walk left me, even though I couldn't be heard, at a loss for words. Approximately 8 steps later, he stands before me, looks me in the eye, and begins to speak!

"Don't worry about us Daddy. We are going to be all right. I will take really good care of Mommy for you. Mommy and I will always love you and miss you."

My premature son's premature yet comforting words brought me to profuse tears. Now I was able to feel emotions. I tried to wipe away my tears because my vision was becoming extremely blurry. I wanted to clear my vision so that I could continue this miraculous and unlikely conversation with my infant son. The more I wiped, the blurrier things became. Finally, the blurring waned. The next thing I know, I am rubbing my wet eyes and looking at the ceiling of my barracks with my neck area completely saturated.

Slightly perturbed, I manage to focus my sight and look around the barracks to see if I inadvertently woke up anybody. There was no indication that anyone was awake. The night was rather tranquil, with the exception of Smith's light snoring. I looked at my alarm clock to see the time. It was only 0300 hrs, and I was pretty certain that I would not be able to resume my much-needed sleep because of my nap earlier in the day and also because of the subconscious out-of-body experience I had just finished enduring. I thought about getting out of bed and beginning my trip home immediately, but even though I would have arrived home much earlier, I would have given up my last opportunity to say goodbye to the guys, which I didn't want to do. I decided to stay in bed and pass the time by reflecting on the dream I had just had. I wasn't too sure how to interpret it or if I should even attempt to make any sense of it. What would be the point of even trying? If anything, I did manage to extract one important lesson from my dream—I did not want to cause all the pain and suffering that my parents, my in-laws, my wife and my son were subjected to because of my passing. I was going to do everything in my power to make it out of this war alive and well.

As 0400 hrs slowly approached, I began to hear the rustling of waking soldiers. Usually one of us sets his alarm for the benefit of all, but with last night's festive mood, this was apparently overlooked and forgotten because I didn't hear the once dreadful beeping that I, as well as many others, so openly grew to distaste. Little by little and one by one, each soldier eventually began his monotonous morning stretching and waking ritual, of course, with the exception of me. It felt awkward to watch everybody prepare for another day while I just casually sat on my bed and observed.

"Are you finding it hard to leave Perez?" Morales asked as he wiped the crusty rheum from his eyes with his index finer.

Jaime Perez

"Yes and no. I am anxious to leave, but I didn't want to do it without saying my goodbyes to you bastards. Although I've been trained to become a stonehearted soldier, I guess the small remnants of soft-heartedness that I still possess impeded me from leaving last night or earlier this morning. I'll be out of here very soon Morales."

Within half an hour, I was in my car and ready for my nearly half-day drive to my family. I said my hasty goodbyes to everybody, even to the few soldiers that had never spoken a word to me as well as the one soldier who had never spoken to anybody but me, Private Brown. Before leaving I even got to say goodbye to Sergeant Mills as he walked out of his room. He was usually the first one dressed, ready and out the door to passionately begin his daily duties. Farewells to soldiers, I noticed, are much shorter than the type of goodbyes given to family members or close friends. In fact, saying goodbye to my barracks brothers almost seemed perfunctorily heartless. Only a firm handshake or a tap on the back generally accompanied the most intimate and heartfelt of goodbyes. There were no phone number or address exchanges, no tears, no painful reluctances and no hugs, just a frigid, inhumane coldness that I wasn't expecting. Maybe human detachment is an advantageous and quintessential tool when living the life of a soldier; this was something they obviously forget to teach me in basic training.

Today would have normally been a day that I would have called V. I usually made my customary call at about 1800 hrs, but today, by 1800 hrs, I should be in the comfort of my own home. No call was necessary. I had left Ft. Sill without eating breakfast. My plan was to grab a bite to eat on the road whenever it was time to gas up. As soon as the surroundings became unfamiliar to me, I stopped at a gas station, purchased something to drink, filled up with gas, and reached for the glove compartment to get my Texaco Road Map. I was pretty certain that I was headed in the right direction, but I was just in need of a little reassurance. As I open the folded map, a little piece of paper falls from within and onto the passenger's side floor mat. I was the last one to use the map, so I was naturally intrigued by the unfamiliar paper and quickly wondered what it was. It appeared to be an unused, oversized white napkin with writing on it. Even before I had completely unfolded the napkin, a smile came to my face because I knew that the writing was V's. She had an elegant and distinctive penmanship, unlike any I had ever seen before. She must have premeditated this perfectly to coincide with my trip home. She likely anticipated my using the map for my drive home and therefore placed this little note inside the map to surprise me. This type of playfully romantic display was characteristic of V. The note read:

My brave soldier,
Surprise!! If you are reading this, you are probably on your way home now. I want to wish you a safe trip back and to tell you that I am eagerly awaiting your arrival. I wrote this note and placed it in the map while you were in training because I didn't want you to catch me red handed. I know I have told you many times what I am about to say, but I am going to say it again because I never want you to forget it. The only difference in what I'm about to tell you is that this time it is in poetic form.

Those Thoughts
Whenever I think about the past…
I always see you in those thoughts.
Whenever I think about the present…
I always see you in those thoughts.
It's not surprising that whenever I think about the future…
I always see you in those thoughts.
And it is those thoughts that make smile for no apparent reason.
It is those thoughts that make me look forward to tomorrow.
It is those thoughts that make me cry of happiness because those thoughts are all of you.

O.K. I know I am not exactly Shakespeare, but that doesn't mean that these words are not coming from the bottom of my heart. I can't wait until you get here where you belong with Gilbert and me. So stop reading this and start driving home!!
Love you and be safe,
V and Gilbert Perez

My wife was right—this poem was definitely not Shakespeare, but unlike Shakespeare, I could understand and therefore feel this poem. It took me a few minutes to mentally return from my evanescent moment of wonder and contentment. When I finally did come back to my senses, I put V's note in my pocket, perused through my map and took a much-needed sip from my RC cola. I was on the right path home. V's note instilled anxiousness and heightened my desire to get home. These next several hours were going to seem like a painful eternity. I turned on the

Jaime Perez

radio in hopes of it taking my mind off of my unduly tedious drive. I dialed through the radio frequencies and finally found something to help me get on with my journey. I was going to resume my drive, and my friends *Jan and Dean* were going with me.

Chapter 10

I was only about 2 hours into my drive, which meant that I had approximately 8 hours left of lonely, desolate road to travel. Dealing with silence when it is not desired is difficult for me, so I had to keep my music search going on the radio as I drove. I am very finicky when it comes to listening to music. V used to tease me about having my right hand on the radio dial just as often as my left hand was on the steering wheel. This thought made me laugh a little because she was absolutely right, and I had just noticed that this very moment.

I have never been a lover of road trips and lengthy drives, but I knew the destination of this particular trip was different than any other. Previous to being drafted, I had never been away from home or my family for more than a week, so the extensive displacement I had just experienced was alien to me. As a matter of fact, it was probably also alien to V as well. She had willingly decided to join me at Ft. Sill when she could have just as easily stayed home. I thought it was going to be challenging to convince V to come with me because I wanted her to be with me, even though I would have to spend the majority of the day at the fort. I remember not knowing exactly how to approach her with my unappealing invitation to accompany me to Fort Sill.

"V, I have been assigned to Lawton, Oklahoma for on-the-job-training at Fort Sill after I complete my basic training in San Antonio." I said slowly and carefully so as to not seem so rushed and presumptuous.

Without even waiting for my invitation, she boldly asks, "So when do *we* leave?"

I responded to her question with a smile, and as she noticed my smirk, she asked, "What's so funny? You are going to train for a war you don't care for and you are laughing. Baby, maybe you should get mentally re-evaluated so we can make sure you are actually whole and functional. You

63

Jaime Perez

might get lucky and be forced to stay home if your results are not up to par." Her unmatched wittiness never ceased to humor me.

"I thought I was going to have a hard time convincing you to go with me. After all, it's not like we are going to the Bahamas; it's Lawton, Oklahoma!" I said sarcastically.

"I know, but you are going to be there, and I feel we should be together. It's as simple as that. I'm not staying here while you go off and leave me brooding on how you're doing every single night. I will go insane. Plus, I want you to be with me when I give birth. If I stay here, we won't be able to share our miracle together." V made complete sense.

"I'm glad you are coming with me. I wouldn't have it any other way." I assured her of my concurrence.

I approached a sign as my pleasant reminiscence came to an end. The sign read, "Ft. Worth 40 miles, San Antonio 302 miles." I still had a seemingly insurmountable drive before me. My destination, McAllen, Texas, was roughly an additional 400 miles farther south of San Antonio. I didn't even want to begin mentally calculating the hours because this would have exacerbated my already engrossing impatience.

I must have lost track of the radio while I was thinking of V's and my conversation because under normally perceptive circumstances I would not be listening to the song being played on the radio. I don't know exactly who it was, but it certainly was not to my liking. I began my search for something on the radio that could help keep my mind off this seemingly incessant journey. As I approached Ft. Worth, Texas, I began to lose reception to most of the radio stations I was previously enjoying; this fostered a new search for new radio stations in the Ft. Worth area. I must have spent at least half an hour searching with disappointment for something that I could at least tolerate listening to because finding something that I actually enjoyed was proving to be impossible. Just as my right hand was losing sensitivity and numbing up from having it reach for the radio dial for too long a period of time, I finally found it. I was beginning to conclude that people in Ft. Worth had embarrassingly poor taste in music, but then I came across KFTW—Ft. Worth's Grooviest Station. This was their self-proclaimed slogan, and judging from what was exuding from my 8-inch speakers, I was not about to argue this accurately pretentious claim because this radio station sliced completely through the wrists of ennui. For the next several minutes, the power of music had resuscitated me from the darkest depths of boredom and dullness. It was as if I was KFTW's own deejay. They were playing everything I would play if I had the liberty of doing so. The Hollies, Simon and Garfunkel, The Bee Gees, Jan and Dean, The Beatles, The Four Tops, The Kinks, The Rolling Stones and even Wilson's supposed brothers, The Beach Boys were all in for the ride. I was in a momentary aural paradise. Hell, even the commercials between songs were entertaining and upbeat. Unfortunately, the closer I got to San Antonio and the farther I drove from Fort Worth the less clear KFTW's reception became. Surely something in San Antonio would suffice to keep me entertained, or at least I hoped so. As I reached to take a sip of my drink, I noticed that my sweatless aluminum can of RC Cola was empty, and I was beginning to acquire an impressive thirst. I still had several miles to go before arriving in San Antonio, but I was not too convinced that the amount of fuel I was running on was enough to get me there. I could see a protruding Phillips 66 sign up ahead, and this was my chance to refuel both my car and me.

After filling up the red Corvette's tank, I entered the gas station and browsed around for something to snack on. I was hungry, thirsty and I didn't want to have to stop again until after I passed San Antonio. An elderly man wearing a cap with some kind of World War II inscription on it was having a troublesome time getting the door opened to exit the store. As I noticed this, I hurried my pace to get to the door so that I can help remedy this man's predicament. The man notices my Army attire and shrewdly gazes at me and makes it a point to observe me from head to toe.

"Good day Sir." I say to him with respect as I enter the store. He, on the other hand, failed to reply for some reason.

Two seconds after I entered the store, the usual, everyday sounds that one would expect inside of a gas station went completely silent, as if the volume knob of life was turned all the way to the left. Everyone, customers and employees alike, simultaneously turned towards the entrance to look at me in my military uniform. The obvious and awkward silence puzzled me as I approached the soft drink cooler towards the rear of the gas station to find energy in a can. After grabbing another RC Cola, I strolled down to the potato chip aisle to get a bag of Lay's Brand Potato Chips. Directly in front of the potato chip display were two boys contemplating their selections. They immediately moved aside and made space for me to have all the room I needed to observe the snacks before me. It seemed as if they were stepping aside to signify respect as one would to a king, queen or person of royalty, but the grudging looks on their faces seemed to suggest a sentiment quite contrary to esteem and laudability.

65

Jaime Perez

As I approached the cashier to pay for my items and gas, I could faintly hear the two boys behind me gossiping about me like immature schoolyard kids. Considering these boys were in their late teens, their conspicuous behavior protruded more than expected. Their discussion was too indistinct for me to construe, but I had a good idea that it wasn't anything polite or anything that I had deserved. Aside from the boys' ill-mannered giggles, all else was as silent as when I initially entered.

"Hello." I greeted the female employee behind the cash register who kept me discourteously waiting for a few minutes while she counted and recounted dollar bills as if she had not noticed me. She, like the elderly man at the door, was non-conversational.

"I'll take care of this one. Go out back and throw the trash." An overweight bald man with a faded tattoo of an American flag on his right arm, probably the gas station's owner or manager, directed the female who I had just greeted.

Reaching for my wallet, I notice anti-Vietnam War propaganda on the counter by the cash register: bumper stickers, Zippo cigarette lighters, caps and a few other items. The man, who is now behind the counter, charges my items and takes my twenty dollar bill but not before grabbing one of the caps on the counter and putting it on his head. The cap read *Viet-NO*.

"How 'bout a cap soldier boy?" He condescendingly offers with a bogus smirk.

"No thank you." I respond with a feigned smile.

I didn't take his gesture very kindly, and I didn't really feel like having my day ruined by another mindless yet over-opinionated anti-war advocate. I, too, had my strong doubts about this controversial war I was being sent to fight, but I was sick ad nauseam of having to hear all the opposition. The people's and the media's opinions aren't going to change anything. This war will resume, and I have been chosen to provide my services. There is nothing I can do about this now.

The obnoxious man behind the counter slowly gives me my change and seems as if he is about to finally find me worthy of his undesired utterances because he takes a deep breath, the kind one takes before initiating a conversation, but I hastily grab my things and my change and make my way to my car before he can begin muttering his garbage. Although it was a little inconsiderate and rude of me to leave as I did, it was well deserved; plus, I figured that the sooner I got out of there, the sooner I would get home.

Just as I thought that I could consider this unfriendly encounter as a

Through You

thing of the past, a little boy, who must have been no older than 5, is sitting in the back seat of his mother's Chevy Impala and ecstatically waving to me as his mother pumps gas in her car, which was parked behind mine. I naturally wave back to the little boy, as he sticks his head out of the car and yells, "Look Mommy, one of Daddy's friends!"

The excited little boy eagerly jumps out of the car, much to his mother's disapproval. "Get back in the car this instant Timmy!! I'm not going to tell you again." The mother sternly ordered in failure.

The little boy, Timmy, stands directly under my shadow with a serious look and gives me a firm military-style salute. His innocent cuteness almost compels me to laugh, but I didn't think Timmy would have taken my laughter kindly. I saluted him as well.

Timmy's mom explains. "I'm sorry Mister. My son can get a little excited whenever he sees a solider like his father. He wants to follow in his father's footsteps and be a soldier one day, but I don't plan to let that happen, not over my dead body. I'm sorry. I didn't mean that out of disrespect."

"No disrespect taken mam." I assured her that her reference to a dead body was taken metaphorically and not literally. "If I may ask, is Timmy's father stationed overseas?"

"No, he is too old to be doing the dirty work that you younger men do. He is a Sergeant at Ft. Sill. Fortunately for me, he won't be leaving the country this time around."

"Your husband wouldn't by any chance be Sergeant Mills, would it?"

"Why…yes!! That is my husband. Are you stationed at Fort Sill?" She asks showing a newfound concern for our conversation.

"Yes mam, I am." Forgetting that Ft. Sill was no longer my place of temporary residency. "I mean, I did my OJT there, and now I am on my L.O.A."

"Well isn't this a coincidence," says Mrs. Mills.

"You see Mommy, I told you he was one of Daddy's friends. He even talks like him with all those letters and stuff." Timmy bursts out.

I smirk as Timmy points out my impulsive use of abbreviations and acronyms, which likely didn't seem noticeably odd to Mrs. Mills since she is the wife of a Sergeant.

"Timmy thinks that everyone he sees in a military uniform is one of his Daddy's friends."

"In a way, we are friends, family, brothers and confidants all at the

67

Jaime Perez

same time. Your husband is a good man Mrs. Mills. This country is extremely fortunate to have him serving." I say in all seriousness.

"Why thank you…Officer Perez." She says as she reads my name from the patch on my chest.

"Well, I better get on my way. I am going to visit my family in McAllen, Texas before being sent to Vietnam. It was a pleasure meeting you Mrs. Mills, and you too Timmy."

"You take care of yourself Officer Perez. I will keep you in my prayers."

"Thank you mam." I said to Mrs. Mills before giving Timmy one more salute before leaving. He returns the salute with his lips pouted, as if to accentuate his sternness.

Chapter 11

I resumed my painfully long road trip, but not before opening my bag of chips and taking a healthy sip of my RC Cola. I loved the thirst-quenching volcanic eruptions that cold colas produce in one's throat. It's just as invigorating, if not more so, than the time I had to be given smelling salts in El Paso, Texas at Fort Bliss after fainting during one of our many hellish physical endurance tests. Although, I'd have to say that I would gladly prefer a refreshing cola to nasty smelling salts any day.

As I veered back on to the highway, I couldn't help reflect on how much Timmy resembled his father. Not only his physical features, but also his mannerisms were as similar as possible, considering Sergeant Mills has to share Timmy's time with military time and therefore wasn't always there to model his behavior. I instinctively began thinking of Gilbert's appearance and whom he might begin to resemble. The first few days after the baby's delivery, V would playfully attest that Gilbert had more of her features than mine; of course, I would argue the contrary. Sadly, I vaguely remember what my son looks like. I mean, I didn't spend as much time as I would have liked holding him and marveling at his existence. By now, I'm sure Gilbert's features have drastically changed since the last time I saw him. He probably doesn't even resemble any of the now outdated photographs I have of him. My permeating curiosity was commanding my thoughts, and this did nothing to appease my anxiousness to get home. I was now approximately 3 hrs north of San Antonio, as I calculated from the road sign that read "San Antonio 170 miles".

I mentally returned to Ft. Sill and wondered what my fellow soldiers were doing at this very minute. It was around lunch time, so I couldn't help but picture all of them eating and sitting at their usual table as Capelletti, Morales and Smith made fun of Wilson while Brown preferably kept his usual silence. As a food service specialist, I didn't have the chance to fully

69

enjoy their company during lunch because us 94 B20s didn't eat until everybody started clearing out of the cafeteria.

The seemingly incompatible and sometimes intense characters of these men, Wilson's slowness bordering on mental retardation, Brown's selective muteness, Capelletti's excessive machismo, Smith's anti-war outspokenness and Morales' pro-patricidal desires along with his philosophical outlook on life somehow fused together well enough for them to inexplicably get along without killing each other, although they came close to this disposition many times. This anomalistic group of men, although I may never speak another word to them, would forever remain in my thoughts. They never realized it, and I never told them that it was their eccentric friendships that helped me endure and survive my tumultuous times at Ft. Sill. I wish I had been a little more expressive with them so that they would know the significance and profundity that each one of them had on my life.

I had a regrettable habit of not saying what is on my mind a lot of the times, and now my self-detested reticence has surfaced again to establish superiority over me. We were undoubtedly more different than similar, but we formed a strong symbiotic bond of brotherhood that kept us from relinquishing to the grips of insanity that often and inexorably clasp many unfortunate soldiers. I hope I had some sort of positive or pleasant effect on them. I don't really care if they remember me when they hit 90 years of age, but I just hope they enjoyed my company at least half as much as I enjoyed theirs during the brevity of our time together.

Out of nowhere, a blinding blur suddenly covered my windshield. Without the foreseeable warning of dark clouds, an impressively inundating downpour began aggressively striking my windshield, so I quickly turned on my windshield wipers. Although the dreadful rain sounded as if it was accompanied by hail, I couldn't clearly detect anything solid smashing my vehicle. Just as I had begun to veer off the road to weather the deluge, it abruptly stopped. The rain probably lasted a little less than a minute, but when one is subjected to an impressive downpour on the road while driving 55 miles an hour, a minute of obstructed vision seems like an hour. My windshield was clear, but my vision was still relatively blurry. This is when I realized that there was another source to the blurriness, my eyes. I wiped my previously unnoticed tears, and then everything seemed clearer. At home, I didn't have any brothers, only two older sisters, so the depressing effect of my detachment with my temporary, government-assigned brethren was not a surprise.

The multiple-hour drive between Ft. Worth and San Antonio was mostly soul soothing and surprisingly therapeutic, unlike the experience inside the Phillips 66 gas station south of Ft. Worth. I had smoothly breezed through Waco, Georgetown, Austin and San Marcos. This stretch of my trip didn't feel like 3 hrs at all. Soon enough, I was now only 8 short miles from San Antonio; I had just realized that I had made this portion of the trip with the radio off. The previously unnoticed silence ostensibly yielded me with time for additional thoughtful reflection. Mom, Pop, V and Gilbert all ran constantly rampant through my mind. I wasn't even paying very much attention to whether or not I was driving in the right direction. The road was a relatively straight path, so this didn't concern me too much.

One of the thoughts that crossed my mind was the first time V met my parents. It was the week before my Senior Dance at high school. We had been seeing each other for several months, and I had already met her parents because they knew me from the grocery store where I worked and where they also shopped. My parents had been irritating me endlessly to bring her to meet them since they had heard a lot about her, but never met her. This was her first time meeting a boy's parents, and she was struggling with this far more than I thought was possible. She was sweating profusely; her heart rate was pulsating more rapidly than normal, and she was practically on the verge of tears. Her frantic behavior reminded me a little of the unruly and frenzied reactions that women would unashamedly display in the front row of an Elvis Presley concert as the king of rock and roll would sing and dance through his tunes, musically hypnotizing his frantic female fans.

"Beltran, I don't know why, but I can't do this today. Can't we please do this tomorrow? I am going to mess this up completely, and they are going to think I am weird. I want them…I need them to like me. I know I will be better prepared to handle this tomorrow. I promise." V begged.

"What's the big deal? Why are you so uptight and intimidated? It's only my parents. They are going to like you. I know it." I tried but failed to convince her.

Her anxiety had us debating outside my house's front door for about 30 minutes. Even though I had promised my parents that I would introduce V to them that night, I thoughtfully gave in to V's convincing pleads and spared her of her unnerving internal inferno.

Just as I had agreed to drive her back home and attempt this tomorrow, my dad opens the door to supposedly check the mail and sees us standing directly outside the door on our front porch.

71

Jaime Perez

"What are you doing out here Son? Did you forget your house keys? Well...who do we have here?" My father redirects his attention from me to V.

Just as I was about to formally introduce my father to V, my mother suddenly makes an appearance as well. "What? A party in front of my home, and I'm not invited?" She rhetorically and jokingly asks with a motherly smile.

I, without much of a choice, begin introducing V to my mother and father. The rest of the evening went much more smoothly than V had probably expected. My parents had a natural way of making people feel comfortable and welcomed. We ended up having enchiladas for dinner, and we continued with small talk as the television aired episodes of *The Andy Griffith Show*. The entire 3-hour long event went much better than V had anticipated. Her unfavorable expectations were likely just rigid products of her unbending fear. After V realized it was getting a little late, she politely gave me a look that wordlessly expressed her need to leave. I informed my parents that I needed to drive V back home before it became too late. They got up, said their prolonged goodbyes and invited her back whenever she felt like visiting.

"You see. That wasn't so bad was it?"

"I'm sorry Beltran. I am just not accustomed to this type of thing." V sincerely stated.

"Well, it's all behind us now, and you can now resume the rest of your life contently relieved." I said as I started my car.

V only lived a few houses down the street, but I, like every male teenager in the world who owned his own car, tried to use every excuse I could conjure to get in my car and drive. As we approached her house, we said our goodbyes, and she got out of my car. I courteously waited until she entered her house before I drove off. We waved goodbye to each other, and I resumed home. I had a funny feeling that my parents were going to be waiting for my arrival to unnecessarily recapitulate the evening's event. I must know my parents better than they think because they were both sitting in the dimly lit living room anticipating my walking in the house. They didn't even bother keeping the television on to at least make their façade a little more believable.

"Since when do you guys check the mail on Sundays?" I asked Pop jokingly. "You could have come up with a better excuse than that Dad. Come on...really."

"Well son. I couldn't think of any other excuse to use. I just knew that

I had to do something quick because you and V had your mother and me with our ears against the door for so long that, after about 20 minutes, our ears started to sweat against the wooden door. You were killing us with your procrastination." My dad admitted as my mother laughed along with him in slight embarrassment. They had sneakily eavesdropped on V's and my lengthy conversation outside our house before they went to "check the mail" on a Sunday. I laughed along with them, not because they had admitted to listening in on my conversation with V but because picturing them both with their ears glued to the door seemed a little amusing yet at the same time childishly mischievous on their part. This is when I realized that my eavesdropping on my sister's conversations late at night outside their bedroom door when I was much younger was likely a hereditary inclination that was biologically passed on to me. I couldn't be blamed for that.

Traffic started to suddenly look more active and congested. This was a sign that I was approaching the San Antonio city limits. I hadn't been paying enough attention to all the road signs, but I was pretty certain this was the San Antonio atmosphere. I was never particularly fond of big city traffic; so numerous cars were easily passing me by left and right. To my left, I could see a brand new, blue Ford Mustang approaching through my side door mirror. As I looked to see the driver of this car, the man in the driver's seat honked his horn to get my attention and screamed something to me that I couldn't quite decipher due to the boisterous sounds of traffic. Judging by the man's cheerful manner, I assumed that his comment was nothing humiliating or rude. A few miles up the road, this man veers in my driving lane and resumes driving directly in front of me. I was close enough to notice a bumper sticker on his rear fender that read, "Support our troops...I do." He probably noticed me in uniform as my left arm hung out of the car window, showing my camouflaged Army jacket sleeve. Although I would probably never know what this man was making a valiant attempt to tell me while we were driving, I had a good idea that it was something I would have liked to have heard, something to offset the unavailing disapproval I had received hours before at the gas station.

As I drove through the bustling of San Antonio, I began to think again about the anti-supportive gas station incident as well as the apparently supportive man in the blue Ford Mustang. These sentiments of ambivalence concerning the Vietnam War were prevalent everywhere. The media never seemed too convincing as to inform on the dominance for the war or against the war. When we had the chance to watch the

73

Jaime Perez

news at Ft. Sill or Ft. Bliss, we were all left with confusing contradictions. One day the war seemed like the right thing to do; the next day the news would show country-wide protests scorning the inevitable war efforts. People's inflammatory opinions varied to no end. Even within our own government, contradictions in opinions were common. Everybody was in disagreement, governors, senators, state representatives, soldiers, the rich and the poor, but the men at the top felt it was in our best interest to police Vietnam and aid those in need, even though Vietnam was not the United State's property.

I hated being a part of something that I wanted to have no part of, especially when I was supposedly a free man, who wasn't allowed a free choice on the matter. It was like being forced to honor a prearranged marriage where one was forced to spend the rest of his/her life with someone he/she didn't love. Or maybe even being forced to practice any given religion simply because one's ancestors were once devotees to a practice that one doesn't completely find suitable anymore. I felt like a puppet with no strings, a choiceless servant, and a victim of government agenda, where incompliance was considered unpatriotic and the incompliant were considered cowards.

Mom and Pop tried to justify my drafting with ineffective and inconsolable religious comforting. "This is all part of God's plan son. Accept this because the Lord will take care of you and watch over you."

I don't know exactly how much of this my parents actually and wholeheartedly believed, but I found it challenging to contain myself from openly shunning and discounting their preposterous advice that reeked of utter unreason and ill-founded illogicality. I know their words were well intended, but they seemed about as plausible as the existence of Santa Claus, which needless to say, as a child, they also assured me of his existence. Out of respect to my parents' good intentions, I restrained my disbelief and anger. This was no time to stir up a needless argument. All I could think about was, "If God were truly watching over me, I wouldn't be sent off to train to kill his children in Vietnam. He could surely do this himself without putting my life in jeopardy."

The first few days after receiving my draft notice were the most difficult and resentful of my life. I was just out of high school, just married and ready to start my new life as a husband and a father, not a soldier and a murderer. What should have been the most blissful and highly-anticipated point in my life quickly became the most sordid instead.

Suddenly, from my right side, a baby deer jumped about 25 feet in front on my red Corvette and hopped along to my left side, but driving at the speeds that I was, 25 feet felt much shorter than it actually was. I pounded on the brakes and turned my steering wheel to the right to avoid both killing the fawn and damaging my car. I closed my eyes; my car came to a stop on the shoulder of the road after skidding for several feet, and suddenly there was no deer in sight, no blood, no cracked windshield, nothing. Luckily for me, the road was desolate, and nobody within view was driving behind me or ahead of me. I remained idle on the side of the road for a few minutes to gather my thoughts as well as my breath.

Roughly 10 feet in front of my car was another sign. This one read, "Three Rivers 12 miles". I was just south of San Antonio now and less than 4 hours from home. My excitement and anticipation were increasing by the minute. I looked at my gas gauge and noticed it was almost time to fill up my vehicle again. I drove the 12 miles to Three Rivers and decided to fill up there.

I had driven many times to and from San Antonio when I was younger to visit family and friends, so the road I was on was relatively familiar. I knew there was a Texaco in Three Rivers, so I stopped to gas up there and prepared myself for any kind of reaction from those inside. This time I was ready for whatever came my way.

After pumping my gas, I head towards the door of the gas station. Just as I am about to reach for the door handle, a fellow soldier in his United States Air Force uniform and his wife or girlfriend are cheerfully laughing together as they open the door on their way out. I step aside and allow them to continue on their way. The soldier notices me in my uniform and stops to talk.

"Good afternoon soldier. It's good to see another soldier like myself every once in a while." He tells me in a very stern and confident voice as we salute each other.

"You got that right soldier. I've been receiving dirty looks just about everywhere I go. It's almost like we are at fault for what is going on overseas. Where are you stationed?" I asked him.

"I'm heading out to South Vietnam in two days. I'm on my L.O.A. and visiting family here in Three Rivers. I am Private Olson, and this here is my future wife Elsie." She kindly offers her hand with a smile.

"It's a pleasure meeting both of you. I am Private Perez. I'm also on L.O.A., and I'm making my way home to McAllen, Texas to see my parents, my wife and my son before being sent to South Vietnam as well."

"McAllen, Texas...that's about 4 hours south, huh?"

Jaime Perez

I nod affirmatively and add, "I am almost there. I can practically feel it."

"Best of luck to you Perez. Be safe on the ground, and I'll do my part in the air." He saluted me before making his way towards his car with his wife.

I answer. "Good luck to you Olson. Let's make sure we make it back in one piece." I saluted him before I entered the store. I wasn't really hungry this time. Maybe the fear of nearly killing a wandering fawn had left my stomach a little uneasy. Just as the man behind the cash register was about to greet me, Olson swiftly reappears and sticks his head through the front door of the Texaco and says, "Hey Dad, give Officer Perez the gas on the house please. A brother in warfare shouldn't have to pay for his gas."

I look at the man, Private Olson's father, with a look of slight surprise and unexpectedness. "You heard my son. The gas is on the house. Be safe and God bless you." He said with a hasty and tenuous salute.

I smiled, put my money back in my pocket and thanked him as I returned the salute.

As I exited the Texaco, I got to see Olson and Elsie one last time as they drove off and waved goodbye from Olson's convertible Chevy Camaro. I smiled and waved to them as they gradually faded in the Texas heat.

I once again resumed with my strenuous drive, which was now about 4 hours away from concluding. I was sure that the last hours 4 would likely seem like the longest 4 hours of this drive. As I continued down the scorching road, I thought about how happy Olson and Elsie appeared to be. I couldn't help but think that there had to be a little hidden despair and lingering apprehensiveness in both their minds. They were planning on getting married, and Olson was set to leave the country in two days, which lead me to deduce that they were going to get married upon Olson's return—granted he did return. My pervasive pessimistic predilections yielded me to think the worst. What if Olson didn't make it back? What if Elsie found someone else while Olson was away serving his country? What if Olson made it back a changed man, maybe missing a limb or mentally unable to cope with post-war life? Would Elsie feel compelled to fulfill her relationship's obligation?

I suddenly couldn't help but notice the undeniable parallels between Olson and Elsie's relationship and V's and my marriage. For some odd reason, I developed a sense of empathy for Elsie, when V was just as likely to experience what Elsie might. It was very possible that V would be put through trying situations while I was gone as well. After all, misfortune is

Through You

not biased when it comes to inflicting its afflictions upon the unfortunate. Sometimes it's a little easier to see things from an external and unattached perspective, as I had with Olson and Elsie.

Now that I had indirectly observed and contemplated the potentially pressing hardships that a girlfriend of a soldier has to face on a daily basis, it was easy for me to convey these tribulations relative to V. It must be equally difficult for a parent as well. I began to feel guilty and somehow responsible for subjecting V to such hardship even though I didn't really have an option to refuse serving. V not only has to constantly worry about me, but she has to raise our fragile son alone while I'm off killing strangers in their own country.

A sudden surge of selfishness overcame me as I approached a road sign that read "Alice 11 miles". I felt as if I owed V an apology for what I'm putting her through. It's not fair that she should have to endure a psychological war at home while I endure wars of my own overseas. This is when I truly came to realize that it takes an unusually special kind of woman to spend the rest of her life with a soldier, constantly worrying about his well being, losing sleep over uncertainty, enduring nightmares of her own, afraid to answer the phone or answer the door with fear of being given notice of her husband's demise. All of this is unduly unjust, not just for my wife, but for Elsie, Mrs. Mills, and every other wife, fiancée, parent, brother, sister, cousin and friend who must somehow be expected to inhumanly endure the unendurable. I heard a saying once when I was in grade school. It went, "What you don't know won't hurt you". I am not sure who the visionless visionary was who came up with this fallacious adage, but whoever it was must not have known or been related to a soldier because I don't think this applies to the wives, family and friends of soldiers. Not knowing, in this case, can still cause unbearable, immense pain.

I had managed to once again exasperate my own emotions as was evident with my tears. I don't consider myself to be melodramatic or overemotional, and I am usually pretty good about concealing my emotions. So these recent ambushing outbursts of moist and mixed sentiments had taken me by surprise. It's almost as if I have become someone else during the passed few days, someone else who I didn't know I was capable of becoming. I was often told that war has the power to change a man for better or for worse; in actuality, I was already beginning to undergo a change even before truly experiencing the unrelenting horrors of war.

Chapter 12

I was now approaching Alice, Texas, which was approximately 2 tolerable hours from home. I had never actually stopped in Alice, so I didn't know much about the area other than what I would see from the backseat of Pop's car whenever I would pass by as a child on summer family vacations. The only notable piece of information I knew about Alice, Texas was something I heard from a friend of mine who had transferred from Alice to Pharr-San Juan-Alamo High School, my alma mater.

Francisco Garza transferred schools about midpoint during my junior year in high school. He sat next to me in my U.S. History class, and I also had him for my physical education class. He was the type of boy that gave off the impression of being a troubled loner; he was definitely not an initiator of conversation. Although when someone would spark a conversation with him, he could effortlessly carry that conversation forever, regardless of the subject matter. He was taller than most of our classmates, so he naturally stood out amongst the rest of the student body like an irritated pimple on the middle of one's cheek, a blemish that Francisco often wore with little or no concern. He appeared to be the type of loner that exuded confidence, not the type that gave off vibes of dejection or hopelessness. It was almost as if he was a loner because he was too good for everybody else, but once you broke through his thin shell of capricious solitude, you would realize that he wasn't too bad of a guy. I thought it was a little peculiar that a student would transfer schools during the middle of the school year instead of just completing his year and starting fresh at the beginning of the next school year, so my inherent inquisitiveness was what actually triggered our friendship.

"Hey man, I'm Beltran Perez. Where are you from?" I asked Francisco as I offered him my hand in friendship while changing into our gym clothes in preparation for running during our physical education class.

"My name is Francisco Garza. My friends call me 'Frankie' by the way." He answered as we shook hands.

"Good to meet you Frankie. If you don't mind me asking, from what school district did you transfer?" I shamelessly began my invasive, yet innocuous inquisition.

"I'm from Alice, Texas. Are you familiar with Alice, Texas?" He asked in a rhetorical tone even though I didn't know much about Alice other than the fact that it existed.

"All I really know about Alice is that it's pretty much the halfway point between here and San Antonio. Whenever my family and I travel upstate for summer vacation, we use Alice as a landmark to gauge our progress. We don't actually stop there unless it's to fill up with gas or pick up some snacks." I answered; in actuality, I didn't remember seeing anything else in Alice other than the gas stations.

"Well, then you haven't heard of the protesting that's been going on there, huh?" He asked as I developed a newfound interest in our conversation.

"No, what are you talking about?" I asked him as Coach Murphy commanded us to begin exiting the men's locker room and begin 'dragging our fat and lazy asses' to the track.

"There has been a lot of discriminatory bullshit going on with the school district up there. I wasn't affected by it first hand, but my parents didn't want to wait until I was soon a targeted victim. My parents are the ones that know the specifics since they try to stay overly involved with anything and everything I do. They sat me down one night after completing my English homework and informed me that we would be leaving Alice to begin a new life in a more racially tolerant and culturally accepting area. The very next day they withdrew me from enrollment, while they spent the next few days getting things situated down here for us. I stayed home for about 10 school days, which was fine by me! I was pretty bored to death at home doing nothing, so I would listen to the radio in my room to keep me entertained. On one of the local radio stations, I heard a report that Mexican-Americans were protesting the school district and accusing the district of being discriminatory towards Mexican-American students and parents. If you ever get to meet my parents Beltran, you will initially notice that they don't take shit from anybody, especially when it comes to anything that may even minutely harm or slightly affect their one and only son, me. The radio reports were particularly vague, but I had a good idea that my parents' decision to transfer and begin anew was likely

Jaime Perez

due to the type of things that I had heard on the radio. It's cool being an only child sometimes, but it can also wear you down, especially with stifling, overly protective parents like I have. I know they mean well. Are you an only child Beltran?" He asked. His question caught me off guard because I was focused on the surprising racial tension that was supposedly taking place just a short drive from where I lived.

"Uh, no. I have two older sisters, Diana and Sarah. Well, I don't think you are going to have too much of an issue with discrimination here. I'm sure it exists everywhere to some degree, and if it does exist here, I fortunately still haven't witnessed it first hand." I tried to comfort him, although he didn't seem to need my consoling.

"Are you little girls done with your gossiping, or would you like me to allow you some more time to start kissing? We don't have all day Perez, you too Mr. New Guy. You guys can save your chitchatting for one of your other classes. I need to get you ladies into prime shape, and you both are making it extremely difficult for me to accomplish my task." Coach Murphy sardonically yelled to Frankie and me as we both laughed and proceeded to catch up with the others. Murphy had a way about sounding funny even though he was humiliating you. I don't know if it was his voice, his delivery or the shorts he wore that were so short and tight that they looked like they belonged to his daughter, if he had one. I was so intrigued by Frankie's story that we both didn't realize that we were the only ones who had not begun running our daily mile.

Frankie was a nice guy. Good friends like him often cross my mind during random moments of reflection. I wonder what became of him after high school graduation. Coach Murphy is probably still doing his best to simultaneously humiliate his students with his harmless yet spiteful jocularities. As a matter of fact, Coach Murphy would have been a great military officer. He would naturally fit right in with the likes of Sergeant Mills and many others.

This next stretch of road was intimately familiar because, if you traveled westward through one of the narrow intersecting rural roads, you would eventually end up in Rachal, Texas; this is where my family's ranch was located, the same ranch where my first experience with death occurred back in November of 1960. Rachal was considerably small; if you blinked while driving through it, you would likely miss it. This area mainly consisted of farms and ranches. You had to inconveniently drive to surrounding towns to get groceries, buy clothes, purchase gas and to acquire all the other often overlooked daily necessities that people in bigger areas take for granted.

Up until I was 12 years old, memories of the ranch were enjoyable and often brought a genuine smile to my face. The Easter egg hunts, the barbecues, the horse rides, the Thanksgiving dinners and the beauty of the local nature were all now just marred memories densely clouded by the accident of my Uncle Raymond's death. After a few years, the traditional familial celebrations were resumed at the ranch, but to me they were never really the same. Only one thing would cross my mind while at the ranch, the thought of my Uncle Raymond. A dear place that once yielded profoundly fond recollections of my youth continued to bring forth poignant sentiments, only now the sentiments were riddled with undeniable grief.

The street signs along the road were often distractions that made me abandon whatever it was that was currently on my mind. In this case, I welcomed the distraction because it helped momentarily remedy the sorrow that now accompanied my memories dealing with Rachal, Texas. Another street sign approached; this one read, "Edinburg 36 miles". It has been a long while since I was this close to home. If Edinburg was only 36 miles away, then McAllen was about 42 miles or so. My undeniably fervent anticipation to reach home was evident in a variety of ways: my sweaty and shaking hands, my rapid thunderous heartbeat pulsating throughout my body and my minor exceeding of the speed limit. It was elating to imagine that I would be in my wife's arms in less than an hour. I felt the sudden urge to listen to music, which I surprisingly hadn't done for the majority of the trip. This last stretch of road would seem shorter and less sapping if I utilized the magic of music to carry me home. As the speakers blasted my ears with the sounds of Elvis Presley, I glanced around at all the warmly familiar sights that were presently encompassing me. With windows rolled completely down, I deeply inhaled the South Texas air as if it were a euphoriant that bore an undeniably intoxicating redolence.

I was down to a quarter tank of gas, but I wasn't about to further delay my arriving home, especially if I was certain I could make it with the amount of fuel I had. For me, arduous drives, such as the one I was about to complete, were usually soporific. So I expected to feel sluggish and lethargic by journey's end. On the contrary, I felt rejuvenated and full of vim, which my adrenaline was primarily responsible for inducing. It was close to 1600 hours, and I had been on the road for roughly 11hours.

For some reason, all the radio stations within reception were airing

Jaime Perez

news programs that often voiced the opposition for the Vietnam War that was prevalent among many in our country. I didn't want to end my trip by once again listening to the overstated and ineffectual opinions aimed at the U.S. Government, opinions which they constantly chose not to heed. I used to think that maybe if the public expressed enough convincing disapproval and condemnation for the war that the U.S. Government would listen to reason and abandon the war efforts. I have since given up hope on this unlikely idea; the war is taking place whether the public likes it or not, and I happen to be one of the lucky ones expected to somehow procure a victory to another country's battle.

Just as I reached to turn off the radio, two much-needed and comforting things happened: a sign reading "Entering McAllen City Limits" appeared, and a particular song began to play on the radio. This was no ordinary song—this song was Capelletti's favorite. He made it known to us every time it aired on the radio back at Ft. Sill.

"Hey. Turn that radio up. That there's my favorite tune." Capelletti would admit after trying to get everybody within listening distance to shut their mouths so that he could revel in the sounds of Bobby Vinton.

The song was *Coming Home Soldier*. I couldn't think of a more appropriate song to be playing at this exact time. At the very second that I first saw the McAllen City Limits sign, the first notes of *Coming Home Soldier* began to sound. It was as if I was in a movie, and this song was playing in the background as I made my way home. I don't know what Capelletti is doing this very moment, but right now, *I* am a soldier that is coming home.

Two songs later, I was in the parking lot of my apartment complex in my much-missed hometown, McAllen, Texas. I grabbed my duffle bag from the car, and proceeded to walk to my apartment. This moment felt ominously familiar, like the déjà vu of a bad dream. Then I remembered that this is exactly what it was, a vision from one of the many dreams I had back in Ft. Sill, except this dream was the most vivid and realistic one of all. As silly as it seemed, I looked for yellow flowers on any of the apartment doors, especially apartment #17. Much to my encouragement, there were no flowers of any color hanging on any of the doors. The apartment complex seemed a little vacant, much like the desolate atmosphere one feels when entering a ghost town, but this was likely attributed to the fact that most of the tenants at Ivy Terrace Apartments were still at work or on their way home from work.

I grabbed my keys and resumed to unlock and open the door with caution because I didn't want to hit Gilbert with the door if he were crawling in our living room by the apartment's entrance. Slowly I squeaked in; the apartment was uncommonly calm and silent for an apartment with a newborn. The ticking clock on the adjacent wall showed that it was 1632 hours. It was odd that V and Gilbert would be out at this hour. She didn't like taking Gilbert outside in the middle of the Texas heat, so she often waited until after sundown to avoid unnecessarily exposing our son to the irritating heat and humidity. I quietly placed my duffle bag on our brown leather recliner and continued lightly walking on the hardwood floors, listening for the sound of anything. Aside from the ticking clock, the only other thing I could hear were the soles of my boots along the creaking wooden floor.

At the end of the hallway was our bedroom, which also contained Gilbert's crib. I noticed that the door to our bedroom was partially open. As I surreptitiously peaked through the opening of the door, what I saw nearly brought me to instant tears, my wife asleep with my son on her belly, their rhythmic, tranquil breathing in unison. Although this was an unforgettable sight that I could marvel at for hours, I was compelled to disrupt the serenity because I couldn't wait any longer to hold my wife and son in my empty arms. In any other instance, I would have let them rest, but this time I was going to have to gladly interrupt them.

V was facing me with her eyes closed, but Gilbert was facing away from me, which led me to believe he was asleep. Seconds before gently reaching for V's face to avoid startling her, Gilbert, as if sensing my presence, turns around on his mother's stomach and gives me the most welcoming and adorable smile I have ever witnessed. His reaching for me with both his tiny arms roused V from her nap. I took my son and held him for the first time in several weeks. V smiled in a sleep-interrupted disarray and asked me to pinch her so that she could be certain she wasn't dreaming. I reached over and kissed her to eliminate any doubts of her being conscious.

"Well hello soldier. I was just dreaming that you had arrived home, and to my surprise, you are here." V said while wiping her eyes and focusing her vision.

"I guess dreams do come true sometimes, huh? I know one of my dreams came true when I met and married you." I said as she blushed with a smile as I joined her and my son in our inviting bed.

"You didn't call to let us know you were coming. I wanted to make your arrival a little extra special by having our families and friends here

83

Jaime Perez

to welcome you, maybe have a little barbecue." V admitted with a bit of disappointment.

"Well we have plenty of time to organize something nice like that. I will be here for 10 days; we'll make the best of it. Anyway, being with you and Gilbert right now is already breathtakingly special." I assured her as I looked directly into her deep brown, watery eyes.

"Ten days?! That's great. I thought you were only going to be able to take a week-long furlough." She stated and looked at me as if I was teasing or losing my sense of time.

"I was only going to be granted a week, but Captain Benson called me in his office yesterday to inform me that he had kindly expedited and lengthened my L.O.A. So I now have 10 days instead of only a week." I said to eliminate any doubts that she was being the subject of a prank.

"That's great. And the fact that you showed up without calling beforehand was you practicing for a classified, covert operation?" She said with a slight giggle.

"What? Where did you learn the phrase 'classified, covert operation'?" I said in amusement.

"I was reading an article in an issue of *Time Magazine* while I was waiting for Gilbert to be called at the doctor's office about some military stuff, and I liked the way that sounded—'classified, covert operation'. Are you going to be doing any of that stuff?" She looked burdened as she apprehensively asked.

"Unless the United States Government is planning on covertly sneaking in some unauthorized consumables for us to snack on, I don't think that is too likely." I said as I kept my eyes on Gilbert.

Gilbert had grown significantly from the last time I saw him. He used to be able to easily fit in one of V's shoeboxes, which is relatively small since V wears a size 6 in women's shoes, and now he would probably have a little trouble fitting in one of my shoeboxes. Unfortunately, Gilbert's premature birth was not the only pressing issue concerning our son; his congenital heart disease was now the primary concern. I was extremely eager to hear what the doctor had told V when she took Gilbert to his regular doctor's appointment, but I honestly wasn't expecting any promising information concerning my son's malformed heart. In addition, judging by the fact that V hadn't freely revealed anything to me from the past doctor visit, I assumed there was nothing optimistic to share. Rather than dampen the present moment, I preferred to ask her at a later time and keep the mood joyful, even though I really wanted to know immediately.

84

Through You

My son was obviously not an insomniac because he quickly fell asleep in my arms as V and I spoke. Holding my son as he peacefully napped on my stomach felt euphoric and indescribable, especially when the only thing I had recently held in my arms was a lifeless, metal device designed to give a false impression of comfort and protection. I knew that cherished moments like this were numbered because of my brief visit. The serenity, the togetherness and the gratification were ineffable. I didn't want to wake my son from his precious and much-needed rest, and I was pretty sure that V wasn't sleeping normal hours having to adjust to a newborn's sporadic and arbitrary sleep schedule, so I decided to remain in bed with my sleeping son and restless wife.

I didn't need a welcome home party, a crowded house of friends and family or any other form of festive celebration to commemorate my short visit home. All I actually wanted was exactly what I had this very moment, to spend some quality time with my wife and child. I had no idea what was going to happen after I left here in 10 days, but I knew that I was going to have to enjoy and relish these priceless moments because I had realistically come to terms with the brutal and ugly truth that these may be the last 10 days I ever see V and Gilbert, as well as all my other family members who I hold dear. I was going to live these next few days as if they were my last, but I was going to do everything in my power to avoid making them my final days.

Chapter 13

For the rest of the day, V, Gilbert and I stayed home and did nothing but relish each other's company. I was drained from my long drive; V's sleeping had been erratic at best, and Gilbert seemed content to stay home with us and do nothing. V and I realized that our sleep was going to come whenever Gilbert's did.

After a few hours of rest, Gilbert's resounding weeping woke us. It was still early in the evening, just after sundown, and it was time to feed Gilbert. I prepared a bottle of milk for my son and turned on the television as I fed Gilbert in my arms and quickly took notice of all the little things that I had surrendered as a soldier: a comfortable bed, fluffy pillows, your own refrigerator, your own shower, your own toilet and many more of the little things that I was sure to notice the more time I spent at home.

I hadn't spoken to Mom and Pop since I had arrived, so I dialed their number to let them know that I was home and that I would like to see them sometime tomorrow. It was good to hear their voices. Naturally, Mom started to display her uncontrollable emotions when we spoke, and Pop welcomed me home with more earnestness than I was accustomed to receiving from him. I even spoke to V's parents briefly afterwards as well. Both V's parents as well as mine would be coming over tomorrow to spend some quality time with us.

I noticed a folded piece of paper held by a magnet on our refrigerator door. It was a reminder for a doctor's appointment tomorrow at 10:00 AM with Gilbert's doctor, Dr. Richards. I was really kept in the dark and uninformed with Gilbert's current condition because V rarely mentioned anything in her letters or on the phone when I would call her from Ft. Sill. She was probably just trying to help me maintain my focus on my military duties. I was pretty sure there was a reason for her lack of information;

86

tomorrow I would find out just exactly how slim Gilbert's chances of recuperation are.

We were candidly warned at the Ft. Sill Hospital of Gilbert's meager possibility to survive his condition. Being born premature and having a malformed heart with a hole in it were two daunting obstacles that were going to take two miracles to surmount. All we could do was statically hope for the best and take each day as it came. Gilbert quickly finished his bottle, and I took him to sit with me in our brown leather recliner. I looked around and felt an uncomfortable eeriness, an eeriness that carried me back to one of my dreams. The last time I pictured my living room, albeit subconsciously, my whole family was in bereavement over my death, and my son was somehow comforting me and assuring me that he and V would be all right. Everything was exactly the way it was in my dream, except I was alive, very much alive.

V startled me as she grazed my crew cut from behind the recliner. I hadn't had a home-cooked meal in a while, so she offered to make some tacos with all the trimmings. After eating dinner, the three of us lay in bed and watched late night episodes of *The Cisco Kid* until we all finally fell asleep. It wasn't until 4:00AM that Gilbert's crying woke us up. The television was still on, although programming was off the air, and it was time to change Gilbert's diaper and feed him once again.

We miraculously managed to get a few additional hours of sleep before needing to wake up to visit Dr. Richards and find out the inevitable. I made V some of my cinnamon/pecan pancakes for breakfast before starting our day and heading out for the appointment. Once at the doctor's office, we calmly sat in the cold and overcrowded waiting room until we were called. Gilbert was surprisingly calm throughout the whole ordeal; then again, he had routinely done this many times before, although it was new to me. We had patiently waited for approximately 30 minutes when an assistant in green hospital scrubs came from behind closed doors and called our name. Now it was our turn, and I felt a swift blanket of goose bumps engulf me as we entered another room to await Dr. Richards. I wasn't expecting to hear anything favorable, so I went in expecting nothing but the worst.

I never had the privilege of meeting Dr. Richards before because he became Gilbert's doctor upon returning home with V while I was still at Ft. Sill, so today would be my first time meeting this man. V and Gilbert had recently increased their doctor visits at Dr. Richards' request from twice a week to every other day. After a short wait, Dr. Richards walks in the room and looks surprised to see me.

Jaime Perez

"Good morning Mrs. Perez," he said as he reached for Gilbert's little hands. "I see you brought a guest this time. You must be Mr. Perez, or should I call you Officer Perez?" He asked with obvious intentions of making light of our situation as he firmly shook my hand.

"You can call me Beltran, Doctor." I informed him as I tried to display a genuine smile to momentarily disguise my unsettling concern.

"Let me have a quick listen here." Dr. Richards said as he placed the metal stethoscope on Gilbert's tiny chest. Gilbert was startled by the uneasy coldness of the stethoscope and tried to move the instrument away from his skin. Dr. Richards' subtle facial expression gave me the unsettling impression that he did not like how things sounded, yet he didn't make a comment.

The doctor had a folder in one hand with several papers and x-ray sheets sticking out of it. The folder had 'Gilbert Perez' written in red marker on the front. He began thumbing through the x-ray sheets as he placed them in front of a lighted wall to help further explain the diagnosis.

"Let me get you up to date Beltran, since you have been away on military obligation. Your wife has already seen the test results I am about to show you. In my possession, I have all the x-rays that I have had done on Gilbert's heart since your wife and child started coming to me. The only way I can tell these x-rays apart is by the date because all the x-rays look identical. This is both a good thing and a bad thing. It is good because the hole in your son's heart, which you can clearly see here, is not getting any bigger. On the other hand, this is bad news because there is no sign of the hole getting any smaller. As your son continues to grow, his body will demand more work output from his heart, and this will likely pose a problem. At this stage in his life, there is very little we can do aside from continuous monitoring of his heart. I would seriously consider having little Gilberto in your prayers every single day. I'm not going to stand here and tell you that things look positive Mr. and Mrs. Perez, because they really don't." Dr. Richards said in an impassively mechanical yet honest way that I somehow found genuinely truthful and therefore had to appreciate.

I really didn't know what to say or if I was even expected to say anything. I looked towards V and noticed that her head was hung low in dejection as she held our son in her arms. After Dr. Richards made his statement, the cold white room remained completely silent for about 10 uncomfortable seconds; then V lost her composure and began unbearably sobbing. Shortly after, Gilbert joined in on the crying. Although the news was heartbreaking, I didn't cry partly because of shock and partly because

88

I had been bracing myself for the worst-case scenario, which I felt I had just received.

"So you are saying that there is absolutely nothing we can do but just wait for our son to die?" I asked with despondency.

"I wouldn't advise you to literally just sit and wait. I am sorry to inform you that the inevitable is going to happen sooner than later, and it is practically impossible to give a time line for your child's life expectancy. It could be one day, one month or one year. I recommend that you both enjoy whatever time you have left with your son. Live it to the fullest. I am truly sorry." The doctor advised as he put his hand on my shoulder in attempt to offer some kind of solace. Nothing, and I mean nothing, could have softened the verbal blow that Dr. Richards delivered.

I looked at my slowly dying son as he rested in V's arms. By looking at him, you wouldn't be able to detect that there is anything physically wrong. He looks just like any normal baby with a normal heart, except he isn't.

"I have Gilbert and Veronica coming in every other day as a precaution. Since there has not been a significant change in your son's condition, you can resort to bringing him in whenever something doesn't feel right or something concerning arises. I will leave your next visit up to you. As soon as anything seems abnormal, feel free to come by, and we will squeeze you in the day's appointments. Are there any questions you have for me?"

I looked at V to see if there was anything she wanted to ask the doctor before leaving his office. As she wiped the tears from her bloodshot eyes, she tried to bring forth a smile as if to signify that she was fine and had no questions at the time.

I briefly looked towards Dr. Richards and nodded as if to say 'no'. "Thanks for the honest advice Dr. Richards. We will keep a close eye on Gilbert at home for the time being." I deferentially offered a departing handshake, as did V.

On the way home, V and I had decided to keep Dr. Richards' disheartening information to ourselves. Having to hear it was difficult enough; having to repeat it to everyone else would be unnecessarily overbearing.

Later that afternoon, Mom and Pop came by to visit. About half an hour later, my in-laws showed up with a German chocolate cake. Virginia was a great baker, and she obviously remembered that German chocolate cake was my favorite. V had decided to make her undeniably delectable enchiladas for dinner.

The whole evening seemed like friendly interrogation from my parents

Jaime Perez

and in-laws. I mentioned my eclectic barracks brothers, the daily grind to which we were monotonously subjected, the far below-average tasting food and anything else that would give them the impression that things weren't as bad as they expected it to be. This, of course, meant that I would deliberately leave out any mention of nightmares, homesickness, near fatal dehydration, innocuous yet pervasive racism and the public's anti-war sentiments that I was often pestered by, as if I had anything to do with us going to war.

Throughout the entire evening, we enjoyed each other's company and shared more than a handful of laughs as we ate. One thing seemed irrefutably peculiar; something didn't seem right about any of the laughter I heard that evening. It was almost as if everybody was using the unconvincing laughter to disguise deeply hidden, genuine emotions. I knew that V's and my laughter was being used to conceal and avoid discussing the depressing revelations from Dr. Richards concerning our son, and my parents and in-laws seemed to be using their laughter to cover up something of their own. Maybe they were uneasy with my being a soldier, or maybe they were secretly concerned about my being sent to South Vietnam and therefore having my chance of survival drastically reduced. Whatever the reason, it remained undiscussed yet obviously present through the entire evening.

Pop wasn't exactly one to stay up very late, especially when he had to wake up early the next day to go to work, and Al and Virginia seemed a little worn out as well. As the evening waned, we said our goodbyes to V's parents and made plans to meet again before I left. Mom and Pop left shortly after, but not before saying goodbye to their grandson. Just as we were about to close our apartment door, Mom unexpectedly calls and gets our attention before shutting the door.

"I forgot to mention. If you guys would like to spend some time alone together, your father and I can take care of Gilbert for you while you catch up." She said with a motherly look.

I looked at V to see what she thought. Although I hadn't spent very much time with my son, I thought some time alone with V would be rather enjoyable. V looked at me and said, "It's up to you Babe."

"I'd like to take you up on your offer Mom, but I want to wait a few days so that I can spend a few more days with Gilbert." I said as I held and looked at my son.

"Oh sure. That's understandable. Just know that we are there for both of you when you need us." Mom assured us.

"Thanks Mom." We will call you soon.

Mom and Pop gave us one more goodbye as they drove off in Pop's Ford pickup truck. I waited by the door with Gilbert as they drove off and faded away, Gilbert waving bye until he could no longer see their vehicle. As we entered the apartment, the phone rang; it was my sister, Diana.

"Hello little brother." She said.

"Hey there Sis."

"What's this that I hear of V and you having a feast with Mom and Pop and not inviting your two loving sisters? Has our relationship shamefully boiled down to this?" She rhetorically asked in her usually sarcastic manner.

"Ha. Ha. Damn, word spreads fast doesn't it? I figured you were at work. Are you still working the late shift at the hospital?"

"Yeah, but I will be off the next 3 days. Sarah and I would like to see you, Veronica and Gilbert sometime very soon. When can you fit us in to your busy, yet short schedule?"

I asked V if we could see my sisters tomorrow, or if she had other plans for us.

"Baby, those are your sisters. Of course, we can see them tomorrow. I haven't made any plans for any of your days here. I want you to spend them as you wish. Have them come over tomorrow after they get out of work if you want." V recommended.

"Can you both make it tomorrow?" I asked my sister.

"I know I can. I'm pretty sure Sarah will cancel any previous plans to visit our little hero. How does six o'clock sound? Oh wait, don't you guys say it '0600 hours' or something like that?" Diana said jokingly.

"If you plan to be here at 6:00 AM, which I seriously doubt, then you would say 0600 hours. I know you haven't suddenly become a morning person since I left to Oklahoma, so I am going to assume that you meant 1800 hrs. That would be 6:00 PM." I said with a slight chuckle.

"Uh, yeah. That's what I meant. There is no earthly way that I will be there at 6:00 AM. I will pick up Sarah, and we will be there at 1800 hours. We will bring food, so tell V not to make any supper." Diana offered.

"That's sounds great Sis. I am looking forward to seeing both of you at 1800 hours."

"O.K. Give your wife and my nephew a hug for me, and I will see you tomorrow."

"You got it. Good night Sis." I said as we hung up the phone.

I carefully placed Gilbert down to let him crawl freely on the living room floor. V had already started washing dishes, so I gave her a gentle, chill inducing kiss on the back of her neck and helped her with the dishes. After the dishes were done, the 3 of us lay in bed as we had begun ritualistically, yet enjoyably, doing every evening. While in bed, V and I discussed potential ideas for what to do with our time alone while Mom and Pop took care of Gilbert for the day, and we eventually decided to spend our time alone at South Padre Island, which was about a little over an hour drive from McAllen. We hadn't been there since before we married, so it would be nice to return to one of our most memorable locations together. After feeding Gilbert for the night and putting him to sleep, V and I apparently lost consciousness and woke up in each other's arms the next morning as Gilbert cried us awake a little before we would have liked to have begun our day.

The next day was completely impregnated with massive rains. The rain clouds must have sneakily traveled by night because there was no sign of possible rain yesterday. The torrents continued for the entire morning and part of the early evening. Unless we were in hurricane season, rain wasn't particularly common in our part of the country, but when it did rain, it usually came down hard. V, Gilbert and I stayed in all day and watched the rainfall from our bedroom window.

Rain was a new concept to Gilbert, so he appeared to be breath-taken and intrigued at the same time. His little brown, wide-open eyes looked liked glossy marbles absorbing the seemingly intriguing and unfamiliar spectacle. As a matter of fact, I didn't recall V mentioning rain in any of her letters to me, so I think this might have been the first day of rain since Gilbert's birth. He didn't appear daunted, just curiously excited. One might not think that looking out a window and observing rain exactly qualifies as a noteworthy or memorable moment, but today it was exactly that. Sharing a new experience with my son was something that I was badly lacking.

I came to the realization that I would likely not be around for many of Gilbert's 'first times' in life, so I was understandably enraptured in what might seem to be an uneventful banality. This is what fatherhood was, being there to witness and share the little things in life with one's child. I kissed my son on the cheek as if to nonverbally apologize for not being able to be there for him like a good father would. My son had to endure the complications of a premature birth, the pains and hardships of being born with an incurable congenital heart disease, and now I had to rob him of a real father. Gilbert looked at me as if confused when I started to cry next to him by our bedroom window. He started wiping my tears with his tiny little hands. It was almost as if he were comforting me to assure me that everything was going to be all right. Judging by his reaction, Gilbert seemed, although highly unlikely at this age, as if he were noticing the similarities between the rain and my tears. The comparable drops of moisture with their amorphousness, their constancy and their natural acquiescence to the force of gravity were alike in many ways, but my drops were induced by pain, discouragement and feelings of impotent fatherliness. Gilbert stared at me intently as if trying to construe the reason for my episode of sadness; maybe it was better that he not know. I would not want to add to the already lengthy list of oppressions I was forcibly imposing upon him.

V came out of the shower and noticed me crying. She didn't bother asking me what was wrong because she knew that I lately had a tendency to suddenly become an emotional wreck. She simply continued where Gilbert left off, wiping my tears. Afterwards, she carried Gilbert off to feed him and to give me a moment alone to gather my emotions. I had to get over the pervasively recurring anguish during my short stay, or I would ruin it without getting to fully enjoy it. After I showered away the melancholy, I came out a new person as I waited for my sisters to show up.

As a child, my two sisters, Diana and Sarah were overly protective of me when it came to girlfriends. Since I was their baby brother, I guess they felt obligated to protect me from potential heartbreak. Sometimes they were simply rude and irritating to any girl who I would mention, simply because I mentioned them in conversation. They were worse than Mom ever was. Diana and Sarah could be complete sweethearts one minute then total tyrants the next when it came to protecting their little brother. Much to my surprise when I mentioned V one day, they both seemed to encourage me and persuade me to pursue V instead of discourage me from seeing her. I don't know what the reason was for the sudden change of heart, but they apparently liked V from the very beginning. My guess was that my sisters knew a lot of personal things about other girls, and they would use this information to determine their worthiness of my affection. My sisters never openly maligned any of the girls they disfavored; at least I never actually heard them speak maliciously of any of them. They would just simply tell me, "She's not for you. You are not her type. You can do better. No way, not her." They never gave justifiable credibility or substantial reasoning for their frank and unwanted advice; they just offered it. I don't know why my sisters hated all these unsuspecting girls because they never told me, and they never told me why they were partial to V. They must have sensed V's

Jaime Perez

thoughtfulness and felt her worthy of their little brother's time, effort and companionship. The only thing I know is that I am glad they approved of her because I would have pursued V without their blessings, and that could have turned out to be an ugly and regrettable chapter in all our lives.

Chapter 14

Gilbert must have heard or felt something because he ecstatically half crawled and half rolled towards the front door. Seconds later, the doorbell rang; it was Sarah and Diana.

"Oh my God your hair is so short Belty!!" Sarah said as she grazed my prickly head before embracing me.

"Gilbert came out of Veronica's womb with more hair than you currently have!" Diana jokingly added as she followed Sarah's lead.

After their expected yet friendly attempts at humiliation, my two witty sisters gave V their jubilant hugs and were shocked to see Gilbert once again. I believe the only time they had seen Gilbert, other than in pictures, was the day that V and Gilbert came home after leaving Oklahoma, and at the rate that Gilbert was now growing, they appeared surprised and awestricken.

Of my two sisters, Sarah was the oldest. She was two years older than Diana, and I was two years younger than Diana. We were all approximately two years apart in age, give or take a few weeks. They were both excellent cooks who loved to proudly flaunt their edible masterpieces wherever they went, which is likely why they both decided to give V an evening's rest from the kitchen and bring their own dishes. Their contributions were still warm. Sarah made her popular chicken parmigiana (she liked to refer to it is as "worldly renowned"), and Diana brought her homemade bread and freshly squeezed lemonade. My sisters knew that I loved Italian food and that my favorite beverage of choice was lemonade, especially when it is freshly squeezed. As for the bread, I could live off of it if I had to. Whether it was sweet bread, sour bread, corn bread, French bread, wheat bread, it didn't matter; I savored them all.

We all sat at the table, ate and discussed each other's lives while Gilbert merrily played with some random toys on the floor. For a baby, Gilbert

Jaime Perez

seemed relatively independent. He didn't constantly demand or request V's or my attention, rarely asked to be carried and liked to play on his own. According to my parents, these were qualities that I possessed when I was young as well. I smiled at the thought of my son being like his Daddy and quickly brought my attention back to the conversation at the table to which I had become oblivious.

"Well, what's the latest with the doctor's appointments? Any good news?" Sarah asked with the concern of a protective and curious older sister as V and Diana turned to me to listen to my response.

"Dr. Richards said that we don't have to resort to visiting him on a regular basis anymore. He advised that we could monitor the situation at home and to notify him of any concerns." I said after waiting a few seconds to swallow my partly masticated food.

"That sounds like good news to me. It's usually a good sign whenever a doctor tells you that he doesn't need to see you as frequently. At least that's my experience at work." Diana mentioned as she used her nursing experience to further extrapolate Dr. Richards' advice.

I looked at V and gave her a little flirtatious and comforting smile as she exhaled deeply as if to inadvertently convey a sigh of relief. She smiled back at me and continued to devour my sister's scrumptious chicken parmigiana. That was one of V's many cute idiosyncrasies, her shamelessness when it came to eating. She wasn't afraid to show others when she enjoyed whatever was on her plate. Then again, I don't know of anybody who could actually resist from being compelled to express a sign of excessive laudation for Sarah's culinary gift. It was actually Diana who gave her the memorable recipe after refusing to share it with her for several years.

After about 3 hours of continuous and joyous reflection, my sisters decided that it was time for them to leave so that V and I could spend time alone with Gilbert. I had suddenly remembered that V and I were planning to visit the beach at South Padre Island, so I had to check with Mom and Pop to see if it was still all right to leave Gilbert with them tomorrow. Diana and Sarah said their goodbyes as we thanked them for a delicious dinner.

"We need to see you at least once more before you leave Belty. Even if it is just to drive you to the airport." Sarah commanded.

"That sounds like a good idea. Maybe Mom and Pop can also come along with V to send me off on my journey." I suggested.

Just as Sarah had opened the door to her Chevy Impala, Diana came running back towards me and began crying in my arms. I must admit that although Diana was usually extremely emotional like our mother, I didn't expect her to lose herself like she did.

"I know you are not leaving until next…week, but you…better come back from that war or…I will be very, very… pissed off at you Belty. I'm not…going to lose my little brother to a senseless war." Diana faintly uttered with a painfully cracking voice in my ear as I felt her tears running down my side.

"Hey…don't worry about me. I need to come back for more of that fresh baked bread and homemade lemonade, so I plan to be back." I tried to amusingly assure her.

"Come on Diana. Don't start with your emotions, or you are going to get me started too. I really don't feel like crying tonight." Sarah ordered our sister so as to avoid a symphony of sobbing.

She kissed me on the cheek and unfastened her tight embrace as she said goodbye one last time for the night. I waved goodbye to both of them as they returned the gesture through the car window. V was waiting for me by the door with Gilbert in her arms as we continued inside.

"I was honestly just waiting for Diana to explode emotionally. She took longer than I expected." V mentioned.

"Yeah, she gets like that every once in a while. That's my emotional sister. It's no mystery from whom she inherited that trait. Which reminds me, we need to call Mom and Pop to reconfirm that they are still taking care of Gilbert tomorrow so that we can split for the Island first thing in the morning." I said to V.

"Go ahead and do that while I take a bath and bathe Gilbert." V suggested.

I proceeded to call Mom and Pop. Pop answered the phone with a loud and uncontrollable laugh. He was probably watching one of his many favorite television shows; judging by the barely discernable audio in the background, my guess was that he was watching episodes of *Rowan and Martin's Laugh In*. Pop was a loyal viewer to this comedy sketch program to the extent that he even memorized some of the more memorable lines. He even made it a point to watch all the reruns, and he would somehow manage to genuinely laugh just as hard the second time around as he had the first time.

"Hello." Pop managed to answer after he caught his breath.

"Hey Pop. It's me. Let me guess. You are watching *Laugh In*." I said.

"Damn, this stuff is funny Son. Is everything all right?" He suddenly sounded concerned.

Jaime Perez

"Oh yeah. I just wanted to make sure it was still okay to leave Gilbert with you and Mom tomorrow."

"Yes, of course. Your mom and I are up by about 6:00AM every morning, so you can come over anytime after that. I have to go to work, but your mother will be here all day." He assured me.

"Thanks Pop. Tell Mom we will be there at around 8:00AM. V and I appreciate you and Mom doing this Pop." I expressed with gratefulness.

"Of course Son. You and V enjoy yourselves while your mother and I enjoy our grandson."

"Okay, we'll see you tomorrow then. Thanks." I said and soon after hung up the phone.

From the kitchen, I could vaguely hear V's voice in the bathroom. I thought she was calling for me, but when I got to the bathroom, she was in the tub with Gilbert singing to him. I stood by the doorway and continued to watch this touching display of motherly affection. Listening to V singing brought memories of the days she used to sing for the school choir. She rarely sang publicly anymore, but when she did, the sensation her voice projected was nothing short of aural ecstasy. V and Gilbert were almost entirely immersed in bubbles, which somewhat resembled a dense clutter of clouds in the sky as if they were two angels sent to me to give me a rejuvenated sense for life.

"Do you take requests?" I jokingly asked as she finished her miniature vocal solo.

She looked startled, not having noticed my standing by the door and eavesdropping. "Yes, I do actually. You can take Gilbert and dry him off for me." She said as if to dodge any potential requests from me for a song. I carried my son to our bed and I dried him off with a towel, put on his diaper and allowed him to comfortably rest in our bed.

"Did you talk to your parents?" She asked while towel-drying her hair in her favorite robe, a remarkably soft yellow robe that I had given her for Valentine's Day a few years back.

"Yes. Everything is set for tomorrow. I will pack Gilbert's bag of necessities along with some of his toys so that he can stay occupied at my parent's house."

V proceeded to pack a few things we would need for our trip to South Padre Island. I lay down with Gilbert in bed as I fed him his bottle of frothy milk. He was on my chest, and I could feel his fragile little heart palpitating along with mine. That was the last thing I remember before being awoken by Gilbert in the middle of the night, 2:32 AM according to the alarm clock. I got up with Gilbert and walked to the living room to hopefully avoid disturbing V's sleep.

I looked outside our living room window and noticed an inviting sense of tranquility outside, so I proceeded to enjoy the evening's aura with Gilbert in arms. Gilbert obviously hadn't witnessed the outside world in the dark, as his astonishment with the incessant clear sky and the countless number of bright stars seemed to entice him. He naively reached for the illuminating stars as if there was the possibility of him grabbing a tiny handful of them. At this moment, I so dearly wished that I could hold a conversation with my son and tell him all that he means to his mom and me. After a bit of contemplation, I realized that it wouldn't hurt to tell my son anyway. Even though he wouldn't be able to construe anything I was saying, there would be no harm in expressing myself in the middle of a calm evening with nobody to question my behavior.

As Gilbert rested his tiny, little head on my shoulders, I began to unashamedly begin our first actual father to son talk. "Son, I don't know exactly how things are going to turn out here. I wish I did. It all seems so insurmountable. If it were up to me, I would do everything in my power to be here to see your first steps, hear your first words, and care for your first cut from your first fall. I would make every sacrifice to give you a better chance of survival. In other words, I would, without hesitation, die for you my son. Unfortunately, some things are beyond our control. I have tried so hard to look at the bright side of things, but there is little if any brightness. You don't deserve to be in the situation that you're in. Nobody does. It just isn't fair. It literally kills me to think I may not make it out of this war alive, and therefore I may never get to see, hold, or speak to you again. If I do survive, there is also the chance that I still might not make it back in time to hold you in my arms like I am doing right now. This is why I feel it necessary to speak to you even though you understand none of this. I don't mean to be so negative, but the truth is that I am just trying to be realistic about everything, even if this entails being rationally pessimistic. This is how I cope with things. You have changed my life and your mom's in ways that we never thought were possible, and you don't even realize it. I can even see the happiness in your mom's eyes when she looks at you or talks about you. She sparkles more now than she did before you came into our lives. Gilbert, I live my life for you and your mom; that is what gives me purpose. If there is one thing I wish you could understand, it's that I want to apologize ahead of time for what may become, and I want to let you know that I love you beyond description Gilbert. I only wish you

Jaime Perez

could understand that, but just because you can't understand me, doesn't make this any less true. You are a part of me, and you will always remain so, no matter what."

I came to realize that my words might have come off a little too dark and frank to share with a child, but I am at a point in my life where I have determined that it is best to fully and honestly express one's self because you may not get the opportunity to do so later. I waited for my tears to dry naturally with the sporadic night breeze before returning to bed. V was still sound asleep, and Gilbert seemed to approach the same state; his eyes appeared heavy and only halfway open. It was now 2:58AM, and V and I had planned to wake up at 7:30AM. I closed my eyes for what seemed to be a couple of minutes, and then I opened my eyes to see that 7:30AM was already here.

The 3 of us woke up at about the same time. Most of our things were packed and so were Gilbert's things. V made breakfast for us while I prepared Gilbert's bottle. I figured that I should call Mom and Pop to let them know that we would be arriving there shortly. Just as I was reaching for the phone, it rang.

"Hello." I answered as V surprisingly looked at me like I was a psychic who could tell beforehand when the phone was going to ring.

"Hey Son. I was just wondering what time you were going to drop Gilbert off. Your father has left for work, and I could use a little company."

"We are just finishing up with breakfast, and we should be there within the hour. Is that okay?" I asked to make sure it was not an inconvenience.

"Yes, that's perfect. I will see you soon then."

"Okay Mom. Bye." I hung up the phone; well actually, Gilbert took it from my hand and hung it up for me.

"Mom says she is ready for us." I told V.

"Great. We'll leave as soon as we finish breakfast." V stated.

After breakfast, we all got in the car and headed for Mom and Pop's. We weren't too sure how Gilbert was going to react to being without V or me and being in new, unfamiliar surroundings. Gilbert wasn't used to these types of arrangements. As we drove up to the covered driveway, Mom's familiar face waiting by the door eased any apprehension Gilbert may have had. We stayed and chatted with Mom for a few minutes while Gilbert seemed to scrutinize the photos on Mom's wall. Photos of Gilbert, Sarah, Diana, wedding photos of Mom and Pop, wedding photos of V and

100

I as well as many other photos all adorned Mom and Pop's living room walls as if her walls were a personal family museum.

After several minutes of random conversation with Mom, V and I were ready to leave to the island, but we had a feeling Gilbert was going feel uncomfortable and become unruly as we began to leave his sight. V quickly took out his toys and placed them on the living room floor in hopes of diverting Gilbert's attention from us. The plan worked; we quietly waved goodbye to Mom as we carefully made our way out the front door and into our car.

Being alone with V felt a little alien because, as of late, we were either never alone or miles apart from each other. Instead of having the radio entertain us during our drive, V and I just talked about anything and everything through the entire drive. We both admitted feeling a little badly about sneaking out on Gilbert in such a deceptive manner, but we felt it was the best way to leave without making it too difficult on everyone. In addition, I don't know if V and me would have been able to handle Gilbert's pleading cries for us to stay.

South Padre Island hadn't changed much from the years past when V and me would come more frequently. Come to think of it, to me, it appeared exactly the same. It had taken its share of ravaging hits from a few havocking hurricanes, but the resilient people of the area always managed to get through any regressive hardships and continue to move diligently forward. V and I had our usual spot on the island where we would park, and lucky for us, that same spot was available. We situated ourselves on our folding chairs after setting our umbrella and rubbing each other with much-needed sunscreen.

Sitting here basking in nature's opiate with V made it seem as if I were on an entirely different planet from the one I was in last week. Although, Fort Sill was soon going to seem like a rapturous paradise compared to the blood-drenched hell I was going to in the next 6 days.

"You slept like a rock last night. Did you notice that Gilbert and I had left you alone for a bit?" I asked V.

"No, I didn't. I have been sleeping very contently since your arrival. I feel safer with you here, and I can therefore sleep much more peacefully than when I am alone. I don't like to be alone Baby. I hate it."

"I'm sorry. I will do everything I can to make sure you will not be alone." I tried to assure her as she held my hand.

"Baby, I want you to know that, although I am your wife, I am your best friend as well. If you need to talk about something or want to get

Jaime Perez

something off of your chest, I am there for you. Nothing is off limits with us." V kindly offered as she displayed her impulsive altruism.

"Thanks V. I have always felt that way as well." I said as she looked at me as if she was waiting for me to say more. She continued to look at me, expecting a continuation of this conversation.

"What's the matter? Is there something you want to ask me, or something you'd like to discuss?" I asked with hopes of feeding and fulfilling her obvious, lurking curiosity.

"Actually, yes." She said as she swallowed to clear her throat before continuing. "I noticed you were crying yesterday as you and Gilbert looked out the window during the rainstorm. I didn't want to say anything because I wanted to let it pass and not appear to be nosy, but at the same time I felt like I was being inconsiderate and didn't want to seem stolid. Would you like to talk about what was bothering you?" V asked in a non-imposing tone as several seagulls nimbly flew over our umbrella.

"Sure. I mean, I was just a little inundated with all that is happening. I started thinking about how I didn't feel like I was being a good father to Gilbert or a good husband to you. I began to feel ineffectual and lacking because of my absence. I felt as if I had started something but was unable to finish it. I enjoy being with and holding my son, yet it's very distressing to know that I am limited to what I can give you and Gilbert. I want to be everything that both of you deserve. I want to give both of you everything I have to offer, but I can't even begin to be that person because I have to leave you both in a matter of days. I thought about how it was unfair to leave you to parent a child single-handedly, and how this wasn't anyway to raise a child. I thought about how hopeless I felt that I couldn't do anything to change things for everyone. There are many things in life that seem trying and insurmountable, but I have come to realize that leaving behind the ones you love is far more difficult than anything I have experienced as a child, man or soldier. It often gets the best of me and weighs me down sometimes, but I always manage to overcome it. That is why you saw me in tears that afternoon." I explained to V.

The whole time I was explaining this, I was being entranced by the hypnotic, undulating waves of the soothing beach and therefore not looking directly at V. It wasn't until I heard her sniffle a few seconds after I was done speaking that I noticed she was in tears.

"Hey, did I say something wrong? I didn't mean to make you cry." I said in attempt to pacify her uneasiness.

"Now I feel bad because you have been going through all of this mental anguish by yourself. I am supposed to be there for you, and I have done absolutely nothing to offer you any comfort. I told my parents the day that I accepted your marriage proposal that I was going to make you the happiest man alive, and I have already failed miserably." V managed to utter between sobs.

"V, it is because you make me so happy that this hurts so much. It is because I love our son so much that this is so difficult. You have done nothing short of being the perfect mother to Gilbert and the perfect wife to me. Don't ever think that you have failed either of us. It's just that I sometimes feel like I am fighting multiple wars simultaneously. The fight against my son's illness, the fight for my son's life, the fight of being apart from you and the fight to be a good father to Gilbert and husband to you all seem to unravel the fabric of my sanity more times than not. If you notice, I haven't even begun to mention the deadly war that I am being sent off to fight in less than a week. I am not cut out for this killing thing V, and that scares me because it makes me a weaker more vulnerable soldier. It is these indomitable, vexatious truths that keep me in constant shambles. My grueling pains have nothing to do with you failing me; they have to do more with me being a failure to you and Gilbert. I wouldn't necessarily call myself a control freak, but I really don't like being subjected to so much lack of control, especially when so much is at risk of being lost. I am sorry for not sharing this with you earlier. I just know you have enough on your mind as well, and I didn't want to dispirit you further."

V got off her folding chair and approached me. She sat on my lap and hugged me tightly like she had no plans of letting go anytime soon.

"Thank you Baby." V whispered in my ear.

"For what?" I asked with sincere uncertainty.

"For being you." She tersely responded.

Several minutes passed before either of us said anything else. I think we both ended up being caught up in the pleasure of being so close to each other that we just resorted to enjoying the silence, the peacefulness of the singing seagulls and the cool, breath-taking breeze that naturally embraced both of us.

Chapter 15

For the next several hours, V and I enjoyed the actively pounding waves and the tan, fine sand that the Gulf of Mexico perennially bestowed to its guests. The day couldn't have been any more ideal for a trip of this kind. We walked along beach hand in hand for miles and returned back to the inviting shade under our umbrella. I don't know the length of our gait in miles, but we realized that we had walked for four straight hours up and down the beach. Time didn't seem to feel the same whenever I was with V. Our four-hour walk didn't feel as lengthy or tiring as one would suspect of a walk of this distance, not even the last quarter mile when I carried V on my back as she held on tightly above my shoulders.

The surprisingly lengthy walk produced an undeniable hunger that led us to voraciously attack the ham sandwiches that we had prepared the night before. The first time V and I came out here we brought ham sandwiches with us, and we have kept this mini-tradition going ever since. It was practically impossible to eat a sandwich at the beach without a few stubborn grains of sand being consumed as well, but V didn't complain. Considering the crap I was used to eating at Ft. Sill, this SANDwich was ambrosial; so you weren't going to hear any complaints from me.

Our reflective stroll was delightfully therapeutic. We even managed to collect a few eye-catching seashells as well. V had a collection of small seashells from all our previous trips to South Padre Island. She would clean them when she got home and toss them in a clear jar where she would accumulate them. She liked to call her little ongoing art project "the jar of memories".

"Turn the car radio on Baby." V requested. "Let's listen to music together. I've have always liked doing this, especially here at the beach."

"I can do better than that. Remember this?" I grabbed my portable, battery-powered radio from the back seat of our Corvette. The radio was

104

the first gift V had ever gotten for me. It was a Christmas gift from 3 years ago.

"Wow!!! You still have that thing?" She asked with a smile.

"Heck yeah. I'm taking it with me to Vietnam too. This may be the secret to maintaining my sanity amongst all the rampant insanity to which I will be exposed." I assured her.

"What's the point? You won't be able to hear any English music over there will you?" V asked.

"You know what, I never thought of that. I don't know what I will catch on the radio, but anything is going to be better than listening to bullets, bombs and death. Even the sound of endless static would be preferred." I responded.

"This is going to sound stupid, but I wish I could go with you." V said while placing her hand on my cheek.

"WHAT? I know you don't mean that. As much as I don't want to be miles away from you, I would not let you go with me if you were somehow able to. It would be selfishly cruel of me to drag you along in this inferno. The guys at boot camp and OJT have told me some of the most horrendous, inhumane stories about this war and previous wars. We would sometimes stay up at night and share anything we knew or had heard about war. Some of them had grandfathers, fathers or uncles who served in World War I, World War II, Bay of Pigs or Korea. Many of these men returned a different person, and their transformation was in no way for the better. War screws with your head, your life and your emotions, with everything. What's even more terrifying is that the things I've heard are daunting enough to elicit recurring, lifelike nightmares that can wake a grown man and have him in a cold sweat screaming for his mommy. I wish I could say that I am prepared to face whatever gets in my way, but the truth of the matter is that one can never be truly prepared for the many vile and unpleasant aspects of war. The reality of it is far worse than any of the stories I was told. War cannot be orally duplicated or accurately recounted; the only way to truly feel the essence of war is to be right in the middle of the whole damn thing." I abruptly stopped speaking because I felt as if I was rebuking or lecturing V judging by the attentive and humbled look on her face.

"I'm sorry V. I didn't mean to get carried away with my explication."

"No, it's fine. I was just enthralled by the passion in your delivery. I could almost see the visions of war in the reflection of your sunglasses. I

Jaime Perez

think I changed my mind; I don't want to go with you anymore. Sorry." V added.

"You and Gilbert stay here and wait for me to come back. Otherwise, I have no reason or desire to return. Will you do that for me? Will you wait for me to come back?" I asked V.

"With open arms Baby." She assured me.

After our conversation and after having eaten our sandwiches, V and I listened to the tunes on my constantly reliable portable radio. We both found it extremely soothing to lay down on the beach with the radio at a low volume as we simultaneously absorbed the sedative sounds of the nearby waves. Being in the shade under the umbrella as the Gulf's fresh breeze blew by us was exactly what we needed. I closed my eyes for a brief moment with V at my side. When I opened my eyes, apparently a few hours later, V and I had front row seats to the most gorgeous sunset I've ever seen in my life. It was the type of sunset one only sees in paintings or jigsaw puzzles. It was a masterpiece of nature. I am going to assume that it was equally as impressive to V because a sight like this could not be matched in all its grand beauty.

It was still early in the evening, and we hadn't really given my parent's an estimated time of return so that we could pick up Gilbert. V and I waited for the sunset to vanish completely, as if covered by the endless blanket of waves, before even speaking to each other. It was almost as if V and I telepathically agreed that speaking during the sunset would have been disrespectful towards nature's breathtaking offering.

"Do you think we should start packing up and heading back home?" I asked immediately at the conclusion of the astounding visual extravaganza.

"I wish we didn't have to leave, but I know we should." V responded.

"We'll come back when I complete my year of service in Vietnam." I said with a tone of confidence to help ease any worries or doubts V may have about my returning.

"Promise?" V asked with a slight tone of hope.

"Yes. We have to continue adding seashells to your jar of memories. The jar is barely half full; you can't stop now. Your masterpiece is incomplete. That would be like DaVinci not finishing the Mona Lisa." I joked lightheartedly with V.

"Okay, let's gather our belongings and go pick up our son." V said as she folded her lawn chair and placed it in the trunk of the car.

The drive home with V by my side was peaceful and relaxing, unlike the solitary, arduous drive from Lawton to McAllen. We made it to Mom's and Pop's a little before 2100 hours. As we entered the house, we noticed that Mom and Pop were watching the local news as Gilbert slept in the extra bedroom.

"Well look who's here! Did you have fun out there?" Pop asked.

"Yes it was great; thanks to you for helping with Gilbert." I added.

"It's the least we could do. Son, I've been watching the news, and things don't seem to be getting any better in Vietnam." Pop said with a trace of slight concern.

"That's probably why they are sending me over there, to save the day for all mankind." I somehow managed to utter with an unexpected sense of humor. "A lot of the stuff that the news reports is inaccurate Pop. I don't want you worrying about what the media is saying."

I don't know where my sudden confidence came from concerning the war and my future, but it caught me by surprise. It was as if spending time with my loved ones caused a revival of good spiritedness and optimism. It took a few days for the sensation to completely infiltrate my being, but it finally has. I never really thought about this, but it makes sense. If one is constantly surrounded by weapons and soldiers who are preparing and training for a war, one becomes controlled by the idea and horrific essence of war. You inhale the gusts of war, speak the terminology of war, smell the stench of war, dream the abominations of war and fire the weapons of war. War and its demons are ubiquitous in surroundings such as boot camps and military training facilities.

On the other hand, being away from everything I've been exposed to for the past several months brought me back to a calmer sense of reality. The darkness of war is still present within; it just isn't as dominantly controlling and oppressive. I feel an ability to cast light upon the shadows of war and maintain significant influence over my emotions. I am certain that this optimism will likely wither once I land in Vietnam, but at least I might be able to enjoy the few remaining days I have to spend with my family. My Pop used to tell me when I was younger that "...family can help one overcome the most dire consequences in life, so never turn your back on your family. Never". I have a good idea that his wise words have just come to fruition.

I went to the extra bedroom to get my son and continue home because it was getting late. Gilbert was still asleep, which meant that V and I had a long, unrestful evening to look forward to. We said our goodbyes to Mom and Pop and thanked them again for babysitting our son.

Jaime Perez

"Let us know if you need our help with Gilbert again before you leave." Mom graciously offered.

"Thanks Mom. It was a little difficult for both V and me to be away from Gilbert, especially with his state of fragility. We'll probably just spend the rest of our time together at home as a family, so you and Pop make it a point to drop by sometime before I leave." I stated.

"How many more days do you have before you leave?" Pop asked.

"I leave in 6 days, which will probably feel more like 3 days." I added.

"We will drop by before that; we promise." Mom spoke for both her and Pop.

"Okay. Have a good night." I said as I hugged and kissed my parents.

I didn't want to prolong our leaving because I noticed the look on Mom's face; it was her precursor to sorrow. I could always foresee when Mom was going to get emotional and begin to cry. There was a certain look in her eyes that accompanied what appeared to be a squinting-like gesture. I hated to see my Mom cry because I always felt futile for not being able to prevent her sadness like any loving son would. We wisely got in the car and left before she was able to shed a tear.

Although the day at the beach was wonderful, it was equally draining and enervating. By the time we got home, Gilbert had woken up from his short nap. After showering, V and I played with our son and enjoyed his sorely missed company. Approximately 3 hours later, the 3 of us simultaneously fell asleep. That night I had no trouble going to sleep. It may have been due to being out in the sun the majority of the day, but it may have also been the contagious optimism of being around my family for a continued, albeit short, period of time. Regardless of the reason, it felt good, and I hoped things would continue this way.

Gilbert woke us up twice during the evening. His resting with Mom and Pop during the day was probably in excess of what he was used to sleeping, so it was logical that V and I would now have to deal with those consequences. As we jointly fed Gilbert the second time he woke us, I began to notice that he was beginning to get a little heavier. It was as if I could accurately relive the first time I held him at the military hospital in Oklahoma and compare the difference in his weight then and now. He was slowly approaching 5 months. Being a father for the first time, I was not sure what a 5 month-old infant should weigh, but at least Gilbert's weight felt normal, which was comforting. My experience with Gilbert was my

108

first with ever actually seeing a premature baby. Gilbert probably weighed less than V's schoolbooks when I would carry them home from school for her when we first started dating.

Upon waking up that morning, my 5th day home, I woke up with an idea that I wanted to pass by V. During a tasty breakfast of bacon and eggs, I brought up my idea to see what she thought.

"V, I was thinking. What do you think about the 3 of us getting a family portrait professionally taken today? I think both of us have something a little extra nice that we can wear, and we can stop by Montgomery Ward's to get a spiffy outfit for Gilbert because I don't think he has any attire that borders on formal." I asked even though I knew V would love the idea.

"Don't we need to make an appointment days in advance for something like that?" V asked after she expressed a partial smile and nod of implicit concurrence.

Then both of us simultaneously and almost in perfect unison suggested, "We could go where we got our engagement pictures taken."

The photography studio where we took our engagement photos belonged to the father of one of V's and my mutual friends from our childhood neighborhood. I don't recall the man's name, but he was always very cordial and never failed to wave to us with a big smile as he would drive by the house in his black Plymouth Barracuda. Surely, he would cater to our unexpected plans without the need for an appointment.

"Well let's begin getting ready to start our day." I advised.

Before leaving the house, I went ahead and called the photography studio to reassure that our neighbor would be able to fit us in his scheduled appointments. The man on the other end of the phone immediately recognized my familiar voice after I introduced myself. I apologized for our not having made an appointment sooner and explained that this was something that we had whimsically thought of this morning. He mentioned that one of his early afternoon appointments had cancelled on him, so he would be able to fit us in at about 1430 hours. This would work out perfectly. I thanked him several times and assured that we would be there at exactly 1430 hours, or 2:30 PM in normal time.

The search for Gilbert's outfit at Montgomery Ward's didn't last long. V saw something that she found irresistible within minutes and therefore had to succumb to it. It was as if the outfit was screaming for V to notice it, and she did.

"Oh my God! This would look absolutely adorable on Gilbert, and they have his size!" She stated as if she couldn't believe the fortuity.

Jaime Perez

I agreed that it would look really nice on Gilbert, so rather than to wander the retail store desultorily for a tiresome eternity, we purchased the outfit and resumed to our car to change Gilbert into his new clothes. We still had some time to spare, so we decided to have lunch at a local restaurant. I began to realize that this was the first time the 3 of us had ever eaten out together as a family. Even though Gilbert would have to pass up steak and potatoes for his bottle of milk, it felt comfortingly normal to do little, often overlooked things together such as shop for clothes and eat out. Although normalcy may not seem like the type of circumstance that is particularly exciting or longed for, it was exactly what I needed in my life because the abnormalities that have immersed me the passed few months were internally tearing me apart.

We took our time eating as the majority of those around us shared their favorable reactions and admirations for our son. For close to two hours, V and I heard everything imaginable, and all the comments were so gratifying that I could literally sit there for several more hours and just absorb the continuous esteem.

"He's so cute. He's got your eyes. He's adorable. Look at the cute little baby. How precious. He's an angel. Look at that smile. He's gorgeous." Many openly shared as they passed us by. My son was everything and more that these kind strangers said he was, and I was relishing every comment to the fullest because in a few days, there would be little to relish.

It was slowly approaching 2:00PM, so we decided to begin heading towards the photography studio. We arrived with some time to spare, so we entered the studio and greeted our neighbor as he stood behind his camera, apparently inserting some film.

"Hello sir." I said with V and Gilbert following behind me.

"Well hello Mr. and Mrs. Perez, and I see we have a new addition to the family with us as well. Hey there little fella. You must be Gilbert." He said as he reached for Gilbert's infant hands. I felt kind of bad and embarrassed that he knew my son's name, our name, and I didn't know his first name. I just new his son was Fernando Gomez, so I simply called him Mr. Gomez.

"We appreciate you seeing us with such short notice Mr. Gomez." I said.

"Oh don't mention it. I'm always glad to help a neighbor out, even though both of you have since moved out on your own. I still see your parents quite often as they water their yards, check their mail or go for a walk around the block. Oh, by the way, call me Fernando. I don't feel so

110

old when people call me by my first name." He said with a rough laugh as I realized that his son was named after him.

"I spoke to your father a few weeks back. He mentioned you are a soldier. I myself fought in World War II. Being that I survived the worst hell known to man, my respect and best wishes go out to you my son. God bless you, and those who fight by your side. I know you don't want to hear about war or anything having to do with the military right now, so if I start digressing towards my military experiences, feel free to tell me to shut up." He said jokingly and with a warm smile as he began to show us the various photo backgrounds he had to offer.

As V and I glanced through the backgrounds and decided on a few different ones, Mr. Gomez began adjusting his lighting and whistling a song that I was familiar with but could not identify. I began taking notice of Mr. Gomez's jolly manner and life-loving disposition. By looking at him, one could not tell that he was subjected to the most unspeakable of obligations, war. Seeing Mr. Gomez instilled hope about being able to mentally, emotionally and physically overcome the hardships and tribulations that lie ahead for me.

"Have you all decided on at least 3 different backgrounds?" Mr. Gomez asked.

"I think we'll go with these." V answered after a little deliberation.

"Good choices. I will take 3 different poses with each background for a total of 9 different options for you to choose from when I get the proofs ready for you." Mr. Gomez explained.

With ease and meticulousness, Mr. Gomez positioned the 3 of us in various poses as he changed the backgrounds behind us. Gilbert was surprisingly calm and agreeable throughout the photo session. For some reason, the flashing lights provoked Gilbert to laugh freely and unrestrainedly after each photo was taken. It was as if he was enjoying the illumination's effect. This proved to be beneficial because it assured that Gilbert would be smiling for the proceeding shot. All Mr. Gomez had to do was test the flash immediately before and then take the real photograph while Gilbert was still laughing away. This unexpected reaction caused V and me to laugh and smile along with Gilbert more than we would have liked.

After all the photographs were taken, we filled out the information sheet for Mr. Gomez. I was fully aware that a sitting fee of $10.00 was to be paid the day of the photography session, so I took out my wallet to pay Mr. Gomez. Much to my surprise, he sternly refused to take my payment.

Jaime Perez

"Oh, no. I'm not taking your money Mr. Perez. We'll settle this when you and your wife decide on which package you want and which poses you select. I will waive the sitting fee. Consider it my gift to you for serving our country."

"Uh, thank you Mr. Gomez. That is rather kind of you." I said in surprise.

"I should be the one thanking you son. Soldiers don't get enough public respect because there is a widespread ignorance on a soldier's everyday duties and life threatening routine. The media cannot effectively convey what is really going on in a state of war because the media are not soldiers; they are merely reporting spectators. Just like spectators at boxing matches cannot truly feel the blows being given and received in the ring; they can only see and hear them. There is much more to war than what one sees and hears. People who have never been in a war only imagine what a soldier's life is like. Their conceptions can never begin to truly comprehend the calamities that soldiers have to bravely persevere every single minute of their serving lives. Damn, you were supposed to stop me when I began yapping like a maniac Mr. and Mrs. Perez." He said as he appeared to be slightly abashed and disconcerted by his momentary digression, an insightful and enlightening digression that I was actually enjoying. I wish he had continued because I liked what he was saying. It made total sense, and this man knew what he was talking about because he has been there.

"So how long are you on L.O.A. Mr. Perez?" He asked suddenly to help somewhat change the subject.

"I will be leaving next week Mr. Gomez."

"I don't expect to have the proofs before you leave, so I will call Mrs. Perez when the photograph proofs are ready so that she can come by and decide on which ones to purchase. Is that fine Mrs. Perez" He looked towards V.

"Yes, that's fine Mr. Gomez." V responded.

"Very well then. I have all your information, and I want to thank you for your business once again. Both of you say hello to your parents for me. Tell them to come by for some family portraits; I will give them a good deal." Mr. Gomez said as he looked at V and me as if he was thinking of something else in the back of his head.

"We will Mr. Gomez. Thank you again for everything." I said as V, Gilbert and me began exiting Mr. Gomez's studio.

It was close to 3:30PM, so V and I decided to go home and change

112

into something more comfortable. Even though Gilbert wasn't being particularly fussy about his outfit, I was pretty sure that he would rather roam our apartment freely in nothing but his comfortable diaper. We didn't have anything else planned for the remainder of the day, so this meant that we would likely stay home, watch television and enjoy our son's company.

For the rest of the day, the 3 of us just lounged slothfully in bed. Gilbert fell asleep in my arms during an episode of *The Twilight Zone* as V lost consciousness on my left shoulder. It was moments like these that I was going to long for the most when away. I began to doze off, but I didn't want to get up to turn the television off and possibly awaken V and Gilbert. I allowed myself to doze off with my wife and son. A few hours later, the OFF AIR notice that the local ABC affiliate aired after all the day's programming concluded startled me. I was surprised that V and Gilbert remained at rest during this annoying sound. Before I could get up to turn off the television, I noticed that Gilbert was a little warmer than usual. I felt uneasy about what I was feeling, so I quickly woke V and asked for her opinion.

"V, I think Gilbert is running a slight fever. What do you think?" I asked as I let her feel his warm body.

"I think you are right. I have some medicine Dr. Richards prescribed for him. We'll give him some and see how he feels in the morning. If he doesn't appear to get better, we should pay the doctor a visit." She said as she poured a red, syrupy liquid into Gilbert's mouth.

It was almost 4:00AM, and we would likely wake up again in about 4 hours. If Gilbert's fever didn't begin waning significantly, our morning would be spent at the doctor's office. I didn't like the fact that Gilbert was not crying. Normally, a baby cries when something is wrong, and it was obvious that he was running a fever. His disquieting calmness gave me the impression that he was submitting to his fever, as if he was overpowered by his current state of health.

Approximately 4 hours later, I instinctively woke up and immediately reached for my son's forehead. He appeared to be getting even warmer. I hastily woke V, and ordered her to get dressed because we needed to pay Dr. Richards a visit. Within a half hour, we were in Dr. Richards' waiting room doing exactly that, waiting.

Chapter 16

Gilbert cried the entire time we helplessly and anxiously waited. Nothing seemed to appease his anxiety. It was as if our efforts were ineffectual. At home he seemed calm yet ill, now he appeared ill and feisty, kicking and screaming unlike anything I had ever witnessed from my son. The more he cried, the more I worried. I wasn't sure if his crying had any effect on his heart. I was concerned and uncertain if there was any correlation. Does crying demand any additional strain on the heart? Could my son's heart stop if he continued with his illness-induced boisterousness? V sat next to me looking as concerned, dejected and hopeless as I felt. As a parent, you try to do everything in your power to nurture and care for your child. This reaction is not learned; it is simply humanly inherent. Sure, life is filled with many uncertainties that are inconveniently beyond our control, but when it comes to one's child, the inability to offer comfort and to remedy your child really makes one feel feeble and worthless, like a blind and deaf watchdog.

"Gilbert Perez." The doctor's assistant called as she opened the squeaking door with some documents in her hand.

I looked up at the round clock on the wall as we got up and noticed that we had only waited for about 8 minutes, although it seemed much longer with a sick child in your arms, throwing an impressive fit. Dr. Richards was already waiting for us in the room to which we were directed.

"What is wrong?" He immediately asked with an obvious look of concern as he approached Gilbert without even looking at or greeting V or me.

"Gilbert had a slight fever last night, and it seemed to get worse this morning when we woke up." I responded.

With meticulous alacrity, the doctor took Gilbert's temperature and checked his heartbeat. He looked at the folder he always carried with him

114

during all of Gilbert's visits and began jotting down some new information as Gilbert continued to kick in angst. Finally, the doctor explained his findings.

"Okay. You're son is running a fever of 102.3 F°, and his heartbeat is more abnormal than before. Since you started bringing your son to us, your son's heartbeat has always had a slight deviation; it appears to have become more noticeable. It is difficult to tell if his current state of agitation is primarily responsible for the increased deviation or if his heart disease is responsible. In addition, the fever is likely not a symptom of his heart disease. The fever is likely a commonality of infancy. I don't think your son will calm down until after he has slept. I would like to check him when he is not as exasperated so that I can accurately and effectively compare his heartbeat patterns. I would like to see him tomorrow before lunch. I'm going to give you a prescription to help remedy the fever, but my biggest concern is his heart. His fever should subside before early evening. Monitor that closely. If the fever persists, I want you to call me at home. If the fever subsides, return tomorrow as scheduled. I will set you up for tomorrow at 11:00 AM. Is that fine with you?" The doctor asked after his comprehensive explanation.

"Yes, that is fine." I answered, overwhelmed by all that I had just heard.

"So if the fever continues through tonight, we call you at home. If it goes away, we just come back tomorrow at 11:00AM." V asked for reassured clarification.

"Yes. Get this prescription filled on your way home and administer the drug immediately. Your son will gradually become calmer as soon as you do this. He will need rest. After he awakens, check for the fever. He should return to his normal temperature soon after. Any questions?" Dr. Richards asked with an unconvincing and partial smile that was nonexistent up until now.

I looked at V before saying, "No. You've made everything perfectly clear." I said with slight disingenuousness. When it came to my son, I always had questions and concerns. Even when all questions were answered, new ones surfaced.

The doctor proceeded to give me the prescription, as well as his home phone number, as he led us out of the patient room.

"Thank you for seeing us with no appointment doctor." V added.

The doctor then said, "There is no need to thank me when it comes to doing my job Mr. and Mrs. Perez. I too had a sick child, one with the

Jaime Perez

same condition as Gilbert. So I have a good idea what you are struggling through. My daughter's condition is what motivated me to become a doctor. I didn't want others to go through what my wife and me had to endure."

I wanted to know so much more about Dr. Richard's situation, but I know it was not my place to ask and pry into his personal life. His sharing what he did was probably difficult to do, but he did it anyway in hopes of probably instilling some much-needed solace in V and me.

V, Gilbert and I drove to the local pharmacy and filled Gilbert's prescription. Gilbert appeared to be drained and tired out from his intemperate outbursts, but he was still warm and in need of rest. V gave Gilbert his medicine in the car, and by the time we arrived back home, Gilbert was fast asleep.

V and I hadn't spoken since we left the doctor's office. The quietness wasn't odd, but it wasn't very common between us either. I had a lot I wanted to say, but the compelling force to resort to silence prevailed, until we placed Gilbert in his crib.

Surprisingly, it was V who broke the deafening silence. "Well, what did you make of our doctor's visit? It was definitely different, wasn't it?" V asked as if waiting to receive my affirmation.

"Different is a good way to put it. I didn't quite get the impression that things were going to be all right like the last visit. You have been to the doctor's with Gilbert more than I have, and you felt a sense of peculiarity or doubt as well?"

"Yes, that's exactly it. It was peculiar, or weird. I don't know. It's difficult to explain." V seemed perplexed.

"I was really shocked that Dr. Richards revealed what he did about his daughter. His voice sounded as if he was trying to disguise something unsettling. Did he tell us about his daughter to assure us that he was able to understand our situation? Did his daughter survive? If she didn't, was he trying to prepare us for the worst because he felt Gilbert's chances of survival were dismal? What was the point of his revelation? " I confoundedly asked V.

"The phone number part is what got me the most. Dr. Richards didn't seem to voice too much concern, yet he gave us his home phone number, which seems like something he would do if there were a serious concern. I think he was trying to downplay the gravity of the situation in order to keep us at ease." V keenly assessed.

"Well, I didn't like the vibe that I felt today. We can speculate and try to construe the meanings of this all day, but it's really useless. Let's just wait and see if Gilbert's medication remedies his fever." I recommended.

After the doctor's visit, V and I apparently didn't feel like doing much of anything. We watched television the remainder of the day while attentively monitoring our son's body temperature as he rested face down in his crib. Everything had been going particularly well for Gilbert, which is comforting, but it is unrealistic to expect everyday to be without perils and complications, especially with the vexations that Gilbert is inconveniently subjected to on a daily basis. It's funny how it only takes a pivotal second for something pleasant to quickly become unpleasant. If there is one thing you learn as a soldier it's that you should never take anything in your life for granted, never. That is a wise adage by which to live, not just for soldiers, for everybody.

With this in mind, I looked at V as she sat next to me on our couch and kissed her gently on her forehead. She looked at me perplexingly, as if she didn't know who I was or what I had become. This is when I shamefully realized that I don't display enough affection to V. I don't tell her enough how much she means to me, how she makes me feel, how happy I am to be with her and how fortunate I am to have her as my partner in life, my companion, my other half. Her reaction and my realizing that I substantially lacked in my displaying of affection felt like a punch to the throat.

"I love you V." Although I wanted to say so much more, nothing else came out, not because I didn't know what else to say but because the look in V's passionate and glistening brown eyes when she turned to me left me breathless and completely unable to utter another syllable. People often ask, "How does one truly know when they are in love?" Previous to this moment, I never had the answer to that question, but now I do.

A single tear rolled down both of V's eyes. She caressed my unshaven face and, as if she too was witnessing a shortness of breath, kissed me with her rose petal-like lips between my mouth and cheek. After approximately 15 seconds of complete and heartfelt silence, V whispered in my ear, "How do you know you love me? Tell me, how do you know?"

"Because when I look at you I forget that there are others among us. When I touch you, I feel a shivering warmth inside that can only be transmitted by you. When I'm with you, I don't want to be without you, and when I'm without you, I want to be with you. I never really knew what happiness and love were until I met you." I said after I was able to catch my breath and clear my throat.

Jaime Perez

Within seconds, V's single tears were accompanied by many more. Beneath the tears was the only smile that could weaken me to the point of bringing me to my knees, V's smile. She embraced me tightly as she valiantly tried to fight back and control the abundance of tears. After a couple of minutes needed for her to regain her equanimity, she was finally able to say something.

"I wish I had a colorful way with words like you so that I could tell you how I feel." V stated.

"What are you talking about? You do have a way with words. That poem you wrote for me was nicely done. You can't write poetry if you don't have a special way with words. You have to have the ability to make words come to life, and you gave those words a strong pulse. I felt them. What was the title of the poem, *Those Things?*" I asked V as she stared at me.

"*Those Thoughts*. I titled it *Those Thoughts*. Oh my God. I almost didn't give that to you because I felt it was a little immature and laughable. You never told me that you found it." V said as she began turning a slight shade of red.

"I didn't tell you?" I thought about it for a brief moment. "I guess not. Yes, I received it when I opened the glove compartment to grab the map to get a better idea of my route home. I still have it."

"Please throw that away." V pleaded.

"Throw it away? I was hoping we could sell the rights to it so that we can be rich!" I said with sarcastic yet playful tone.

"Very funny. I thought you went to military training, not comedic training." V said as she harmlessly punched my shoulder.

"Now who is the funny one?" I asked her.

"I don't know what got into me that day. I had some ideas in my head that I wanted to express to you, and the next thing I know, I have a very rough draft of some poem. It's been a long time since I tried writing of any kind." V explained.

"Well, you still have the gift. I don't see why you should stop writing if you are good at it and you enjoy it. I'll tell you what. Why don't you write another one for me to take to Vietnam? You wrote a poem for me for my trip home. Now write one for my trip to Vietnam. I think it will really help me get through some of the unspeakable adversities I expect to encounter overseas. Will you do that for me?" I asked non-rhetorically.

"If my husband wants a poem, my husband will get his poem. I'll work on it sometime soon. I promise." She said with a smile as she grazed my prickly head.

I got up to feel if Gilbert's temperature was decreasing at all. It appeared that the prescribed medicine was working. It was already time for Gilbert's next dosage. V brought the medicine bottle and prepared the dosage as I picked Gilbert up from his crib. His little eyes opened, but he didn't seem irritated or upset from his untimely awakening. Just as Gilbert began to yawn, V stealthily yet carefully thrust the spoonful of syrup into Gilbert's mouth, forcing him to swallow. Judging by his puckered expression of disgust, it was obvious that Gilbert didn't take too kindly to the syrup's taste. It was also feeding time, so his tasty bottle of milk would disguise the unpleasant acridity that he was unexpectedly forced to take.

"Hey, we are all in need of a shower. Why don't we all take one together?" V asked without any sign of facetiousness.

I looked at her and waited for her to smirk or give off a sign of being nonsensical. She didn't.

"You are being serious?" I asked with a slight shock since we had never done this.

"Sure, why not? You take showers with your military buddies don't you? Why can't you shower with your wife and child?" Even though she had a good point, it didn't eliminate the awkwardness of the situation. I guess part of the awkwardness was the manner in which I was brought up. As a child, I never did this type of thing with my sisters, and I couldn't remember doing this type of thing with Mom and Pop when I was younger. Naturally, I reacted the way I did, but I didn't see any harm in it.

"Sure, get the water ready." I said.

"Really? You're serious?" V asked excitedly.

"Just don't set the water to boil like you usually do, or you will end up giving your husband and son 3rd degree burns." I commanded.

"I won't. No boiling today." V assured me.

For close to an hour, V and I enjoyed sharing the shower with our son as we took turns lightly scrubbing him. Gilbert was never truly afraid of water, but he did seem a little uncomfortable and apprehensive whenever he was bathed. He would constantly stare at the water as if he found the water to be suspiciously wicked and therefore expected some sort of wrongdoing on the water's part, but with V and me in here with him, he appeared to be more at ease and more accepting of the water's mystique. His confidence was apparent.

I leaned over to kiss Gilbert's forehead, then V's neck. I touched her face while I kissed her neck when V noticed my wrinkly fingers.

"How long have we been in here?" V asked with no real idea.

Jaime Perez

"I am not sure. Why?" I asked.

"Because all of our fingertips look like raisins. Look." V said as she showed me her hands, Gilbert's hands and mine.

"I knew your neck had a familiar taste." I joked.

"If I'm a raisin, you're an even bigger one!" She laughed as she kissed my lips.

It was time to get out of the water and begin letting nature and time iron out all of our wrinkles. Considering this family group shower thing was new to me, it wasn't as peculiar as I initially expected it to be. Once in the water, everything felt natural and normal.

Gilbert would probably remain awake until about the time V and I would begin to receive a visit from our nightly friend, lethargy. For the next several hours, the three of us lay down on our bed like we did on several occasions. Gilbert's body temperature seemed to be returning to normal, which brought much-needed solace to V and me. In addition, Gilbert's anxiety and feistiness turned to tranquility and playfulness. The label on the medicine bottle specifically stated that we should continue to administer the medication until the entire bottle was finished. The small bottle appeared to have enough in it for one more dosage, which meant that we would have to inconveniently wake up Gilbert in the middle of the night to administer it in a timely manner.

V always fell asleep before me. She had this gift of being able to reach unconsciousness within seconds of finding an agreeable sleeping position. I on the other hand was a prisoner of insomnia. As I looked at the three of us in our bed, I realized that Gilbert might have fortunately inherited his mother's restfulness and not his father's restlessness.

After a couple of hours, I began to feel sluggish and heavy eyed, so I set the alarm clock to wake us up in time to give Gilbert his last dosage of his pucker-inducing and disgusting red syrup. With Gilbert on my chest, I began to transcend to another state of mind, the state of deep sleep. A state that I rarely visited but always looked forward to attaining on a nightly basis. The last thing I remembered before falling asleep was that V was asleep on my left-hand side and Gilbert was asleep on my chest. The three of us together in bed was becoming to be enjoyably familiar and memorable. This was becoming the kind of memory that I would probably reminisce about while I am sprinting for my life through the damp lands of Vietnam. The problem with familiarities such as this and the joyful amenities associated with familiarity are that when things become unfamiliar, they now often become equally disturbing and difficult

120

Through You

to accept. The following morning as I awakened literally seconds before the ringing of the alarm clock, I felt that uneasy feeling of unfamiliarity when I noticed that V and Gilbert were no longer in bed with me. I was drenched in sweat, and I began to wonder, where my wife and child were?

Chapter 17

The apartment was serenely silent, which meant that Gilbert was probably still asleep. I didn't hear V in the kitchen, so I naturally deduced that she was still sleeping as well. Before anything else, I glanced briefly towards Gilbert's crib and noticed that it was vacant. Half asleep and half perplexed, I walked to the living room and noticed V and Gilbert covered by a blanket and asleep on the davenport. V must have been on the verge of waking because my approaching her caused her to open her eyes. I couldn't believe what I saw when she looked me directly in the face.

"Baby what happened? Are you okay?" I asked in shock from what I saw on V's face.

"I'll be okay. It wasn't your fault." V forgivingly responded as she smiled half-heartedly as if to give me the impression that everything was fine when it really wasn't. The fact that she tried to comfort me by not placing the onus on me made me conversely feel responsible for the dark semi-circle under V's right eye.

Although it had momentarily been erased from my thoughts, that very second I suddenly remembered a vision I had in my sleep. Sometimes my dreams are simply non-linear, unrealistic and preposterous visions or random thoughts. There is no beginning, no end, no story, nothing, just snippets of unconscious, mental fragmentations. Seeing V's black eye brought forth this illusionary sensation. This is when I realized I was solely responsible for her conspicuous contusion.

"V, I am so, so sorry. I really have no control over this. Ever since the first days of basic training in El Paso, I began having dreams, or shall I say nightmares, of being attacked or being coerced by someone or something. I never get a clear look at my assailer, but I always manage to wake myself with violent jerks and convulsions before anything further manifests. I hadn't had one of these ill-fated episodes in a while, so I assumed they were

122

now conveniently a thing of the past. Now I know they have a recurring effect." I said before kissing her gently on the nose.

"It was very scary; I'll admit that. I'm just glad you hit me and not Gilbert." She said as if trying to look on the bright side of the situation.

V's and Gilbert's absence from our bed was all clear now. V must have wisely taken herself and Gilbert to safely sleep in the living room after she received my bruising blow. I immediately went to the freezer to get some ice to put on her eye. I had never hit a woman in my life previous to this day, and the one time that I do hit a woman it ends up being the one woman I would never wish harm upon, the only woman I would gladly die for, the mother of my child, my wife. I felt shameful and unworthy of V. I was so humiliated that I now had a difficult time looking her directly in the face, not because the contusion was strikingly obvious but because I didn't want to see what I had done to her. I was trying to manipulate the guilt by not looking at her too much. This method was faulty and did nothing to appease my burning guilt. I wrapped some ice cubes in a paper towel and put them in V's hand without looking at her. She noticed my shame and quickly eradicated it.

"Hey, look at me." She said as she grabbed my face by the chin and sternly insisted that I make eye contact with her. With her eyes inches apart from mine, she continued. "I know you didn't mean to do this. Hell, you were asleep for God's sake. How can you blame yourself for doing something in your sleep? That's crazy. Don't go beating yourself up for something beyond your control Baby. By the way, you should know me better than to think I am going to feel sorry for myself because I have a little bruise on my right eye. Big deal, I've been through worse. I can deal with it; I just want to make sure that you can deal with it too. I don't love you any less because you had a nightmare; trust me." V authoritatively declared as she simultaneously managed to make me feel slightly better and a little less brutish.

"Thanks for your understanding V. You know I would never hit you intentionally."

"One thing is certain, the military has done a hell of a job training you in self defense. As I got off the bed with Gilbert, I watched you for a few seconds more until you completely stopped your unconscious battering. You were kicking and punching very tactically and systematically. Do you remember any of that?" V asked with slowly melting ice on her right eye.

"Now that you mention it, I vaguely remember a little of it. In my dreams, I can never seem to overcome my attacker. He never seems to

Jaime Perez

contain me either though; it's like a continuous struggle with someone or a force that I can't even see. I feel hands on my neck, fingers in my eyes, kicks on my back, punches on my stomach, but I never seem to actually grasp anything solid or tangible. The only reason I stop is because it eventually, after what seems like hours, ceases, with no gradual weakening, no detectible sign of stoppage. It just suddenly stops, so I stop. I used to get these at least twice a week, but they had stopped for a while now. Sometimes I would wake up in the middle of the night from someone else's nightmares. The funny thing is that no one would mention anything the next morning. It was our barracks' little secret within ourselves, like it never happened." I explained to V. Then I thought, "What are our parents going to think of me?"

"What do you mean?" V asked in confusion.

"I mean, what are my parents and your parents going to think of me when they find out I hit you?" I clarified.

"They don't need to know you hit me. Our parents would never suspect that you would do something like that, so why not just go along with it? I'll think of something to tell them. Just like you had secrets with your Army friends about your nightmares, we can have our little secret too, just you, me and Gilbert." V said.

Although I felt bad about lying to our parents, it was an accident, so we could just use that excuse—it was an accident. No harm done, no reason for concern, just a simple accident.

"I still feel bad V." I told her.

"Well, then you will have to make it up to me later tonight, in bed." She said with a slight blush that actually drew my attention more than her black eye.

"That's the least I can do." I responded with a mischievous smirk and raised eyebrows.

That night, the 7th day of my L.O.A., after constantly focusing on being parents for close to 5 months, we decided to change roles for a while and focus on being lovers. It was a pleasing change of pace from the passionless and stodgy monotony to which V and I had become hostage. Just when I thought I couldn't love V anymore than I already did, she would manage to prove me wrong time and time again. I used to have a History teacher back in high school who would always quote history's great minds as a way of effectively conveying a message to the class. One of the things Mr. Rupert liked to utter repeatedly was, "If you are not loving, you are not living", or something to that effect. I am not sure who originally

124

said it, but I was now able to fully comprehend the intent of those words with utmost clarity and perception.

Minutes after our transcendent, carnal expedition into climactic weightlessness and effervescent ardency, Gilbert's cries of hunger reverted us to normative reality—a reality that was so much more meaningful with both of them around with which to share my life. I unraveled myself from the damp bed sheets to tend to my son's needs while V remained in bed. It was 0235, which was a frequent waking point for Gilbert. Before going to the kitchen to get his bottle, I went by his crib to reticently feel his body temperature. Much to my relief, his little body temperature felt normal.

I carried Gilbert to the dark living room and sat with him in my arms as we lightly swayed on our recliner until he quickly sucked his bottle completely dry. I briefly closed my eyes and enjoyed this sweet and silent moment together, just a father and his son. I must have dozed off for a few minutes during Gilbert's feeding because upon opening my eyes Gilbert was once again asleep. I placed him in his crib and returned to bed with V.

"V, are you awake?" I whispered.

"I am now. What's the matter?" V whispered back.

"Are you sure you want to do this?" I asked.

"Do what? Sleep?" V asked sarcastically.

"Sleep in the same bed with me. What if I have a nightmare again?" I asked, but V seemed too fatigued and incoherent to respond. "Don't worry, I'll sleep in the living room. It's my turn anyway." I said as I kissed her.

Suddenly with a tight, unexpected twitch, V grabbed my forearm and said, "I am not going to have you sleep in another room like quarreling, unhappy spouses for the last days that I have you just because of an uncontrollable freak accident. We'll be all right." Then after a slight pause, V asked, "Will it help if you sleep on your stomach?"

"I don't know. We can try it. If I start throwing punches, punch me back." I responded jokingly.

"Ha ha, very funny." V whispered with an unconvincing tone. "Baby, will you do me a favor?" V then asked.

Yeah, sure, what do you need?" I asked expecting her to request a glass of water to replenish her fluids or for me to turn on the radio, something V occasionally resorted to in order to help her fall asleep faster.

"Do you think you can take Gilbert to the doctor's on your own. I don't want to really be seen publicly just yet." She requested.

"Be seen publicly? What do mean?" I asked in confusion.

125

Jaime Perez

"My eye, I don't want to be stared or gawked at by others in the waiting room as if I am a victim of husband abuse. I would rather just stay home for this appointment. Is that okay with you?" She asked with the sweetest voice that disallowed me to deny her anything she requested when she used this particular tone of expression.

"Yes, of course. That's a good idea actually. I had already forgotten about the eye. Sure, I'll take Gilbert with me. Consider it a guys' day out on the town."

Within seconds, I could vaguely hear V's heavy breathing, assuring me that she was already asleep. I turned to assume a prone position as V recommended. Several hours later, with the comfort of not remembering any subconscious visions or struggles, I look at the alarm clock and notice it is already 10:15AM. I literally jump out of bed to check on Gilbert. As I am half way to his crib, V laughs and says, "Where do you think you are going in such a rush?"

Because of my impulsive and hasty reaction, I had not noticed that V and Gilbert were lying next to me in bed. I was not used to sleeping this late in the day, as an insidious giddiness was now taking its toll on me from my sharp movements.

"I noticed the time, and I realized I was late in feeding Gilbert. I didn't notice the two of you were in bed with me." I said as I glanced over her body to peruse for additional bruises.

"The way you jumped out of bed I thought maybe you were having a dream that you were being chased or something. What are you looking for?" V asked as she noticed my attentiveness to her body.

"I'm looking for more bruises. I guess I didn't go insane in my sleep again." I responded.

"Apparently not. You need to begin getting ready to take your son to the doctor's. You have less than an hour to get ready and get there. Take a shower, and I will get Gilbert ready." V recommended.

Without hesitation, I did just that. Before leaving I kissed V and closed the door behind me. Within 15 minutes, Gilbert and I were out the door and on the way to visit Dr. Richards. We had made it just in time. After signing in at the front desk, Gilbert and I waited for approximately 10 minutes before being called. While waiting, I had an interesting conversation with an older lady who was waiting for the doctor to finish with her daughter and grandson. Our conversation was one that I would have rather not had.

I'm not usually one to hold a lengthy conversation with strangers; it was just something my parents instilled in me as a child, but I didn't see any harm in passing time with an elderly lady in the doctor's office. She obviously noticed my dog tags, which I wore everywhere I went to get into the habit of always leaving them around my neck.

"Are you in the military son?" The elderly lady asked.

"Yes mam I am." I tersely responded not expecting this trivial exchange to continue any further.

"My late husband was in the Army. He fought in World War II." She proudly revealed with a reminiscent smile that exuded from her gray, dried and aged lips.

"I'm sorry for your loss mam. It must have been difficult." I expressed as Gilbert sat quietly on my lap as if he were listening in on my conversation with this new unfamiliar face.

"It was. Losing the man you love by his own hand is never easy. You question if you could have done anything to help. You wonder if you were not significant enough for him to want to continue to live. It eats you up and leaves you feeling worthless." Her words left me a bit stupefied and questioning whether or not I had misconstrued what she said.

"Excuse me mam? Your husband didn't lose his life in battle?" I requested clarification.

"Oh no, my husband survived the war, in a way. How can I put this? Physically he made it back, mentally he didn't." She said and must have noticed my befuddled expression because she continued to willingly elaborate. "Five days after his return, he committed suicide in our bed as I slept by his side. It was the blasting, deafening gunshot to his head that woke me up in a panic. I woke up with pieces of his brain on my chest. Every time I tell this story, it's as if I can actually smell the strong scent of blood that covered me in red. Fred was never himself after the war. A woman knows when something is not right with her children and her husband. I knew something was not right in my husband's head, but he refused to discuss anything with me. He just assured me everything was fine. The military took my husband's well-being and therefore took his life. I found a note that he had placed in my hand while I was asleep that read, 'I am no longer the man you married, and I have become someone who isn't worthy of your companionship. This is why I leave you to resume your life to search for the happiness you deserve. I'm sorry, and I forever love you. Until death did us part, Freddy.' That is exactly what the note stated, word for word." She said in a tearless sorrow as her hands trembled.

I didn't know what to say; I was rendered speechless from unexpected

Jaime Perez

shock. How do you respond to something like that? Luckily, the doctor's assistant called us in before I could appear rude for not being able to utter a word, except, "Excuse me mam; that's us they're calling. Uh, have a good day." I pitifully uttered as I could feel myself turn red from embarrassment. I am glad that Gilbert was unable to understand anything the lady was saying because I don't think I would have felt comfortable exposing my son to such nightmare-inducing horrors. I took one more glance back at the lady before the door closed behind us to see if she was all right. She appeared to be in a profound soliloquy as she stared up to the waiting room's ceiling in observance of something undeterminable, or maybe she was looking to God to let him know that she still felt he was there. Regardless of what she was doing, I don't think I will ever forget her story. This is one of those situations in life that hovers in your head like a dry leaf during a windstorm, indeterminably afloat and unassailable.

I had heard a lot of stories about veterans who have returned home in a different state of mind, as if they were never completely released by the stern, pitiless clutches of war. Wilson used to share some of the stories he had heard, but many of us only took about 10% of what Wilson ever said seriously. In addition, the media and other anti-war advocates always used this treacherous tumultuousness as a tool to help strengthen their arguments for abandoning the war. There were many names for this type of mental illness: combat fatigue, gross stress reaction, battle fatigue, etc. I was more familiar with the term "shell shock" because that's the way many of today's soldiers refer to it. I'm sure after the Vietnam War it will be called something else. I think the government gives different names to this same condition to give the misled public the impression that the old condition miraculously vanished or no longer exists. In actuality, this condition is exponentially claiming the soundness of many who risk their lives for this country, and unfortunately nothing is being done about it.

As Gilbert and I waited for Dr. Richards to tend to us in the white-walled, frigid patient room, I felt a little disappointed that I didn't ask the ill-fated elderly lady what her name was. I was so taken by her story that asking her name was the last thing on my mind. I can't imagine V as a widow, so I had every intention on coming home in the same condition I left.

After about 5 minutes waiting, Dr. Richards walked into the room with the usual folder and papers in his hand, his stethoscope hanging around his neck.

"Sorry about the wait Mr. Perez. Where is your other half, Mrs. Perez?" He asked as he flipped through the papers in his folder.

"Oh, she stayed home. She was tired from staying up all night with Gilbert." I responded with harmless dishonesty.

"I remember those sporadic nights of restlessness when my wife and me had our little ones." He said as he began to listen to Gilbert's heart.

Judging by the doctor's content whistling as he began noting information on Gilbert's documents, I was under the impression that things appeared favorable. This was until Dr. Richards called for his nurse to assist him in taking Gilbert to the x-ray room.

"We'll be right back with Gilbert Mr. Perez. I just want to run another x-ray on Gilbert's chest again for precautionary measures. His heartbeat sounds better than it did during your last visit, but of course, it still resumes to be slightly abnormal as expected. Give us a couple of minutes." He said with an unconcerned tone as he took Gilbert from my arms. Gilbert was not accustomed to being taken by strangers, but I realized that Dr. Richards was probably not an unfamiliar figure to my son any more. He was already more exposed to Dr. Richards than he was to my sisters, parents or in-laws, which probably accounted for Gilbert's calmness when he was being taken from my arms.

Shortly after, the friendly nurse brought back my son. Gilbert was ecstatically holding a brown stuffed animal and putting it in his mouth as if it were an item for consumption. At first, I couldn't tell what it was; it was the banana in the animal's right hand that gave it away.

"We gave your son a little friend to play with for being so cooperative with the doctor. Dr. Richards will be right with you Mr. Perez." She said as she somehow managed to smile through every syllable she just uttered.

Gilbert was completely enthralled by his new little monkey friend, even though he would accidentally drop it every minute or so and I'd have to pick it up for him or he would give the forewarning of a potential tantrum.

"Okay Mr. Perez. Let me show you today's x-rays and compare them with those taken previously. We have good news and bad news." As he said this, I began to remember how much I hated being told by doctors that they have good news and bad news. In my opinion, as long as there is bad news, there is no good news. The only time there is good news is when there is no bad news. Regardless, I listened to the doctor's explications of the day.

"Gilbert's heart isn't getting any better, but it isn't getting any worse.

Jaime Perez

He is constantly growing, so I am expecting some change in his heart's formation very soon, hopefully something advantageous and favorable." He said as he showed me the transparencies of my son's insides. "I can see that he no longer has his fever, which is a good sign that his immune system, with the help of medication, is still able to help fight off sicknesses. I want to begin seeing Gilbert at least once a week, unless an unforeseen illness arises, if so, then I want Veronica to bring your son as I had directed before, without appointment. Again, feel free to call me at home if anything pressing should occur. We gave him a little monkey for being brave and well-behaved. Any questions Beltran?" He asked as he grabbed Gilbert's tiny hand and shook it lightly.

"So when is Gilbert's next appointment?" I asked.

"Let's get him in here in exactly one week." He responded as he wrote this down on his appointment slips and handed me the paper reminder.

"Thanks for everything doctor. Barring an AWOL, I will be overseas when Gilbert is due back for his appointment, so she'll be handling the childrearing for the time being. I can't thank you and your staff enough for the hospitality and compassion. It was a pleasure meeting you." I stretched my hand out to shake Dr. Richards' hand one last time before I was deployed to Vietnam.

"You tell your wife that we are here for her whenever Gilbert needs anything. In the meantime, you take care of yourself soldier, and don't forget that regardless of what someone believes about this war, you are still brave heroes who do daring things many others would not or could not do. I should be thanking you instead." He said with a smile.

"Thanks for the kind words. Have a good day." I said as I walked out of the freezing patient room and into the warmth of commonness.

Although I wouldn't expect her to still be waiting, I quickly glanced the waiting room for the elderly lady with the dark and gloomy story; she was no longer there. Gilbert and I were on our way home when I realized that maybe V would like some "alone time", so I decided to spend a little time with Gilbert at a park nearby our apartment. It was a cloudy, yet beautiful day. The kind of welcomed, cloudy day that seemed to promise tranquility, not precipitation. My 10 days of L.O.A. were beginning to wind down, and although it would have been nice to have V here, I felt it fitting that Gilbert and I have some time together as a father and his son rightfully deserve.

While at the park, I placed Gilbert on my lap as we swung on the swings and later raced down the curving slide together. Initially, he

130

appeared daunted with the unfamiliarity of these amusements, but after a few minutes, he was practically crying for me to supply him with more of this uncommon rush. We spent close to an hour at the park, and just as I began to feel as if it were time to put an end to the fun, I noticed that my son's eyes were becoming a little heavy, like when a child is trying to fight off the need for sleep. I didn't think the slide was particularly helpful with getting Gilbert to sleep, so I returned to the less exhilarating swings and allowed the vacillation to help relinquish Gilbert's efforts to stay awake. Within minutes, I noticed that my plan worked; Gilbert was, as they say, sleeping like a baby.

During our drive home, I began to realize how special and significant our little adventure to the park was. What started out as a diversion to kill time and give my wife some "alone time" ended up resulting in a sincerely momentous occasion. Even though I couldn't help think that this may be the only time my son and me get to spend time at a park together, I knew I would remember this day forever. Holding my son, hearing him laugh, seeing him smile and sharing precious time together were the kind of extraordinary memories that endure time. It was moments like this that simultaneously help define one's past, present and future.

Approaching the apartment, I looked to see if Gilbert was still asleep; he was. I open the apartment door quietly so as to not wake Gilbert, and I notice V was writing something in a notebook on the kitchen table. She quickly closed the notebook and placed both the notebook and her writing utensil in a drawer.

"Hi handsome." She whispered as she kissed me.

"Me or Gilbert?" I responded in a whisper of my own as I sat down on the recliner.

"Both of you silly." She said as she took Gilbert from my arms and placed him in his crib to continue his routine sleep.

"I was beginning to get worried. Where did you guys go?" V asked as she sat on my lap, much like an eager child sits on Santa Claus' lap when taking a picture with Santa at a department store.

"After the doctor's appointment, Gilbert and I went to the park to play on the swings and the slide. I felt it would give you a little time to yourself. Bye the way, the doctor asked for you." I added.

"What did you tell him?" She asked seriously.

"I told him I beat you up because you wouldn't let me watch the baseball game on television." I responded jokingly.

Jaime Perez

After playfully hitting my shoulder, V said, "You don't even like baseball."

"Dr. Richards doesn't know that. Honestly, I told him you were tired from being up all night with Gilbert." I said.

"That was a believable reason. What did the doctor say?" V asked with a concerned look.

"After taking new x-rays, he said there hasn't been much change in Gilbert's heart, and that it's a good sign that he was able to fight off the fever. He wants to see him weekly and also mentioned that you are still advised to call him at home if anything unforeseen should arise." I said as I handed her the appointment notice.

"What did you do while we were gone?" I asked V.

"Nothing." She tersely responded as if she was hiding something.

"And what's this?" V asked as she stuck her hand in my jacket pocket, taking out Gilbert's newest friend.

"They gave him that at the doctor's for being well-behaved and brave. He seemed to really enjoy it. Gilbert and I decided to name it 'V', after his mommy."

"How do you know it's a girl?" With raised eyebrows, V asked to rebut my comment.

"I can tell. They showed us how to accurately determine the sex of all primates while I was at Ft. Sill." I said with the inability to refrain from smiling.

"In a matter of days, you went from being a soldier to being a clown. What a transition!" V sarcastically commented.

"I also said my goodbyes to Dr. Richards and thanked him for everything since I will be overseas during next week's appointment." I added.

"That's right. I don't want you to leave." V said with a child-like pout.

"Believe me. I don't want to go either." I assured V.

"Why don't we take advantage of Gilbert's time asleep and go lie down in bed." V recommended with a subtle look of mischief.

"That sounds like a great idea." I added with a smile of my own.

Chapter 18

I had almost eight days down and two to go. My visit home was rapidly streaming as steadily as I had originally expected. After tonight, my 9th day begins. I needed to make arrangements for my last day; I wanted to gather the family and have one more final moment together before leaving for the airport, all of us.

Speaking of family, I wondered how my military-assigned, non-biological brothers back in Oklahoma were doing. They were probably still giving Wilson hell, all except Nicholas Brown who was likely in his own internal hell trying to cope with and screen his clandestine sexual nature. I hope for Capelletti's sake that he's already been deployed or at least given some sort of dangerously adventurous assignment to quench his thirst for ravaging havoc. Morales would probably like a similar opportunity to add some excitement to his pensive life, and perhaps Smith is still hopelessly trying to convince all those around him that he should be exempt from any more unnecessary and inhumane violence since his people have endured enough. Sergeant Mills, the queen bee of all the aforementioned worker bees, is probably listening in on his colorful bunch with his ear glued to his door to keep himself entertained with all the outrageous stories and discussions that take place amongst this specific group of soldiers. I can't truthfully say that I really miss being in Oklahoma, but I can honestly say that I sincerely miss the company of the men I met there.

Once again, Gilbert served as our own personal human alarm clock for V and me. I got up this time to do the honors of preparing a bottle for Gilbert. As I was on my way out of the kitchen and heading to Gilbert's crib, I suddenly stopped when my attention was drawn to the kitchen drawer that V had hastily hid her notebook when Gilbert and me had returned from the park. My curiosity was compelling me to take a look at what V was so tenaciously trying to keep me from seeing. At the same

133

Jaime Perez

time, I was never the type of husband to inconsiderately pry into my wife's precious privacy, and I didn't want to start playing investigator now. My urge was not driven by distrust; I was just simply trying to appease my inquisitiveness. As I thought about it once more, I decided to let the continual mystery dwell. V's secret will remain just that, a secret.

Gilbert was waiting with open arms in his crib, so I picked him up and fed him his bottle. I was beginning to notice that he was getting slightly heavier. Although this would normally be a welcomed sign for most parents, I on the hand was now dreading my son's growth because I felt that his maturation and growth would likely demand more work of his frail heart. Then again, I am not a doctor nor do I know if there is any truth to the matter. Within minutes, Gilbert had finished his bottle, but he still appeared to be sleepy. I brought him to bed with me and placed him on V's tummy.

"Hey there little man." V spoke to Gilbert as he smiled like he knew what his mommy was saying.

I remembered seeing his monkey friend on the floor by the bed when I got up to make his bottle, so I reached down for it and grabbed it so Gilbert could play with it. He had close to a hundred toys, gadgets, stuffed animals, noise makers, etc, but for some unknown reason, Gilbert loved his banana-eating friend the most. The second he saw it he began joyfully smiling and springing up with glee as he was once again reunited with what seemed to be his long-time, long-lost friend. Although V and me would likely discourage Gilbert from sticking his friends in his mouth and biting them with his gums, we allowed it with this particular friend due to the special circumstances.

"Our son goes crazy for that thing. Look at him. I bet you if we get him an outfit or some pajamas with monkeys on them he would really enjoy them. When you get back from the war and Gilbert is a little older, we should take a trip to the zoo and let Gilbert see real monkeys." V said with a smile.

"I just hope he doesn't want a real monkey when he gets older. That could be a little problematic." I added.

"Well, if he wants a real monkey, he will just have to settle for another brother or sister. I am sure Gilbert wouldn't mind the substitution. We will worry about that when the time comes. For now, the stuffed monkey will do." V mentioned.

"Hey, I just noticed that your black eye doesn't look so obvious. You have to look for it in order to notice it." I tried to comfort her with my honest opinion.

"Thanks. Is there anything in particular you want to do today?" V asked.

As she asked, an idea came up. "Why don't we go watch a movie? We haven't done that in at least a year. There has to be something of interest showing. I could ask Mom to take care of Gilbert today. I am sure she will have no problem with it, especially since I leave tomorrow night. What do you think?"

"That would be nice, but I don't like the idea of imposing on your parents on such short notice." V voiced with concern.

"Well, let's ask and see. I need to call Mom and Pop anyway to make sure we get together tomorrow before I leave. I will call my sisters as well, and you can call your parents. Maybe we can have a special dinner before I have to leave to the airport. I am scheduled to depart on an evening flight from the McAllen airport. I believe my flight is scheduled to depart at 9:35 PM."

"All right, ask your parents, and I will look in the paper to see what is showing. If your parents are busy, maybe we can ask mine to watch Gilbert." V suggested.

"Sounds good. Look for a comedy. I would like to avoid any dramas if at all possible; I need something lighthearted to ease the tension of leaving." I said as I reached for the phone while V flipped through the newspaper and Gilbert played with his stuffed primate.

I dialed my parents' phone number and waited for Mom or Pop to answer. "Hello." Mom answered after the 3rd ring.

"Hey Mom. What are you and Dad doing?" I asked.

"Wow. What a surprise! Your father and I were just talking about you and Veronica." Mom said with an unfeigned tone of unexpectedness.

"What exactly were you talking about? Is everything all right?" I asked in concern.

"Oh yes, everything is fine. Your father and I were just contemplating calling you and Veronica to see if we could have Gilbert for the afternoon, but your father said that you would probably like to spend as much time with Gilbert before leaving as possible. He has the day off today, so I just thought it would be nice for both of us to spend some time with Gilbert since the last time you brought him over your father had to work." Mom explained.

"Wow. Actually, V and I just finished discussing the possibility of

Jaime Perez

taking Gilbert to stay with you while V and I go to the theater to watch one last movie before I leave tomorrow." I responded with my own tone of unexpectedness.

"Sure. Bring him over whenever you are ready." Mom advised.

"Oh, before I forget. I would like to get all of us together, Diana and Sarah included, to have one last supper before I leave. My flight leaves tomorrow at 9:35 PM. If possible, maybe you can all come to bid me farewell after we eat. What do you think?" I mentioned to Mom knowing that she would like my idea.

"That's a great idea. I will call your sisters and order them to cancel any previous obligations they may have had." Mom said authoritatively.

"Thanks Mom. Let us get ready for the movie, and we will see you in a bit. We'll be there in about half an hour." I said.

"Okay son. Goodbye." Mom said before hanging up.

"Mom and Pop are fine with taking care of Gilbert." I screamed to V thinking she was in our bedroom when she was actually right behind me in the kitchen.

"All right. There is no need to scream." V said sarcastically.

"Sorry, I thought you were in the other room. What did you find in the paper?" I asked.

"They are showing *The Odd Couple* in an hour and a half. Do you want to see that?" V asked as if she had her fingers crossed behind her back because I knew she was a big fan of Jack Lemmon.

"Sure, but why do want to see a movie about us? Isn't reality good enough for you?" I joking asked.

"Very funny. Is that a yes?"

"Yes. I have heard on the television that it is really funny. This could prove to be a much-needed therapeutic experience. I'll get Gilbert's bag ready while you get dressed. I'll make sure to include his little monkey." I recommended to V.

"Did you mention tomorrow's dinner plans to your parents?" V asked in reminder.

"Yes. Mom is going to call Sarah and Diana today to make sure they show up. Hopefully they can go with us to the airport to say goodbye. Make sure you mention it to your parents as well." I recommend to V.

"I will call them when we get back from the movies. Can we get some popcorn at the movies? I haven't had theater popcorn since the last time we went to a movie. I can't remember how long ago that was. As a matter

136

of fact, I can't even remember what the last movie was that we saw at a theater." V said in slight disarray.

"My poor, lovely wife is already suffering from Alzheimer's Disease. When I get back from this dreaded war, I will take care of you my forgetful princess. Hopefully you won't forget who I am." I joked.

"You are really asking for it *Beltran*." V said as she emphatically enunciated my real name, which she only used when she was irate or agitated. In this case, it was just a playful jest.

V wasn't the kind of woman that took hours to get ready for a simple outing, so in 15 minutes, the three of us were on our way to my parents. As we drove to Mom and Pop's, we passed by the park that Gilbert and me had visited the day before. The park was on the corner of an intersection where we were currently stopped. I briefly glanced to the park and noticed fathers playing catch with their sons, parents pushing their children on the swings, children playing on the seesaw, and a plethora of felicitous merriment. Not until that moment, did I realize the park actually had a name and a sign displaying that name: Robert E. Lee Memorial Park. I immediately noticed the irony of my son and me playing in a park named after a war hero a few days before I was being sent to fight a war. I could see V with my peripheral vision looking at me as I gazed intently at the park. She stayed silent and observed me in my reminiscent trance. I don't know exactly how long I stayed in a reverie, but if it weren't for the honking of the car behind us, I may have remained in momentary enthrallment for a short while longer.

Finally, V asked, "Was that where you and Gilbert came to spend some time?"

"Yeah, that was the park." I said as she softly caressed my face while I resumed the drive to my parents' house.

Upon arrival, Gilbert must have noticed the surroundings from the last time we brought him over to stay with Mom and Pop because he had a different look on his face, one that hinted at familiarity. The fact that Mom and Pop were anxiously looking out their front windows awaiting us might have heightened Gilbert's anxiousness.

Seeing my parents looking out the window reminded me of when I was younger. As a child, my parents always kept a close eye on me. Whenever I would play with my neighborhood friends, they would watch me like a spider would a fly. Often, I would notice them from the corner of my eye looking out the window to see what I was doing and whom I was with. I wouldn't say that they were overprotective to the point that they hindered my childhood experiences because that was not the case. I was actually granted more privileges and freedoms than both my older sisters. Actually, it wouldn't be fair to use the term "overprotective"; maybe a more appropriate term would be "vigilant". I never spoke to my parents about this, but I had concluded that my parents realized raising a boy was a little different than raising girls. They had already experienced raising two girls; now they had to adjust to my distinct upbringing. I wasn't particularly mischievous or problematic; I just didn't really put safety and prudence on the top of my list of priorities. What young boy does? I suppose that watching your son climbing fully grown trees, jumping from rooftops, play wrestling with older boys and playing tackle football on the street might be enough to make most parents cringe and worry. I assume that coming home with torn clothes on a regular basis, sometimes with stains of blood on my shirt, didn't do much to rid my parents of their concerns either.

Before ringing the doorbell, Pop opened the door with obvious anticipation as we approached their house. Pop wasn't the type to smile much, especially when being asked to do so as in the case of being photographed, but seeing Gilbert always brought a convincing and warm-hearted smile to my Pop's face. Mom, on the other hand, always displayed her tender smile, even when there was nothing really to smile about. Whoever coined the phrase "Opposites attract" must have known my parents personally.

"Hey there little fella. Come to Grandpa." Pop commanded as he raised his arms to take Gilbert from my arms.

"Hey Pop, hey Mom." I said as I hugged Mom.

"Hi son. Hi Veronica." Mom said with her motherly and welcoming smile.

Everything appeared to be normal, like any other visit to my parent's house. It wasn't until V took off her sunglasses that the normalcy quickly turned to utter concern.

"Oh my God! What happened to you Veronica?" Mom asked with a troubled tone as she noticed V's gradually waning black eye, which judging by V's reaction, she had obviously forgotten about.

"Huh? Oh, the eye thing. Yes, I had a small accident. It's nothing to worry about. It has actually gotten much better." V attempted to comfort Mom and Pop as I could see that she was mentally trying to concoct some convincing and plausible explanation for the semi-conspicuous blemish.

"What are you talking about?" Dad's poor vision was no longer deniable.

"Look! She's got a black eye. Don't tell me you can't see it?" Mom asked.

"Oh, that. Of course, I can see it." Dad responded in an unconvincing manner as he squinted to hopefully acquire some sort of clarity or a temporary and miraculous remedy for his dwindling vision. "Luckily for you, you are going to the movies where it might go unnoticed in the darkness."

"I'll just wear my sunglasses until the movie begins." V suggested, as she seemed to try to evade any further inquiry and interrogation from my parents concerning the accident. "I should really use the lower kitchen cabinets to store my heavy pots and pans instead of the upper ones." V added as I quickly turned to her in surprise, impressed by her believable excuse.

"What movie are you going to see?" Dad asked in complete shift of subject.

"*The Odd Couple.*" I responded.

"Why pay good money to see *The Odd Couple* when you can sit here with us and observe the odd couple for free?" Dad joked.

"Now I know from where your son gets his wittiness. He suggested earlier that me and him were an odd couple." V added as Gilbert lay on the couch with his best primate friend next to him.

"I'm sure everybody is odd in some way." I added. "We better get going if we want to make it on time."

"You both enjoy yourself, and take your time. If you want to do something after the movie, feel free to do so. You don't have to hurry back right after the movie." Mom suggested as Pop nodded in agreement with Mom's recommendation.

"We'll see what happens." I answered.

"Be careful, and don't forget to put your sunglasses on Veronica." Pop added.

"Okay Mom, Pop. We'll be back shortly." I said as V and me let ourselves out of the house.

I was really looking forward to going to the movie theater with V. We both loved going to the movies, but, for obvious reasons, we hadn't been able to go as often as we would like. Having children changes you like nothing else. It's almost as if you transform into another person in such a short period of time. Your beliefs change, your behavior changes, your

Jaime Perez

responsibilities change, your outlook on life changes and you change. In a way, all these changes also occur when one becomes a soldier, except having a child is beautiful, miraculous and marvelous. I am still finding it difficult to find anything magical or enjoyable to say about becoming a soldier.

Chapter 19

I had requested that V decide on a movie with some humor to hopefully serve as a therapeutic tool to help get my mind off of what was to come. This idea proved to be advantageous. Throughout *The Odd Couple*, V and I laughed away unrestrainedly. As a matter of fact, the entire theater was in a continuous uproar of laughter. This same theater was the very first theater where I had ever seen a movie on the big screen; it was also the only theater that V and I had ever been to together. This theater, I felt, held a part of me within its red-carpeted aisles and granted me a sense nostalgia and solace that I rarely experienced anywhere else. It was a place for essential escapism that allowed me to enjoy the little things in life without taking everything so seriously. For some reason, life's weighty burdens didn't seem so oppressive and stifling; actually, they virtually vanished into the theater's unintimidating darkness.

Although V and me were still considerably young, not even 21 years old yet, I did feel older that I actually was. A big part of that was becoming a father, and the other part of that was becoming a soldier. Regardless of how old or mature I felt, sitting closely with V in the theater, holding hands, sharing a fountain drink and tossing popcorn into each other's mouths made me feel like a carefree youngster once again. Gone were the worries of war, the dwellings of death and the broodings of bloodshed, at least for a moment.

"What did you think?" V asked me as she always does after a movie to get my opinion.

"It was a good choice and definitely funny. The movie critics were right about this one." I responded favorably.

"I didn't hear you laugh out loud even once!" V stated in minor shock.

141

Jaime Perez

"You know I don't laugh aloud. I am more of a silent laugher, but it was funny." I explained.

As we began walking to our vehicle, abruptly and unexpectedly V said, "I don't want to go home yet. Do we have to? Can we spend a little more time together, just a little bit?" She gestured with her index finger and thumb to show just how much more time she wanted to spend together. The look on her face was unforgettably cute. She looked like a little girl pleading with her parents to buy her a new dress she had fallen in love with, her drooping, puppy dog eyes making it almost impossible to deny her wish.

"It's still early. I don't see why we can't prolong the evening for a bit. What do you have in mind?" I asked her.

"You." V responded.

"What?" I asked because I wasn't quite sure I had heard her correctly.

"You asked what I have in mind; I have you in my mind." V slightly elaborated.

When V said things like this to me, I often felt short of breath and unable to speak. I am not usually the type of person to be at a loss for words, but V was probably the only person in the world who had the ability to clear my mind thoughtless by simply uttering a few hypnotizing words.

After an ephemeral paralysis, I was finally able to respond, "You drive me crazy when you say things like that."

"Don't blame me for your craziness. I met you this way; you were already crazy." V joked.

"Well now I am even more crazy, thanks to you." I retorted as I looked V directly in her deep brown eyes and proceeded to kiss her nose.

We drove around in our car, desultorily yet content. As long as we were together, it didn't really matter what we did. For a little over an hour, we just drove and drove with nowhere to go, enjoying each other's company as we so often did.

When you get to really know a person, you can sometimes sense the slightest of aberrations or feel a certain uncanny vibe in their speech, their look or their mannerisms. I was getting this exact sensation from V right now. The whole evening was fine, until now. I didn't want to force the issue, so I allowed the anomalistic aura to serenely lurk until V was ready to unveil it, whatever it was.

"Can you park the car for a bit?" V asked with a sudden shift in tone, as if she was about to explode emotionally.

I noticed she was appearing a bit anxious as she began biting her self-manicured nails, something she rarely ever did unless something extremely pressing was bothering her. I entered the first parking lot I noticed and parked in an empty parking space. Not a second after I shifted the car in park, V jumped out of her seat and attacked my right side. She began crying vehemently. She tried to speak, but her speech was inaudible due to her heavy sobbing and hyperventilating.

"Hey, take it easy. Breathe. Talk to me. Tell me what's on your mind." I said as I opened the car window to allow some fresh air to circulate and assist V with her respiration. Up until our aimless drive, I honestly didn't foresee this change in V's disposition; it came out of nowhere. Obviously V was holding something in that she was not telling me, and it eventually became too overwhelming for her to contain.

V finally regained her composure and lifted her head off my chest. Her eyes were completely bloodshot, and her cheeks were saturated with tears. She seemed to have better control of her breathing as she began wiping her tears on her blouse. After several seconds, V caressed my face but still didn't say anything.

"Take your time Baby." I stated even though I was extremely anxious to hear what was on her mind. I grazed her moist face softly with the back of my hands as I allowed her all the time she needed to repeat what she initially and inaudibly tried to say earlier.

With a disheartened look, V made direct eye contact with me and began to take a deep breath before attempting to speak again. "I'm really sorry honey. I've tried to be strong, but I can't anymore. I didn't want to make things any worse for you than they already are, but my emotions had to come out. I know you have a lot on your mind that is already taking so much out of you. Because of this, I did my best to keep everything in with hopes of facilitating matters with you. I thought I could remain calm throughout your visit and appear to be handling everything well, but I drastically misjudged myself. The truth is that I have cried myself to sleep ever since Gilbert and me returned from Oklahoma, every single night previous to your return. I am so scared about you leaving and possibly not coming back. I couldn't even manage to watch the news because there was always something negative and gruesome about the war, so I had to constantly shut the television off. For the sake of comforting myself, I have tried to imagine myself without you, and I just can't; it's impossible.

Jaime Perez

You are not supposed to be absent from my life. That's not how things are supposed to be. I can't even begin to explain how much all this hurts. A few times I had to call Mom to come over and just be there with me to talk to and to listen to me. I told her not to tell you how difficult of a time I was having coping with all this. I don't even think my father knows about the mother/daughter discussions we had. I was able to contain my outbursts since you arrived, but now I no longer have the capacity to appear composed. That's it. That is what is wrong. That is what is why I am here crying by your side."

We sat in our seats in complete silence for about another minute or so with no exchange of words. I was trying to absorb everything V had said. Although I had no control over this, I felt somewhat responsible for putting my angel through a hell of which she didn't deserve. I had clipped her wings, and because of me she was suffering an emotional freefall. I had to say something to comfort my wife, anything to make her feel optimistic about the most trying situation we have ever been through. I wasn't the most eloquent of men, but I rarely had trouble expressing myself. This time things were different. My mind was completely blank.

Suddenly unbeknownst and without really thinking, I unpremeditatedly said, "V, for the next year we will be apart physically but not mentally. For the next year, I won't see you with my eyes, but I will see you with my mind. For the next year, my wife, the woman of my dreams will be with me in my dreams, and for the next year, I plan to do everything in my power to return to you. After that year is over and when all the dust has settled, I will be back so that we can continue to live our lives where we left off. Everything will return to normal, and all this hardship will be behind us." I said as V looked at me with a diminutive look of hope.

After a long, heartfelt hug, V said, "Well then, for the next year, I will be waiting for you."

Finally a semi-convincing smile shined from her face. Seeing V's reaction to my leaving was fervently powerful. Her pain demonstrated just how strongly she felt for me, and it simultaneously evoked an enlivening rejuvenation that yielded a strong sense of consolation for our future. Many unfortunate individuals wander through their empty and discontent lives in search of their other half, their soul mate, their partner for life. I was fortunate to have found mine. I just had to come back the same way I left, alive.

I hadn't realized that V and I had been parked for close to an hour in the parking lot of a local drug store. I didn't want this moment to end because I knew there weren't many more of these left before leaving tomorrow night. I assumed that V felt the same way because she had been leaning over to my side of the vehicle with her head on my shoulder for several minutes. At one point, I thought she might have actually gone to sleep resting on me.

"Are you asleep?" I whispered.

"Yes." She facetiously whispered back as I felt her manage to produce a smile. "I know we should leave, but let me enjoy this moment for a few minutes more. Please." V requested, so I graciously granted her request without a response.

After 10 more minutes of warm embracing, V sat up straight to silently signal that it was time to leave and pick up our son. We drove towards my parents' house and noticed Mom and Pop outside with Gilbert playing in the front yard. After parking our vehicle, Gilbert arduously crawled towards us on through the thick, verdant grass with a big smile as if recognizing our vehicle.

"Hey big guy." I said as I picked up my son before he stumbled onto my feet.

"How was the movie?" Pop asked.

"It was funny." V and I both responded at the same time.

"You need to take me to see that movie." Mom stated to Pop with a stern voice.

"Did you get a hold of Diana and Sarah, Mom?"

"Yes, they are free tomorrow to spend some time with us. What time do you want us over?" Mom asked.

I looked at V before answering. "The sooner you get there, the more time we get to spend together. My flight leaves at 9:35PM. Maybe everyone can get there by 5:00PM. We can have a nice dinner and then head on to the airport together." I suggested.

"That sounds good. Are Virginia and Al going to be there Veronica?" Mom asked V.

"I totally forgot to mention it to them, but I am sure they will be there too. They aren't going to miss Beltran's departure." V answered.

For the next several seconds, there was a peculiar silence amongst the 4 of us, 5 if you include Gilbert. It was as if everybody had something to say, but nobody was saying it. I think the reality and gravity of my situation was beginning to truly manifest itself. Leaving to boot camp and basic training for several months took some adjusting from my family, but leaving for

Jaime Perez

battle for an entire year many miles away in potentially harmful territory was completely different for obvious reasons.

"Okay then. We better get going. Mom, Pop, thanks for helping us with Gilbert." I brusquely said to break the momentary interval of silence. I didn't want things to get weird right now. I was pretty sure tomorrow was going to be emotional enough, and I didn't want to aggravate sentiments one day before leaving as well. In addition, I could tell that Mom was about to begin getting teary eyed, and I preferred to avoid that from escalating. It's not that I was being insensitive or heartless; I just hated being the cause of such pain and somberness, especially to the people I hold most dearly, my family.

Finally, Pop helped drag me out of this silent quandary by adding, "It was our pleasure son. You bring Gilbert back whenever you feel the need Veronica. Don't hesitate to ask." Pop directed his comment to V.

"Thank you Mr. Perez. I appreciate the help that you and Mrs. Perez graciously give." V responded before making her way to the door.

"Don't forget, tomorrow at 5 o'clock. V and I will have dinner ready at the dining table. Don't be late or we will have to start eating without you." I said jokingly to try to dissipate the sorrowful aura.

"We'll be there son. You can count on it." Pop responded with Mom by his side.

If we would have stayed a few minutes longer, I was pretty certain that we would have all ended up in tears. I could already see them start to exude from Mom's eyes, and I don't think Pop would have been too far behind.

We waved goodbye as I reversed out of the driveway. The drive home was just as silent as the few final minutes at Mom and Pop's, except this silence was not foreboding of any melancholy. This was sweet, welcomed silence. It was the kind of silence that felt right, with no need of disruption— Silence, no sporadic gunfire, no crying souls, no flying aircraft, no ravaging explosives, just glorious and magnificent silence.

Chapter 20

Upon arriving home, V and I noticed that Gilbert had fallen asleep in the back seat of the vehicle. Apparently, Gilbert felt the same way I did about the silence so much that he welcomed it to the point of reaching unconsciousness. It was time for Gilbert's usual bedtime anyway. We placed him in his crib, his primate friend watching and guarding him as he slept.

V and I proceeded the evening with a memorable, soothing and sensual shower that I knew I would be able to vividly visualize while away. This pleasurably lengthy encounter coupled with the hot water began to produce a mist from the evaporation that gave the appearance of us floating amidst thick celestial clouds. As we embraced and caressed each other, I knew that there was no other place I would rather be than where I was right now. I had often heard a saying as a child that went something like, "One might need to go through hell before arriving to heaven." At this very moment, I was to experience the exact opposite. I was being escorted by my wife through heaven, before being sent away to witness the essence of true hell. The remainder of that passionate night was nothing short of magical ecstasy and euphoria.

Our explosive expedition together must have caused us to lose track of time because just as V and I were beginning to unwind from the shared exhilarating exhaustion, Gilbert was waking from his sleep. I got up to perform my routine fatherly duties. By the time Gilbert was done feeding, V was already asleep, as I had expected. It was encouraging to see that V was able to achieve a good night's rest, especially considering the stirred state she was in just a few hours ago. I placed Gilbert in bed with us and sandwiched him between V and me as I slowly crawled next to my wife and admiringly watched her as she lay in bed next to me, breathing softly and calmly.

147

Jaime Perez

"I love you." She whispered to me, unconsciously.

Although it didn't occur too often, V was known to talk in her sleep. This was one of those instances. I had witnessed this a few times before since it always took me longer to fall asleep than V. It wasn't problematic or anything like that, and it was usually just a few words or sometimes just one word. Tonight, she had unknowingly uttered 3 words. Whenever I would question her the morning after hearing her, she would claim that she didn't remember saying anything. Initially, she thought I was playing a prank on her, but after a while, she realized that some of the utterances I told her about were actually from her dreams. This is when she knew I was being genuine about my claims.

Even though I knew she couldn't hear me, I went ahead and told her, "I love you too."

Somehow, it seemed as if she reacted to my response with a heartwarming smile. Maybe my eyes were deceiving me, or maybe the light shining through the window created an illusion of some sort. Regardless, I'd like to think that she did smile, that she did hear me, and that she did mean what she said.

The following morning, my final morning with my family, the 3 of us got dressed and did some shopping to get some items we needed to have our dinner. I was really looking forward to this evening. It's really sad that the only times we get together as a whole like this is when have to meet at a family funeral or somebody is dying in the hospital. Although in this case, nobody was dying, and nobody was planning on dying.

Something about V looked different, but I couldn't quite put my finger on it. She caught me staring at her in wonder, so she asked me, "What's the matter?"

"Nothing, it's just that you look different to me somehow." I responded.

"Could it be that you can no longer see my black eye?" She said as she turned directly to me so that I could get a better look at her face.

"That must be it. Did it disappear completely?" I asked surprisingly since it hadn't been too long since I gave her the blemish.

"It has faded away enough for me to be able to conceal it with make-up. It looks good, doesn't it?" V asked with a slight tone of self-confidence.

"Yes. You did a great job of hiding it." I agreed with sincerity because I didn't' want anyone asking V about the accident tonight at the dinner table.

I had previously told myself that I was not going to mention the "I love you" comment from the previous night to V, but I couldn't help myself. My curiosity got the best of me. After leaving the grocery store on the drive home, my inquiry unfolded.

"Do you remember talking to me in your sleep last night?" I asked.

"No, I don't, but I have a good idea what it was that I might have said." She said surprisingly confident.

"What do you think you said?" I was now fully attentive.

"I told you that I loved you. Even though my dream was a little morbid and dark, it was still pleasant." She added.

"How could something morbid and dark be pleasant?" I wondered.

"Wait a minute. Was that what you heard last night? Was that what I said?" V requested confirmation.

"Yes, it was. You whispered it once. How did you guess?" I inquired.

"Because my whole dream was in silence except for those 3 words. It was morbid and dark because I was in my deathbed. There were others around, but their faces were a distorted blur. I really couldn't make out who else was in the room with us, although the silhouettes of the figures appeared to be of two men who were by your side, comforting you. The important thing is that you were there and that was all that mattered." She added.

"And how is you dying pleasant?" I was eager to know.

"We were already old. I was dying of natural causes, and you were on your knees by the bed, firmly holding my hand, pleading for me to stay with you, to wait for you. I thought that was very romantic, in an odd kind of way. If this isn't pleasant enough, you being there next to me signified that you made it back from the war alive. It was comforting to know that you returned to live a full life with me even though I wasn't able to recollect our life together in the dream. I remember blacking out in my dream right after I told you that I loved you. That's how it all ended. I can't really tell you anymore, but that's what I dreamt. I know it was just a dream, but I have a funny feeling about this dream—a feeling that you will make it back home to me. It all seemed to vividly real, real enough to establish a bit of comfort concerning this whole war thing. You will make it back to me, and I no longer have to worry about becoming a widow and losing you." She said with a smile as she held my hand and kissed the back end of it.

"Wow. That is dark, morbid and pleasant, all into one." I agreed. "Let's hope that if one dream in your life comes true, it will be this one."

"Yes, let's hope. I just don't know whom the two men were who were

Jaime Perez

standing beside you. Oh well, you were there, and that was enough for me." She added.

Knowing that V was now temporarily convinced of my survival and safe return was a comforting relief. I didn't care if I was convinced or not, as long as she was. That was all that mattered. I can take care of myself when I'm away, but I can't take care of her or my son from such a broad distance. This would hopefully ease some of the worries I would likely have of V when I was too far away to assure her that everything would be all right. I wanted my wife to live the next year content and normal. I didn't want her to be in complete anguish and distress over me, therefore wasting away a full year of her life.

Once at home, there was still some time to spare before V and me needed to start preparing dinner, so we decided to play with our son in bed as we had become so accustomed to doing. This would truly be the last time until next year that I would have the pleasure of doing this. For the next 3 hours the 3 of us did nothing but laugh and enjoy each other's company. Hearing my son's jovial giggles brought me much contentment that it almost brought me to tears. We even managed to achieve a small nap of maybe 30 minutes or so. It was one of those short naps that seems hours long, the kind that leaves you startled and in disarray about what time it is after you've awakened. After all, I didn't want to be running late with our dinner preparation on my last day at home. The 3 of us awakened almost simultaneously like the untimely awakening of soldiers in unison at 0430 hrs at Fort Sill, something that I knew I didn't miss at all but knew I had to get used to once again.

While preparing dinner, the phone rang, and V answered it. It was my sister Sarah. She had asked if she or Diana should bring something. V told her not to worry because everything would be taken care of and that all they needed to bring was themselves. Ever since I was a kid, I had always loved my Mom's mouth-watering chicken fried steak. While V and I were engaged, V asked my Mom for the recipe so that she could prepare the dish for me in as much the same way my Mom would. While V was preparing the main portion, I was making mashed potatoes from scratch and heating up some corn. I glanced at the clock on the wall and saw it was a quarter 'til five. Just as I turned down the gas stovetops, the doorbell rang.

"Hey. Come on in." I said as I answered the door for the whole clan. Apparently both my sisters had decided to ride along with Mom and Pop. I could see Virginia and Al's vehicle driving up as well, so I waited by the door until they approached our apartment.

150

"Thanks for coming Mr. and Mrs. Saenz. Your joining us for dinner means a lot to me." I expressed sincerely to my in-laws as they made their way to our doorstep.

"It's good to see you son." V's father said as he shook my hand firmly. From the very first day I met him, he has always called me "son", rarely anything else. I then hugged V's mother, who looked like a mirror image of V to the point that many would often mistake them for sisters. Although I am pretty sure that V mentioned that it was unnecessary for her parents to bring anything to dinner, Virginia was carrying a covered platter or dish. It was shaped as if maybe it held a German chocolate cake. My mouth was beginning to water already.

"I brought your favorite." Virginia said. Now I knew my guess was correct. It was a German chocolate cake. V and I had completely forgotten about preparing a desert, so this surprise was delightful.

Even though our family dinner was primarily in honor of my leaving, Gilbert received his share of attention. V's parents had not seen him since before he had hair, and everybody was in complete admiration of our son.

"All right, let's start eating. I hope you all brought a ravenous appetite." I announced as I approached the kitchen to help V serve our guests.

"Woah, wait a minute. You sit your butt down little brother. Let us take care of this. You've been serving your country for the passed few months; now it's time for you to be served." Diana stated as she escorted me to the living room with Pop, Al and Gilbert while the women took care of setting the table and serving our plates.

I don't exactly know what Al and Pop were abstrusely talking about in the living room before I entered, but judging by the last words spoken by my father-in-law, I could tell that it had something to do with me because I heard him ask my father how he and Mom were handling everything. Their conversation came to a complete and silent standstill. Rather than to allow my presence to induce an awkward moment of silence amongst us, I went ahead and hastily broke the silence by initiating a conversation with my father-in-law, a conversation to which he instantly changed the topic.

"How is everything at work Mr. Saenz?" I asked him.

"Son, I want you to know that you are a very brave man, and you will be in our prayers every night. With the Lord, everything is possible." He stated as he totally disregarded my question, or maybe what I asked didn't register because he had anticipated an entirely different topic of conversation. V's parents were extremely religious, and I wished I could

Jaime Perez

tell Mr. Saenz that if everything was possible with the Lord, why was it not possible that this war end today? Why was it not possible that I could stay home and comfortably live my life with my family without being subjected to military punishment? Why was it not possible to achieve peace in Vietnam without a war? Although these thoughts were running amuck in my head, I did the respectful thing and thanked my father-in-law for his kind words, in spite of how implausible and irrational they actually were.

"Come and get it guys." Mom called as she placed the final item on the table, the quintessential bowl of mashed potatoes.

Pop, Al and myself must have been equally famished because we each hurriedly got up and grabbed a chair. Gilbert remained in the living room playing with a plastic set of toy drums that he had received as a gift from my parents. Our guests noticed Gilbert's uncanny independence.

"Gilbert is so independent. It's amazing that he can quietly be by himself and not be bothered by it." Sarah said.

"I remember Veronica used to need us every second of her infant life. If she saw us going to the bathroom or walking to answer the phone, she would begin whining until we would return to her." Mrs. Saenz revealed.

"Yes, she was a very needy child. I think she inherited that trait from her mother." Mr. Saenz interjected jokingly, leading us all to laugh, V included.

"I remember Beltran being just like Gilbert as a child. We would offer to play with him or carry him, and he would prefer to be alone." My oldest sister Sarah recalled.

"I probably just didn't want to play with dolls, that's all." I added.

"Yes. Beltran was always the most self-sufficient of our 3 children." Pop added.

"I remember Beltran would wake up in the morning, prepare his own bowl of cereal and sit down two feet in front and in center of the television to watch cartoons on Saturday mornings while his two older sisters had to come barging in to the bedroom to wake us up to ask us to make them a bowl of Corn Flakes. He was so well-behaved and responsible." Mom said with an emotional smile that was obviously accompanied with some enjoyable reflections of the past.

"And us? What about us?" My sister Diana asked in longing for some laudatory comments about her and Sarah.

"You were extraordinary in your own special way." Pop responded with a smile while the rest of us, except Diana and Sarah, laughed at Pop's failed attempt to assuage my sisters.

152

Although I really didn't want to continue discussing embarrassing points and moments about my childhood, I felt that I would relish this moment of sentimental reminiscence and enjoy these intimate revelations despite their tendency to cause me to blush in innocuous embarrassment. This is what family gatherings are supposed to be, an enjoyment of each other's company along with the manifesting of memorable childhood eccentricities that were once thought to be safely buried in the past. At this point, I was just glad that Mom or Pop didn't bring any of those ancient photo albums that contained abasing visual memories, many of which had begun to turn a light shade of brown from their aging.

V's mom was anxious for us to try her cake, so as soon as all of us had finished with our meal, Virginia wasted no time slicing the cake and offering everyone a generous portion. As I observed Virginia meticulously slicing her mouth-watering, moist masterpiece, I noticed the clock on the wall behind her now read 6:32PM. Our time together seemed to be elapsing quicker than normal. Time was flying by, and soon I would be flying away. I had already packed my bags with all my necessities so that I wouldn't have to spend any time doing this while my family was here.

Virginia's cake was delicious, which is probably why she was so eager for us to try it. We had all left our plates crumbless, and I, as expected, boldly helped myself to a second serving since I would likely not have anything this delicious waiting for me in Vietnam. Military food isn't exactly known for its unparalleled scrumptiousness.

After desert, which approximately sucked another half hour of our dwindling time, our conversations turned a bit more serious and less amusing. I had a feeling our discourse would eventually turn to this. Our tears of laughter would now become tears of anguish, fear and inevitability.

After all the dishes were put away, nobody got up from the table. We all just sat there as if expecting something else to take place. Mom grabbed my hand and as expected, she was the first to relinquish to her emotions. I knew this was going to be extremely difficult for everyone, but the most softhearted person I have ever known was Mom. Just seeing her cry was enough to compel everyone else to join her in her episode of tearful moroseness. I felt that I had to remain as mentally and emotionally strong as possible in order to leave my family with at least a minute feeling of hope and optimism. If I were to cry with them, they would then witness my insecurity, my trepidation and my apprehension, which would inundate them with more fear and concern. If I couldn't be strong here, there was no

Jaime Perez

way I was going to be strong in battle, which would likely amount to my dying. My courageous display of strength needed to permeate and pierce through my family's bones and into their soul in order to successfully accomplish my intentions.

"I know as your father, I don't tell you that I love you enough Son, and for that I am terribly sorry. Throughout your younger years, your mother and I have instilled you with many of life's lessons and expectations. Now that you are a young man, we have naturally strayed from the parental duty of giving you advice and instilling beliefs in you because you are old enough to choose such matters for yourself. It's been a long while since your mother and I have given you any words of wisdom or asked you to do anything for us because you are living your own life now. With this in mind, there is one more thing that I am commanding you, not asking you, but commanding you to do for your mother and me, and that is to never forget how much we love you and how proud you have made us." I looked towards Mom because I noticed her hand was trembling uncontrollably as I held it. Pop was speaking for both Mom and him because Mom was probably incapable of speaking right now. She often had a difficult time speaking whenever she would experience fits of tormenting agitation. Dad appeared to want to say more, but nothing else was coming out of his mouth. He appeared dazed and in a hypnotic state as he stared motionlessly without blinking at the center of the table.

My overprotective yet well-intentioned sisters had some comments of their own to share as well. "Beltran, you have always known us to be very protective of you because we are your older sisters; that's what we do. It's in our nature. Lately, we have felt as if we've failed in our sisterly obligations to keep you from harm's way. If there were anything in our power that we could do to safely keep our little brother here with us, we would do it without question. Unfortunately you are being taken from us, and there is nothing we can do about it." Sarah stopped for a moment to blow her nose and catch her breath. In the meantime, Diana proceeded, "As silly as this may sound, Sarah and I hope you are not mad at us for not being able to do anything to help you. We know you are coming back when all this is over, but it is still agonizing to know that our little brother is being painfully and inconsiderately seized from the grasps of our comfortable lives. Hurry back so that things can come back to normal again because without you normalcy is impossible." Diana concluded as both her and Sarah came to my sides to simultaneously kiss both my cheeks and embrace me in a sibling sandwich that usually grossed me out and left me with a

154

disgusted look on my face, but today, today was different. I gladly let my sisters kiss and hug me without end, much to their surprise.

Al and Virginia also had a few words of their own to share, words that I had never heard from them before. As Al said, "Son, it is never easy for a mother and father to let go of their only daughter so that she can begin living her own life in her own way. I used to have nightmares of the day that my little girl would ask to leave the house or the day when her boyfriend would ask for her hand in marriage. It's just something that I always dreaded; it actually made me sick to my stomach in some cases. Then Veronica brings you home one day. I don't know what it was about you, but Virginia and I felt at ease the moment we met you for the first time."

Virginia interposed, "After you left our house, I remember asking Al if he thought that Veronica and you were serious, and he surprisingly answered, 'I hope so.' Inside, I was thinking the very same thing. I never thought that Al would ever think that anyone was good enough for our little girl, but I was pleasantly mistaken."

Al continued, "Son, marrying you was the wisest decision our daughter ever made, and both her mother and I are glad that it was you with whom she decided to spend the rest of her life. The only problem is that she still has a lot of life left to live, and you need to return so that my daughter can smile again like only you can make her smile and so that she can continue to live the rest of her life with you." My father-in-law stopped, possibly prematurely, because he appeared to be attempting to control his emotions. I have never seen Mr. Saenz display as much sincerity as he had just finished displaying. He always appeared impassive and expressionless, almost robotic, but today, as he shared a few words with my family and me, I came to see a different yet empathetic side of Mr. Saenz—he was as human as the rest of us.

The table was silent. Everybody had spoken, except V. I was a little overtaken by all the kind words being directed towards me. I was about to thank everybody for the kind words and thoughts, but I unexpectedly noticed that V was slowly walking towards me as if to whisper something in my left ear. Her lips touched my earlobe, but she said nothing. She just stood there motionless with her soft lips against my ear for roughly 5 seconds as I began to feel tingly goose bumps all over my defenseless body.

She then sat down and smiled at me. V didn't say anything to me that moment in my ear; she didn't need to. I knew exactly what she was

Jaime Perez

thinking, exactly how she was hurting and exactly how she felt for me. Even though she whispered nothing in my ear, her silence still managed to generate an earnest smile from my face.

Again, I was about to begin speaking when I noticed Gilbert playing with his monkey on the living room floor laying face up on his plush baby blanket. He looked perplexingly at the dining table where all of us sat. I think he wasn't accustomed to seeing adults crying, especially so many at one time. I went to pick him up and bring him to the table with me, so that I could resume with my response.

As I placed him on my lap, he looked at me as if he was waiting to hear what I had to say. I kissed my son's forehead as he sat quietly and seemingly attentively. "I am really touched by all of your kind words, and I sincerely feel blessed to have the family that I have. I want to ask all of you for a favor though, one little favor. I ask that each and every one of you go about living your life to the fullest while I'm away. Try your best not to worry about me because I will be back. I have too much here at home waiting for me, perfect parents, the best two sisters in the world, understanding in-laws, my beautiful wife, and this little guy needs me to play catch with him, to show him how to ride a bike, to take him fishing and to take him to his first baseball game." I said as Gilbert looked up at me while I spoke and as he wiped away a tear from my face that I told myself I would do my best to contain. "Believe me. Each and every one of you will be in my thoughts daily, and it is the thoughts of you that will help me endure and persevere the horrors that await me. Regardless of what confronts me overseas, I live through you, and I live because of you." I was done saying what I had to say, and it was not a minute too soon. As I remained the center of attention at the dinner table, I managed to catch glimpse of the clock. It was 8:03PM, and I had to be at the airport an hour before to assure a smooth boarding process. In other words, it was time to leave.

Chapter 21

In order for everyone to bid me farewell, we had to take two vehicles to the airport. I rode with V and her parents in Al's vehicle while Diana and Sarah rode with Mom and Pop. My 9:35PM flight from McAllen, Texas would take me to Seattle, Washington and arrive at Fort Lewis. I would be given more specific orders there, and from there I would fly to Japan, and finally arrive in Vietnam roughly 30 hrs later with all the time-consuming layovers. Even though I wasn't even in the air yet, I was already eagerly anticipating my arrival in Vietnam. It wasn't so much that I was looking forward to landing in a hostile environment and risking my life; it was more of the idea that the sooner I arrive in South Vietnam, the sooner I come home. I wanted to begin my service so that I could get it over with once and for all.

I sat quietly in the back seat of Al's vehicle with V by my side. V was resting on my shoulder and grasping my left arm as we rode with the car windows completely down while I allowed the fresh, untainted air of a free country to invigoratingly flow through my airways. Gilbert sat on my lap and seemed to enjoy the air grazing his little face. We passed by the Robert E. Lee Park, and I couldn't help but remember Gilbert's and my first genuine father and son moment from a few days before. I stared at the park intently so that I could attempt to vividly remember as many details about it in hopes of being able to mentally picture it overseas and possibly use it to help me take my mind off any unwanted wantonness. I realized that it was going to be the little details and memories such as these that may just save me from returning home early in a body bag.

Gilbert startlingly turned to V as if he had heard her calling him, but she hadn't. I think he sensed that his mother was in a state of obvious distress because she was gently quivering in the Texas heat as if she were freezing. V was silently crying, doing her best to hold in her anguish, but

157

she was unable to subdue her insurmountable emotions. My left army jacket sleeve was drenched with my wife's tears; tears that I wished would never have to dry off. I held my son's head in my right hand and my wife's hand in my left hand as I brought them both to my chest to embrace them. This specific moment, this exact second was the type of moment that had the magnitude to forever imprint itself in my mind and subsequently become a life-long memory that would never be forgotten. Rare picturesque and poignant moments like this give life substance and purpose and often instill an unrelenting drive and desire to live life. I naturally relished it.

As we approached the airport parking area, I confidently felt that I was ready to confront and embark in this volatile stage of my life. It was as if I had suddenly yet mysteriously developed a strong tolerance and acceptance for the uncertainty that lies ahead. I wasn't scared. All fear had now waned; I was ready as I could possibly be.

Immediately after my father-in-law parked the vehicle, I opened the door to grab my belongings from the trunk. Pop parked his vehicle in the vacant space next to Al, and we all proceeded to the airport entrance. As my familial entourage appeared somewhat melancholy and apparently struggling to contain their runny noses and watery eyes, I walked slightly ahead of them with self-assurance, wife by my side, son in one arm and military duffle bag in the other. It was a quarter 'til 9:00 as I proceeded alone to the ticket counter to check in my belongings. The plane was on schedule, and all I had to do now was patiently wait until the announcement was made to begin boarding. There were several available areas for us to sit and talk until I had to leave; we chose a quiet, secluded area slightly apart from the rest and all sat down. The blue vinyl sofas in the airport waiting areas were positioned in a circular shape, and every one grabbed a sofa and placed them closer to me to face me.

"Well, this is it, huh?" Pop took the initiative and asked to break the uncomfortable silence among us.

"I guess so Pop. This is what it all comes down to." I really didn't know what to say. We had all expressed ourselves minutes earlier at the dinner table, and we all seemed at a loss for words, especially V. The only things coming out of her were quivers and tears. As I sat on the sofa, I noticed V positioning herself closer to me as all others followed her lead. My sisters fell to their knees in front of me as each one grabbed hold of my knee closest to them. V and Gilbert squeezed in with me on the sofa I was sitting on, Mom and Pop were to my left and my in-laws stood closely to my right.

"Mr. Perez, if you don't mind, I'd like to say a little prayer before OUR son leaves for battle." Al requested the honor from Pop.

"Of course Al, be our guest." Pop graciously permitted Al to pray on behalf of all of us.

While Al was conducting prayer, I focused my attention on my son so much that I didn't even register most of my father-in-law's words. Throughout the prayer, everyone but my son and me bowed their heads and closed their eyes. I would have joined them in prayer, but just as I was about to bow my head, I noticed Gilbert curiously staring up at me as if he knew I was about to leave him. He was obviously too young to know what was going on, but the unforgettable look on his innocently adorable face seemed to emanate a sense of sincere sadness. He reached for my face with his tiny hand and grabbed my nose, eyes, cheek and lips as if he were doing it for one last time.

Seconds after Al's prayer concluded, the announcement to begin boarding resounded. I got up first, and everybody else followed. I hugged everyone one last time, saving V and Gilbert for the end. I knew I had to leave, but I didn't want to let go of my wife just yet. It was apparent that she didn't want to let go either. She didn't deserve any of what she was being put through, and neither did my son. Through the entire drive to the airport as well as while in the airport, I noticed that V hadn't spoken a word, yet I knew what she wanted to say and how she felt. Sometimes a person's actions and behavior can effectively express a lot more than words. Words are restricted by their inherent meanings and can therefore fall short of truly conveying one's feelings. It was V's stentorian silence that clearly spoke volumes of the unspeakable misery she was bearing.

As I slowly began approaching the tunnel to board the plane, I thought I would stop and take one last look at my family and wave goodbye. When I did, V was making her way towards me, walking hurriedly. She opened her arms, and we embraced for several more seconds as other airplane passengers were passing us by.

"I love you. I'll be waiting for you." V finally uttered softly in my ear as I received goose bumps from her lips touching my sensitive earlobes.

She touched my lips, kissed them and walked away before letting me say anything to her. I stood there as if paralyzed, completely motionless, as I watched my wife slowly fuse into the cluster of other travelers hastily attempting to catch their flights.

Without further hesitation, I resumed to my plane, found my seat and patiently waited for liftoff. I closed my eyes for what seemed to be 5

Jaime Perez

minutes when I was awoken by the flight captain welcoming us to Seattle. I was surprised that I slept through the whole flight because I wasn't physically tired, but I was mentally drained from all the deep thoughts that had been crossing my mind for the past several days, weeks and months.

Upon exiting the plane, I was to look for a man wearing camouflage and holding up a sign that read "Fort Lewis". Due to the fact that he was surrounded by other soldiers in camouflage, he wasn't too difficult to locate. I presumed that they sent this soldier to pick up several others while at the Seattle airport.

"How was the flight Perez?" The soldier with the sign asked me in an obviously uninterested and inconsiderate manner.

"Restful sir." I said before reading "Martin" on his Army jacket.

"You were the last one we were waiting on Perez. I am Captain Martin, in case you can't read." He said in a rude, belittling tone. "I was sent to pick up four soldiers, and I've got four soldiers. This means my mission is partly complete. The vehicle comfortably fits four, but we are five. Unfortunately, one of you is going to have to sit on someone's lap like a bitch at a strip joint. I'll let you guys decide who sits where. Don't kill each fighting for the front seat because we need you in Vietnam." Martin said with a subtle tone of sarcasm yet with enough sincerity to acknowledge that he was being serious as well.

The entire ride to Fort Lewis was spent glancing in silence at the area's landscapes as we rode through the empty, desolate streets of Washington State. It had apparently just finished snowing, something I had never before witnessed in South Texas. The scenery and temperature were a nice change of pace from the snowless, scorching weather back home. The white ice gave the area a peaceful, serene feeling that was somewhat welcoming, even though Martin's unwelcoming and nauseating 2nd-hand, cigar smoke was annoyingly making its way through me. Although the other three soldiers were observing our surroundings as well, I could tell that snow was nothing new to them as they watched casually.

Several minutes later, the vehicle stopped. "All right men, we are here. Bring your bags, and I will show your sorry asses where you need to be." Martin coldly and heartlessly ordered. I don't know who or what most of these soldiers think they are, but it seemed as if many of these men lack manners and normal social skills, almost as if it were a learned contagion that gave them strikingly similar, impersonable personalities. Cordiality and hospitality were now somehow institutionally uprooted from within most of these intolerable men and replaced with seeds of ill will that grew

160

like unyielding weeds, forever damning their once fertile, now tainted gardens of humaneness.

I usually take my time when meeting someone new to make a judgment about their character, but only minutes after meeting him, I could already tell that Martin was not the kind of man whose company I enjoyed. I didn't expect to be in Fort Lewis very long, so I wasn't too disheartened by the thought of his undesired presence.

We all jumped off the Jeep and followed Martin to a barracks. The fort was silent, which was expected considering it was only a few hours before Washington's sunrise. I had never flown before, and I therefore was unaware that flights would land at such an ungodly hour.

Martin led us to a half-full barracks and ordered, "Find an empty bed, get some rest, and I will see you in the morning with further instructions. Sleep tight you bitches."

"What an asshole." One of the other new arrivals whispered to himself after Martin left and slammed the door behind him.

Some of the sleeping men woke up with the door slam and with Martin's abnormally scratchy voice; others remained calmly asleep and undisturbed by this man's unpleasant impudence. It took a few seconds for our eyes to adjust to the permeating darkness and for us to feel our way to an unoccupied bed. All four of us eventually found one. In the meantime, I restlessly waited a few hours before Martin was to come in with orders at the top of a new day. Sleeping proved to be too much of a challenge for me that night. Like many times before, I acquiesced to my insurmountable insomnia. It wasn't surprising that I ended up staying up the whole evening because of the impressive, deep sleep I had during my flight. The bed I chose was the nearest to a window that provided me with a rather decent view of Washington's attributes. I simply stayed up all night looking at a snow-covered mountain in the distance that was lightly illuminated by the slowly passing moon just enough to witness and appreciate the beauty of this part of the country.

I wasn't exactly sure what time it was, but I knew it was closely approaching 0430 hours. A few of the men began sluggishly waking up one by one, until finally one individual got up and turned on the light, eventually waking up all the others. This laconic group of men quietly began their daily morning routine. Nobody said much of anything. I glanced towards the other 3 men who arrived with me earlier that morning. We all appeared to be in a state of bewilderment because we weren't sure if we were to join this group with their agenda or if we were to await our own

Jaime Perez

orders. Just as I was going to approach the newly arrived soldier who slept two beds from mine, Martin brashly bolted in to remedy our uncertainty and confusion.

"Wilkins, Perez, Anderson and White. Put your make-up on ladies, and meet me at headquarters in 5 minutes. Hurry your asses; time is money, and I have neither of both." Martin announced and quickly left without making eye contact with anybody in the barracks.

After grabbing our duffle bags, the four of us went to the facilities to perfunctorily wash our faces and attempt to give the false impression of being fully cognizant. Although I failed to get any sleep, I still felt lost and out of place, similar to when one wakes up not knowing what day it is, what time it is or even where one is. The other 3 soldiers appeared groggy and zombie-like, so I assumed they were actually able to fortunately achieve a few short hours of restrictive, restorative restfulness. There were others in line waiting for the shitters and the sinks, so we didn't even have enough time to brush our teeth and make it to headquarters in 5 minutes as ordered.

Half asleep and half puzzled, we walked in to headquarters. Towards the back of the edifice, a stern-looking man with more honorary, military medals on his chest than I knew existed sat in his office behind a wooden desk and in front of a U.S. flag. His door was open, and he could see clearly to the entrance of headquarters.

"In here gentlemen." He ordered with slightly more respect and a non-threatening tone than Martin had. We saluted him and remained standing until he asked us to sit on the only other 4 chairs in his office. "Have a seat men. Welcome to Fort Lewis. I am Lt. Col. Chandler, and I will make this very brief. As you know, you are not staying here. You were brought here to receive the specifics for your drop offs." He said as he handed each of us a stack of papers. "In a nut shell, you will be leaving here and arriving in Tokyo, Japan. From that flight you will be taken to South Vietnam to truly begin your service overseas. Everything you've trained for will be implemented and necessary for survival from this day forward. I will have Captain Martin, who I'm sure you had the pleasure of meeting, personally drive you to the airport. In case you didn't notice the departing military vehicles on your stroll to headquarters, there will be many others being deployed from this Fort as well as others across the nation. If I'm not mistaken, your flights are scheduled to leave at 0700 hours, which means the four of you should hit the road very soon. Any questions?" I had a plethora of questions, but I assumed he was being rhetorical and therefore spared the possibility of looking moronic by actually responding.

He continued, "Good. I hate questions; I like answers. Best of luck men and make our country proud." He said as he got up and saluted us. We saluted him without saying a word as we grabbed our bags and began our way out of headquarters.

"I feel like I just got screwed without any foreplay." White commented to the 3 of us as we all smirked at his metaphor and approached the headquarters exit.

"Now you sound like my wife." Anderson responded as we all couldn't contain our laughter.

"What in God's name is so damn amusing ladies?" Martin asked with his annoying, scratchy voice as he waited for us immediately outside the headquarters entrance, sitting in the military vehicle with the motor already running.

"Shit." I heard Wilkins subtly mutter to us in disappointment of having to ride again with Martin.

None of us were particularly interested or desperate enough to interact with Martin. Nothing pleasant ever seemed to spew out of his mouth, so I think Wilkins, Anderson, White and myself all did the smart thing, remained silent through the entire drive back to the airport.

Upon arriving to the airport, we noticed several other military vehicles arriving and departing. Martin didn't bother parking; he just briefly stopped and ordered us out of the vehicle.

"Good luck bitches." He said as he began driving off before I had the opportunity to grab my bag from the back of the Jeep.

I had to run after the Jeep and jump on its rear in order to grab my bag as Martin inconsiderately continued to drive off without hesitation. I walked back towards Wilkins, Anderson and White, since they waited for me.

"I swear. If I were to see Martin in Vietnam, which I'm sure I won't, I would fucking kill him myself." Anderson commented with a convincing look of fidelity.

We realized that the four of us were on 3 different flights, all going to South Vietnam. White and I were on the same flight and actually in neighboring seats. This airport was much bigger and enigmatic than the one back home in McAllen. After deciphering at which gate we had to be, we all wished each other luck and gave one last salute before White and me collectively went our separate ways from Anderson and Wilkins.

163

Jaime Perez

The gate numbers were chronological and easy to see. We had to be at gate 22A.

"I have to take a piss Perez." White commented.

"I might as well go now too." I responded.

We still have about a little over an hour before our flight's departure, so we weren't too concerned with being late. As we exited the men's room and resumed to gate 22A, I noticed at least a hundred or more soldiers throughout the airport dressed in their camouflage attire and carrying military duffle bags.

Something appeared awkward on the way to our gate. I noticed a man walking a little further down from gate 22A who was dressed like a religious monk, with sandals, a rope around his waist, what appeared to be a black, hooded robe and a Bible in his right hand. I suppose someone dressed like this during the times of Christ would appear to be normal, but it was a little out of the ordinary in 1968 in an airport in Seattle. I hadn't noticed until a while later that the individual was also carrying a military duffle bag in his left hand. He got on top of a chair and began preaching to a growing circle of curious onlookers. The airport security took note of the ruckus and quickly asked the man to step down from the chair and to leave the premises if he was not here to board a plane. I tapped White on the arm and pointed to the unexpected situation as we both continued towards the gathering to feed our curiosity.

"Sir, I am going to have to ask you to leave. We don't take to kindly to disruptive behavior in airports sir." The security stated.

"Are you a man of the Lord? Are all of you children of the Lord?" He asked as he turned his attention from the security to everyone within listening distance. He continued, "You can not be of the Lord if you kill the Lord's children. The Ten Commandments clearly state that 'Thou Shall not Kill", but soldiers like myself are being sent to Vietnam to sinfully kill the Lord's greatest creation, man."

Not until I heard the enraged man say, "…soldiers like myself…" did I notice whom the boisterous individual mimicking a monk was. "Holy shit!" I said not intending the pun. "Look White; that's Wilkins."

"It can't be." White responded with a tone of uncertain ambivalence.

It was difficult to recognize him at first because of the hood enshrouding his head, but the military duffle bag and the way he walked back and forth on his platform led me to believe I was right. Just as White and I continued towards the crowd, the preaching man took off his hood. White and I simultaneously turned to each other in shock.

Through You

"It is Wilkins!" White finally concurred in disbelief.

Wilkins continued with his religious diatribe. "John 3:15 reads, 'Whosoever hateth his brother is a murderer; and ye know that no murderer hath eternal life abiding in him.' I refuse to kill another man regardless of whom he is because we are all the Lord's children. Proverbs 28:17 reads, 'A man that doeth violence to the blood of any person shall flee to the pit; let no man stay him.' I pledge to thee that I will not kill a man at the request of another, unless God almighty himself asks this of me. The war in Vietnam is a precursor to many other cataclysmic events that the Bible warns about. For example…"

Wilkins didn't get the chance to complete his public tirade because the airport security finally subdued him from behind as they placed a cloth over his mouth that knocked Wilkins out cold. They carried his body away, and that was the last that we saw of him.

"Wow. That was a rather eccentric and theatrical attempt to dodge the war. I wonder if it worked. What do you think?" White asked as the crowd dispersed and we resumed to gate 22A.

"I don't think he will be going to war in Vietnam, but I do think he has started an entirely new war for himself here at home. He will probably be court-martialed, possibly imprisoned or subject to a multitude of military laws. You can't screw with the military and expect to only receive a light slap on the hand. He just screwed up his life." I responded.

"Even though I didn't really know the guy, I felt badly for him. I had no idea he was such a holy roller." White added.

"I don't think he was particularly devout White. I think he just came up with a plan to get out of having to go to war. He had to contrive this plan ahead of time. He must have changed clothes in another restroom and transformed from soldier to monk in matter of minutes. He wouldn't be the first one to hypocritically turn to God in a trying moment of desperation. I wonder if God is caring for him now." I said to White as we gave our tickets to the airline attendant.

"Not particularly religious, are we Perez?" White asked with subtle sarcasm.

"I guess not." I answered.

"That makes two of us." White mentioned as we both approached our seats.

Our flight was full of soldiers, some eager, some fearful, some praying and some reading. Walking down the plane aisle I could read a few of

165

Jaime Perez

the jacket patches: Parker, Williams, Coulter, Sanchez, Moore, Evans, Lewinksi, Davis and De Leon to name only the ones I was able to read.

White and I put our bags away and sat down. Last night's skipping of sleep was beginning to insidiously come over me, so I figured this would be a good time to catch up on some much-needed rest. My sleep schedule was now completely and understandably disoriented, and it would only get worse when we arrive in a completely different time zone in Vietnam. I was about to ask White for a blanket from the overhead compartments, but he was already snoring before the plane was even off the ground. As sleepy as I was, I could have slept on rocks, so the pillow was only a luxury I didn't actually need. I closed my eyes for several hours as I peacefully slept through miles and miles of unturbulent air travel.

Upon waking, I stretched in my tightly uncomfortable seat and noticed the button on my left jacket pocket was not fastened, which I found odd because I never used my pockets. I figured that maybe it became unfastened when V washed the jacket back home. I reached to fasten it but stopped when I noticed something was in my pocket. It was a piece of paper, something I hadn't put there.

Chapter 22

"Can I get you something to drink sir?" A blonde-haired stewardess asked me seconds after waking up. Her nametag read "Virginia".

"Yes. I'd like some water please. Virginia, that's my mother-in-law's name." I added.

"Really. My parents moved to Virginia a few weeks before I was born, so they named me after the state I was born. Was your mother-in-law born in Virginia too?" She asked with the over-exaggerated tone of false happiness and an over-expressed smile that all the other attendants seemed to implement even though they still hadn't quite mastered the art to the point of making it believable.

"No, she's actually from Mexico. Do you know if we get meals on this flight?" I asked as I heard my stomach growling from not having eaten.

"Yes, this 15-hour flight serves two meals. We already served one, and the other is not until another 4 hours. Right now we are just offering beverages." She answered and feigned that same sterile smile of sarcastic elation from before.

How could anybody display such a fake smile for such a long period of time, especially when telling a customer that you are just serving beverages? I was so overtaken by her lack of genuineness that I almost didn't discern what she had just said about the meals.

"Did you just say that you already served one meal?" I asked for clarification.

"Yes sir. You must have been asleep when we came by your section. We don't wake up sleeping passengers, and we won't serve again until another 4 hours." She continued smiling.

"How long have we been in the air?" I asked in disarray.

"We've been airborne for roughly 7 hours now sir. If everything proceeds as scheduled, we have approximately 8 hours left before touching

Jaime Perez

down in Tokyo." She responded and gave me the water I requested as I looked out the window in search of the sun to get an idea of what time of the day it was.

"All right. Thank you. If I fall asleep during the serving of the next meal, will you please wake me up? I'm starving." I requested of the attendant.

"Of course soldier." She answered as she continued down the aisle after noticing that White was asleep.

I resumed drinking my water as I tried to get my mind off of my growing hunger and looked over to White as I saw him reaching inside his pocket. He pulled out a candy and gave it to me.

"Here Perez, maybe this will hold you over for the next 4 hours." He said with his eyes closed.

"You mean you weren't asleep?" I asked as I took his offering.

"I'm a very light sleeper. I was asleep until I heard the attendant speaking. She must have thought I was asleep too because they didn't offer me the first meal." White explained as I began unwrapping the Tootsie Roll he had kindly offered me. "Let me know if you want another one. I always carry a shit load of Tootsies with me. I don't do any drugs, but I am definitely addicted to fucking Tootsie Rolls. I'm surprised I don't piss them out whole." White added as I almost choked on the Tootsie Roll from laughing at his last comment.

"Yeah, I can see how they can become pretty addicting." I assured him.

I savored the candy for as long as I could and let it evaporate completely in my mouth before taking the last gulp of my water. I reclined my head back on the cushioned seat and began crumpling up the candy wrapper to throw it away when I suddenly remembered the piece of paper I had felt in my jacket pocket.

I never really got the opportunity to take it out because the attendant sidetracked me when she came by to ask if I wanted something to drink. I reached in my pocket and took it out. It didn't look remotely familiar, and it was folded as many times as humanly possibly. I knew I hadn't put it there. I looked at my jacket patch to make sure I was wearing my own jacket and not someone else's accidentally. As I gradually began unfolding the paper crease by crease, my curiosity began to heighten. Suddenly, a familiar aroma began to permeate before me, an aroma that brought a smile to my face. It was the scent of V's perfume. I don't know what it was called, but there was no doubt that's what it was. I eventually finished unfolding the whole note and noticed its contents. It was the poem that

168

V promised she would write for me. I though she had forgotten about it, obviously my wife is a woman of her word.

Just as I was about to begin reading the poem, White opened his eyes and looked to me.

"What is that smell? It smells like a women." White asked with a contorted look on his face.

"It's my wife's perfume. She must have sprayed it on this paper for me." I explained.

"So what does it say?" White nosily resumed his pervasive inquisition.

"It's a poem. My wife likes to write me poems." I answered, hoping he would hinder his prying.

"Interesting." White responded as if he was hoping I would elaborate on the subject.

"Are you married White?" I began my own counter-interrogation so that he would cease his.

"Nope. If I survive this bullshit, maybe I will. It must be pretty hard on your wife to have to let you go, I mean, not being able to do anything about you fighting in this war." He deduced.

"Yeah, it was. I mean, it is. She is a strong person. I just have to be as strong as her, if not stronger."

"Wake me up when these chicks begin serving the 2nd meal." White requested.

"Sure." I responded, as he appeared to continue his sleep with little trouble.

In the meantime, I decided to take advantage of White's unconscious state by reading the poem that V wrote for me. The poem was titled, "Now That You Are Gone", and I curiously began to read.

Now That You Are Gone

When I am with you
I feel complete.
When I am with you
You make me smile.

When I am with you
I need no other.
When I am with you
You give me comfort.

Jaime Perez

But now that you are gone
My mind begins to wonder.
Do you miss me, because I miss you?
Do you think of me, because I think of you?
Do you cry for me, because I cry for you?
I can't wait until you come back...now that you are gone.

I read my wife's touching poem at least 5 more times and deeply whiffed the aroma of her perfume before resuming to fold the paper the way I had originally found it. I placed the poem back in my jacket pocket and fastened the button so that I would not lose or misplace this memento. This keepsake might be the kind of keepsake that helps me keep my sanity in the most insane of times.

I closed my watery eyes and began to think about what my wife and son were doing at this very moment. I wasn't even in Japan yet, and I already began to miss them sorely. Thinking of them away from me made me begin to feel indignant resentment towards my government for dissecting me like a laboratory animal apart from my family. I suddenly felt consumed by a pervasive aura of malignity, and I began to wonder if this was a similar type of sentiment that drove Capelletti to become so hungry for war. Maybe these emotions would fuel me through my days in battle. This could only be possible if this ardent malevolence would endure within me and become the norm, or it could simply dwindle to nothingness as an ephemeral emotional reaction. If it became the norm, I would obviously transform into a different type of man, a man I had never before become. Then I began to wonder, what is exactly is the norm in a state of war? How could anything be considered normal when men are asked and expected to heartlessly take another's life?

I still had my eyes closed, and I noticed that the passionate tears from reading V's poem were now mixed with tears of anger and frustration. I quietly sniffled my runny nose and wiped my eyes when I felt White moving.

"Are you crying Perez?" White sounded surprised as if he expected me to be beyond the ability to show emotions or produce tears.

"I guess. I'm just a little pissed off, that's all." I responded realizing that I had obviously not sniffled quietly enough.

"Your wife's poem pissed you off?" He asked in confusion.

"No. I'm just thinking of how we all seem to be government-

170

manipulated puppets without the option to live a normal, non-combative life back home." I explained.

"You mean you got drafted? You didn't ask to be here?" White suddenly opened his eyes and gave me all his attention. White's queries sounded as if he couldn't imagine anyone not wanting to fight overseas.

"I was drafted right out of high school. I don't want to be here." I explained and resumed to ask, "You mean to tell me you actually signed up for this?" I asked White.

"Hell yeah Perez. I come from a family of soldiers. I have a soldier in my lineage for every single war that the United States has been a part of, and now I do my part by joyously participating in the Vietnam War." He said with apparent pride as I suddenly noticed how odd it was to hear a form of the word 'joy' in the same sentence with the word 'war'.

"Sorry. I seem to forget that there are those who take pride in serving in the military, and I respect that. I just don't think that anyone should be forced to go to war. If I were the cause of the war, I would understand my mandatory participation, but I didn't start this war. I don't even actually know what we are doing in Vietnam." I explained myself to White.

"You have a valid point. I guess if I were married I would reconsider being away from my wife as well. Do you have any kids?" He asked.

"I have one son. He was born about 6 months ago." I feel like I haven't gotten to know him enough to be away from him.

"Six months Perez. Damn, he's an infant. I now see the reason for your distress. I wouldn't want to be here either if I were a husband and a father. You need to do everything in your power to stay alive my friend because your wife and child need you to return." White explained with an honest and fervent tone.

I just simply nodded without saying a word. White was absolutely right. I needed to do everything in my power to return safely to my family. I'll serve my country, but I don't plan to die for my country. Let the other guy die for his country; I've got too much life left to live.

I killed a little bit of time with some reading material that the stewardess offered me. All the magazines she offered were filled with war-related articles, and I really didn't feel like reading anything having to do with the war. I must have expended more time by reading than I imagined because the attendants were preparing to walk the aisles with our 2nd and final meal.

I shook White to wake him up, and he jerked himself to consciousness, as he screamed, "No!"

Jaime Perez

Everybody in the plane looked towards him to see what the problem was. He was gripping my left wrist tightly as he observed every single passenger and attendant wondering what the screaming was about. White was trembling as dots of sweat seeped from his facial pores. After most of the soldiers noticed his disconcerted appearance, most of them simply ignored the unexpected outburst as if they all knew exactly what had just occurred.

"Damn Perez. I dreamt I was eating a corpse! It felt so real!" White explained as he wiped the sweat from his face with a handkerchief he had in his back pocket.

"You mean soldiers who welcome the war also have bad dreams?" I asked in all seriousness.

"Not really. I don't know when the last time was that I had a dream like this. I dreamt I was captured by two Viet Cong soldiers who were hiding behind me in some dense elephant grass. They took me to this room and locked me up with a bunch of decomposing corpses of allied soldiers, many of them American. There was another P.O.W. who spoke English, rather chopped up but understandable. He said if I planned to stay alive I would have to eat my comrades because I would not be getting food. Instead of picking up the partially decomposed corpses, the Viet Cong would force the living prisoners to eat the remains, which simultaneously kept the soldiers alive and eliminated the need for the Viet Cong to have to clean anything. That's when you woke me up. I was about to begin chewing on the least decomposed body when I felt you shake me. The funny thing was that I didn't really hesitate in my attempt at cannibalism. That was pretty screwed up. Damn I'm hungry." He said as I almost laughed by his side at the irony.

"I'm glad to hear you didn't lose your appetite White. I would have probably lost all desire to eat for days after that dream." I explained.

"Perez, there are two things that you must know about me: I can eat like a starved horse, and I can sleep for days. After I eat this here 2nd meal, I plan to sleep until we arrive in Japan. I've always been this way." He said as he began wondering what the stewardesses were serving the passengers in the rows slightly ahead of ours.

"You have a gift White, or shall I pluralize that and say that you have gifts."

"Maybe you're right. I am a little on the fortunate side." He said as he grabbed his plate of fish fillets and green beans and appeared as if he was about to drool over his pre-heated, mass-produced feast.

Through You

I wasn't too fond of fish, but my hunger superseded my finickiness. I ate everything on my plate and began to wonder what time it was back home. Adjusting to the time difference in Vietnam was going to be awkward and arduous. I've never been to the other side of the planet, and I needed to be able to adjust to sleeping at night and staying up during the day because my survival might be dependent on that. I don't think adjusting to sleep was remotely bothering White as he too finished his food.

"See you in Japan Perez." He said as he placed his Army cap over his face, rested his head back and resumed to sleep for the remainder of our flight to Tokyo.

As I wiped my mouth with my napkin, I was able to smell the lingering scent of V's familiar perfume from the poem she had hidden in my pocket. I began to wonder if this poem was what she was hiding from me in the kitchen drawer when I had arrived by surprise with Gilbert that one afternoon. I never did take a look in that drawer to see what V was trying to conceal.

For the next several hours, I filled my head with pleasant thoughts of home, my wife, my son, my parents, my in-laws, my sisters, my high school friends, my neighbors and anything else that was reflective of my short yet precious life. I constructed a mental montage of all the components of my life that made life worth living. Although I was currently being flown to a place that was nothing short of hell on Earth, I was much better off than many of my fellow soldiers. I had overheard the two soldiers in the row ahead speaking to one another before receiving my insipid and bland fish fillets. I overheard one say that he was using the war as a way out of his shitty life back home. His girlfriend had left him and eloped with his best friend, and his alcoholic father was abusive to him and his mother. The other soldier added that he was convicted of armed robbery a few months back. He was trying to rob a liquor store in his neighborhood and didn't realize that an off-duty police officer was in the store shopping when the soldier tried to hold up the store. His lawyer told him that if he would sign up to serve his country in Vietnam, the lawyer would see what he could do about clearing his record of the armed robbery charges. It must be very disheartening to feel that one needs to go to war to make a better life for one's self or to leave behind unbearable circumstances by running from them. I am glad that my life is not so shitty that I actually feel as if I have to enter hell to make it better.

Chapter 23

I was unexpectedly awakened by a voice over the intercom that stated, "Welcome to Tokyo, Japan. Please remain in your seats until the plane has come to a complete stop." I must have dozed off for several minutes because I felt a little vertiginous and displaced. White was also awakened by the announcement as he uncovered his face and looked around to see what was going on.

"Japan already? Are you going to get off Perez? I believe we have an hour layover here. I want to take a dump in a normal-sized toilet, and I would like to get a few snacks because I don't know how many meals we get from Tokyo to Vietnam." White was right. We had about an hour before we took to the air again. I had originally decided to stay on the plane to avoid any anti-war sentiments from the Japanese, but I decided to join White in his little stroll through the Tokyo airport.

A few other soldiers were making their way off the plane as well, when one of them began to tease the lone Asian-American soldier on board. "How does it feel to return home Chang?" An officer whose name I could not see rhetorically asked Officer Chang with a disparaging tone. A few of the other soldiers laughed at the comment.

"I'm not Japanese; I'm Chinese bitch." Officer Chang responded defensively as the conversation now got everyone's attention and had most soldiers laughing.

"What? You're a Chinese bitch?" The officer continued to taunt.

"No. You are a bitch. I am Chinese." Officer Chang attempted to clarify. He didn't particularly seem offended by the other soldier's racist comments.

"Chinese, Japanese, what's the difference? You all look alike to me." The officer brazenly asked.

"I think the Chinese have better food." Another soldier added his ill-

174

humored and unnecessary comment as the majority of the soldiers were now taking part in this silly discussion.

"No way, Japanese food is much better. Nothing is better than sushi." Officer Lippold added.

"Sushi is gross Lippold! The Chinese definitely outdo the Japanese in the area of cuisine. At least the Chinese take the time to cook their food, unlike the Japanese who prefer their shit raw." Another responded as the conversation slowly began to continue outside the plane as the soldiers exited to get a brief glance at the airport.

I lost track of the Japanese/Chinese discussion once I was out of the plane. I figured that I might never return to Japan, so I might as well enjoy it while I'm here. The Japanese civilians stared at us absorbingly as we strolled through the airport. In truth, I felt a little uncomfortable with this reaction, but I suppose it was expected and far less vocal than what I had witnessed in Texas. There was no doubt that they knew who we were and where we were going. I wasn't too sure what the Japanese sentiments were on the war and our participating in it, but I assumed that they were probably the same as they were back home, some for and some against. Because of the language barrier, it was difficult to determine what they were communicating to one another. Judging by their disposition, the Japanese people weren't yelling any profanities or shouting out any acrimonious comments, at least it didn't look like they were. If there was any fervid opposition to American occupancy in Vietnam, it was definitely being impressively concealed by their reserved and restrained nature.

"Do you think they hate us as much as our own countrymen do back home?" I asked White as we approached the men's facilities.

"I don't give a shit Perez. They probably still have a grudge over what happened at Hiroshima, which I personally think they brought on themselves. If they want to start some shit, let them. I'll sign up for that tour of duty too." White expressed with the same gung-ho attitude as Capelletti used to display back at Ft. Sill.

After handling our matters, we searched for something to snack on and resumed back to board the plane. Out of nowhere, a little girl came up to me and tugged on my pants. It caught me by surprise because I wasn't expecting to socialize with anybody at the Tokyo airport other than my fellow soldiers. I didn't know what to say to her because I didn't speak any Japanese, and I didn't know if she spoke any English.

"Hello." I slowly enunciated and smiled as I glanced around concernedly looking for the girl's parents.

Jaime Perez

She smiled back without saying a word. She pulled something out of her dress pocket and stretched out her hand to give it to me. I opened my hand. She placed some kind of cloth-like amulet with some designs woven on it and walked off without saying anything. I took the gift and placed it in my pocket to further study it in the plane. I didn't know what it meant, or what it was, but I wish I could have somehow thanked the little girl for her kind gesture.

White had gone on ahead without me and did not notice my interaction with the young Japanese girl. Before getting back on the plane, I looked back one more time for the seemingly unaccompanied little girl; she was nowhere to be seen. It was almost as if she mysteriously dissipated into thin air like morning dew in the final minutes of dawn.

I sat down in my assigned seat and took out the red, cloth-like trinket. White noticed the item in my hands and immediately took interest. "What's that Perez? Did you buy that out there?"

"No. A little girl came up to me and gave it to me. I don't know what it is, but it seems like it took some time and skill to make." I responded.

"Why don't you ask Chang to see if he knows anything about it?" White asked with an innocuous tone of oblivious racism.

"Chang is not Japanese; he's Chinese." I reminded White.

Our conversation was apparently not as discreet as I had thought because Chang overheard our conversation. Officer Chang was assigned a seat a row directly in front of us. He suddenly popped his head over the seat and quickly wanted to know what White and me were discussing.

"Are you guys talking about me too? What is it with you Americans hating us Asians? I'm helping your country fight a war, and you still try to bring me down." Chang expressed prematurely and defensively.

"Woah. Hold on there my little Asian friend. We weren't saying anything bad about you. I just wanted Perez here to ask you to see if you knew what the hell this was." White defended us and pointed to the intriguing article in my possession.

"Let me see that. Interesting." Chang expressed with a tone of intrigue and mystery as he grabbed the item from my hand, examining its intricate weavings and texture of the cloth. He held so close to his eyes that for a second I thought he was going to lick it or put it in his mouth.

"Well, do you know what it is?" White asked.

"Yes and no." Chang answered, causing more confusion than clarity.

"What kind of a retarded answer is that?" White sounded upset and impatient.

176

"This is a Japanese *omamori*. I am not Japanese I tell you. I am Chinese. It's totally different. I am not an expert on this, but I know a little bit." He said, continuing to feel the trinket as he held it carefully in the palm of his hand.

"It's a what?" I asked.

"An *omamori*, where did you get it?" Chang asked.

"A little girl gave it to me in the airport. She handed it to me and left without me getting a chance to show her any appreciation for her kind gesture. It is a kind gesture, isn't it Chang?" I asked with a little doubt.

"It looks like some type of voodoo thing." White had to interject.

"Like I said, I don't know too much about it. I do know that they are generally used as good luck charms or for protection. I think the color and the design on it determine the specific purpose of the *omamori*. Some of them are to protect you from harm; others are for prosperity with love, money, health or a number of other things. I can't tell you what this particular one means, but whatever it means, it is probably something favorable and not wicked like voodoo or anything like that. You must have made a good impression on the little girl. She must have liked you." Chang said as he gave me my *omamori* back.

"I don't see why. I didn't do anything." I stated. "Thanks for the information Chang." I added after I realized that I now had more questions than answers about this little piece of art.

"No problem. I'm sorry I don't know more. It's not my culture; I just know from what I have read in books. These things go way back in history. I think they are tied to deities in some way, but because they were supposedly used so long ago, the facts about the *omamori* have been embellished, twisted, lost in translation, forgotten and possibly lost forever." He said, as he sounded disappointed to not have more information for me.

I don't know the little girl who gave me this *omamori*, and I never will. I do believe this may be the first and only time that I am given something like this, so I put it in my other jacket pocket, the pocket opposite the one that held V's poem.

It was time to begin boarding our plane again. This time all the passengers remaining on the plane were soldiers. We had approximately another 8 hours to go before landing at the Tan Son Nhat Airport in South Vietnam. I wasn't particularly fond of teasing anyone, and I began to feel bad for Chang. He seemed perfectly able to shun off any offensive remarks and defend himself from all of these obnoxious soldiers, but that didn't

Jaime Perez

lessen the sympathy I had for him. Before I put my seatbelt on, I reached over to the row in front of White and me.

"Thanks Chang." I said as I tapped Chang on the shoulder to show some type of gratification for his input.

"Sure man. No problem." He responded with an addled look on his face as if he wasn't accustomed to being shown any gratitude or being thanked for anything. With the ferocious unmannered monsters aboard this flight, he was probably never shown any respect or consideration, much less be treated like a normal American, which he indeed was.

The Captain got on the speaker and asked us to remain in our seats and prepare for take off. I knew I was only 8 hours away from entering a war zone, a hellhole from which I already had the displeasure of suffering many, countless nightmares. Somehow, I felt at ease and composed. I looked around at the soldiers that I could see from my seat, and I noticed some of them praying, some reading, some doing crossword puzzles, some sleeping and some already shaking and sweating from the obvious imminence that was in store for all of us aboard this flight. It was funny how everyone handled a likely confrontation with death and uncertainty in a completely different manner. We were all going to the same country to embark in slightly similar endeavors with the same result in mind, to come out successful and alive, preferably with all the limbs and body parts with which we had originally entered Vietnam.

When I was much younger, Pop used to tell me, "You can't fully enjoy today, if you are busy worrying about what tomorrow will bring." This was never truer than right now. I needed to enjoy this moment and not think about what was to come when in Vietnam, or I would sadly end up self-consumed in things that were beyond my control.

For the next few hours, I closed my eyes and enjoyed the soothing, constant purr of the airplane engine. I never thought I would ever consider the sounds of an airplane to be soothing, but considering what was in store for me, the sound of an airplane engine was far more serene and tranquil than rapid gunfire and random explosives. It was time to eat, and this time I heard the stewardess as she came by to offer us our only meal for this connection flight from Tokyo to Tan Son Naht. White and I both ate our small steaks and resumed the rest of the smooth flight in sleep. It wasn't until I felt the plane crash against the ground that I woke up. We were in South Vietnam now; it was time to be a soldier.

178

Chapter 24

Arriving in Tan Son Nhat was a rather frenetic experience. I remember seeing a movie when I was in middle school that had a scene in which mail was being distributed to prison inmates who waited in an overly anxious cluster and frantically reached for their uplifting correspondence as their name was called. I can't seem to recall the name of the movie, but the atmosphere here was similar; soldiers were bunched up waiting for their name to be called to be given specific orders on where to go from Tan Son Nhat. It seemed as if there were hundreds of us from an obvious accumulation of several other planes that had arrived earlier from other areas. Everyone appeared restless and impatient from not knowing exactly where in Vietnam our next year was going to be wasted.

Suddenly, from within the camouflage chaos, I heard my name being called by a familiar voice, and it wasn't from the individual giving out our orders. I glanced around for several seconds, not noticing anyone familiar other than White, Chang and a few of the others who were flying with me, but it wasn't them. Again, my name was being called, this time a little louder and from a closer distance than the previous calling. In the military, most are referred to by their last name or a condescending and ridiculing nickname that has been forced upon them by the handfuls of countless and heartless soldiers who get off by being assholes. This familiar voice was a friend because I wasn't being called by my last name or anything unfriendly and unkind.

"Beltran! Beltran!" I couldn't figure out who was calling me. It had to be me they were calling because really, how many Beltrans could there be here, waiting to be sent away?

I was so distracted and captivated by the fact that someone was calling me that I actually tuned out the voice of the man giving us our orders, which is to whom I should have been listening. Just as I saw a military cap

179

Jaime Perez

being waved atop the crowd in a distraught manner to get my attention and slowly approaching me, it abruptly came it to me like a delayed epiphany. I couldn't believe my eyes. It was my high school friend, the transfer from Alice, Texas, Frankie.

"Beltran!" He yelled once more as I finally made eye contact with him.

"Frankie. Man, what a surprise!" I said as we shook hands and hugged each other. I hadn't seen my friend since our high school graduation ceremony, which actually wasn't too long ago, yet it seemed like forever. I had heard that he had gotten married or was engaged to be married, but I never had that rumor confirmed.

"Beltran, how have you been?" He asked with obvious elation to see me.

"Struggling but surviving." I answered with a smile.

"Ain't that the truth. I guess it wouldn't be survival if there weren't some kind of struggle to accompany it. I had no idea you had signed up for this bullshit. You must be crazy." Judging by his comment, I assumed that Frankie was a draftee like me.

"I am a draftee. I don't have a choice but to be here. Believe me; I would rather be at home with my wife and son." I responded before noticing his look of uncertainty.

"You have a kid Beltran? Did you end up marrying your high school sweetheart? What was her name?" He inquired as if he wanted to catch up and reminisce as much as possible in the brief amount of time before our names would likely be called.

"Veronica. Yes, we got married and had a baby boy on August 22, 1968. His name is Gilbert, and he is my pride and joy." I responded as he appeared to be overwhelmed with felicity for me. Frankie was always a thoughtful person who seemed sincerely concerned with the well being of others.

"I'm so happy for you Beltran." I didn't want to dampen his current state of being, so I refrained from revealing any more than I had to, leaving out all the sordid gloominess of Gilbert's illness.

Just as I was about to curiously ask about him, we heard his name called. "Francisco Garza."

A rapid aura of melancholy covered me like an old, blanket that had lost its ability to comfort anyone or anything. I was glad I got to see my friend, but I felt like he, like everyone else of importance in my life, was being taken away from me. We said our hasty goodbyes and gave each other one last embrace.

As I witnessed Frankie slowly vanish into a camouflage green sea of squirming eager bodies, I noticed that he seemed anxious to get this part of his life over with. He didn't appear daunted or apprehensive about going to war. He actually strolled with a noticeable swagger of a confident soldier returning home from war, not one going to war. I couldn't help smile at seeing my good friend once again as he dissipated quicker than I could completely exhale a sigh of comfort. We had some good memories and laughs together in school. Maybe if we both managed to survive this fiasco and we could somehow locate each other, we could get together and talk a bit more about the good old days. A few minutes later, my name was called. It was now time to receive my destiny on a piece of paper.

As I reached for my orders, I heard White's named called as well. I was being sent to Long Binh, Vietnam. I didn't know how to react, encouragingly or discouragingly, because I didn't know much about the country. I just knew that the North Vietnamese were trying to force Communism upon the South Vietnamese, and we were being sent to help the South Vietnamese to maintain their way of life. To me, all of Vietnam was equally dangerous.

"Where are you headed Perez?" White asked.

"Some place called Long Binh. What about you?" I asked.

"You lucky bastard." White said with a smile.

"Why am I lucky? Is Long Binh supposed to be a calm sunny, dreamlike paradise with aqua blue beaches where it never rains?" I sarcastically asked.

"No. You are lucky because you get the spend the next year with me man." He said as he offered his hand for me to shake, as if we had met for the first time again.

I shook his hand as I nodded and smiled. In all honesty, I was somewhat glad that White would be near me. I don't know how frequently I would get to see him, but at least he was going to be within the vicinity that we would likely hear the same explosives and smell the same rotting corpses. As odd as that sounded, it was no less comforting. After receiving orders, groups of soldiers were being taken in crowded truckloads to their designated stations.

"OK soldiers. Everyone assigned to Long Binh, come with me." A soldier with a rifle strapped on his shoulder yelled. It was easy to see which

Jaime Perez

soldiers had been here and which ones had just arrived because the ones who had been here all had guns, the rest of us didn't.

We proceeded to our designated truck and began driving to Long Binh. As much as I hated guns, I didn't feel safe being driven so nakedly conspicuous without carrying a gun of my own, at least not here I didn't. Obviously there was reason to carry one because the previous arrivals brought theirs with them. I felt like a defenseless, moving human target. I don't recall how long it took us to get from Tan Son Nhat to Long Binh, but being defenseless as we were made the drive seem like an uncomfortably unnerving timeless eternity. The bumpy dirt roads and dense jungles alongside the road didn't do anything to create a sense of welcomed hospitality. I felt the funny feeling that we were being closely watched from within the brush. I don't know if my eyes were playing tricks on me, but I could swear that I would see pairs of shiny spots flickering in the leaves as we drove down the dusty road. It reminded me of the way a cat or dog's eyes appear in the dark when light reflects off of them, except the concerning risks were far greater than being lightly bitten or slightly scratched.

There were about 20 of us sardined in the back of the truck, and most of us seemed to be conscientiously and silently examining our surroundings. The only ones who appeared indifferently numb to our surroundings were the two soldiers riding with us in the back who had already been here before us. The rest of us were foreigners, unfamiliar to the land, and to me, Vietnam seemed like an entirely different planet. Every once in a while sporadic rounds of gunfire could be heard in the distance. I couldn't help think that there was a good chance that the gunfire I was hearing likely forced somebody to breathe for the last time. Although we were traveling at a rapid pace, especially for a packed truck traveling on rough, unpaved roads, it didn't quite seem like we were traveling fast enough to provide us with the comfort and confidence that we would actually reach Long Binh before being killed. After a few more pulsating rounds of gunfire, we were finally at our new home, Long Binh.

"We are home ladies. Everybody get off and follow me. The first thing is first. We need to introduce you to your new best friend." Stated one of the soldiers who was already in Vietnam.

We proceeded to a shack-like room and were assigned our rifles. I had never before been so pleased and comforted to see, feel and hold an M-16, but today was a different kind of day. On the other hand, I also simultaneously felt an uneasy ambivalence about attaining a sense of comfort from acquiring a rifle. As much as I disliked guns, I was somehow not too fazed with the fact that I was in a situation where having a gun made me feel better than not having a gun. Only on a hostile battlefield could I understandably accept such sentiments. I've heard it time and time again, "War can change a man." I hadn't been in Long Binh more than one hour and already I was transforming into someone with the desire and willingness to unwaveringly embrace a gun and at the same time express a deep sigh of relief.

"Hell yeah. Finally, we get guns. It's about time. Let the games begin." Many of the soldiers in line excitedly expressed their satisfaction at receiving their rifles.

After everyone was armed, we were assigned to a specific area to meet with our commanding officers and received a quick, crash course orientation. We were under a canopy encircling a table and listening to our commanding officer when all of a sudden shots were being fired at us. I don't think I have ever been so scared in my life. My heart felt as if it had fallen to my feet, and I felt as if I could actually hear my heartbeat amidst the gunfire and yelling soldiers. I recognized the soldier who had taken us to the shack to get our guns and saw him running towards a nearby trench. I instinctively and frantically followed him because I assumed he knew what to do since I didn't. Another soldier already in the trench was signaling others his direction to provide them with a better chance of surviving this unforeseen ambush. Even though I had undergone several months of training for this exact type of scenario, I don't think that anything could have substantially prepared me for what I was witnessing. Nobody is trying to kill you in training; here thousands are trying to kill us.

I don't know how long the ambush lasted, but I do remember the ambush occurring close to the onset of dawn. I remained with my head ducked down in the trench for what seemed to be several hours. I could hear soldiers yelling and some screaming in pain. The trench was full, but there was no way that it could have contained all of us. There were still many who were left outside to shoot it out. Initially the gunfire was nonstop, but after several hours, the shots began to diminish gradually, along with the pandemonium that accompanied the attack.

"Is he dead?" I heard someone say as I regained consciousness and opened my eyes to a wall of dirt. My face was buried in the soil as I firmly hugged my rifle. I felt someone shaking me from behind.

183

Jaime Perez

"Are you alive? I don't see any blood on him." The same soldier who was shaking me asked.

I wiped away the dirt from my face and turned around to face him. The first thing I noticed was a salient pitch-black sky; this encounter had lasted much longer than I had anticipated.

"Are you shot up? Talk to me soldier." The concerned soldier asked.

"No. I'm all right. I don't think I'm shot." I replied.

"Well, if you were shot, you would definitely know it." He stated without an overly concerned tone. "I think you actually slept through most of this; didn't you?" He rhetorically asked as he offered me his hand to help me up.

"I wish I could sleep through all of this." I sarcastically uttered.

"Yeah, don't we all." The soldier said with a slight laugh. "Are you one of the new arrivals?" He asked as he tried to read my name on my chest.

"Yes." I responded.

"Go ahead and situate yourself over there." He pointed to a nearby room.

As I resumed to my assigned area, I noticed my duffle bag was still on the floor in the exact same spot where I had dropped it at the beginning of the surprise attack. I picked it up and entered my barracks. I couldn't believe that I had managed to effortlessly sleep in an outdoor trench in Vietnam through the commotion of an unexpected attack. I must have been extremely tired, or I must have fainted. Whatever happened, I was glad it did.

I came to Vietnam with prefabricated notions of inhumane hellishness that was supported by pervasive media coverage and my own countless, graphic and disturbing nightmares. Now my notions were supported by real life, actual situations. I overheard a few guys in my barracks mention that only 3 of us had died in the attack. Only 3 of us!! This perturbed me immensely. In my opinion, that was 3 soldiers too many. That could have very possibly and very likely been 3 daddies, 3 sons, 3 brothers, 3 husbands or all of these. A few others continued outside to gladly pile up the bodies of the dead enemy. The rest of the evening I stayed in bed staring blindly at the ceiling and hoping that tomorrow would start off much better than today did. I didn't socialize with anybody the first day; I just wanted to survive this first day in hopes that it would make the proceeding days less difficult with which to cope. The next morning I realized that I had survived one day, and I now had 364 more to go. Lucky for me this wasn't a leap year.

184

Through You

The next morning I was assigned my usual duty, food service specialist. I did the same thing for a couple of weeks, cooking and cleaning at the cafeteria, which we called the Mess Hall. The monotonous routine was welcomed because I realized any interruption of the norm likely meant we were being attacked or were going to attack. I was having a difficult time adapting to the different time zone as well as getting up at 0430 hours again, but by the middle of breakfast, I was completely awake and cognizant.

There was an overstaffing at the Mess Hall due to the fact that there were too many cooks at our base. It became apparent that many of us were waiting motionlessly for something to do and therefore standing around doing nothing most of the time. I tried my best to keep busy to help make the day appear to go by faster. After my 2nd week in Long Binh, a superior officer noticed that I was hustling and working at a productive pace, so to reward me and help change my day's routine, I was deservingly offered the additional duty of helping to transport kitchen police (KPs) to our base.

The KPs were South Vietnamese allies who would help us with doing much of the dirty work that we preferred not to do, cleaning restrooms, washing dishes, maintaining the showers, throwing out the trash, etc. Some of them would help me organize the ration room. We had a day and night shift for ration room organization, and I was in charge of the morning shift. Shaklee and Warren would drive the vehicle, while I endured the bumpy and dusty ride in the back with the KPs. Normally I wouldn't think of such an assignment as enjoyably gratifying, but it did allow me to get some fresh air and get away from the base for a while every morning. At first, I was a little apprehensive because it was difficult for any of us to distinguish between the North and South Vietnamese people. It had been mentioned that the North Vietnamese Army (NVA) and the Viet Cong (VC) had made several attempts at disguising themselves as South Vietnamese with intentions of killing the transporters or even at attempt to infiltrate the base. Because of this, I had to be extra cautious and keep my 3rd eye open at all times. For my remaining duration here, I was part of the KP transport crew and was also in charge of maintaining and organizing the rations room. I don't mean to brag, but I did a hell of job keeping that room structured and orderly. Being meticulous, inside the rations room helped me get my mind off of the ruthlessness that was taking place all around us. It also kept me from having to smell the permeating stench of the dead NVAs who were literally just a few feet away.

At night, I would do my best to write to V and inquire about anything

185

Jaime Perez

and everything that was happening at home. I didn't get to write to her for the entire first week upon arriving at Long Binh because of my struggle with trying to stay awake. I would hit the bed in the early afternoon and stay there until morning. I began to feel as lethargic and rested as White usually was. Upon becoming accustomed, I wrote to V every chance I had, even if I hadn't heard from her yet. I would also write to Mom and Pop and stick both letters in the same envelope. Writing to V helped me cope with the things with which I was dealing, such as fear, sleep deprivation, ambushes, homesickness and death. I realized that I had never written as frequently in my life as I was writing now. I also quickly realized that writing was the most normal thing a soldier could do to offset the grossly abnormal life of a soldier during war. I've heard that change is difficult, but as a soldier, it's not only difficult—it's mandatory. I must admit that I did not like the soldier life. I was constantly on the lookout for someone who wanted to kill me, displaced thousands of miles away from home, carrying a gun 24 hours a day and 7 days a week and slowly becoming numb to the sight of dead bodies. At times, I felt like an animal with the inability to do what is right because I was forced to do what I had to do, even if it seemed cruel, barbaric or apathetic. There was nothing remotely normal about my current situation, so I wrote frequently to seem human again. The ability to write is unique to the human species; so writing helped eliminate the self-assessed notion that I was a heartless animal.

My first response from V arrived towards the end of my first month in Vietnam; it was a package that I quickly ripped open in anticipation to see what she had sent. I felt like an ecstatic 5 year-old opening a present on Christmas morning, and I probably looked like one as well. I really wasn't expecting anything more than a letter from my dearly missed wife, so I was particularly intrigued by the contents. I wanted to contain myself and open the package carefully so that I wouldn't damage anything potentially fragile or breakable. The first thing I noticed was a cassette tape. At first I thought that V had recorded some music for me that I might enjoy while away. She knew everything about me, and she would certainly be able to compile some of my favorite tunes to help compensate for my lack of aural enjoyment. I read the cassette's label and noticed that V had written "Guess Who" in black marker. This was inscribed on both sides of the 60-minute tape. The Guess Who was a fairly new Canadian rock band that I had heard on the radio several times.

Although I did enjoy some of their music, I don't think I ever gave V the impression that I was a fanatic of the band to the point that she would feel it necessary to record any of their music. She knew The Beatles were my favorite band, but she probably also knew that I had just about every release with which the godly Beatles selflessly bestowed upon this unworthy world. The bulk of the package was a black Holy Bible with V's letter in it. I opened the Bible to the first page and saw a note written on the inside cover from my in-laws, Virginia and Al.

Son, January 1969

Virginia and I hope you are doing well overseas. We want you to know that we have you in our daily prayers. Your life is in the Lord's hands now, and he has his best intentions for you. We have sent you a gift, the Holy Bible. This Bible has been in our family for generations, and now we give it to you. The words in this Bible are a big part of our lives, and you are a big part of our life as well. The power of this book's messages can help you conquer any hell because it has helped us overcome many of our family's hardships. God bless you Beltran and be safe.

The Lord loves you and so do we,
Al and Virginia Saenz

Although I wasn't exactly known to be the type of person to carry a Bible, I was grateful for my in-laws' kind and thoughtful gesture. I know giving this holy heirloom to me was a big sacrifice on their part. I was going to keep this under my pillow, and I might even get a chance to brush through it for entertainment value. Within the Bible's pages was V's 4-page, handwritten letter. As I opened the letter to anxiously read it, a photograph fell facedown out onto the floor. I picked it up and turned the face over, it was one of the photographs that we had taken while on my L.O.A. at Mr. Gomez's photography studio. I'm not particularly fond of taking photographs, but I was glad we had taken these. I glanced at the photo for several seconds and felt myself having to inhale deeply after a while because I was left breathless by what I was seeing. The 3 of us looked like a happy family, even Gilbert was smiling as if he knew it was expected of him. Him in his little outfit and my wife displaying the same alluring smile that made the temperature rise a few degrees, or at least that's what it seemed was occurring.

For the next few minutes I simply held the photo in my hand and

Jaime Perez

stared at it with utter enthrallment. It appeared to have a magical ability to convey me to a reverie in which I was momentarily reverted to the exact day the photo was taken; I remained in vivid reflection as an unexpected tear hit my son's face. I quickly wiped the photograph so as to not ruin it with moisture. After a while, I placed the photograph in the Bible for safekeeping.

I turned my attention to the most important part of the package, V's letter. In it she mentioned that Mr. Gomez had done his best to get the photographs processed as quickly as possible in hopes of getting them to us before I flew out, but he was unable to accomplish this. He didn't even charge us for any of the pictures. V wrote that Mr. Gomez said, "Your husband is paying me for these pictures with his service. It would be greedy of me to take anymore from either of you. Just tell him to hurry back." That man's warm-heartedness blinded you with its brilliance. I wish I were there to thank him personally. V also mentioned that Gilbert grew two whole inches since I last saw him, and he was becoming more vocal and expressive. I didn't have the luxury of being home long enough to be a part of Gilbert's initial stage of language development. I wished I could hear at least a little of my son's mumblings; it would be a welcomed change from listening to superior officers yelling out aspersions, listening to men scream in their sleep, listening the resounding echoes of gunfire, or in general, listening to the perennially pervasive, unsettling sounds of war.

Apparently my sisters were visiting V and Gilbert frequently to keep them company. V mentioned that they would go out to eat on occasion and shop for clothes together to offer each other's imaginary fashion expertise. I couldn't help smirk at the thought of this scenario. I just hope V, Sarah and Diana weren't clothing my son in pinks, yellows or violets. The thought of this was dreadfully amusing. My poor son, being cruelly subjected to multiple self-proclaimed fashion experts, was bleakly defenseless. In all honesty, I was grateful that my sisters were spending time with my wife and son. They had busy schedules of their own, so I knew they were making substantial sacrifices to make time for V and Gilbert. Although my primary focus is generally and understandably on V and Gilbert, I do miss everyone back home. In an inexplicable way, I even miss that funny looking monkey that Gilbert grew so fond of for some reason.

Mom and Dad were doing fine. V mentioned that Mom would call V sometimes and begin crying on the phone for me to come back. Mom was the epitome of pure kindness and motherly affection. If she could, she would, without the slightest hesitation, switch places with me in an instant just so that her son wouldn't be in harm's way. Mom would do anything for her children. If it were possible, she would do it. If were impossible, she would make it possible or die trying. Who could ask for anything more in a mother? I missed my Mommy, and I know that she is probably undeservingly hurting more than anybody about my being at war. Picturing her crying pissed me off to no end. It angered me to think that mothers and fathers had to endure the unwanted and, in this case, unnecessary stripping away of their sons, all in the name of abstracts such as patriotism and honor. It is not right for parents to have to bear witness to the burying of their children. It shouldn't even be considered natural. Subjecting Mom to this unequaled and ineffable horror would surely leave her forever heartbroken, and I didn't plan on leaving my mother in such a depleted and dejected state.

V went on to mention that the Bible her parents sent me was over 200 years old! Had I been aware of this, I would have opened it with much more care and precaution. I now realized the magnitude of my in-law's offering. I would have liked to return it to them when I returned home as a gesture of appreciation, but Al wrote in it, for me. He wrote in a 200 year old Bible and sent it to me! The thought of them willingly sacrificing and selflessly offering a priceless heirloom to their daughter's husband made me feel an unignorable warmth that flushed throughout my body.

V expressed feeling empty without me. She longed for me and couldn't wait for me to get back to resume our happy lives together. I had mentioned to V in one of my letters to her that I had found the poem in my pocket during the flight to Vietnam. I asked where she had hidden it all this time; she revealed having hidden it from me in the kitchen drawer in a notebook—just as I had expected. In her letter, V claimed that she missed me, but I don't think it was possible for her to miss me anymore than I missed her. In a matter of a few hours, I sadly went from holding her warm, soft, pulsating body to holding a cold, lifeless, heavy piece of metal. The only similarity between the two is that they both had the ability to keep me alive through this tumultuous and worrisome period in my lonely, displaced life.

Gilbert hadn't gotten sick since I left; that was very comforting to me considering my son's proneness to illness. Another thing that V mentioned about Gilbert is that she felt that Gilbert noticed my absence. There was something different about his reaction lately that V noticed, something that she associated with my leaving. Gilbert would crawl on our apartment floor and explore the entire apartment in search of something or someone, but

Jaime Perez

he appeared unable to find what or who he was looking for. V mentioned that Gilbert would do this several times a day, maybe expecting to increase the chances of me eventually appearing if he attempted this more than once. Although one might interpret Gilbert's doting to be a sweet sign of affection on my son's part, I didn't focus on my son's affection but rather on my absence. My son was looking for me, and I was nowhere to be found. He wanted me to be there for him, to carry him, to hold him, to play with him, but I failed to fill my son's void. Being there for your children in their time of need should be the simplest part of being a parent, and I couldn't even manage to do that.

I put the letter away inside the Bible it came in and proceeded to take out the photograph one last time to take a quick, yet necessary glance at it. Every night before going to bed, I would continue this ritual. This provided me with an ephemeral sense of completeness and allowed me to better contain the strenuous strife that seemed to effortlessly and profusely circulate through me and steadfastly permeate my porous spirit. Every soldier here had a trustworthy ritual or an uncanny manner in which to maintain their sanity and keep their hopes up. Just like at Fort Bliss and Fort Sill, some prayed, some read, some did word puzzles, some smoked and some listened to music; I simply pulled out my photograph on a nightly basis and gazed at it euphorically until I was eventually overtaken by a welcomed and peaceful desire to gladly relinquish to unconsciousness. I honesty don't know how else I would have managed to stay alive.

Chapter 25

Ever since I started basic training in El Paso at Ft. Bliss, I had begun having my chilling nightmares that often rudely awakened me in a sweat-drenched frenzy. Visions of death, struggle, hatred, barbarism and inhumanity all became mentally yet graphically visible in my capricious state of sleep. What was thought to be rest often became restlessness. The uncontrollable terrors were so realistic that I sometimes actually felt as if I could smell the malodorous unbounded wantonness.

I was pretty sure that my dreams were partly attributed to what I would continuously see and hear in the media and partly what I would hear from former soldiers who had been in previous wars. The idea of war is probably the most daunting and dreadful concept I could ever fathom. My expectations for this ongoing malignity were nothing short of horrific. I don't know what is worse, partaking in full-blown battle or anticipating full-blown battle. In full-blown battle, all it takes is a shot to the head and it's over. It's quick and uncomplicated. The anticipation of full-blown battle, on the other hand, could completely immerse you in a debilitating insanity. Even before you begin physically fighting for your life, you have already begun mentally fighting to stay alive. Although one may argue that there is nothing worse than death, there is many a soldier who would tenaciously disagree and claim that slowly going crazy from realizing that death may be waiting for you behind a thick brush is far worse. I think this is exactly what I was currently experiencing. There hadn't been much action in our area since the ambush on the day I arrived. I could hear screams, gunfire, helicopters, planes, rocket-propelled grenades (RPGs) and other explosives all around me; they quickly became a ubiquitous and omnipresent part of the landscape, but nothing had transpired in the past several weeks. It was almost like the lifeless and barren calmness that often exists before a storm, except this storm wouldn't bring forth

Jaime Perez

thunder and rain; it would likely yield torrents of thunderous explosives and raining bullets. This was unbearably discomforting for me; there was really nothing I could do but wait and wait some more.

The atmosphere here in Long Binh was significantly different than at basic training or OJT, and understandably so. The camaraderie here in Long Binh was almost non-existent. I had plenty of laughs and interesting conversations at Ft. Sill and Ft. Bliss, but things here were rather melancholy and bland. Everybody in my barracks pretty much kept to himself and rarely spoke, unless you count all the times someone screamed, cried or prayed themselves to unconsciousness late at night. I rarely got a chance to see White, and the only others I spoke to on a daily basis, other than the non-English-speaking KPs, were Warren and Shaklee. Everybody else appeared to be in a robotic trance of pensiveness that they never came out of. I guess it's difficult to socialize and to display a semblance of gregariousness when any minute may be your last.

Warren and Shaklee were together in another barracks, but they would usually invite me to spend some time with them whenever they would go to the Postal Exchange. The Postal Exchange (PX) was an on-base store for soldiers that provided us with anything from candy to cigarettes and everything in between. One particular day, I realized that I hadn't gotten a chance to hear my Guess Who tape from V. I had a radio, but I didn't have a portable cassette player. I had a little bit of money on me, so I purchased a small General Electric cassette player with the intention of listening to my tape before going to bed. I felt silly paying with the fake money that was used on the base here in Vietnam. We didn't use Vietnamese currency, and we didn't have US dollars; so we were given paper bills with numbers on them that represented their value. Although this pseudo-currency was frivolous to the outside world, these were like gold to those of us here on base.

On the day I bought my cassette player, Shaklee and Warren purchased a few adult magazines with pictures of naked women. Apparently both of them were intimately familiar with this particular publication because there were certain sections and articles that appeared regularly that they were eagerly looking for in between their interruptive and amusing gawking at the erotic photos they observed as they slowly flipped through the pages. Shaklee and Warren could have passed for brothers, but they met here on base. They were very much alike and enjoyable to be around. On the way back from the PX, a soldier from another barracks approached us in

Through You

a businesslike manner and shamelessly pulled out several knotted bags from his jacket.

"You guys want some Mary Jane?" He asked with a scratchy half-whisper.

"No, we already have plenty of women in this." Shaklee gullibly answered before the rest of us burst into laughter.

"What's so funny?" He continued to ask with a perturbed expression on his face.

"Mary Jane is marijuana you dope." Warren explained to him.

"Oh shit. I knew that." Shaklee said unconvincingly.

Shaklee and Warren both looked at me, awaiting my response. "I've never tried it." I said.

"All the more reason to buy some." The dealing soldier added.

"Can we get busted for this?" Warren asked as he reached in his pocket.

"Man, I just sold a couple of bags to a Captain and a Sergeant, not to mention to the boys in my barracks. I'll even throw in some rolling papers at no additional cost. Hey man it's cool; if you don't want this, somebody else does." He said as he began to turn around and walk away.

"All right. I'll buy a bag. Is this enough?" Warren asked as he handed the businessman a couple of bills.

The businessman heedfully thumbed through the bills. "For you my man, it is. It's been a pleasure doing business with you brave men." The peculiar-looking soldier stated as he sauntered in search for more customers.

"What are you going to do with that?" Shaklee asked.

"What do you think we are going to do with it, wipe our ass!? We are going to smoke it. Maybe we can create a little bit of heaven amongst all this hell." Warren said as he shook and flaunted the bag in front of my face.

We went to hide behind a secluded shack towards the outer edge of the base and did our thing. I had never tried drugs before even though I was often curious about them. I never ruled out the possibility of one day trying marijuana, but I never fathomed that my experimentation with the drug would occur while I was in a war-torn country being hunted down by thousands who would like nothing more than to riddle my body with bullets. I was surprised that accessibility and use of the drug was not forbidden, or if it was, its prohibition was not being enforced.

"Is marijuana legal in Vietnam?" Shaklee asked as he watched

Jaime Perez

Warren meticulously role up a tight joint like a professional with years of experience.

"I would think so. In a country such as Vietnam where killing is legal, I don't suppose there is a law against burning natural, God-given herbs. Regardless, we have some, and we will momentarily transcend to another place, a better place." Warren stated as he took out his Zippo lighter from his jacket pocket and began to light the tightly rolled joint.

"Even if this were illegal, what would they do to us if they caught us? Throw us in jail. We are too valuable right now. Every American and ally soldier is needed; it would be ludicrous to imprison us for something so trivial and innocuous. We need every accessible resource of escapism we can find here; otherwise, we are going to surely drive ourselves crazy." I said as I tried to convince myself that what we were doing was not as criminal in our world as it was in the outside world.

"That makes perfect sense to me Perez." Shaklee responded with an odd-looking smile. "Hell, I'd rather be in a maximum security prison than in this shit hole, jungle-like prison we are currently in. Our chances of survival, without a doubt, would be much greater than they are now."

"The way I see it, we are in prison. It just happens to be more of a gigantic, open-air prison. Honestly, I would feel much safer confined within four walls." Warren stated analytically as he blankly followed the evanescent smoke with both eyes and tried to use his index finger to make shapes of the amorphous cloud-like gas.

After the three of us had taken multiple puffs of the easily accessible drug, we slowly began to feel the affects taking over. I had heard many stories from friends about their reactions to marijuana. Many of them admitted to an increased hunger, some to lethargy, and others to chronic laughter. I was beginning to witness the latter. I began laughing at everything and anything. Even my thoroughly-shined boots brought me laughter. Warren and Shaklee obviously incurred the same side effects and were soon also joining me in my mirthless, unbridled laughter. By the time I knew it, the three of us were all rolling on the floor laughing at the shining stars, the grainy dirt, our leather boots, our fingers, our dog tags and everything else that captured our distorted attention. This whole experience was peculiar and completely unenjoyable, contrary to what my drug-induced outbursts might convey to anyone who might be witnessing this spectacle from a distance. My stomach began to hurt after a while, but we kept on puffing on the joint until it completely dissipated into our lungs, our brains and our bloodstream. After about 10 minutes of seemingly incessant laughter,

194

Through You

it all began to get very annoying, but we still continued laughing to the point that the laughter was now beginning to convert to pain, at least to me it was becoming painful. My whole body felt sore and tender, as if I had spent hours lifting weights after not having lifted weights for a lengthy period of time. In addition, I felt nauseous and very close to the point of vomiting, yet I continued to uncontrollably laugh aloud.

"What the hell is going on here men?" A soldier, probably one of superior rank, popped out of nowhere and asked us as he pointed his flashlight on our ruddy faces.

We must have looked ridiculous, three grown men on the dirt floor experimenting with drugs behind a shack at an Army base in Long Binh, Vietnam. None of us said anything, none of us had to.

The soldier wrinkled his nose as he effortlessly picked up on the unmistakable scent lingering among us. "Oh, I should have known," the unknown soldier stated as if he had seen this type of behavior or experienced this exact situation before. "If you boys can't handle drugs like real men, maybe you should leave doing the drugs to us." He advised as he pillaged the bag of leftover marijuana from the floor, and proceeded to walk off with it as he took an impressive whiff of what little remained.

"Well, I guess the party is over men." Warren said as he picked himself off the ground and began dusting off his uniform. Shaklee and I did the same. I could still feel the lurking desire to laugh, but I was somehow able to control it to a certain degree. As the three of us made our way back to our barracks, Shaklee suddenly started laughing again, while pointing at me.

"Aren't you forgetting something?" Shaklee managed to audibly ask underneath his laughter.

"What? Do you want me to kiss you goodnight?" I sarcastically responded as we all began to purge in laughter one more time.

"You wish you faggot. You are forgetting your cassette player you stoned idiot."

"Oh shit. I almost forgot." I said as I sprinted back behind the secluded shack and picked up my newly purchased cassette player. Without this, I would have to ask to borrow someone else's device to listen to my Guess Who tape, and I didn't want to inconvenience anyone in my barracks, especially since I wasn't too close to any of them.

"We'll see you tomorrow Perez. Gotta pick up some more KPs. Be locked, cocked and ready to go." Warren managed to utter with the usual tone of voice he produced when he was not under the influence of drugs.

195

Jaime Perez

I saluted both of them as I proceeded to my barracks with my cassette player firmly in hand. My unrestrained laughter was slowly becoming a mind-exploding headache. I was quickly regretting having experimented with marijuana. I didn't like the side effects of it, the stink of it, and the stigma attached with using such narcotics. My experience slowly turned to guilt and regret. From that point on, I never tried marijuana again; I didn't need it nor did I desire it.

I walked into my barracks, and I became the center of attention as some of my fellow soldiers whispered to each other and stared at me as I walked over to my bed to take off my boots and prepare to unwind and listen to *The Guess Who*. One of them even made a disgusted face and whisked his hand over his nose like when someone is trying to brush away a foul smell. I was pretty certain that they all knew what the hovering and persistent aroma was that penetrated my clothing, and most of them were not very fond of this stink. Those who were not irritated by the stench simply smiled and nodded as if recognizing and approving of my current state of nauseous euphoria.

Every once in a while, the stubborn stench would continue to pierce its way to my nasal passage and bring with it the vexatious nausea. I wasn't going to be able to enjoy any music or get any gratifying rest with this odor on me, so I decided to race to the shower and rid myself of this stink. The quick, cold shower had a purifying effect on me, eliminating the nausea and part of the drug-induced buzz.

I returned to my barracks. By this time most of the others were already asleep, with the exception of a few soldiers who usually read themselves to sleep underneath a lamp to avoid illuminating the entire room and inconveniencing everybody else who didn't need to resort to similar methods to achieve unconsciousness. I quietly and cautiously tiptoed across the hardwood floor in hopes of not making such a grand and attention-getting entrance as I had previously managed to do. I reached under my flat and cardboard-like pillow for my cassette tape, placing it in the cassette player. I didn't want to disrupt anyone's rest or anyone's reading, so I adjusted the volume to a minimum level and placed the device upon my ear. As a child, I had a habit of listening to music to put me to sleep more quickly. I don't know what it was about it, but it never failed to help put me at ease. After pressing the play button, I lay down on my left side, positioning the cassette player between my ear and my poor excuse for a pillow. It took a few seconds for anything audible and discernable to come out of the 4-inch speaker.

I waited patiently for the soothing sounds of music to transport me to a more pleasant realm of tranquil abstractness, but what I heard seep out of the tiny speaker was far more delightful than anything I had ever heard in my life. I quickly opened my eyes and looked around me to reassure I wasn't dreaming. This was no dream; this was real. The tape began with V's voice speaking away from whatever device she used to record. I could hear her in the background saying, "Come on. Don't be afraid. It's only a microphone." Then I heard it, a different kind of music, euphony—the sweet and innocent babblings of my son, Gilbert. I instinctively raised the volume a bit, forgetting about those sleeping around me. My son was beginning to speak in baby talk. I couldn't see myself, but I was pretty sure I was smiling bigger than I had in a long while. Hearing my son's voice for the first time drenched me in tears of joy, and I was unable to contain myself for the duration of the 60-minute tape. The few soldiers who were still awake and reading observed my subtle whimpering, but simply glanced away and resumed as they were. Hearing a soldier cry in his bed at night during a full-blown war was nothing new. As a matter of fact, it usually occurred on a daily basis, more than once per evening. This time it was my turn to release tears of my own. I couldn't understand anything my son was saying, and still, his words kept me in attentive and enthralling wonderment. He sounded so vibrant and full of life. I had no trouble picturing him on the living room floor, wearing his pajamas with his little monkey friend by his side. I missed my son, and I wanted to be there with him to hear everything he had to say to me, regardless of its meaninglessness. My son's voice exhilarated me and kept me awake for the entire night as I ecstatically played both sides of the cassette over and over until it was time to wake up and begin a new day.

The burning redness in my puffy and swollen eyes the following morning must have stood out like a full moon on a pitch-black sky. The combination of staying awake all night, crying throughout the entire evening, and trying marijuana for the first time all contributed to my benumbed appearance. The imprint of the speaker grill on my left cheek must have added additional awkwardness to my already peculiar appearance. I began putting my cassette player away and making my bed when I noticed the clear, plastic cassette case that V sent the cassette in. Once again, I saw the words Guess Who on the lined cardboard insert that helped identify the tape's content. This is when it hit me like a slap in the face. V didn't mean The Guess Who, the band. She was asking me to "guess who" was on the tape. It was a question, not a band. The question

Jaime Perez

mark on the insert had smudged off; otherwise, I would have taken it as a question, not as a reference to the band The Guess Who.

For the next several days, I used my son's unconstruable yet enrapturing gibberish to put me to sleep as I repeatedly heard the tape before going to bed. Each time brought an equally genuine smile to my face, a smile that I believe managed to remain on my face through sleep until morning. At times I would dupe myself into thinking that I could actually make out a few words amongst the hour-long incomprehensible chitchat. Several times I could swear that I heard Gilbert say "daddy". I would rewind the tape and realize that I was just delusionally hearing things that I wanted to hear. Regardless, it was a pleasantness to hear my son speak in his mysteriously whimsical infant language.

Even though I must have looked awkward going to sleep with the speaker of a cassette player ironed to my ear every night with the device's volume set to a point where only I could hear it, I didn't share the contents of the tape with anybody else. I didn't feel truly comfortable with anybody in my barracks. Maybe it was due to the melancholy atmosphere within our confining walls, or maybe it was just because none of us spoke to each other very much due to drastically different duties and specialties. If someone would sneeze, the occasional "bless you" would surface, but not much more than that. This type of atmosphere inside, along with the highly unpleasant and atrocious aura outside that was now so tangible that it could be smelled, felt and seen, was enough to drive the most strong-minded man insane. The only things keeping me from going insane were my letters and gifts from back home and my daily encounters with Warren and Shaklee. There was a certain believable and authentic liveliness about the two of them. They seemed to almost be immune to the hostility, hardship and hideousness that permeated the rest of our vulnerable and fragile bodies with every necessary yet impure breath we took.

The next morning, I told myself that I would ask Shaklee and Warren for their secret to maintaining their sanity and seeming so easygoing all of the time, considering the current circumstances. I approached the vehicle with my M-16 in hand as they both waited in the front seat with the motor running as I hopped on the jeep.

"Morning Perez. What is that shit on your face soldier?" Shaklee asked, but I had no idea to what he was referring.

"What is it? What do you see?" I asked with concern.

"It looks like some kind of skin disease or rash of some kind." Warren extrapolated as he positioned the rearview mirror towards me so that I could see in what they were so interested.

"Oh, that is the grill of my cassette player's speaker. It will fade away in the next few minutes." I said with a smile, forgetting that I probably still had the imprint of the parallel and intersecting lines on my left cheek.

"Let me get this straight Perez. You are sleeping with your new toy?" Shaklee asked as he and Warren laughed in a disparaging yet playful and harmless manner.

I didn't feel like having to explain the whole story to them, so I simply said, "It's a long story guys. I'll tell it you some other time."

"Just make sure you don't share it with us when we are high because we will likely piss our pants from laughter." Warren recommended.

"Although I don't plan on getting high anytime soon, I'll try to remember that wise advice." I responded sarcastically.

"I wouldn't mind getting high one last time before we leave back home." Warren mentioned as I suddenly felt a tinge of curiosity that left me wondering exactly when Warren and Shaklee were expecting to be released from this shit hole.

"And when might that be?" I asked.

"In less than a month, twenty-eight days to be exact." Shaklee informed me.

"Both of you?" I proceeded to inquire.

"Yep. We both started together, and if we don't die in the next four weeks, we will leave together." Shaklee said as he and Warren punched each other's shoulders in excitement. The smile on their faces made me happy for them, but I simultaneously felt sadness because my only real friends here were leaving me behind with a barracks full of dehumanized robots. I disguised my sadness and displayed nothing but elation for them.

"How long have you been here Perez?" Warren asked as we drove down the bumpy dirt road to gather some KPs.

"A month and eighteen days now. I have a little over ten months of this cruelty to persevere before I go home."

"What are you going to do without us Perez?" Shaklee asked jokingly, yet his question had a stunning affect that ran throughout my entire body like the shock one feels when hitting their funny bone. I just simply shrugged my shoulders in uncertainty to Shaklee's deflating question.

"If you're lucky, you will get teamed up with another set of drivers to gather KPs. Maybe it won't be so bad after all." Warren said as if he

Jaime Perez

sensed my disappointment in my reaction when I morosely shrugged my shoulders.

"I'll be alright. Just make sure and write me every now and then." I asked of them, even though I didn't expect them to take my desperate yet honest request seriously. We arrived to the area where we picked up the KPs. This was the scariest part of the day for me because I, like every other American soldier I knew, was unable to distinguish between the North and the South Vietnamese. This is why I kept all three eyes on the supposed KPs during the drive back to base as I tightly clenched my gun with my sweaty and numb forefinger on the trigger for the duration of the return. There was no more talking, no more joking, and no more smiling for this portion of the drive. It was strictly business from here until we got back to base.

Chapter 26

Upon arriving at the base, I now realized why Shaklee and Warren were always in good spirits—they were very close to completing their yearlong duty here in Vietnam. I guess I would be excited beyond imagination to know I was merely weeks away from being released as well, but I didn't want to put too much premature thought into this overly ideal situation because anything could happen in 10 months, especially here. The blandly repetitious day dragged on with nothing noteworthy or out of the ordinary to help distinguish this day from any other, until I got back to the barracks at the end of the day.

As I opened the door to my barracks, I immediately noticed a white envelope placed in the middle of my bed. One of the soldiers must have gotten it for me during mail call while I was away on KP transport. I naturally presumed it was correspondence from V back home. I was right. I hastily ripped the envelope open and began reading V's highly anticipated response. V mentioned her usual longing for me, the fact that Gilbert was getting bigger by the day and unnecessarily asked if I had enjoyed the recorded tape of Gilbert's voice. The letter brought complete enjoyment to my face, but V added a postscript at the end of the letter that somewhat flushed me with concern and anxiousness. She wrote:

> P.S. Gilbert came up with a fever and vomited a few days ago, but Dr. Richards said it was nothing major and advised me to bring him back after Gilbert completely finished his medication. I'm sure it is nothing to lose sleep over. Love you…Veronica Perez

Ironically, even though V said there was nothing to lose sleep over, that is exactly what occurred—I began losing sleep. If this were nothing to worry about, why would V mention it at all? I know V too well; if this

201

Jaime Perez

were nothing to lose sleep over, she would have disregarded mentioning it altogether. I felt she was downplaying this so that I wouldn't stress over it. I know it is difficult to construe tone through one's writings, but the entire letter exuded a gloomy tone, unlike V's previous responses. For the first time, I finished reading a letter from back home without a smile on my face.

Later that night, I went to the on-base bar/club that was there for soldier entertainment. The establishment looked like any other bar back home probably did. It was dark, muggy, and creeping clouds of cigarette smoke often snuck into one's lungs no matter where one was sitting. There was a colorful jukebox that had nothing but songs from back home constantly playing. I never noticed anybody inserting any money in it, but it poured out the familiar tunes all night, much to everyone's content. The cracking sounds of billiards balls being blasted by the cue ball resonated without end. I had been inside a couple of bars during my training back in the U.S., and they all seemed to look the same. As long as I wore my military uniform, I was never asked for identification; otherwise, I would likely be denied entry. I needed to get my mind off the plaguing worry that was infesting my thoughts. Even though I was still a minor, I was able to purchase alcohol without any problem. I guess the government and the general public figured that if I was old enough to serve and die for my country, I should be old enough to be granted the luxury of freely drinking whatever the hell I felt like drinking. After a few moments Warren and Shaklee strolled in and sat beside me at the bar.

"Wanna get high with us Perez?" Warren asked as he and Shaklee laughed loudly.

"I think I am done with that junk for now." I answered with surprise that they would even consider engaging in another session of drug-induced stupor.

"Just kidding. We are done with anymore drug experimenting, unless that drug is alcohol." Shaklee responded as he grabbed his beer bottle and chugged half of his beer down in one impressive, breath-taking gulp.

"In a hurry to finish your beer, are you?" I asked Shaklee as he turned my way, exposing his watery eyes.

"The sooner I get drunk, the sooner the pain goes away." He responded.

I looked at Warren with uncertainty to what Shaklee was talking about. "His fiancé wrote him and called off their engagement, so our friend is a little upset about that." Warren explained, as Shaklee seemed to valiantly do his best to disallow the flow of any more persistent tears.

I honestly didn't know what to say. I didn't know his fiancé; I didn't even know he was engaged. What do you say to a man whose love has broken his heart? I felt worthless in my inability to console Shaklee. I wanted to comfort him, but nothing would come out of my mouth. All I could do was lift my beer bottle towards his and tap our bottles; Warren tapped along with us.

"I'm sorry Shaklee." I eventually and instinctively said without putting much thought into my failed and feeble attempt to comfort my somber friend. I suddenly felt like I should have just remained silent because I felt like a worthless jackass after saying what I did. For several minutes, we sat speechlessly with our sweating bottles in our hands like dejected souls attempting to foolishly drink away their problems. No one said anything until we all finished our beers.

"You know. It's all right. I will manage to persevere through this because I AM A FUCKING SOLDIER!" Shaklee yelled emphatically as he raised his empty beer bottle in the air, everybody in the bar/club glancing our way to visually witness the ruckus.

I wasn't sure how many beers Shaklee had had, but he was beginning to sound as if he had already drunk two too many.

Warren must have noticed my unsocial behavior. "What's wrong with you Perez? You don't look like your normal self. You look the way Shaklee looked when he received his bit of unexpected news." He asked and analyzed me as if he were some kind of behavior expert.

"Actually I did receive some shitty news in my wife's last letter." I responded.

"Is she screwing somebody else??" Shaklee blurted out with an inebriated slur.

"Hey Shaklee. That's not cool bro. Stop your shit now." Warren commanded of Shaklee after witnessing his unnecessary and inconsiderate comment. Warren's voice suddenly projected louder than everyone else's.

Shaklee looked at me with a look of immediate regret. "I'm sorry Perez. You didn't deserve that. I am not in my brightest of moments. That's all. Really, I'm sorry." He offered me his hand, so I shook it to signify my acceptance of his apology. I knew Shaklee was going through a trying time in his life; he couldn't be held accountable for his words after just finding out what he had.

"It's all right. I understand. Actually, although finding out that my wife

Jaime Perez

was screwing somebody else would be heartbreaking and disheartening, I honestly feel that the depressing news I received today is a little worse." I explained.

"What could be worse than your wife getting it on with some bastard while you risk your life for your ungrateful country?" Shaklee asked.

I noticed Warren and Shaklee both staring curiously at me as they neared themselves to me to get a better listen to what I was about to say. I had their undivided attention.

"I don't know if I ever mentioned this to you, but I have an infant son, Gilbert. My son is ill; he has a congenital heart disease. He was born with a malformed heart, and the doctors say that his chances of survival are slim. There is really nothing they can do except to hope for the best. My wife's last letter mentioned that our son had become ill. Every time he gets sick, my wife and I worry that this is just a precursor of the potentially inevitable. It may be nothing serious, but I still worry that every one of my son's illnesses may be his last. I feel like I've abandoned my wife and kid when they need me the most. It gets so bad that I actually lose my appetite just from thinking about it. It really sucks to know that there is absolutely nothing you can do to help your son's chances of survival. I would give him my heart in a second if I could, but I am not given the luxury of giving him life at the cost of mine."

We remained completely quiet and somewhat motionless for a few minutes. It wasn't really what I would describe as an uncomfortable silence, but it definitely was noticeable. The rest of the bar continued with their rambunctious rants and boisterous behavior. The three of us were the only ones in the whole bar who weren't screaming, laughing or yelling our lewd remarks; to be more specific, we probably more accurately resembled ancient statues than soldiers. I realized it was time to call it a night. I wanted to put the day behind me and start anew. I took the last gulp of my beer, downed my bottle, left some money to pay for my suds and slowly got off my barstool to proceed to bed.

Just as I was about to walk away, Shaklee firmly grabbed my arm and said, "Sorry Perez, and thank you."

"Thank you for what?" I asked, not knowing to what he was referring.

"For always being levelheaded and for making me realize that my wife's decision to resume her life without me is not the end of the world. There are things far worse...I hope your son gets better Perez."

Not until that moment, did I realize that Shaklee was still holding on

204

to my arm with a constant sternness. By looking at his face, I could tell that he meant every word he said. I don't know how I could tell—I just could.

"I appreciate your sincere concern for my son Shaklee. You guys have a goodnight, and I will see you tomorrow during KP transport." I shook hands then saluted them before leaving their presence.

For the next several days, I had constant nightmares. Some nights I would dream of dying in this frivolous war, and sometimes I would dream of things back home. Unfortunately, my dreams of home were not pleasant. They often dealt with Gilbert's frail condition, but one time I even dreamt that Mom and Pop had died. I could see their somber funeral from a bird's eye view, as if I was watching from the top of a high tree. I guess I must have died before them because I was not within the group of mourners. I noticed that my son was nowhere to be seen either. V was bereft and sitting in the front next to the hardwood coffin, crying with my two sisters by her side. She, along with Sarah and Diana, were attempting to console each other as they all tried to be the emotionally strongest of the three, each of them failing to conquer the weeping outbursts. The priest began his eulogy, and that was the end of it.

Oddly enough, most of my dreams usually never had a definitive ending. They just turned off like a television during a power outage. When I was a boy, my Pop would encourage me to do my best at everything by telling me, "Dream big Son because sometimes dreams come true." It was in moments like this that I seriously hoped Dad's advice was the furthest from the truth, especially since most, if not all, of my dreams were nothing but disturbing visions of death, despair and disappointment. As odd as this may sound, I was beginning to welcome my once-dreaded dreams. My nightmares helped open my eyes to the fact that my life wasn't as bad as one would think. Sure, I was scared shitless in a country I can't stand, my son is sick, my wife is lonely, I am homesick, and the list goes on. For now, at least, my nightmares were more unbearable and unspeakable than my actual life. The second my nightmares were over, I would awaken to a lesser hell, a tolerable hell, a hell I was beginning to accept as a fact of my life. My living hell burned less than my dreaming hell. In a weird way that was something I could somehow manage to feel grateful about.

For several more uneventful weeks, nothing out of the ordinary occurred. We would hear stories of incidents in other areas, or attacks several miles away or in other cities in South Vietnam, but nothing worthy of mentioning was befalling. There were still the occasional explosives,

Jaime Perez

constant rounds of gunfire, planes flying overhead and the echoes of injured or dying men screaming in agony from within the distant brush, but that was now part of the daily soundscape. It was simultaneously remarkable and somewhat eerie, the horrors that a man can learn to live with and accept as a daily part of his life. I was officially numb; I think we all were. Those who weren't numb yet, would be soon enough. Maybe this was the secret to surviving the all-too-common and unendurable inclination of being driven to insanity that unconditionally afflicted many soldiers. If numbness was the cure, I would at least have a fighting chance of rising completely above the horizons of sheer insanity, pain-free and unscathed.

The undeniable monotony of transporting KPs to and from the base was really beginning to mentally wear on me. If it were not for the accompaniment of Shaklee and Warren, I would have asked to be put back on the universally despised mess hall assignment, but I never did. I just simply tolerated the trite inconveniences and banalities of battle. Maybe after Shaklee and Warren were relieved of their service I could ask for a reassignment, something less robotic and something more human. At this point, I wouldn't even mind burying the neglected and decomposed enemy corpses whose ineffable and ubiquitous stench could be perceived no matter where in the base we were. The offensively pervasive stink became so commonplace that I forgot what it was like to smell fresh, clean and undefiled air. The only positive aspect of this foulness is that it concealed and enfeebled the putrescence of puke, piss and shit that freely lurked in the restrooms. Even after a long, hot shower, I couldn't seem to rid myself of the vile odor. It was as if it had seeped into my pores and was now a part of my being, maybe even a part of everyone else's being.

For the past several days, Shaklee and Warren began counting down their remaining days and ostentatiously flaunting their imminent release. Although they seemed to be getting on everybody's nerves, their showy displays didn't bother me. I was actually very happy for them, even though I would likely begin feeling a void from their absence immediately. It was sad because I didn't really know too much about either of them. The only reason I found out that Shaklee was previously engaged was because of his mood at the bar after he found out that his fiancé had decided to leave him. I didn't know from what part of the country they were, and I had no idea about their families, their hobbies, their religious beliefs, their fears, nothing. All I knew was that they both liked to look at magazines with pictures of naked women, and they were both going to leave me with

Through You

poignant memories that I would probably never forget. They both made the most difficult time in my life a little more tolerable and a little less painful. Sometimes that is all we can ask or expect from a friend. Sure Shaklee and Warren were soldiers, but to me, they were friends first, and soldiers second.

"Ten more days Perez Woohoo!" Shaklee yelled as we embarked on our daily ritual.

"I'm not that bad at mathematics Shaklee. If yesterday you bragged that you had 11 days left to go, I can do the math myself." I said as I smiled and nodded my head at how childish he and Warren were being.

"Damn Perez. You are a genius." Warren said sarcastically.

"I bet these are going to feel like the 10 longest days of our life." Shaklee commented.

"You bet your ass they are. We need to get together sometime before we leave Perez, the three of us. It will be like a going away party. Maybe we can get high again." Warren facetiously suggested because he knew all three of us had an unpleasant experience with marijuana that night behind the shack.

We stopped at our usual pick up point and waited for the KPs to board the vehicle. I am not too sure if the KPs understood any English, but that didn't hinder Warren and Shaklee from attempting to inform the KPs of the fact that they only had 10 days of duty remaining. The KPs just looked at each other in apparent bewilderment as Warren and Shaklee began the drive back to base, laughing gleefully the entire way back.

Warren parked the vehicle just outside the storage room where I was to begin supervising the KPs in the organization of incoming supplies. I was the last one to jump off the vehicle. The second my boots touched the ground I thought I had heard my name being yelled by an unfamiliar voice coming from the area of the base headquarters. I waited to hear it again before reacting, just in case I wasn't hearing things.

I looked at Warren and Shaklee. "Did you hear my name?" I asked them.

"I didn't." Shaklee responded.

"I did." Warren answered.

"Perez!" This time I knew I was not delusional.

"What did you do now Perez?" Warren jokingly asked.

"Nothing. I think. I'll be right back. Watch these guys for me." I asked as I scampered to headquarters from where the yelling was coming.

As I approached the headquarters entrance with my gun in hand, an

207

Jaime Perez

unfamiliar soldier saluted me and ordered me to visit with my commanding officer. I was a little concerned. Maybe I was going to be reassigned to another duty, or maybe I was going on a dangerous mission. An onslaught of thoughts was feverishly racing in my mind. I eventually approached Sergeant Major Dyer's office door. Before entering, I stood at the door and saluted him.

"Sir, you requested my presence Sir?" I asked

"Yes, Perez. Come on in, and sit down." Sergeant Major Dyer ordered of me as he stared intently and intimidatingly into my eyes. Previous to this moment, I had never spoken a word to Sergeant Major Dyer, but everyone on base knew who he was. He was highly respected and highly regarded. I don't know if there is a prototypical image for a soldier, but if there were, Dyer would certainly fit the description. He was considerably tall, stalwart and with a serious disposition that never wavered. I heard another soldier from my barracks mention that he never smiled. Personally, I just think he didn't know how. His abrasive and overly masculine voice matched his physicality. He was a man of few words, but whenever he spoke, you listened. I sat down before him and noticed that I was beginning to perspire and shake a little. I didn't think that I was in any kind of trouble, and surely this meeting wasn't about my experimentation with marijuana. My guessing as to why I was called in to this man's office was overbearing and discomforting, so I sat and waited patiently for him to speak. We were both silent for about 10 seconds, but the silence felt enduring and consuming. After what seemed like a temporary and silent eternity, his commanding voice beheld all my attention.

"Private Perez, I am going to get straight to the point. I hope you pardon my brashness, but I feel that delivering the kind of message that I have been asked to give you has no pretty way of being disclosed. I received a call from a representative at the Red Cross informing me that your son has died. Your wife and family are understandably having a difficult time with your untimely loss, and I have been ordered to grant you a temporary leave. You will be flown back home immediately so that you can attend your son's funeral, after which the status of your service will be determined. I'm terribly sorry Perez. I have been asked to deliver this exact message dozens of times before, and it never gets any easier. This is the only part of being an officer that I detest. I can't begin to imagine what you are feeling because I have not had the unfortunate experience of having any of my children pass away. I need you to pack your things as quickly as you can so that you can be sent on your way

208

home. Your son's funeral is likely to be held in a day or two; so time is of the essence. I don't have much more to tell you; I didn't get the specifics. The Red Cross has all the specifics. Perez, did you hear me? You need to pack your stuff."

I knew Dyer was speaking, but I wasn't construing any of his words. My mind impulsively shut off the second after he told me Gilbert had died. After that I had no idea what he said to me. I was so shocked that I wasn't even able to cry. At that moment, my tears failed me.

"I'm sorry Sergeant Major Dyer. I lost focus; I'm having trouble accepting the severity of what you've just said." I confessed to him.

"You need to begin getting your things ready so that you can make it in time for the funeral." Dyer said.

"I get to attend the funeral?" I asked for reassurance.

"Yes, Perez." He said as if he had just finished mentioning that to me.

"How long will I be away?" I asked, expecting to fulfill my military duty at the conclusion of funeral.

"I would pack as if you are not coming back. I am not saying that you are not coming back; I am just saying that you should pack as if you are not coming back."

I got up and half-heartedly saluted Sergeant Major Dyer before leaving his office. "Permission to be dismissed Sir." I said.

"My condolences Perez. Hurry home." He gloomily stated as I made my way back to my barracks.

In a heavy daze, I slowly walked back to my bed to gather my things. I didn't have much; so packing my things didn't take too long. My barracks was completely vacant; everybody was outside doing their routine duties or doing other things that they shouldn't be doing. After filling my duffle bag with my belongings, I sat at the edge of my bed with my head hung low in wretched dejection. I reached in my bag and took the family photograph out from within the Bible's pages. Just as I was about to sadly gaze at our captured moment in time, the barracks door quickly popped open.

"Are you Perez?" The unfamiliar solider asked.

I nodded in partial cognizance.

"Let's go. Bring your things. I am driving you to the Red Cross facility so that you can acquire more information and be on your way."

I tossed my bag atop my shoulder and proceeded to follow the soldier to a Jeep that was parked immediately out in front of the barracks. We continued to drive to the Red Cross facility that was about an hour drive

Jaime Perez

from the base. As morbid as this may sound, I wished that a Viet Cong or NVA soldier would shoot me directly in the head so that I wouldn't have to endure a man's worst fear, burying your own child. Unfortunately, I wouldn't be so lucky.

Chapter 27

The next hour or so was nothing but a big blur for me. The devastating news of my son's passing rendered me in a zombie-like state. After arriving at the Red Cross, I was placed in some room that seemed like a waiting room; I didn't exactly know what I was doing here, and I didn't care. Although I could hear voices speaking and see my surroundings, I wasn't grasping any words or focusing on anything around me. I couldn't even tell if I was being spoken to because it all sounded like several muffled, disorderly and voluminous oral outbursts being indecipherably uttered at the exact same time, similar to what one would expect to hear within the fervent crowd at a boxing match or other boisterous sporting event.

Suddenly, I regained partial sentience as I heard the clear words of one of three individuals who were in the same room with me. "What do you expect from him? He was just notified that his kid is dead. He's obviously in total shock. Have him sign here, here, and here and he can go. Get this man home yesterday." A man, obviously superior in rank to the other two, ordered as he rashly marched out of the room.

"OK Perez, sign these forms so that we can make this official and get you home in time for your son's funeral." One of the remaining men stated as he gave me a pen to sign my dismissal forms. I looked at his name tag and noticed that his last name was Gilbert. Right now was not the time to appreciate any form of irony. I simply signed the forms and was taken by another Red Cross representative to the same airport I had previously arrived at exactly 2 months and 10 days ago.

The representative kindly took care of all the paperwork and sat with me at the airport until my flight home was ready to depart. He didn't say anything to me; what could he say? At a time like this, words are grossly feeble and inept. Comfort and solace are non-existent. The practicality of silence was the least painful and least irritating manner in which to

Jaime Perez

approach this ineffable horror. Even though I never expressed my gratitude to the Red Cross representative, I somehow managed to acquire a sense of appreciation for everything he was doing for me.

"Can I get anything for you, some water, perhaps a newspaper?" The representative kindly and timidly offered."

I just simply nodded my head in negation. Right now, the only thing I really needed was to return home and grieve with the rest of my family. I comfortably remained in my own little, silent, mental world until it was time for me to board the plane. I had no idea what plane I was boarding, and I didn't even notice the call for boarding. I was still in a shock-induced daze. Had it not been for my new Red Cross friend, I would have likely missed my flight.

"Come on; that's for you." He grabbed my duffle bag and grabbed me by the arm to help me up from my seat in the airport lobby like I was a fragile and elderly man unable to get up on my own. I walked slowly up to the boarding line as the representative spoke for me to the airport attendants. I felt partially comatose and partially hypnotized. Comatose because a part of me had passed away and because of this, a part of me was now dead. Hypnotized because I felt partially hallucinatory, and everything appeared to be dream like and nebulous.

I was next in line to board the plane. I was about to salute the Red Cross representative with the usual impersonal, military salute of hand to head, but at this point I didn't see myself as a soldier. At this specific moment in my life, I was a grieving father still in shock from losing his only child, so I decided to shake the man's hand; a gesture that I felt was more personal and more appropriate.

"What's your name?" I finally asked him as I offered him my hand, realizing that these were the first words I had spoken since I had asked Sergeant Major Dyer for permission to be dismissed from his office after being notified of Gilbert's death.

"My name is Ronald Carlin Sir." He answered as he firmly shook my hand. I noticed a tear was slowly falling from his left eye. I presumed he vicariously felt my pain and was unable to contain it. Oddly enough, it was my son who had died, and I had yet to shed one tear.

I nodded in affirmation, and said, "Thank you."

As I turned around to proceed to the plane, a stewardess grabbed my bag and conveniently escorted me to my seat. Ronald must have mentioned my situation to the flight staff, hence, the special attention. I was seated towards the front of the plane and asked for my flight schedule. I had no idea where my flight was to connect or if I was supposed to board another plane in another airport. I saw Ronald having a few more words with the flight staff before leaving the airport.

"If there is anything you need Mr. Perez, you let us know. We'll take care of everything from here." The stewardess morosely offered with more of a frown than the usual, sterile smile that they were so accustomed to displaying. Stewardesses never fail to smile; this one actually did. I was certain that the entire flight staff knew of my situation because of the superfluous kindness I was receiving.

I was tired, exhausted, shocked, upset, depressed and overwhelmed all at the same time. I was an emotional wreck. I didn't want to talk to anyone, see anyone or hear anyone. I couldn't wait to return home. I didn't know what to expect when I returned; I just knew I wanted and needed to be with V. She was certainly taking Gilbert's passing difficultly. I knew my wife; I could almost hear and feel her pain from hundreds of miles away. Even though Gilbert's frailty was not a surprise, one can never really prepare for the afflicting blow of disheartenment that accompanies the death of a loved one, regardless of how expected it may be.

So many thoughts and emotions were running through my pulsating head that I thought it would be impossible to get any rest. I crossed my arms and closed my eyes in an attempt to hopefully prove myself wrong. As I brushed my arms against my jacket, I felt something protruding out of one of my pockets. It was the photograph V had sent me weeks back, the only photograph I owned of the three of us together, smiling as if without a care in the world. At that exact second, the previously non-existent tears that were obviously amassing with every minute poured out from within, revealing their unmistakable presence. I turned my head towards the plane's window to cover my uncontainable emotions and to unsuccessfully attempt to muffle my sobbing and crying. I couldn't control myself. My outburst of misery seemingly echoed throughout the plane, from the front all the way to the back and back to the front again. I felt considerably warm inside, and I could feel myself trembling and shaking. Right now, nothing but pain existed. No happiness, just pure, unrelenting agony. Between the many attempts at trying to catch my breath through the physically demanding and deep sobs, I could hear the stewardesses speaking to each other.

"What do we do? Is he going to be all right? Should we get him anything?" Several unfamiliar voices asked each other in apparent confusion.

Jaime Perez

"He needs to let this out. Get him some tissue, and put it on the seat next to him. Don't disturb him. This will be cathartic and therapeutic for him." A male voice requested of the others.

That was the last thing I remember before feeling and being abruptly awaken by the unexpected and jerky bounce of the plane landing. I apparently cried myself to sleep for the entire duration of the flight. I had not seen my flight schedule, so I had no idea where I was, what time it was, or if I needed to change flights. I woke up with the photograph in my left hand. I took another gaze at it before putting it back in my pocket. I noticed some tissues on the unoccupied seat next to me. After the plane came to a complete stop and before I began to look around to get someone's attention, the calm voice of the authoritative man who asked the attendants to leave me alone sat by my side.

"Hello Mr. Perez. You had quite a nap there. I am the Captain of this flight, Captain Whitfield. How are you feeling?" He asked with a noticeable and genuine concern, considering he was a complete stranger.

"I am doing as well as possible for the moment." I responded as I flinched my irritated eyes from having felt the giddiness that often accompanies a pounding headache.

"Good. You will be staying with us on this plane until you arrive in the United States, where you will be escorted to your connecting flight that will take you to McAllen, Texas. You will have a Red Cross volunteer waiting for you in McAllen to drive you home. You must be hungry, so I have the stewardess bringing you something to eat because you slept for close to 12 hours!"

"Twelve hours?" I asked for clarification.

"Yes, 12 hours and 18 minutes to be exact. Your food will be here soon, and we will be in the air again in about an hour. Let us know if you need anything Mr. Perez." He offered as he began to get up.

"Captain. Where are we?" I confusedly asked.

"We are in Madrid, Spain."

"Thank you for your hospitality Captain." I said.

"No, thank you." He responded as he continued to the front of the plane.

I had forgotten to ask the Captain where I was going to make a flight change. A few seconds later, the attendant arrived with my meal, chicken fried steak, mashed potatoes and corn. I couldn't help notice that this was what I had with my family on my final day home before leaving for Vietnam a little over 2 months ago. The only thing missing was the

Through You

German chocolate cake, my family and Gilbert of course. Although the airplane meal paled miserably in comparison to the home-cooked meal I had before leaving, at least this meal was more flavorful than the insipid crap we would receive at the military bases. Sometimes I felt the cardboard boxes that the food was shipped in might have had more flavor than what they fed us, especially in Vietnam. After asking her, the flight attendant informed me that this flight would take me to Houston, Texas, where I would connect to return home. I hadn't heard the word 'Texas' in quite some time; it was funny how the enunciation of two syllables can make you feel.

New passengers began boarding the plane. So I naturally assumed it was nearing departure time. I didn't know how long the flight from Madrid to Houston, Texas would be, but I knew I would be back home where I belong very soon. It felt hopeless to know that I couldn't do anything to speed up my flight home. Anxiety was beginning to set in, and I suddenly noticed I was biting my nails, something I hadn't done since elementary school. I needed to be home with my family. I should have been there when my son died and I wasn't. The presence of my absence began to cunningly anger me because I was not there to share my son's last moments with him. I know there was absolutely nothing in my power I could have legally and honorably done to have avoided being sent away, but that did nothing to pacify my current and unstable state of resentment.

Chapter 28

Several hours later, I arrived in Houston, Texas. I waited for everybody to get off the plane before making an attempt to grab my bag and request my schedule from the stewardess.

"You're almost home Sir." An overly friendly voice said from behind me.

"Yeah, almost home." I agreed.

"I wanted to give you your flight schedule Sir. You have an hour and a half delay here in Houston, where you will board Flight 822 to McAllen, Texas. I believe somebody from the Red Cross will be there when you arrive to take you home. Good luck to you Sir and thank you." She said as she handed me my flight schedule. I had an awkward feeling that she was not thanking me for being a passenger but more for the enervating sacrifices that every soldier must persevere.

"I'm sorry for the commotion I created on the previous flight. I'm usually not this emotional, especially in public." I abashedly stated as I began to walk down the center aisle.

"Sir, you have absolutely nothing to apologize for Sir." The older stewardess softly uttered with a shaky and fragile voice. She knew my unfortunate situation, and the tear she excreted from her watery eyes displayed her genuine and thoughtful sympathy. Her unexpected reaction rendered me motionless. My mind was telling me to leave, but my legs were not quite receiving the message. We just stood there. I didn't feel right leaving at that given moment. For some odd reason, I felt that leaving at the moment would be rude. Something told me that the older lady wanted to say something to me that she was having difficulty expressing. Finally, the awkwardness was remedied when she began speaking.

"I'm sorry, but you remind me of my son. He is also serving abroad but in the Air Force. He's about your age. I just hope he is doing all right. I can't

216

stand this whole Vietnam thing. He's my only son, and I am scared out of my wits." She said as she apparently indulged in a momentary episode of pensive reflection while we both stood in the airplane's center aisle. We were the only two left in the plane with the exception of the captain and a few remaining staff members who were preparing to exit the plane.

"I am an only son as well. I'm sure your son is fine. Just keep writing to him because those letters from back home really help us through the most difficult of times." I tried to comfort her. Little did I know that she had a significant reason to worry.

"That's exactly what bothers me. He hasn't responded to his father and me in over two months." She explained while wiping away her solitary tear.

My attempts to console her continued, "I'm sure he is just extremely busy, or maybe his response letters have been lost or misplaced in transport. It happens quite often."

"You're probably right. Best of luck to you Perez." She said as she read my name from my jacket.

"Thank you mam. Have a good day." I said as turned around and I finally made my way out of the airplane and into the bustling Houston airport lobby to await my connection flight.

Even though all airports seemed and looked the same to me, I did get a distinguishing feeling this time when I arrived in Houston. Maybe it was the fact that I was able to predominantly hear English being spoken around me, maybe it was the fact that I was able to read the English headlines of the various magazines and newspapers at the newsstands, or maybe it was simply the fact that I knew I was back in the United States. Regardless, I was closer to being where I belonged, at home and in my wife's arms.

I immediately resumed towards the gate where my connecting flight was to board, and I awaited my departure with jittery anxiousness. I glanced at my flight schedule and realized something; I was arriving at the McAllen airport at 7:15PM on flight 822. I couldn't help notice the irony. I was born on July 15th, and Gilbert was born on August 22nd, which meant that my birthday was my approximate arrival time and Gilbert's birthday was my arrival flight number. Although I highly doubt that this snippet of irony meant anything, it was still something I managed to notice.

I waited impatiently in the boisterous lobby for the boarding of my flight to be announced. Although my delay was a little over an hour, it didn't feel that brief. I could have sworn that I waited for at least 3 arduous hours before the initial announcement was made. I noticed that I was the

Jaime Perez

only one in uniform boarding the plane, probably because everybody else in uniform was displaced overseas and forced to witness sheer inhumanity in all its blatancy. There was obviously still the hovering and overabundant permeation of anti-war sentiment that could be felt in the air like a dark and dense foreboding cloud before a threatening storm. I could feel the occasional stares and impulsive gazes from everyone around me as I formed a line to get on my plane home, but I had other more concerning and pressing matters in my battered mind to keep me occupied and engrossed in deep wistfulness.

With the exception of my previous shameless display of uncontrollable emotions, I felt I was handling my son's passing the best that I could. I had never cried so much in my life, and I had a convincing feeling that there was much more grief to come upon rejoining my family. The flight from Houston to McAllen was about an hour long, and I had never before felt such overwhelming eagerness and anticipation as I was feeling now.

Suddenly as I was just a few feet from entering the plane, I sensed the peculiar feeling that someone was staring at me in a different manner than I had previously witnessed since arriving at the airport. The whole time I was in Houston I had many peoples' attention, but this felt inexplicably different. Something told me to turn my head and glance to my left, I did. About 20 feet away from me, an older man in a wheelchair had his chair positioned so that he could look directly at me. I instinctively stopped and took notice of the intrigued man. He had a small U.S. flag affixed to one of the wheelchair's metal bars that was attached to his seat, and he had on a black cap with some kind of World War II inscription that gave one the impression that he was a war veteran. For about 5 seconds, we motionlessly looked at each other without blinking an eye. I could tell that almost everybody in our vicinity was witnessing our statue-like exchange. Suddenly and patriotically, he firmly saluted me with an earnest look on his face. I respectfully returned the salute, as we remained the center of each other's attention for a short while longer. Although nobody behind me hurried me to continue boarding the plane, I realized I was holding up all the other passengers and so into the plane I continued.

The short flight back home was an opportunity to mentally and emotionally prepare for what would probably be one of the most misery-laden experiences I would ever have to confront. Death was not foreign to me; after all I was a soldier returning from a bloody war, and I traumatically lost an uncle before my very young eyes. This, without a doubt, felt drastically different. Time and time again I've heard that one of the most ill-fated and difficult things that a man could ever be subjected to do is to bury his own son. Here I was, twenty years into life and already having to confront the most dreadful of hardships known to man. It simply wasn't fair, nothing was. I had a difficult time accepting how and why this was happening. Was it by chance? Was it destiny? Was it some kind of sign, or was it just another bullshit random event that was constantly unfolding in a godless, autonomous and misled world? V was going to need me to be strong in order for both of us to get through this without driving ourselves irreversibly mad, so I tried to compose myself the best that I could.

A few rows in front of mine, the vehement and uncontainable crying of an irritated infant resonated clearly throughout the entire plane. I was growing impatient being strapped down in my seat, so I decided to visit the exasperated infant's parents and see if I could momentarily relive the joyous experience of being in the presence of a baby. The baby was resting on the mother's shoulder and facing me with a flushed and restless look. The second the baby saw me rise from my seat the noticeable silence resounded. The seat directly behind the mother's seat was unoccupied, so I sat myself there, smiled at the infant, and asked if I could hold their child.

"Anyone who has the power to stop my kid from crying can hold my kid all they want." She responded as if relieved.

"What's his name?" I asked as the baby rested silently in my arms and played with my ears.

"Jeffrey. Jeffrey Garza. You are a natural with kids. What is your secret?" Jeffrey's mother jokingly and rhetorically asked as her son transformed from one extreme to another in a matter of seconds.

Although I wasn't holding Gilbert, the experience of holding Jeffrey triggered a fleeting reminiscence that took me back several months, to a moment when my life was much more complete and much less empty than it is now. I could tell that Jeffrey's mother was shockingly staring at me in awe as I held her previously inflamed child in a calm and relaxed state. Jeffrey must have been at least a year old, and his deep brown eyes gazed into mine as if he was speaking to me through his eyes.

I didn't how much more of this I was going to be able to take before beginning to exude tears of my own. He seemed so comfortable and at ease, willingly abandoning his exasperation for the time being. Maybe it was the fact that Jeffrey was in the arms of a complete stranger, or maybe it was the eye-catching military uniform I was wearing that kept Jeffrey in a hypnotic daze. Regardless, I don't think his mother knew exactly how lucky she was and how unlucky some others are.

Jaime Perez

"You're child is beautiful mam. Thank you for letting me hold him for a while." I said as I cautiously handed Jeffrey back to his mother.

"Thank YOU for shutting him up. He's been crying since we boarded the plane." She revealed as she brushed his thin hair with her hand.

Just as I was about to make my way back to my designated seat, Jeffrey's mother asks, "Do you have any kids of your own?"

I instinctively hesitated before answering. "Yes, I do." I curtly answered to avoid transitioning to a long and heartbreaking explanation.

"What is your child's name?" She continued to pry as if wanting to prolong the conversation.

"His name *was* Gilbert." I said with an unintended tone of despondency before noticing her facial expression quickly change from a pleasant smile to a disconcerted gloominess. I didn't mean to answer in past tense; it just came out that way, and Jeffrey's mother apparently took notice of my choice of verb tense.

Quickly and awkwardly our conversation ended. She looked as if she wanted to say something more. Her mouth opened as if preparing to speak, but nothing came out. I simply returned to my seat as the captain announced that we would be landing in a few minutes. The flight seemed much shorter than I anticipated, which was fine by me. I wanted to get home and see my family. A few minutes later, we hit the ground. I couldn't wait to get out and look for the Red Cross volunteer who would be waiting for me to drive me home. Unlike the previous flights, I was the first to exit this flight, and with good reason.

There weren't any other passengers on board wearing military attire, so it wasn't too difficult for the Red Cross volunteer to identify me from within the crowd.

"Are you Mr. Beltran Perez?" He asked.

"Yes, I am. You must be my ride home."

"I sure am sir. My name is Robert Betancourt. Let me get your bag sir, and follow me." He eagerly grabbed my duffle bag and started out towards the parking lot.

It was great to be home. Unfortunately, my premature return was made possible by the direst of circumstances. Robert and I made our way to the Red Cross vehicle. I had forgotten what fresh, deathless air smelled like. There was a certain refreshing sweetness to the hometown breeze, almost as if the unmistakable scent of spring was making its way inside me. The drive home was approximately 15 minutes. Robert granted me the preferred luxury of a silent drive home. I didn't feel like conversing with

220

anybody at this specific moment; I just wanted to dwell in the silence that would allow me to gather my thoughts and mentally prepare for a tense and unsettling experience of unmatched grieving.

On the way home, we ended up stopping at the intersection of the Robert E. Lee Park nearby our apartment. It was then that I lost control of my pent up emotions. Tears began to profusely drizzle down my cheek. My silent purge of pain and loss would have likely gone unnoticed for a little while longer if Robert hadn't needed to glance passed me before proceeding into the intersection. I was pretty certain he knew what I was going through and that nothing could be said or done to eradicate the rankling ebullience I was internally beginning to encounter. Robert remained soundless, much to my preference.

As Robert drove up the apartment complex's parking lot, I began to ineffectively wipe away my tears. I didn't want my family to see me for the first time in months in a distraught state of brokenness. I wanted to be strong for my wife so that I could provide her with much-needed comfort. Instead, I softened up like glue with the inability to keep myself together.

"Take your time Mr. Perez." Robert kindly advised as he patted my left shoulder.

I hadn't realized that we had been parked for several minutes already. Robert didn't seem at all in a hurry, but I didn't want to prolong the inevitable any further. I took a deep breath and thanked Robert for everything.

"I'm sorry for your loss Mr. Perez." He said as I entered the back of the vehicle to grab my duffle bag.

I acknowledge the appreciation of his condolences with a simple nod. Eventually, I closed the door to the vehicle and Robert slowly drove away. I stood motionless for several seconds before making my way to apartment #17 and looked around to observe my surroundings. The scenario, the time of day, the walk to my door all seemed so familiar. I had been here before. I felt as if I had already lived this moment, as if I had seen this movie before and was subjected to unwillingly go through this again.

I slowly continued on as I noticed several familiar vehicles in the parking lot. This rather unpleasant episode of déjà vu riddled me with goose bumps, and a surreptitious, fleeting sensation of vertigo suddenly compelled me to stop in my tracks. I felt as if I could somehow feel the earth rapidly rotating on its axis, and a mind-numbing headache ensued. I waited for a few seconds before I resumed my wade to the door but not

Jaime Perez

before hearing the door of apartment #17 open before me. It was my sister, Diana. Being the more emotional of my two sisters, she undoubtedly was having trouble enduring our family's current tragedy. She covered her weeping face with both her hands as she stood outside the door, never looking up and never taking notice of my presence. As I approached her, I slowly dropped my bag on the floor and softly took her hands off her face and kissed her forehead. For two seconds, her sobbing completely stopped as she reacted surprisingly to my sudden presence.

For the next few minutes, I simply and firmly held my sister as she spotted and literally drenched my military jacket with tears of pain. The moment's overweighing essence rendered both of us speechless. Amidst our grieving, I couldn't help but worry about my sister because she was frenziedly and uncontrollably shaking in my arms beyond what I thought was humanly possible. I slowly tried to let go of her and take a step back to allow her to breathe the fresh air freely with concern that she might faint from hyperventilation, but she quickly grabbed me and pulled me to her.

"I...am so...sorry Belty. I...I..." My sister could say no more as she kissed me on the cheek, and I was still speechless.

I reached for the doorknob to enter the apartment with my sister held firmly at my side. In the living room, everybody, except for Pop, was sitting on a couch. A resounding resonance of regret rang loudly and clearly, as everyone appeared to grieve in unison. Simultaneously, everyone glanced to the door, expecting to see Diana reentering the apartment. Faster than I could blink, my entire family raced towards me like attracting magnets, V being the first to reach me. All at once I could hear everyone talking to me, yet I couldn't construe one word—it all seemed incoherently fused together. The only thing I did understand was V's soft and mournful whisper in my ear as she hugged me while we stood at the center of this circle of sorrow.

"We lost him Baby. He just stopped breathing. I didn't know what to do. He just stopped breathing. His little heart stopped beating."

I didn't get a chance to respond with any weak attempts to console my wife because, before I knew it, she had already broken down crying as she lifelessly fell through my embrace and down to her knees. I fell to my knees as well and continued to hold my wife through her shrieks of bereavement. She sounded similar to the way I did on the flight back home, unrestrained in unfeigned unhappiness. We all held each other and cried until we couldn't cry anymore. Little by little, each of us began to silently sit down. I picked V up from the floor and sat her next to me on our couch.

222

Through You

Nobody said anything for about half an hour. Although the grieving quietly continued, the aural atmosphere of our tiny apartment quickly went from loud to silent. It was as if all of us had something important to say, but nobody was ready to say it. Our bodies were in one place, but our minds were in another, very similar to how I had been for the past several months, physically and mentally in two totally different places.

Chapter 29

It was strange. Even though I was surrounded by constant death for the past couple of months to the point that I could even smell it while sleeping, I had somehow managed to put my son's fatal illness aside and not primarily worry about his condition whenever I would think of him. That's what Dr. Richards asked of us. He asked us to enjoy whatever time we have with our son and not to worry over his disease-induced frailty because we would end up damaging the quality of our short time together. So although my son's death should have come as no surprise, it still felt as unexpected and as painful as if we hadn't seen it coming beforehand.

The traveling and difference in time zones left me in confusion as to whether or not I had made it in time for my son's funeral. I didn't get to make out many of the details while I was being told of my son's death because I was only physically in Sergeant Major Dyer's office. I thought I remembered him telling me that Gilbert passed on March 30th; I just wasn't too sure of the actual time of death. My hearing had impulsively shut off at some point in the dismal conversation. In Vietnam, I was approximately 12 hours ahead of the time here at home, so I gained time when arriving here. I didn't know if I had made it in time for the funeral. I didn't know where my son's body was. I didn't know if all the funeral arrangements were made. I didn't know shit. I had so many pervading questions at a time when I felt it would be utterly inconsiderate to ask them, but I needed to know.

I got up to get V a glass of water that I felt she was thirsting for. As soon as I got up, the still and desolate atmosphere in our apartment gradually became less static. Mom quickly walked over to me to and morosely said, "Welcome home Son. We're all glad you're back." The overwhelmingly consuming previous moment of mourning and grieving had left no room for "Welcome Homes", and understandably so.

Through You

"Here you go Baby." I said to V as I handed her a cold glass of water.

"Welcome back soldier." Al said with puffy eyes as he shook my hand with one hand and grabbed my shoulder with the other. Soon enough, everybody had his or her chance to personally welcome me back home. Mom, Pop, Virginia, Al, Sarah, Diana and V were all there to share this trying moment together. Before I was able to shamefully ask the questions that I needed answered, Pop signaled me to my bedroom and followed behind me.

"Son. Gilbert will be buried at Palm Valley Memorial Gardens. The funeral is tomorrow at 10:00 AM, and we all plan to meet here early so that we can all arrive together. We don't want you or Veronica driving, so you will drive with us." He explained.

"And where is my son now?" I shakily asked.

"At the funeral home. All the arrangements have been taken care of. You have nothing to worry about concerning those matters. We are here for you son. Don't forget that." Pop said with his grave and fatherly voice.

Although my Pop and I didn't have the most emotionally revealing relationship, I instinctively reached for my Pop and gave him the biggest hug I had given him since I was a little kid after becoming excited about being able to ride a bike on my own. It felt good to hug my Pop. For years, our love for each other was an "understood" or "manly" love that was usually unspoken and aloof-- not today though. Today, I held my father in my arms and thanked him for everything he had ever done and for the many things he would continue to do.

Mom came in the room and whispered something in Pop's ear.

"Yeah, you're right." Pop said aloud in response to Mom.

We all proceeded to the living room as Pop addressed everybody and said, "I think maybe it's time for us to leave Beltran and Veronica alone." Pop said while signaling to the door with his head to everybody else as if giving them a hint of his intentions to have everyone follow his lead.

"Yes, we should get going as well." Virginia responded as she caught on to Pop's plan of action. Soon enough, Diana and Sarah followed, but not after everyone gave us a heartfelt goodbye. I didn't really want everyone to leave just yet because I felt more at home with everyone there, and I had only spent about an hour with them since I had walked through the door with Diana by my side. Suddenly, as I looked towards my grieving V, I realized that maybe being alone with my wife was the best thing to do for now.

Jaime Perez

Everyone slowly began making their way to the door after making it a point to give V and me an embrace. We would all congregate tomorrow morning and begin our drive to the funeral home to commence my son's obsequy. As we stood by our door watching our families leave and somberly waving goodbye to them, I was overcome by a transitory mental lapse that had me imagining the sorrowful events that I would have to unfortunately face tomorrow at 10:00AM. I could clearly envision a mournful funeral setting with a tiny, black coffin at the forefront of the saddened group in attendance. It was a cloudy, overcast day at the tranquil cemetery, and the invigorating breeze that often bestowed me with an inexplicable essence of liveliness was blowing no longer. A permeating stillness enshrouded, and the suffocating quiescence did nothing to appease the oppressive aura of lifelessness that onerously hovered above and around the morose bereaved. V was sitting and sobbing next to me at the very front with her hands covering her face as she leaned over to my side for me to support her tired and inundated body. I obviously appeared to be in utter shock, as I sat there dormant without blinking an eye, staring at the shiny, gold-trimmed casket that bore the tiny body of my first and only son. Aside from V and me, I couldn't distinguish any of the others among us, but there were many others with us. The otherwise vivid divination began to gradually blur just as my vision had begun to blur only moments before.

I could feel V resting her encumbered head on my left side and could see my family driving away, and even though I was looking straight ahead, I wasn't completely focusing on what was before me. Everything in my path of vision became an indistinguishable blur as I unknowingly continued waving after everybody had left. I noticed V's hazy silhouette appear with my peripheral vision.

"Baby. Baby." She concernedly said as she slowly waved her hand before my eyes to get my attention and withdraw me from my benumbed state. I quickly blinked myself back to the real world.

"Are you o.k.?" She asked as she looked directly into my eyes.

"Yes…Yes. I'm fine. I was just…I don't know. I was just thinking." I assured her.

"Well you've been waving in a zombie-like state at nothing. Everybody is gone. Are you sure you are all right?" She didn't seem convinced at my previous attempt to assure her I was fine.

"Yes V. I am fine." I said with a somewhat forced smile as I hugged her tightly in another attempt to convince her that I was just daydreaming. I took a deep whiff as I inhaled the unmistakable fragrance of her perfume;

226

a familiar sweet fragrance I had longed for and could recognize anywhere, even after more than two months' exposure to death, rottenness, putrescence and insalubriousness.

"Come on. Let's go inside." I advised.

I noticed a bunch of food in unpacked grocery bags sitting on the kitchen counter. V noticed me probing through the bags.

"I'm sorry. I've haven't had a chance to put these away. I was going to put them away when I noticed Gilbert was lying on the living room floor. I thought…he was…sleeping, but he had just woken up…from a nap. So I…" V started stumbling through her words as she probably had just realized that the groceries had been on the table for close to a full day.

"Hey. It's all right V. Leave the bags there; that can wait. Come lie down with me. I'm sure we've both had a long and trying day." I said as I gently touched my wife's damp cheek with the back of my hand. For the first time since my arrival, V managed to muster a somewhat comforting smile, the same smile that I would often reflect upon while many miles away, the same smile that helped me stay sane during the most insane time of my life.

V and I held each other in bed until we both eventually fell asleep. My being in a different part of the world and having to adapt my body clock to the drastically dissimilar time zones of Vietnam left me physically exhausted, not to mention the emotional exhaustion that V and me were undoubtedly experiencing.

Hours later, I opened my eyes in the middle of the night, V by my side. I rubbed my partially opened eyes and glanced over to see what time it was; it was 3:26AM. V was fast asleep, and after a few minutes of listening to nothingness and staring at the ceiling, I suddenly felt wide-awake. I had many reflective and pensive moments like this at Ft. Bliss, Ft. Sill and in Long Binh, more than I could count on both hands. These incidents often kept me awake for hours on end, forcing me to lose precious and much-needed sleep. I knew this time would be no different.

For some reason, I began to take notice that I didn't have one of my infamous and inconvenient nightmares that have so often pried their way into my defenseless realm of unconsciousness whenever something dramatic or disagreeable was developing in my life. In addition, I noticed the highly evident absence of my son's presence in our apartment. Gone were the untimely cries for diaper changes and frequent bawlings for milk in the dead of night. The sweet and priceless inconveniences of parenting that made it all worth experiencing were now only memories, poignant

Jaime Perez

memories at that. The last time I lay on this bed, my son was resting between V and me; tonight, my son was resting elsewhere. I began to feel incomplete and lacking because of this. I went from being a husband and a father to solely being a husband. My experiences in fatherhood were short-lived and unsubstantially brief. I was cruelly and unfairly stripped of my fatherhood status, a welcomed status that filled me with honor and pride to the point that I shamelessly and ostentatiously displayed my newfound prestige.

For the next several hours I did nothing but reminisce of the 10 short days I spent with my son during my L.O.A. Our trip to the park, the admiration my son received from complete strangers, his heart-stopping smile, the deep brown and sincere eyes he acquired from his mother, the memories felt so long ago, so nostalgic, yet there were as clear as if they occurred yesterday.

I began to feel an undeniable yet portentous warmth inside, the kind of stirring sensation one feels at the onset of receiving saddening, heartbreaking news. I knew I was about to emotionally explode, and I didn't want to wake up V. I buried my head deeply in my pillow, turning myself on my stomach. As I attempted to further smother my face and momentarily muffle my misery, I unexpectedly felt something underneath the pillow that I hadn't felt when resting on it. Without even looking at the object, I could suddenly tell what it was. I grabbed it and looked at it in the subtle darkness for several seconds. The unanticipated discovery briefly deferred my inevitable outpour of sorrow.

I decided to leave the bedroom entirely and get some badly needed fresh air, bringing the vestige with me. As I cautiously made my way outside, the wall clock in the living room displayed that it was now 6:35 AM. I quietly opened the door so as to not alarm V and sat on the front steps of our apartment. Even though the presence of dark clouds was threatening to manifest an appropriately gloomy day to coincide with the upcoming gloominess this day had in store for us, the vibrant, bright orange sun was valiantly struggling to pervasively power its way into a new day.

I knew that V would be waking up shortly, and I didn't want her to wake up without me being next to her, especially on a day like today. I decided to sit outside for a few more minutes as I held my son's first true friend in my hands. If there was one thing that my son couldn't live without, it would have to be this little, stuffed primate. I don't think V knew this was under the pillow. Gilbert probably misplaced it there when he was peacefully sleeping with V, as the interim man-of-the house watched over his mother while I was away.

Death often leaves the living with a vicious void and dispiriting dejection that can incessantly infest and infiltrate even the strongest of souls, myself included. Today, on April Fools' Day of 1969, I would bury my son and bid him farewell one last time before physically detaching myself from him forever, although the mental and emotional attachment will never cease. Previously, I had felt that temporarily leaving my family to fight a senseless war was the most difficult situation I would ever have to endure; I was now about to prove myself wrong because the forthcomings of the day were going to displace me in an inhumane, unbearable battle that I would constantly fight but knew I could never win.

Chapter 30

Just as I began to wonder what time it was, the turning of the doorknob behind me signified that V was now awake.

"What are you doing down there?" She asked, as I remained sitting on the floor.

"I'm just getting some fresh air. I couldn't go back to sleep, so I thought I would come outside and inhale some refreshing, non-Vietnamese air, something I hadn't done for more than two months." I explained.

"What's wrong with the air in Vietnam?"

"You don't really want to know. Let's just say the air here is not as nauseous." I added.

"How long have you been sitting out here?" V asked with a look of concern.

"Since 6:35. What time is it now?" I asked as I realized that I had lost track of time.

"It's a quarter until 8. You've been out here for over an hour?"

"Yes. I didn't want to wake you. Look what I found." I said as I showed V Gilbert's little monkey friend.

"Where did you find that? I've been looking for that thing for the past couple of days. Gilbert seemed agitated without it, and I couldn't figure out where he had misplaced it."

"It was under the pillow."

"Gilbert cried frantically for a whole day, and I assumed it was because he couldn't find his favorite toy. The only place in the whole apartment I didn't check was under the pillows! He had been sleeping with me ever since you left, and of course he had to have his friend in bed with him or he would not sleep. Since I never move the pillows while sleeping, I never thought of checking there, and he must have unintentionally stuffed it under the pillow and forgotten about it."

"What time is everyone coming over?" I necessarily and abruptly changed the subject.

"Very soon. We need to start getting ready, or we'll be late to our own son's funeral." V suggested as I began to get up. Before entering the apartment, V purposely stood in my way as if to silently request a hug. Without hesitation, I did just that. Her warm body conveyed a pleasant essence of undeniable love and rejuvenation that traversed throughout my dilapidated and war-torn body.

"I'm glad you're here." She softly said in my ear. "I don't think I could manage to contain myself through this misfortune without you by my side." After a slight pause and a deep sigh, she continued. "Please tell me you don't have to go back. Please." V looked up at me with romantically submissive eyes.

"I am really not sure. I will find out after the funeral. I think I can file for a hardship case and request to serve the rest of my term upstate, but I wouldn't get my hopes up because I don't know exactly how these things work." I tried to downplay any premature excitement on V's part. I kissed my wife on the forehead as she gave me a smile that portrayed a small yet noticeable sign of hope, and we proceeded inside.

Realizing that we didn't have too much time to spare, we hastily began getting ready. For the duration of our preparation, V and I said nothing to each other. I think the fact that we were rushing to begin a distressful day that we wished we didn't have to experience kept us both in a pensive silence that left no room for words. It was an odd and discomforting feeling, having to prepare to engage in the utterly unbearable, but it was something that had to be done. V and I couldn't live to see tomorrow without facing the ineffable inevitability of today, even though tomorrow and the days to come would very likely and unavoidably revert us back to this very day. My life was destined to become a painful, never-ending cycle of gloom and despair, and I was totally powerless against its tumultuousness.

Just as I began to put on my black, leather shoes, the doorbell rang. I proceeded to the door, not expecting to greet everyone all at once.

"Hey everybody. Come on in." I tried to say with a welcoming smile that must have appeared fake and spurious. At a time like this, I don't think anybody could blame me for being unconvincing.

I hugged each and everyone before they entered as V eventually made her way to the living room to greet both our families. Everyone appeared equally haggard, but I looked the worst. My lack of sleep didn't do very much to help lessen my beaten appearance as Pop obviously took notice.

Jaime Perez

"Didn't sleep much last night?" He asked.

"Not really Pop. I've been up for a few hours now, and sleep was rather unsatisfactory. I guess it's going to be like this for the next few days." I explained.

"We are all here to help both of you get through this." Mom added

"I know. Thank you." I tried to genuinely show some sort of appreciation.

"Should we go now?" Al asked.

"Yes. We can't prolong this forever." I said as I grabbed V's hand and placed my forehead on hers.

The short drive to the funeral home was quiet and tranquil, yet it still seemed undeniably unsettling. I had just noticed that V and me had skipped breakfast, and I wasn't the least bit hungry. I am almost certain that V lacked any desire to eat as well. For some reason, I was nervous about this whole depressive situation. I had only been to one funeral before in my whole life, my uncle's, and that one still frequently frets frenziedly in my mind when I least expect it. It's been approximately a long decade since that occurred, and it still sporadically breathes heavily down my neck, causing uneasy chills that tingle down my spine.

V and I drove with Mom and Pop as we sat together in the back seat, holding hands and awaiting what is sure to be the most strenuously stifling experience that we will ever have to face. Right now, this was the calm before the storm. Soon, everyone would be bracing themselves for the upcoming heavy blows that only death can deliver with such unconditional and unwavering ferocity.

Within minutes, we had arrived and parked at the front of the funeral home. Sarah and Diana walked side by side with V as we all somberly and draggingly walked inside the considerably cold and silent building. Mom and Pop walked beside me as Al and Virginia followed closely behind. Immediately upon entering, we were suddenly swarmed by strangers as well as several family friends, some close and some distant, who were here to join us in our time of grieving. Amidst all the peaceful commotion, I noticed something unanticipated towards the back of the room that left me in a staggering awe. I wasn't too certain if I saw what I thought I saw because my path of vision was partially obstructed, so I wanted to get a closer look to reassure myself that my eyes weren't playing tricks on me. Even though I was embracing and greeting the plethora of those who claimed to feel my pain, my attention was centered on something beyond the crowd, something I wanted to make sure was real. I unsuccessfully

232

tried to make my way through the impenetrable barriers of bodies that began to quickly encircle me like vultures on carrion, yet I failed to evade all those around me who simultaneously demanded my attention. After several minutes of condolences and consolatory words of sympathy from many complete strangers, I was able to free myself for a few seconds to see what I had to see. It was exactly what I thought it was, and it left me breathless and unable to speak for several seconds. I wanted to find V so that I could share this moment with her, but I felt a fleeting moment of paralytic motionlessness. I remained in a bewildered daze until I felt a friendly and gentle tap on my back.

"Well, do you like it?" Mr. Gomez's familiar voice asked with a sympathetic smile on his face as his sobbing wife stood behind him.

Before I could even answer him, I gave him a much-overdue hug for all the things he had done for V and me for which I had never been able to show my gratitude.

"I love it Mr. Gomez. I didn't know we ordered this one." I said, as I must have appeared puzzled in addition to sleep deprived.

"You didn't. I took the liberty of having this one made for you, compliments of me and my wife." He explained as his wife took off her veil to kiss me on the cheek and give me a consoling embrace. She looked as if she wanted to say something but preferred to refrain from speaking, probably because she was afraid that more than just words would forcibly come out if she tried.

"Has my wife seen this?" I asked without taking my eyes off of the picture.

"I don't believe so. I had it sent over here this morning." Mr. Gomez replied.

At that exact moment, V walked up and stood next to me, completely stationary and stunned with the same apparent awe I was overcome with when I initially saw the impressive-sized family portrait. The portrait must have been about 3"X4" with incredibly vivid color that remarkably imitated real life. It captured an eerie yet pleasant liveliness that poured out from the wooden frame. Gilbert almost appeared to be able to jump off the photograph and crawl into my arms. V and I stayed silent from the stupefaction, and apparently Mr. Gomez was becoming a little concerned with our seemingly unexpected reaction.

"Is there something wrong with the portrait?" He asked.

"No." V and I quickly answered simultaneously as we both jerked free of the gripping and captivating stupor that shortly silenced us.

Jaime Perez

"It's beautiful Mr. Gomez. It looks so real." V added.

"That's what I get paid for, to bring memories to life. By the way, our condolences for your loss Mr. and Mrs. Perez. We are right down the street whenever you need anything." Mr. Gomez offered with a somber yet caring gesture.

"We appreciate it Mr. and Mrs. Gomez." I said as they made their way in to view the body.

"Are you Mr. and Mrs. Perez?" A stranger in a suit asked us.

"Yes." I responded.

"I'm Martin Simmons. I am the funeral director who will be overseeing your son's funeral ceremonies. We are about to get started, and we would like you to make your way to the front of the room with us."

I took a deep, acquiescent breath and prepared for whatever was to come. V grabbed my arm with noticeable firmness as she looked up at me with a look of defeat and despondence. We made our way to the front of the room, walking in the center aisle that lead directly to Gilbert's gold and black, open casket. About half way to the front, V began to proceed sluggishly and began to feel weighty. My attention was on my son's coffin, but I was noticing a slight pull and hesitation in V's walk. A few steps more were all she could endure. Within a couple of feet from our son's coffin, V violently dropped to her knees as if she had plunged from the skies. I did my best to keep her from falling completely to the ground as Al, Pop and I collectively picked her off the floor and to the front of the funeral home's ceremony room.

"Are you all right V?" I asked with concern.

Before she could comfort me with an answer, another gentleman in a suit kindly brought V a glass of ice water and a paper fan and quickly walked away before I had a chance to thank him. After a few more minutes, the delayed ceremony finally commenced. As the funeral director delivered his condolences and paid his respects from a podium directly in front of us, I was still distracted by my son's coffin and contemplating whether or not to approach the open casket for a viewing before my son was to be seized from me forever. I hadn't had a chance to view my son's tiny body, and I wasn't too sure if seeing my son's lifeless body was going to fare well with my ability to cope with all this. I had pleasant memories of my son, memories that brought a smile to my face, but I was afraid that seeing my son in his present position would erase all the happy memories and leave me with only one gloomy vision with which to remember him by, a disturbing vision of him in perpetual sleep. In addition, I didn't think that

V was going to manage to remain conscious through such an emotional ordeal, especially if she were to decide to view Gilbert. My wife was a strong person, but she wasn't without limits.

I looked to V to see how she was handling all this. She looked utterly devastated and pallid as her bloodshot and glassy eyes appeared ready to burst from so much engulfing anguish. Although I probably appeared attentive and composed throughout the duration of the ceremony, I was lost elsewhere, in a dark and lonely world of unwilling acceptance. I must have been in a trance-like, contemplative state for longer than I thought because the funeral director seemed to be making his closing comments. It wasn't until the unfamiliar yet grieving cries of strangers behind me startled me that I realized the ceremony was coming to a close.

V looked as lively as a mannequin, drearily dormant and vacantly vapid. I didn't exactly feel kindhearted about leaving her alone at a time like this, but I had made up my mind about viewing my son's body. I was going to do it; I had to. Once we leave, the casket would remain closed forever. I hadn't seen my son since I left for Long Binh, so now was my final opportunity.

It was now time for us to resume with the procession to the cemetery. Mourners began to slowly exit the building, but I wasn't ready to leave yet. V, as frail and feeble as she appeared, maintained a strong grip on my arm as if expecting to fall without being able to use me as support. As we both got up to take part in the procession, I began to make my way towards the small casket when V hindered my progress.

"I can't do this. It's too much for me." V said with a pleading shiver in her voice.

"That's fine. You don't have to, but I do." I explained while looking deep into her eyes.

"We'll wait for you in the back Son." Pop said as he heard V's and my conversation.

Nobody in my family had decided to view the body before leaving, except me, and I don't blame them. I dejectedly bowed to my knees and touched my son's little head for the first time in over two months. Without saying a word, I simply gazed at my own flesh and blood for what would likely be the very last time. I didn't know what to say, nor did I think I was capable of speaking just now. I hoped that by simply being by my son's side, my thoughts and sentiments could be spiritually or magically conveyed to him.

Even though I could see a group of men in suits with the corners of

Jaime Perez

tear-filled eyes waiting to carry my son away, I wasn't altogether ready to conclude my wordless homage. Although I was perfectly aware of what their job was, I wasn't content; I wasn't acquiring a sense of closure. What do you say to your son when he has been taken away from you? Is it even possible to acquire even a trace of closure in a situation like this? I made an effort to rise back to my feet, but my leaden body quickly returned to its bowed position. I felt dizzy and vertiginous as hundreds of black spots began to seemingly ricochet off of each other before my closed eyes, exacerbating the discomforting nuisance of my whirling giddiness. With the help of two of the suited men, I managed to get up, keep my balance and stay on my feet.

"Are you okay? Sir?" One of them asked.

I simply nodded in affirmation.

"Take your time Mr. Perez; we don't mean to rush you." The other kindly offered.

"No, I understand. I've already selfishly delayed the inevitable long enough."

I took a slow and reticent step back from the coffin as the men began to close the casket before carrying Gilbert off to the hearse. Just as the casket was inches from being shut, I remembered something.

"Wait. Not yet. I'm forgetting something." My abrupt and unforeseen outburst grabbed their attention.

I reached in my coat pocket; this, I hoped, would bring the closure I so desperately needed and deserved. I approached the coffin once again, as the men kindly placed the coffin back down. I knew I was forgetting something; I just wasn't sure what. If my son were to be able to talk, he would have asked for one thing and one thing only—the company of his best friend. I took the stuffed monkey out and placed it under my son's little arm as he often closely held it whenever he would go to sleep or lay in his crib.

"Here you go son. I'll miss you." Was all I could manage to say as I once again began to feel weighted and emotionally oppressed. I wiped my eyes before turning and walking away in order for me to clearly see where I was going. Although it was impossible for Gilbert to smile, I was pretty sure that he was spiritually smiling inside now that he had his best friend to accompany him. I hadn't noticed that all my family was watching me and still waiting for me at the end of the aisle; they too had to wipe away their excess of emotions.

"I'm sure he would have liked that." V said as she apparently witnessed me place the toy in the coffin.

"Yes, I am sure he did." I concurred with a dejected smile as we now prepared to begin the procession to the Valley of Palms Memorial Cemetery. This was far from being over.

Chapter 31

A viral, undeniable void had begun slowly infecting me from the inside out ever since I received the life-changing news of Gilbert's death, and although I've often heard that time heals all wounds, what is failed to be mentioned is that some wounds, although healed, will leave deeply-engraved scars that will forever remind one of the atrocious misfortune that time failed to completely eliminate. My son's passing was likely just one of many more emotional scars that I would have to endure throughout my existence. I will never understand why certain things happen the way they do. Some foolishly claim that everything happens for a reason, but I feel that there can't be reason in the unreasonable. Regardless of why things happen, the truth of the matter is that they do happen, whether we like it or not. I have quit trying to make inane excuses for the inhuman cruelties we face on a regular basis; they are just part of the irresolvable enigma we call life, or in this case, death.

The procession to the cemetery was a little longer than I had expected, as I noticed an impressively long line of vehicles behind us. Apparently the news of my son's death had gotten quite a bit of local publicity, and therefore many complete strangers joined my family in our bereavement. Many couples came with their children; a group of nuns and priests exited a church van, and I noticed a camouflage, military truck brought a truckload of men in military uniforms as well. Easily over a hundred unfamiliar individuals joined us to help say goodbye to my son in addition to those I knew.

"Do we know all these people?" V looked at me in wonderment as she continued to wipe away her tears.

"I don't know, but they obviously know who we are." I responded as many came up to express their sentiments to V and me.

It took us several minutes to finally reach our seats at the front of the ceremony because we were constantly being girded and embraced by crowds of sympathizers. It all seemed so surreal, like the funeral of a former president or worldly renowned celebrity. Except this was more than a president or celebrity could ever mean to me, it was my only son.

The notions of sympathy and abundant heart-felt condolences were thoughtful yet futile in their attempt at bestowing us with a semblance of solace. For the next 30 minutes, a monotone priest gave his final words before interring my son and officially taking him from us forever. To be honest, I paid little attention to what was being said because my mind hasn't been in the same place as my body lately. If it were not for the shuffling sound of bodies behind me and V's placing of her head on my shoulder, I would have remained detached and unaware the speech had concluded. The final goodbyes took longer than the priest's actual sermon-like speech. Strangers placed flowers and toys all about my son's coffin before it was slowly lowered and eventually immersed 6 feet below in cold, dark and lifeless soil.

I was really surprised at how well V was taking all of this. It was as if she had hurt all that she could hurt. The same applied for me; we probably looked as numb as we felt. The constant pain and sorrow quickly became the norm; therefore, we appeared stoically inanimate. It was as if the pain was so strong that it had a numbing affect. As the many vehicles began to drive away, I held V's hand to assure her that we still had each other and that we would somehow get through this most depressing of personal tragedies. I didn't exactly know how, but we had to. We looked at each other, still in shock and partial denial at what we had just witnessed. Everything around me seemed hazy and blurry, like I was inebriated by unparalleled wretchedness.

It was over; it was finally over. The return home was silent; nobody spoke a word. At a time like this, words are generally useless and often unnecessary, so the silence was convenient. I had never imagined how gloomy one's life could be until today, when mine plummeted to its lowest point possible. I had an amazing wife, a loving family, and I managed to survive a senseless war, at least for the time being, yet I still didn't know what was to transpire now that I was back home. I was granted an excessive leave of 16 days to return home, spend time with my family and get an opportunity to attend my son's funeral. I was oblivious to what was going to happen next in my life. I did know one thing, a lousy 16 days was not going to be ample time for me to put everything I've gone through behind

Jaime Perez

me and resume with my life as a soldier as if everything was copasetic and splendid.

The next few days were dull and uneventful. V and I weren't really up to doing much of anything. Who could blame us for reveling in our complacency? In the back of my mind, I kept wondering what was going to happen next. What now? V didn't want me going back to Vietnam, and I never wanted to be there to begin with. Then one evening I woke up in the middle of a dream. Actually, it was more of a subconscious mental visualization than a dream. There was no plot, no chronology, nothing, just a clearly audible phrase of words that somehow managed to strike me awake. When I woke up, it seemed as if the words were spoken right into my ear while I slept.

"Pack like you're not coming back..." was all I heard before my sleep was disrupted. The resounding words of Sergeant Major Dyer distinctly echoed in my head. I wasn't too sure what he meant by that. Honestly, I do recall that I wasn't really cognizant and attentive at that given moment, due to what he had just revealed to me seconds before. It was 4:10 in the morning, and V was sound asleep. The past several days had been unproductive, but today was going to have a purpose. I needed to find out what happens next. I was going to make some calls in the morning to find out what I could do to remain home with my wife and family.

For the next few hours, the rest of the evening was spent fidgeting in anxiousness and awaiting sunrise so that I could start ascertaining for necessary information. I felt a combination of excitement and anticipation because there had to be something that I could do to avoid going back to war.

"Are you talking to yourself?" V asked as she woke up from her solid sleep.

"Uh, I don't know. Was I? What was I saying?" I asked in all honestly.

"Something about making phone calls and getting information about something. What are you up to?" V asked with her raspy, sleepy voice.

"Sorry. I didn't mean to wake you with my thoughts. I just felt that it was time to make some calls to find out what can be done to avoid going back to Vietnam. I remember Sergeant Major Dyer telling me to pack as if I was not coming back. Now I have an onerous and unsettling curiosity to find out if I have to go back." I explained.

V quickly straightened up out of bed as if stunned. "That would be

240

great Belty. Can you call now?" She asked as she grabbed my hand in bed.

"I don't really know with whom to talk about this. Let's eat breakfast, and I will make some calls afterwards."

V quickly rose out of bed and prepared a complete breakfast in less time than it took me to shower and brush my teeth. She appeared excited and hopeful about my plans. I just hope she doesn't get her hopes up too high just in case I don't acquire any promising information.

After breakfast, I started perusing through all my military paperwork to see if I could find a number or contact information. In haste, V threw the dirty dishes in the sink and proceeded to walk outside.

"Where are you going in your robe?" I asked in a distraction.

"I just realized I haven't checked the mail."

"It's too early for the mail right now." I explained.

"I haven't checked it since…since Gilbert passed. I totally forgot." She explained with a slight somber hesitation.

"OK then, maybe you better check it." I reasoned.

Several seconds later, V comes in slamming the door behind her. "You got something in the mail. It's probably from yesterday, and it looks rather important."

"Let me see it." I glanced at the official business envelope with a nice gold seal on it. It was from our state representative.

"It looks important." V added.

Without speaking and breathing, I perplexingly ripped the envelope open, and immediately began to think that the contents of this envelope were relative to what I was seeking concerning the possibility of my avoiding a return to war. I was supposed to be in Vietnam, so any official government mail addressed to me was probably from someone who knew of my return home. V and I were silent as I read the letter to myself. I could see her furtively trying to decipher the contents of the letter by scrutinizing my facial expression. The letter wasn't particularly lengthy or verbose; I just felt the need to re-read it to avoid any possible misconstruing.

"What's taking you so long?" V blurted out impatiently as she obviously noticed the terseness of the letter and probably didn't understand what was taking me so long to finish reading through it.

Without a superstitious bone in my body, I answered her. "This is funny. This letter has the information I was seeking. It's a letter from our state representative, Kika de la Garza, informing me of what I need to do if I plan to file for a hardship case. This letter is a sign. This is so ironic."

Jaime Perez

I handed the letter over to V; she read it and exuded a tear that dropped onto the letter. It didn't take her quite as long to read the letter as it did for me. "This is good right? I mean…you don't have to go back…do you?" She asked with a tone of overabundant hope and uncertain optimism.

I didn't want to get my hopes up too high, but the letter did sound promising. I was being asked to drive to San Antonio to personally apply for a hardship case. This allowed me to stay closer to home yet still complete my tour of duty. I wasn't too sure if a hardship case, such as mine, had ever been turned down. I was assuming that my chances of being granted a hardship case were promising; otherwise, I wouldn't have received this letter.

"If I am granted this hardship case, and I stress the word 'if", then I will likely be able to serve my tour of duty here upstate. Anything is better than having to go back to Vietnam."

Just as I was about to turn to look at V, she violently and ardently embraced me harder than I thought she was capable. "When can you apply?" She eagerly and unabashedly asked.

"Well, I can go today. The day is still young. We don't have anything planned today, do we?"

"No, not really." V responded with slight excitement.

San Antonio was approximately a 4-hour drive. I could drive up there, submit my paperwork, and arrive back home a little after sundown. Normally, I wouldn't find being on the road for a total of 8-hours to be very appealing, but this grueling drive would be different. It would be fueled by anticipation, possible liberation and excitement.

"Then I will go today." I knew that V wasn't too fond of traveling by car for any extended period of time, so I refrained from asking if she would like to accompany me. Without further delay, I got dressed and gathered my things to begin my spontaneous trip to San Antonio in hopes of having my military-assigned noose loosened for the duration of my service. Minutes later, I was kissing V goodbye and starting up my Corvette.

Throughout the entire solitary drive, I felt my heart racing faster than it had since the day we were ambushed, literally minutes after arriving in Long Binh. I could swear that I felt my heartbeat lightly tapping at my sternum. I was very hopeful and confident that I would be granted a hardship case. My wife was in need of me, and my infant son just passed away. Wouldn't this be the epitome of hardship? How could I be denied? Surely even a heartless brute would empathize with me in a situation like this.

As much as I tried not to worry about being denied a hardship case, I could do little to thwart the persistent onus. Not even the usually reliable radio with all its volume could sidetrack my burdensome thoughts. My plan was to simply keep driving non-stop until I arrived in San Antonio. I would worry about eating on the way home. I had been in San Antonio quite a few times before, and although I wasn't exactly too sure about where I was to arrive for my hardship application, the address on the letter sounded strikingly familiar. I think I remember the address from the time I had to report to Fort Sam Houston in San Antonio for my military physical before even being considered for military service.

Town after town and city after city, my destination was slowly within my desperate and anxious reach. When I had previously arrived home, I was hopeless and dejected. I was previously fed up with life and all of its haltering hardships, which had attempted to choke me to the point of lifelessness. Now, although I was still tender and fragile from Gilbert's passing, an invisible yet undeniable force of hope and possibility was driving my desire to fan away the dark, dense hovering clouds of dismay and make room for the delightfully brilliant rays of renewal and optimism.

I had lost complete track of time. For the duration of most my drive, I was lost in thought, but I was quickly brought back to reality. Had it not been for the street sign that read, "Entering San Antonio City Limits", I may have driven past my destination in obliviousness. I looked at my watch; I had been on the road for a little over 3 hours. My efficient and advantageous plan to drive without hindrance proved to be a wise approach. Now that I was gradually entering the bustling city limits of San Antonio, I reached for the letter I had received this morning to glance at the address of the offices I was to visit; it read 1432 San Pedro Avenue. Just as I directed my attention to the winding and intersecting routes before me, I noticed the exit sign for San Pedro Avenue. I immediately veered left to avoid passing it; within minutes, I was there.

I parked my Corvette in the only vacant parking space available. My hands were sweaty and spots of perspiration were profusely gushing out from my forehead. I looked in the rearview mirror, and I appeared to have just completed a grueling marathon in the middle of the Texas heat on a summer day. I wiped my faced with a napkin I had in my car. I was nervous, but I really didn't know why. I guess I was just worried about not being granted a hardship case, even though my current situation would seem to beg for it.

I didn't want to waste anymore time, so I shook off the nerves and

Jaime Perez

exited my vehicle. Just as I was about to open the door to the offices, I realized I had forgotten the all-important letter in the car. I quickly returned to my vehicle and grabbed the letter from the passenger's seat. This letter was my ticket to freedom, at least I hoped it was.

"Can I help you sir?" A young lady with a warm smile asked as I approached her information desk.

"Hi. I received this letter in the mail, and I would like to find out some information about filing for a hardship case."

The lady took the letter and read it. Apparently she decided to re-read it because it took her some time until she returned it to me with her eyes watery. "Follow me sir." She requested with a shaky, frail voice.

She took me to a room and asked me to wait for the individual in charge of this type of procedure. I sat on a comfortable and rather elegant black, leather couch in front of an oak desk as I waited eagerly. The scenario reminded me of the time I met with Sergeant Major Dyer back in Vietnam as he mentioned my son's passing. The display of the U.S. flags on the two opposite corners behind the wooden desk heightened the similarities between the two situations. After about two minutes, a tall, thin man walked in and introduced himself.

"Hello. I'm Mr. Simms. I understand you are here to apply for a hardship case. Is that right?" He asked as he shook my moist hand and glared at me intently through his thick bi-focal eyeglasses.

"Yes that is correct sir. I also have this." I answered as I handed him my letter without further waiting.

"Where did you get this?" He asked as he glanced through the letter with obvious perfunctoriness.

"I received it in the mail sir." I answer, not understanding the relevance of the question. "Is there a problem with the letter sir?"

"Not at all. It's just that a letter like this is usually requested, especially when it's from a state representative. I guess somebody did you the favor of requesting it. Either that or God is working in his mysterious ways again." He heathenishly said with a somewhat sacrilegious sarcasm. "Fill this out. When you are done, leave it on my desk along with your letter. If you are granted your request, you will be notified in the mail in the next few business days. Oh, and I'm sorry for your loss." He impassively expressed with about as much sincere sympathy as a cockroach, as he half scampered out in an obvious hurry to resume whatever important task he was previously engaged in before my inconvenient arrival interrupted him.

Within a few minutes I was done filling out the two-sided form. While filling it out, I couldn't help but wonder how this letter ended up in my hands. Who requested this? I simply thought that it was sent to me because my situation may have become known within the military, but then I realized that the military was always in need of soldiers; therefore they probably wouldn't encourage the dismissal of a soldier unless it was requested and absolutely necessary and justifiable.

For some reason, I was under the delusion that completing the necessary paperwork for my hardship case would appease my aggrieving anxiousness. I guess I was expecting an immediate response to my request; now I had to wait all over again. I placed both sheets of paper under a paperweight on Mr. Simms' cluttered desk that looked as if it had been struck by Hurricane Beulah, twice. That was it. The purpose of my multiple-hour drive to San Antonio was fulfilled in less than 10 minutes. Now I had to drive back home with more unanswered questions and more unsettling uncertainty than I had when I came up here. I felt as if I had taken one step forward, only to find myself three steps back. With my luck, I would probably receive word of my hardship acceptance after I flew back to Long Binh and therefore be kept overseas to complete my tour.

Before beginning my drive home, I stopped for a burger and took a leak so that I could resume my return non-stop. I had told myself that I wasn't going to worry about anything that I couldn't control and therefore, I would do my best not to needlessly burden myself with the outcome of this disappointing adventure. I was going to valiantly attempt to cherish my time back home with my grieving wife. Whatever happens happens. That's really what it boils down to. Three and a half lonely and radioless hours later, I was at the doorstep of our apartment. As I unlocked the door, I noticed all the lights were off, and all I could hear was the echoing silence. It was early evening and much too early for V to be asleep. I tried to blindly make my way to our bedroom through the gibbous hallway to avoid waking V if she indeed was asleep; she wasn't. She wasn't even home. Being that we only had one vehicle, I extrapolated that my sisters or Mom and Pop probably picked her up to help take her mind off of things.

Whenever V would leave somewhere, she would often place a note held with a magnet on the refrigerator door explaining her whereabouts. Since I hadn't glanced towards the refrigerator when I walked in, I naturally went to the kitchen to look for such a note. As I somewhat expected, she was at her parents' house.

Jaime Perez

I am at Mom's. Miss you. V

The ungodly and arduous drive left me drained and in much need of a bed, but I had to pick V up from my in-laws' before even beginning to consider getting any rest. After washing my face to help splash a little liveliness in me, I got back in my 'Vette and headed to Virginia's and Al's. I felt a little disappointed that I had driven for almost a third of a day and had no clue as to what my future held. Like much of my life thus far, I was forced to wait, and without the luxury of a choice, wait was exactly what I did.

Chapter 32

As I turned the corner to enter my in-laws' neighborhood, I could see V and my in-laws sitting on lawn chairs on the front yard, Al reading the newspaper and Virginia sipping on a glass of what was probably homemade iced tea. V's parents liked to spend quality time together outdoors, even if it was just to bask in the stifling Texas humidity that was often unbearable to visitors or outsiders. Before I had a chance to turn off the ignition, V was anxiously standing by the car door.

"Well, what did they say?" She asked immediately after releasing me from a firm hug.

"I should be getting some kind of notice in the mail or a phone call in the next few days. Hardship cases aren't granted immediately upon receiving a request." I responded.

"What do they need to do that takes a few days to determine approval?" She asked with a bit of warranted agitation.

"I honestly don't know Baby. We'll just wait and see." I said as I resumed to hug my in-laws.

"Good afternoon Mr. and Mrs. Saenz."

"Welcome back son. How was the drive?" Al asked.

"Not bad, just a little tiring."

"Well, you made it back safe. That's what matters." Virginia positively added as I took the extra chair next to them and anticipatorily threw my weary corpse on it.

"Something was brought to my attention regarding my letter."

"What letter?" Al asked with attentive concern.

"The letter I received from our state representative in the mail this morning. It was somewhat of a reference letter stating my case, kind of like a proof of my situation. The funny thing is that these letters aren't just mailed out; they are requested. Mr. Simms, the cold man I spoke to in San

Jaime Perez

Antonio, brought this to my attention. Someone had to have submitted paperwork or requested this for me. It wasn't by any chance you, was it?" I asked my in-laws, hoping for an answer to this possibly life-changing mystery.

"No, it wasn't us. I wish I could say it was us, but I can't." Al truthfully answered.

"It has to be somebody we know, somebody who was aware of our situation." V deduced.

"That's is exactly what makes this even more awkward. Somebody did this for me, or for us, and I have nobody to thank. I was just expecting to come for Gilbert's funeral, spend a few extra days here, and return to Vietnam. Filing for a hardship case would have totally slipped my mind, especially with everything else on my mind. If I am granted this hardship case, or even if I am denied, I feel indebted to at least show some gratitude for such a kind and thoughtful act."

"Somebody is bound to mention it sooner or later." Virginia added with a tone of practicality.

"You must be tired. Are you ready to go home?" V asked.

"Actually I feel very worn out. A cozy bed would be nothing short of germane.

"Then let's get going so you can rest." V suggested.

"All right. May I use your restroom before we leave Mr. and Mrs. Saenz?" I asked unnecessarily to show respect.

"Of course. Go ahead Son; you know where it is." Al affirmed.

I made my way to the restroom and relieved myself. I splashed a little more water on my face to prolong my cognizance at least until I arrived home. I had black bags under both my eyes; I looked more dead than alive. I now knew why Virginia and Al had a peculiar look on their faces when I first approached them outside. The day's drive was relentlessly continuing to take its toll on me. On my way to the front door, I walked through my in-laws' living room and noticed stacks of newspapers scattered on a corner table. They must have been from previous days because I had keenly noticed that Al was reading today's paper. I thought this was particularly odd because Virginia was not the kind of woman who would allow a stack of old newspapers to accumulate in any part of her home, especially one that is clearly visible to company. She was too tidy for such inexcusable unsightliness. One of the corners of a newspaper was jutting out more than the rest, so I, for some odd reason, grabbed that particular edition and began skimming through it desultorily. I wasn't really reading any of the

248

articles or looking at any of the pictures; I was just flipping through the pages as if I had taken a course in speed reading, yet I was not retaining any of the information before me. As if my hands were being inexplicably manipulated, I abruptly stopped grazing through the paper and arrived at a page that appeared to be of no interest to me. I began hastily skimming the articles when I came across a group of bold-faced words that almost knocked me to the ground. I wisely sat myself on the adjacent couch to catch my breath and maintain my composure. I knew I was exhausted and in dire need of rest; therefore, I might be a little incoherent, so I took another reaffirming glance at the heart-stopping article heading to make sure my eyes were not playing tricks on me. Although I couldn't believe what I was reading, I couldn't take my eyes off the page. I was visually glued to the paper by shock and disbelief. Before reading any further, I needed reassurance that I was not going insane.

"V!!!! Come here now." I commandingly bellowed from my in-laws' living room with an unintentionally impudent tone. I never addressed V in such a rude and disrespectful manner, much less do so in front of her parents. I was in a state of utter confusion, and I was beginning to feel dizzy.

"What? What's the matter?" V came concernedly running in with her parents half a step behind her.

I didn't speak for a few seconds; I couldn't. I just gazed without blinking straight ahead into nothingness. V grabbed my hand; it was then that I noticed I was slightly trembling. The newspaper had fallen to the ground, as did my soundness. I wanted to explain to them what I had just come to realize, but my mute words failed to project even the faintest of tones. For a moment, everything felt like a picture, still and free from the unwavering and inconvenient restraints of time. Then, the clock began to tick again. I was beginning to breathe normally, and my mental whirlwind had subsided for the moment.

"Baby talk to me. You are scaring me. What's wrong?" V sounded worried.

"I'm sorry." I said as I deeply rubbed my eyes in hopes of restoring my equanimity.

"What's wrong Son?" Al asked as my mother-in-law approached me with a cold glass of water.

"Somebody please read this article to me." I requested as I picked up the paper from the floor and pointed at the article with my face turned away.

Jaime Perez

V was too concerned with my unexpected behavior that she didn't even take her eyes off of me. Al grabbed the newspaper and seemed to skim the section for the correct article. It took him a while to begin reading. He had likely noticed what it was that had left me momentarily disturbed and shocked because after about a minute he said, "Oh my God!"

"What is it Daddy? What the hell is going on? What does the paper say?" V was beginning to sound agitated and upset at all the uncertainty.

My father-in-law looked over at me with obvious disbelief. He then glanced over to Virginia and V and noticed their justified exasperation. It was their revealing facial expressions that wordlessly screamed for some kind of explanation. This compelled him to read the article, this time aloud. He looked at me one more time before reading as he cleared his throat.

Violence in Vietnam Continues

The death toll overseas continues to increase as hundreds of American soldiers at the US Army Base in Long Binh, Vietnam were killed in a surprise ambush. According to military personnel, the ambush occurred on March 31, 1969 at approximately 0600 hrs. All the recovered bodies will be arriving back to the United States and Puerto Rico for proper burials. An unidentified spokesman for the U.S. Army described the attack as "devastating and unavoidable". "Our condolences go out to the families of the following incomplete list of fallen heroes: Captain Wesley H. Smith, Private First Class Jose Hernandez, Lieutenant James Crowe, Private First Class Lester W. Branch, Sergeant William M. Johnson,...

Without warning, my father-in-law suddenly stopped reading before reaching the end of the list. He looked at me once again as if wanting to ask me what I expected him to ask, but he remained speechless even though he appeared to have a mouthful to say. His curiosity must have been too strong for him to finish the article. He had read enough.

"Why did you stop?" V asked her father before turning her attention to me. "Where those your friends Baby?" She asked me, oblivious to the details of the article.

Whenever I would write my letters, I would always include my base name or location at the top right-hand corner. It was a habit that Capelletti had instilled in me back at Ft. Sill. He used to always include this information in his correspondence just in case something were to happen to his group and the names of soldiers were lost, forgotten or misprinted when mentioned in the papers back home. Al had apparently paid close attention to the details in my correspondence, especially the upper-right hand corner, because he obviously made the subtle connection between the article and my letters.

While V's consternation was intensifying and Al and I were sitting like stones staring at one another, Virginia had gone to a drawer in the kitchen and pulled out one of my past letters from a month before. She had caught on to what had rendered Al and I inanimate as well as to what we were thinking.

"That's your group Beltran, isn't it?" She asked me as she showed Al the letter, pointing to the upper-right hand corner.

V instinctively and somewhat angrily grabbed the letter from her mother's hand and gazed at it as it shook unsteadily in her hand. She too was now as dazed as the rest of us. She finally grasped the reason for our shared stupefaction and eventually joined the three of us in our moment of shared trauma. Everyone was completely silent; all I could hear was my heartbeat as it pounded resonantly through me, sending vibratory sensations throughout my body. I felt like I wanted to cry, laugh and scream all at the same time, but my mind was unable to transmit the cluster of dissimilar reactions to the rest of my body. Instead, I just sat there lifeless, like the pile of North Vietnamese corpses that would accumulate at an alarming rate directly outside my barracks' window in Long Binh.

Without thinking I broke the silence and bluntly uttered, "That was my company. I was supposed to be there. It happened the very next day after I was allowed to return home. I literally evaded death by a few hours."

V sat next to me and didn't say a word. She didn't have to; her firm and fervent embrace expressed her unspoken appreciation for my being alive. Seconds later, both my in-laws joined their daughter in hugging me. As we huddled together overwhelmed by disbelief and emotion, I couldn't help but feel badly about not knowing more of the listed soldiers on a more personal level. We slept under the same roof, and I didn't recognize most of the names. I could only faintly mentally envision the jacket name patches of the few names I did recall. If I hadn't haphazardly grabbed this particular edition of the local newspaper, I may have overlooked the entire article and continued the rest of my life oblivious to my miraculous fortunateness. I realized that my chances of surviving this ambush would have been very slim.

I honestly wasn't prepared for what I had just learned, and I couldn't

Jaime Perez

ignore the frequentness of which death was affluently blossoming into my slowly dwindling world like unwanted weeds, leaving their unmerciful unpleasantness to test my willpower and soundness. The government had taken away the latter part of my teen years; disease had taken away my son, and North Vietnamese adversaries had killed hundreds of soldiers from my assigned Army base. It was easy to succumb to death and drown in its perennially undulating crimson waves. Many soldiers have lost their sanity and therefore lost control of their lives by dangerously and often unintentionally becoming victim to the cancer-like enervation that resides in one's dark and inhumane recollections. For whatever reason, I was alive and given a chance to continue living as normal a life as I possibly could after all that I had been through. At that very instant, I had decided that I would conquer every obstacle of sadness and climb over every wall of regressiveness that would dare appear before me.

Like coming out of hypnotic trance, I suddenly shook myself to normalcy and departed the reflective world of damaging memories. V and my in-laws simultaneously let go of me and each took a step back to observe what was happening to me. I felt the relief one feels when resurfacing after holding one's breath underwater for as long as possible. It was an invigorating and enlivening sensation that brought goose bumps to my skin. I was breathing in deep breaths.

"What's the matter? Are you okay?" V asked with concern as she obviously noticed a change in my character.

Al added, "It felt as if you were coming back from an out-of-the-body experience. There was a surge from within you that almost gave off the sensation of a harmless electric shock. Did you feel that as well?" Al asked V and Virginia.

"I did feel something pull me away." Virginia responded as V just slowly nodded in agreement amidst her dubiety.

"I feel fine. Everything is fine. Don't worry about me. I'm the one who survived the ambush and made it home for the time being." In a sudden change of tone and subject, I added, "I feel really good about being granted that hardship case. I don't why, but I do."

"Let's hope so." Al said as he put his hand on my shoulder.

"Are you ready to go home V?" I asked as my restlessness started to make its presence felt again.

"Yes, I am ready when you are." V responded in a partial state of stupefaction.

"Mr. and Mrs. Saenz, do you mind if I keep this portion of the newspaper? I would really like to keep it as a memento of my good fortune."

"Sure, take it. I meant to throw it away after I read it, but I just hadn't gotten around to it." Al responded. As he handed me the entire newspaper I realized the advantageousness of his uncommon procrastination. It was almost as if I was randomly meant to find and read the article.

"Thanks." I said as I got up off the couch to prepare to leave while noticing that V was still trying to comprehend what had just happened. She looked benumbed and silently got up to kiss her parents goodbye. I did the same, and soon after we continued home. I had a gut feeling that V had so much to say, or so much to ask, but she remained silent for the duration of our short drive home. She held the folded newspaper on her lap and appeared to endure the entire drive without a blink or without a breath, totally lifeless and robotic. I knew my wife; if she wanted to talk about something, she would bring it up herself. Her silence would likely subside once we arrived home.

We both made our way to the doorstep as I began to get the door key out to open the door. As I shuffled through the keys, V grabbed my hand firmly and looked at me with utter dread and profound trepidation. I could feel she was trembling as she began to speak.

"I need to tell you something." She finally broke her silence.

"All right. Go ahead." I granted.

"Not out here. Let's go inside. You may want to sit down for this." V instructed as she grabbed the keys from my hand and quickly unlocked our apartment door. I was beginning to feel a lucid yet intangible tension, the kind of uneasy tension that is often coupled with uncertainty. My stomach was beginning to make funny noises, and I suddenly acquired a loss of appetite even though I didn't remember when I had eaten last. I sat on the couch and waited for V to join me. She finally did, and before she began speaking, she took an impressive sigh.

Chapter 33

The phone in the kitchen rang once, and V raced to answer it before I was even able to begin getting up from the couch. Judging by V's responses, I assumed that it was her parents checking to see if we arrived home okay.

"Yes. We just walked in a minute ago. Sure. OK Mom. I love you too." She quickly hung up the phone with a force bordering on a slam. "That was Mom checking to make sure we made it home all right."

"So, what did you want to tell me that is so staggering that I have to sit down?" I asked V with calmness even though I was trying my best to conceal my growing curiosity.

V looked as if she was trying to mentally choose her words before uttering them, and this process took her a short while. After several seconds of contemplation and continued silence, she apparently gave up on the idea of scheming the delivery of her disclosure.

"I don't know how to say this without seeming weird, so I am just going to say it however it comes out."

"Okay, I'm all ears." I said.

"I dreamt the tragedy that occurred to your company. I've had many dreams and nightmares before, but none of them have matched the realistic feeling that this one had. I saw the bloodshed, heard the gunfire, and it seemed that I could even smell the stink of blood. It was horrible Beltran. It was as if I was witnessing the entire attack from a bird's-eye view. I could see everything so disturbingly clear. Vietnamese soldiers were shooting American soldiers even after the American soldiers were obviously dead, almost as if using the soldiers' lifeless corpses for target practice. Some were shoving grenades in the mouths of some of the American soldiers and piling them up face down while they waited for the grenades to go off to scatter the bodies so they could eagerly and excitedly view the mangled and marred remains. One of the Vietnamese soldiers was carrying a camera instead of a gun. It seemed that his sole purpose was to take pictures of the Vietnamese soldiers posing with dead American soldiers. It was like a big bloody game; they were laughing and enjoying themselves like carefree children at a play park. After a while, the ground looked like a garden of shredded corpses. Not one American soldier was left breathing. I woke up in the middle of the night crying from what I had subconsciously witnessed as well as crying from the little comfort of the fact that I didn't see you slaughtered in my dream."

"Why didn't you tell me anything?" I asked concernedly as I brushed her hair away from her face.

"I didn't want to further agitate our situation. We had just returned from the funeral, and I didn't see any reason to bring up a silly nightmare that I felt had no substantial significance. Besides, you were sleeping next to me, so the nightmare wasn't as terrifying as it would have been had you still been in Vietnam. Please don't be upset." She responded.

"I'm not upset." I assured V. Then I realized something. "Wait a minute. You dreamt this the night of the funeral, after we buried Gilbert?" I asked as I began to yield calculations in my head.

"Yes, why?" V asked with one solitary tear flowing down her cheek.

"You might have been dreaming this at about the time it was actually happening!" I answered.

"I didn't think of that." V said with surprise. "I didn't want to say anything to you at first, but after you found that article in the newspaper, I felt I had to share this with you because it was just remarkably coincidental." She explained.

"Yes. The dream itself is a remarkable coincidence, but dreaming it as it is occurring, which may have very well been the case, is beyond a remarkable coincidence. It is impossible, yet it seemingly became possible." I said, as I was about to get up to get V a glass of water.

"And…" V said, grabbing my arm and pulling me back down to her. "I had another dream that same evening."

"A dream or a nightmare?" I asked.

"A dream. I dreamt that you were granted a hardship case, and you didn't have to go back Vietnam. The weird thing is that you couldn't stay here; you were sent somewhere else other than Vietnam. This dream was more like constant visual flashes that seemed to randomly appear over and over again until I woke up. It was like a series of broken thoughts, but it was enough for me understand what was happening."

"And you dreamt this the same night?"

Jaime Perez

"Yes. That's the weird part." She added as she nodded in agreement, obviously thinking the same thing I was.

"Very weird because I hadn't even received the letter from our state representative in the mail yet. The letter arrived the following day." I said as V and I stared at each other for a short while.

"It's all so surreal that it has me feeling a little uneasy from the awkwardness." V explained.

I didn't know what else to say because I too was overtaken by V's divinatory and premonitory manifestations. So I said the first thing that came out of my mouth. "Well let's hope that your dream about the hardship case comes true; that would be a nice diversion into a more optimistic and pleasant future. We've had enough grief for two lifetimes." I said as I kissed V on her wet cheek, momentarily comforting her with my affection.

Several days had passed, 8 to be exact, and I was now halfway though my military-granted borrowed time. I was only allowed 16 days for the funeral leave, and I was beginning to worry about the granting of my hardship case more and more with each dissipating day. I began to wonder whose brilliant idea it was to boldly calculate that 16 days is an ample amount of time for a father to move on with his life in hopes of achieving some semblance of normalcy after burying his child. How are these numbers decided? Who votes on these types of things? Surely, these ignoramuses have never had a child or have never witnessed the crippling displeasure of living through what I am.

I lay in bed with my hand behind my head, detachedly staring at the ceiling before me as V breathed heavily in her sleep. I could tell by the light penetrating through the maroon bedroom curtains that it was a little later than our usual wake-up time. If V didn't have a good reason to get up, she could sleep endlessly. I, on the other hand, had a capricious sleep schedule that most soldiers unfortunately contracted like an inconveniently non-fatal disease or condition that one learns to eventually live with, like diabetics or asthmatics, except we didn't have anything to help us cope with our conditions other than perseverance, or suicide if that was one's preferred remedy. War was enough to drive even the most solidly sound soldier to insanity, and if you mix this with the paranoia, hallucinations and incoherence from sleep deprivation, it quickly becomes the deadliest concoction one could attempt to swallow.

I don't recall the soldier's name, but one of the men in my company in Vietnam who has probably passed away used to always say, "The one thing the government forgot to implement in basic training and boot camp was

Through You

a much-needed training in sleep deprivation." He used to always utter this notion as if it were something new that none of us had heard from him before. Because of this, I believe he was nicknamed "Sleepy", but I never did learn his real name. Although I am not sure if such training or coping methods exist, Sleepy did have a legitimate and interesting point because every soldier I ever met, even those who claimed that they weren't afraid to die, had an impossible time trying to sleep with the nearby sounds of explosives and gunfire that were likely intended for them or anyone else on the same side of this war.

It was already passed noon, and I realized that I was not going to have the luxury of achieving another restful sleep. I hated lying in bed wastefully, even when ill and especially when my visit had its time constraints. I decided to get up and once again check the mail as I had everyday since my return from San Antonio but this time with the hopes that I would receive some news about my hardship case.

I walked to the apartment mailboxes in my wrinkled sleeping attire without a care of what anybody who saw me thought. Nothing, our box was empty. I instinctively slammed the mailbox door shut and began to make my way back to bed with V, while hiding the slight disappointment from the lack of news. As I approached our apartment door, I noticed a familiar, rustling sound approaching down the street, but its source didn't quite register in my head. I ignored the sound until I arrived at our doorstep and slowly looked back; it was our mailman in his weathered and aged yet reliable mail-carrying vehicle. He must have been running behind schedule because the mail was always delivered by this time. I walked back to the mailboxes and greeted our cheerful mailman who I hadn't seen since before I became swallowed in the military life. He had been our mailman ever since V and me moved to these apartments. His name was Charlie, which was simple to remember because he had a dark moustache like Charlie Chaplin. This always left me wondering whether Charlie was his real name or simply a nickname that he eventually and probably reluctantly accepted after realizing that it could not be shunted away. Regardless, all the tenants called him Charlie, and he always cheerfully responded without seeming to be bothered or irritated.

"Morning Charlie." I mistakenly greeted him.

"You mean good afternoon Mr. Perez. I am running a little late today, as I am sure you noticed. Here is your mail. How are you and the Mrs. holding up?" He asked.

257

Jaime Perez

"We are doing as well as we can considering the circumstances." I answered.

With a sincere and morose look, he said, "My condolences to and your family Mr. Perez. If there is anything I can do, please, don't hesitate to ask."

"Thank you Charlie." I said as I made my way back to the apartment with my mail in hand.

"Tell your father I said, 'Hello'"! He yelled as I reached for the doorknob.

"I will." I loudly responded and waved back with my free hand. Charlie and Pop had gone to grade school together, and Charlie never let me forget it. I tried to slowly creep back inside to avoid waking up V.

"You will what?" V asked as she sneakily embraced me before I could completely turn myself around after closing the door behind me.

"I will tell Pop that Charlie says, 'Hello', again." I responded with my attention not entirely on V but on a tan envelope stamped *URGENT.* V must have noticed my profound gazing at the envelope as I probably appeared to be temporarily paralyzed and immobile.

"Go ahead; open it." V excitedly ordered in much the same way as she did whenever she was surprised about giving me a gift and wanting to see my reaction. "I want to know if I am psychic or not."

I was really surprised at how calmly she was taking this. Normally this was a nail-biting and breath-holding situation for V but not this time.

"Why don't YOU open it?" I asked as I slowly handed V the envelope.

Without thinking twice about it, she grasped it from my hand and began tearing it immediately. It didn't take her very long from the time she took the letter to the time she read enough of the letter to know whether or not I was granted or denied the hardship case, but when your heart is at a momentary standstill, seconds seem like minutes.

For several seconds, V didn't speak, didn't smile, didn't laugh, didn't cry, didn't anything. Her objectivity was strikingly unexpected. For a while, I thought V was trying to mentally construct exactly how to deliver the disappointing news. It wasn't until she jumped on me like a lion on a helpless and unsuspecting gazelle and flattened me on my back that she gave any type of disclosure.

"I knew it!!!! I knew it!!!!," was all she said as she clenched my helpless body on the living room floor. A reaction like this could only mean one thing. I was granted the hardship case.

258

"So does this mean I've been denied?" I sarcastically managed to utter through the shortness of breath I had acquired from both the anticipation and the unforeseen yet amorous trampling with which V landed on me.

"I'm not at liberty to say Officer Perez. This is classified information that I am unable to share with you at this time." V playfully said with an unconvincing deep voice and a lip pouting as if trying to imitate a male soldier.

"Oh yeah. Well maybe this will help you share the information." I said as I started to tickle V on her rib cage, a weakness to which she conveniently had no defense.

After I resumed the torture for a few more seconds, she resumed with her soldier-like mimicry and said, "Officer Perez, I believe you have been granted your hardship case as requested. Congratulations, you have been given your life back."

"I think the receiving of this news doesn't make you a psychic; it made you a clown!"

"A psychic clown. Thank you very much." V corrected me.

"There's an interesting combination." I said as I reached for the letter and began meticulously reading it for myself. After rereading the letter, I confessed to V, "I have married my very own female Nostradamus."

My first instinct was to call my parents, my in-laws and my sisters to inform them of the pleasant news. I must have taken more time to repeatedly read the letter than I thought because V was getting off the phone from making her 2nd phone call; I hadn't even realized that she had made a previous first phone call.

"Who did you call?" I asked with a smile.

"I called your parents and mine. I just need to call your sisters. I promised everybody that I would call them to give them the news as soon as we knew for ourselves. I am just keeping my promise." She simultaneously answered and dialed one of my sister's phone numbers.

Although receiving this news was nothing short of rapturous, I began to experience a slight feeling of guilt. I had just buried my son a few days ago, and here I was feeling joy and elation so soon after Gilbert's burial. I didn't feel right about feeling happy. Betrayal and ignominy began to slowly permeate through me like a life-sucking, virulent toxin with the ability to control one's thoughts and feelings. This was supposed to be a moment of relief, contentment, and hope; instead, I felt a compressing stomachache, and a subtle nausea was beginning to loom inside me. V was busy on the phone laughing and jumping up and down like a child as

Jaime Perez

she fulfilled her promise. I didn't want to spoil her, I mean, our moment, so I did my best to conceal my discouraging disagreeableness and wear a façade of favorable fortuity for the time being. Although I was pretty sure I would be able to successfully screen my external temperament, it was my churning and rankling insides that were going to be much more problematic and challenging to contain.

Chapter 34

Although the granting of the hardship case was something to cheer about, I still wasn't completed exonerated of my military obligation. My tour of duty would resume in San Antonio at Fort Sam Houston at the end of my funeral leave. As far as leading a normal, civilian life goes, this was going to be as close to normal as I would be afforded, at least for the next few years. Anything was better than returning to Long Binh.

I still had close to a week left of my funeral leave, but oddly enough, I was longing for my leave to conclude. It wasn't so much that I didn't want to be here with my family because that had nothing to do with my wishes; it was more of the need to move on with my life, finish my tour of duty, and attempt to make my life as sound and salubrious as I could. I was desperate to see how things were going to turn out. I wanted to know that things were going to be all right, but I couldn't even manage to mentally construct a picture of a favorable future without ultimately thinking that I was being overly optimistic and unrealistic. As soon as I can put these tragic times behind me, then, and only then, will I be able to realize what lies ahead for V and me. The sour and dry aftertaste of sadness was still lingering in my mouth, and I was unable to spit it out. Only time could yield me with this satisfying luxury that bordered on being a necessity, and the uncertainty and volatility of my future, along with my guilt for feeling an inkling of ephemeral joy, were beginning to devour me from the inside out.

"Come on. We are meeting at your parents' house in 15 minutes to celebrate your news." V slammed the phone down and ordered as she dashed to the bedroom to apparently get dressed.

The last thing I felt like doing right now was the very thing I was about to do. It would be utterly rude to refuse to show up to a small family gathering in my honor, so I half-unwillingly and half-graciously succumbed to the tenacity of forced acquiescence. If I could somehow

Jaime Perez

manage to conquer and soar over the vast, internal mountains of guilt that were presently impeding me from moving on, everything would be fine.

The night slowly and painfully crawled on like a lost and legless soldier in sand, but I managed to endure the evening's all but festive occasion. My unsettling ungraciousness was unnoticed as I did my best to disguise my unlikely dispiritedness. For a little over 2 hours, we sat and discussed everything about nothing in my parents' living room. That evening, it was decided that V would initially stay with me onsite in San Antonio every other week so that she wouldn't be alone at home so much.

For the remaining days of my leave, V and I did nothing but begin packing things and driving them up to San Antonio during the day, and driving back home during the evening. I had to complete some paperwork to make the granting of my hardship case official, so I did that the first chance I got. Soon after, we drove to our new temporary home, Fort Sam Houston. I was allowed to begin transferring my things even though I wasn't expected to be there for another 5 days.

"I guess once you've seen one Army base, you've seen them all." V lightly and understandably uttered to me as she wiped her hair away from her eyes and stood in the relatively brilliant December Texas sun, gazing at the surroundings, acknowledging and accepting all their familiar blandness.

Without saying anything, I simply smiled at V's comment and was suddenly overcome by a flurry of anxiousness. This is what I had wanted, the beginning of a new chapter in my life, in our lives. A new decade was upon us, and for the first time in quite a long while, I was looking forward to the future with hopefulness and anticipation. I kept my newfound excitement to myself; otherwise, V would have probably thought I was going insane, especially with such a display of genuine mirth at an unexpected time like this.

To facilitate matters a bit, my sisters kindly made the remaining trips to San Antonio with us in another vehicle packed with my necessities and V's luxuries. What would have taken 5 days only took 2 instead. This gave us time to enjoy V's and my last day at home with our families. This time I wasn't hiding any unwanted sentiments; thus, the bona fide smiles and carefree laughter came easily.

I was officially to report onsite in San Antonio to my superior by 0500 hours on Wednesday, and although it was only Monday, V and I had decided to leave early in the afternoon tomorrow to minimize the tediousness associated with the drive. This still allowed us some time to spend with our families before leaving. As we sat on my parents' couch, I realized it was getting a little late when V subtly gave me the familiar look she always gives me when she is about ready to put an end to a day's events. Just as I was about to verbally suggest to everyone that V and I needed to leave, my parents' phone rang, and Mom raced for it. I decided to hold off on our departure until Mom was off the phone. I wasn't paying any particular attention to Mom's conversation, but apparently V was.

"Your mother is being rather grateful to whomever is on the other end of that phone." V whispered in my ear as everyone else resumed with their respective conversations.

Before I turned around to look at Mom, she gently called to me with tears in her eyes. "Son, somebody wants to talk to you."

"Oh shit, not again. Not more bad news, not now." I thought to myself as I made my way to the phone. I began to wonder who would be calling me at my parents' house. Mom tremulously handed me the phone with one hand as she wiped away her tears with the other and tried to manage a smile. I knew my mother well, and this smile was not a smile of pain or grief; it was definitely something else. The room was now as silent and as a soundless dream, and all my family's eyes followed me like a shadow with every step towards the phone. Mom handed me the phone and gently placed her hand on my cheek.

"Hello." I answered intriguingly.

"Welcome home soldier," said the person at the other end.

Immediately after hearing the first syllable I knew to whom I was speaking. It was my godmother Mary. I hadn't spoken to her since I was about 12 years old, but I knew without a doubt that it was her. She was a good childhood friend of Mom's who was unable to have children of her own because of some hereditary condition with her reproductive system. I never knew the exact details, but Mary would always tell Mom that if she could have a son, she would want him to be just like me. At that time, I never fully absorbed the magnitude of a comment like that, but now that I'm older, I realize the fondness and affinity that Mary had for me was ineffable. It was cruelly ironic because if anyone had the innate gift of being an exceptional mother it was definitely Mary. It was Mary who approached Mom about bearing the responsibility of becoming my godmother. She told Mom that it would be her honor to be granted the obligation. I don't see how Mom could have denied her request without feeling selfishly heartless. If there was anyone 'worthy' enough who Mom and Dad trusted to raise and care for me if anything terminal were to happen to them,

Jaime Perez

Mary was the one. Her sweet and unforgettable voice resonated through the phone and into my ear with aural delight like hearing once again from a special friend whom you didn't hear from too frequently but you knew you would vividly remember until the day your life ceased.

"Mary?" I rhetorically asked as I smiled and looked at Mom.

"Wow. How did you know?" She surprisingly asked with an unpretentious tone.

"I never forget the voices of those whom I hold dear."

"You sound so grown up now. The last time I spoke to you, you had that random pubescent squeakiness in your voice that everyone used to make fun of. Now you sound, I don't know, manly?" She said, and I couldn't help but laugh at her word choice.

"Yes Mary. I am manly and all grown up now." I assured her.

"Listen Beltran. I don't want to take up too much of your time because I know you are having family time together to commemorate your great news, and I am already up to my shoulders in long distance bills. I just wanted to make sure that your hardship was granted so that I could have some peace of mind."

Suddenly it dawned on me. "When did you talk to Mom or Pop? Mom didn't mention you calling recently. How did you know about the hardship case?" I asked even though I had a hunch what she was going to say. I just wanted to hear her say it. And she did.

"I haven't spoken to your parents in years, but I heard about your son's passing from my younger brother. I'm so sorry for you and Veronica, my condolences. I used to think that there was nothing worse than not being able to have any children of my own, but now I know that far worse things do exist. I had heard about the requesting of hardship cases and the process of doing so on some news program; I think it was *60 Minutes*. The process of submitting the paperwork seemed simple, so I went ahead and took the initiative and sent off the initial forms, putting your return address, which I acquired from my older brother."

Even though Mary had explained a lot, she left me with more questions than answers. I knew she had to hang up, so rather than prolong this conversation with questions, I did what I had to do, thanked her for literally saving my life and allowing me the chance to start a new one.

"Mary, I know you have to go. I just want to thank you from the bottom of my heart for doing this for me. I had so much on my mind that the last thing I was thinking about was filing for a hardship case. If not for you, I would be getting ready to fly back to Vietnam. It was hard enough

264

the first time, but I don't know if I would have been able to maintain my sanity a second time. Thank you."

"You're welcome Beltran. That's what godmothers do, watch over their godsons." She modestly responded. "Tell everyone there that I love them. Tell your mother that I will call her soon. It was a pleasure talking to you after all these years. I am only sorry that we couldn't speak more. Enjoy the gift of life Beltran. Goodbye."

"Yes, it was a pleasure Mary. Goodbye." I stood motionless with the phone in my hand and my back to my family for a while before hanging up the phone and mentally returning to my parents' living room as well as to my previous state of mind.

Finally, I now knew who had filed the initial paperwork that allowed me to be considered for the hardship case for which I was so grateful, but another question surfaced; who were Mary's brothers? As I spoke to Mary on the phone, I felt happy to hear her voice once again yet sad because she was not here with us to relish a moment for which she was primarily responsible. It was as if speaking to her over the phone exacerbated a compelling longing for her that now left me with a deep internal void. Mary treated me more like a son than some mothers treat their own sons. My godmother created an opportunity for me to have a fighting chance at a life with considerably less pugnacity, and I wasn't content with my display of gratitude over the phone or lack thereof. I hope I didn't come off as being ungrateful or shallow.

"Are you okay Son?" My Pop asked after noticing I hadn't said a word since Mary hung up the phone.

"I'm fine Pop." I answered with a slight smile in hopes of making my response more convincing and went straight to Mom in expected bewilderment. "That was Mary Pop."

"Yes, you're mother told us." Pop said.

"She was the one who submitted the paperwork for my hardship case." I mentioned, still in somewhat of a state of shock at the surprising revelation. I felt indebted to Mary, but felt incapable of doing anything about it. I had so much to say to her, yet I didn't even know when I would get the chance to speak to her again.

While I was speaking to Mary, Mom must have told everyone else about Mary's thoughtful deed because everybody was looking at me with partial smiles as if waiting for me to say something. I didn't know what to say. There was too much going on in my head that I couldn't contain the mental disjointedness long enough to allow myself to utter anything

Jaime Perez

relevant. I just simply laughed to myself, took a deep breath and tried to allow all this information to settle.

V kissed me on the cheek, and Mom followed right behind her and waited for me to say something to her. Even though I was still speechless, she innately knew something onerous was on my mind. After all, she was my mother, and detecting instincts was her proven mastery. She kept staring at me as if to somehow magically extract the thoughts from my head. Eventually, her magic worked.

"Mom, Mary mentioned some things to me that left me a little confused. She told me that her younger brother had mentioned Gilbert's passing to her and that her older brother had given her our home address for which to send the hardship paperwork, but our conversation transpired so abruptly that I didn't get to ask about her brothers. Do I know her brothers?" I asked Mom, almost certain that she held the answers I was seeking.

Mom looked towards Pop as they smiled at each other. That familiar motherly smile told me that Mom, as well as Pop, knew the answer to my questions. Even Virginia and Al leaked a subtle smirk, making me feel as if I was the victim of a friendly joke. The only ones who looked as confused and uncertain as I felt were V and my two sisters.

Mom finally answered. "Mary's brothers are Carlos and Fernando." Her response did nothing to appease my curiosity; it only exacerbated it.

"I'm afraid I still don't understand. Carlos and Fernando? Who are they?"

"I believe you may know one as Charlie and the other as Mr. Gomez." Mom revealed with no further enlightenment to me.

My resurgent perplexity must have become more apparent with my silent reaction, or lack of reaction. Suddenly, a light turned on, and it all became as clear as spotless glass.

"Do you mean Charlie the mailman and Fernando the owner of Gomez Photography?" I asked before Mom, Pop, Virginia and Al began to nod in agreement. By this point, my sisters and V had already figured out what I was just now piecing together as their smirks now resembled everyone else's.

Even though nobody verbally answered my questions and just gave me nods of affirmation, their smiles delivered a voiceless yet loud response that assured me I was correct. Charlie probably knew just about everyone's mailing address in his route, and Mr. Gomez probably spoke to V when she picked up our family portraits and likely kept in touch with Mom and Pop.

I can't say that I was previously losing significant sleep over the mystery of the submitted hardship case paperwork, but it was relieving to finally know how all this came to be. It was like not knowing the origin of human life and wondering how we got here or why we are here. One could still fully enjoy the sweet fruits of existence with such a burdensome and tremendous ignorance, but it would be comforting to be able to vanquish such pervasive ignorance once and for all.

The evening was young, but it seemed like an appropriate time to begin thinking about getting home to get some rest. I was somewhat physically fatigued from the multiple trips to San Antonio, not to mention the loading and unloading of heavy boxes. As if she could read my mind, which I wouldn't put past her, V reached for my hand, gazed into my eyes and suggested, "Do you think we should go home and get some rest? We have to get ready to begin our new life together, again."

"You don't have to be there until the day after tomorrow, don't you?" Al asked, surprising me with the fact that he hadn't forgotten that bit of information.

"Yes, but we have to be there at 0500 hrs, so we need to be settled in the day before." V responded as her response drew laughter from everybody in the room except her and me.

"What's so funny?" I asked as V and I looked at each other with befuddlement.

"Our daughter is starting to sound like a soldier now." Virginia responded between giggles.

After a few seconds, I realized V's use of military time was a little amusing. I had already gotten used to the terminology being used in my presence, but I can completely understand how the rest of our families would be a little amused by her comment, especially since V wasn't by any means trying to be funny. She was just obliviously revealing that she was the wife of a soldier, in her own cute way.

"That is probably a good idea. We would like to get there about noon and enjoy the rest of the day together to go sightseeing or maybe have a nice dinner." I responded as V quickly turned to me with a slight look of childish excitement.

"All right you two. You know how to reach us if you need anything." Pop said as everybody began lining up to give V and me warm embraces.

Jaime Perez

Mom began sobbing as she usually did during goodbyes or any other emotionally stirring event.

"I'm only 3 to 4 hours away Mom. You don't need to cry." I told her as I saved her embrace until the very end because I wanted to try to comfort her in any way I could before leaving.

"It's not how far away you are that tears me to pieces; it's simply the fact that you are away." She hugged me once again. I could feel her body trembling and quivering as if she were outside during a winter storm. I didn't know how to respond to Mom's comment, so I simply held her for a few seconds more without saying anything. I supposed my embrace did more to comfort her than anything I could have said.

"You all keep in touch frequently." Al ordered us with his authoritative fatherly voice.

"Oh we will. Love you guys." V and I responded in accordance as we waved goodbye and made our way to the door.

As we made our way to our almost vacant apartment, I got the optimistic feeling that things were going to work themselves out for the better. V and I had already embarked in this type of lifestyle before, being away from our parents while fulfilling my military obligations. There was one big difference though. When we had previously done this, it was only going to be a matter of time before I was to be deployed to a hellish Vietnam, many miles and hours away from home. This time, it was only going to be a matter of time before I would be released back home to resume where my previous civilian life had left off. This, I was looking forward to with utmost anticipation. A new and bright beginning was upon us; I could feel it and almost embrace it as if it were a tangible dream just waiting to come true.

Chapter 35

Before the sun protruded its brilliance the next day, V and I were ready to begin our drive. There wasn't much to take with us since the majority of what we were taking was already waiting for us in San Antonio. Much of V's belongings stayed behind since she was going to be coming back home every two weeks to help alleviate her with her proclivity of chronic homesickness. So after a quick breakfast and a filling up of fuel, we were on our way. V wasn't normally the type to beat the sunrise in the morning, so it didn't really surprise me when she slept for the entire drive, almost 4 complete hours of what appeared to be uninterrupted and solid, deep sleep. The always-reliable radio kept me company for the duration of the familiar drive, and watching V somehow miraculously managing a peaceful sleep through the constant music, random traffic stops, various twisting turns, unexpected potholes and through the rhythmic, unintentional tapping of my hand on the steering wheel as I followed along with the tunes, added to my comforting completeness.

"Wake up sleepyhead." I whispered into V's ear after parking the 'Vette.

"No way! We are here already?" V looked around in obvious incoherence and disbelief as she wiped her hair out of her face.

"Welcome home." I somewhat sarcastically stated as I opened V's door and helped her out of the car.

The rest of the afternoon was spent taking things out of re-taped, cardboard boxes and trying to get situated and settled in to a point that V and me could feel as cozy as we possibly could, considering we were at a military facility. We had done good time, and leaving early proved to be an advantageous idea. After unpacking the necessities, V and I took a short nap to allow us some rejuvenation for our evening together, although I don't really think V truly needed any additional rest than what she had

269

Jaime Perez

already received in the car during her previous and lengthy adherence to Hypnos, the Greek God of Sleep. I often wished I had the convenient ability to sleep at will, as V was so accustomed to displaying almost as if she were playfully flaunting it in my face.

Our evening together was everything I had hoped it would be. We had an ambrosial dinner at an Italian Restaurant called Gino's. It wasn't a very big place, but what it lacked in size it made up for in taste. I've never been to Italy to actually try Italian food in that setting, but I don't see how the food in Italy could have been any better than Gino's. V would have probably orally concurred, but she didn't say a single word through the entire meal. V usually speaks during meals, not this time, which lead me to believe she too felt the same about how scrumptious the meal was.

Afterwards, we attempted to talk off some of our indulgence with a romantic, evening horse-carriage ride through downtown San Antonio. V rested her head on my shoulder as the horse trotted us along the paved streets. I closed my eyes, wishing that this moment could be somehow paused or prolonged so that I could relish the pleasure and perfectness of it a little while longer. The night was fresh, and the cool, clean, familiar Southern breeze reminded me of what it feels like to be back in Texas. There was almost a subtle sweetness to the redolence in the air that I felt I could actually taste. I was so overtaken by the purity and invigoration of the night breeze that I almost mentioned to V that it was nice to not have to inhale the putrescence of rotting carcasses with every necessary yet reluctant breathe, but I refrained so as to not ruin the felicitous moment.

I looked at my watch, which was a high school graduation present from Mom and Pop, and noticed it was later than what I had anticipated. V felt me lift and glance at my wrist.

"It's late isn't it?" She asked with her cute little pout of disappointment.

"A little late." I fibbed.

"How long is this carriage ride?" V asked.

"The man charges by the half hour, so he's not going to stop until we tell him." I answered.

"You need to get up early, and I don't want my handsome soldier struggling on his first day back at Fort Sam Houston." V quickly straightened up as her smooth skin appeared like regal silk against the dim light of the full moon.

"You're right." I agreed and nodded as I gently grabbed V's hand.

The night was already perfect, so maybe ending it on such a high

270

point would be best. I called to the gentleman in front of the carriage and signaled to him that we were ready to be taken back to our vehicle, which was only a few blocks away. Within a few minutes, we were back to driving ourselves to our new temporary residence.

Once home, I had a difficult time sleeping. Part of it was due to my nap, and the other was due to resuming my military obligations with a whole new group of soldiers, officers and attitudes. It was very much like the nervousness one feels when beginning a brand new year in grade school. Even though I had already been subjected to a lifetime of pain and displeasure and so much had transpired since I was in grade school, it was approximately only two short years since I had to sit at a desk on the first day of school and wait for my name to be called so that everybody could see me lift my hand and eventually associate a name with the face. Those normal and delightfully ordinary days seemed so long ago and therefore a part of my distant past, yet they are still vividly remembered and very much alive in my thoughts as if they had occurred yesterday.

I lay in bed, waiting for the persistent restlessness to relinquish and bestow me with a little satisfaction. As I stared at the ceiling, which I often did when unable to sleep, I thought I had heard V mumble something with her sleepy, raspy voice. I assumed she was asleep, so I ignored it and continued on with my lengthy yet unsuccessful battle with the implacable demons of unrest. Again, V mumbled something. It wasn't until she placed her hand on my chest that I realized she was actually awake. V didn't wake up very much during the middle of the night; she could sleep through thunderstorms, hurricanes, passing trains, and probably through most of the explosives and gunfire that kept me awake in Long Binh. I grabbed her hand and kissed her palm.

"Why are you still awake?" V mumbled again, this time directly in my left ear and with slightly more audibility.

"My being awake is more plausible than your being awake. What are you doing awake?" I answered and asked.

"Let me show you." She responded.

V, slowly, sensuously and seductively, slithered her way on top of me like a snake soaring in air. Although my eyes were still facing the ceiling, my thoughts and sensations were elsewhere. Physically, I was lying with V, but the rest of me was now in a place that V and me loved to visit together. It was a place of mesmerizing rapture and surreal ecstasy. There were no wars here, no sorrow, no worries and no worldly concerns, yet it was still beyond description, beyond words, simply ineffable. Even referring to it

Jaime Perez

as 'heavenly' would likely be insufficient. This was beyond perfection, beyond life.

Several timeless minutes later, V flimsily and exhaustedly allowed herself to completely collapse on me as if fusing our two bodies into one. I could feel her pounding heartbeat more than I could mine, and I could feel her quiverings of vulnerability flagellate throughout my entire body like harmless and subtle currents of electricity. That morning, V and I simultaneously woke up in the same exact position that I remember being in only a few hours before. V's hair was still in my face, and her arms were still around my moist neck as she blanketed me for the duration of my brief sleep. Even though I knew I hadn't slept more than 3 hours, I felt alive and ready for anything.

"It's time for you to get ready, isn't it?" V whispered in my ear with her sexy, sleepy voice.

"Yes." I said as she slowly rolled off me and allowed me to get up while she moved over to the dry side of the bed.

I quickly took a shower and began embarking in my glorious monotony once again. Nothing outrageously exciting happened for the next few months, and I welcomed the calm, uneventful routine. It was much preferred over the violent and unpredictable extravaganza overseas. The chances of me being shot at within minutes of reporting to duty like I was in Vietnam were highly improbable, and this was the type of comforting routine I could quickly grow to enjoy. Everyday I woke up, did what was expected of me, and went to sleep. Nothing fancy, nothing to brag about; it was just my life now, and I was beginning to finally get another chance to relish and lead a somewhat normal life. Sure, I was still a soldier, but I was now a different soldier. My brief time at war provided me with a thicker and harder shell to protect me from all the daily bullshit that us soldiers have to smell everyday. In addition, the prevalent anti-war sentiments of the many civilians didn't bother me as much as before; actually, they didn't bother me at all. I guess the war numbed me to the futility of all the disagreeable rants. I would rather be shouted at than shot at.

The weeks quickly passed like the wind, sometimes going unnoticed. Weeks turned to months faster than I could notice them transpiring. My beautifully boring service at Fort Sam Houston began in mid-April, and before I realized it, we were already in December. If it were not for the holiday decorations adorning the streets of San Antonio, Christmas would have gone unbeknownst, as all the previous holidays had earlier that same year. If a holiday occurred during V's time with me, we would just spend

Through You

our time together without the weighty commitments to holidays. If a holiday occurred during V's time away, I simply passed the time by lifting weights, jogging or thinking to myself at the base's mess hall. I was away from my family, and holidays just weren't the same without everybody with which to share them. In addition, I wasn't really looking forward to holidays since Gilbert's passing. One could argue this point, but I felt it was still too soon to begin celebratory rituals. There would be many more opportunities to festively celebrate the holidays—maybe next year, but not now, not yet. Considering what we had already lost, V and I didn't feel like we were missing out on much of anything anymore. As long as we were together, there was nothing to complain about.

I kept to myself at Fort Sam Houston for the most part, fulfilling my duties, and eventually I became head cook. I spent a lot of time in the mess hall because of my specialty. Serving and preparing food allows one more than enough time to ponder on things, both pleasant and unpleasant. My preference was to be confined within my own little reminiscent world, but whenever I ventured out, I would notice that others were noticing me more than I was noticing them. I had this peculiar feeling that everyone at Fort Sam Houston knew why I was here. Nobody actually said anything to me; it was more of their body language that spoke loudly. Soldiers would laugh and joke with each other like children without a care, but whenever they were in my vicinity, their sudden silence was the only thing I could hear. It was as if they knew my son had died, and they didn't feel comfortable or respectful laughing in my presence. Sometimes I could feel them secretly discussing my situation whenever they would eat. I am sure I was the topic of conversation for most of the soldiers, if not all, at one point or another. To be quite honest, this bothered me about as much as it probably bothered the government to send me off to die against my will—none whatsoever.

For New Year's Eve, I was graciously allowed to come home for two measly days. I figured it would be nice to come home and see everyone once again. I hadn't been home or seen my family, with the exception of V, for about 10 months, but I did keep in touch with everyone by phone on a weekly basis. I had no idea when I would again be afforded the luxury of visiting home, so I didn't think twice about visiting now, just in case it would be another 10 months before the next opportunity.

Nothing drastic had changed since I was last here. Everybody was doing fine. The only minor and surprising aberration, if I could call it that, was that my sister Diana was suddenly taking a big interest in music and kept persistently harassing me for my extensive collection of 45-RPM vinyl

273

Jaime Perez

records, which I adamantly refused to hand over, but other than that, I'd have to say that things were normal, at least for now they were.

The 48 hours at home with my family felt more like 12 hours, and soon enough I was on my way back to San Antonio. Since it was V's turn to spend two weeks with me, we drove up together so that she wouldn't have to take the bus like she had been so accustomed to doing every two weeks. Once again and as expected, V fell victim to the commanding grip of lethargy, a grasp to which my wife so often succumbed. I kind of hoped that she would have stayed awake and kept me company because I wanted to discuss something with her that I've been meaning to bring up for a while now; I just never had the nerve. Maybe it was better that we didn't have this discussion in a moving car while driving. I could bring it up later. I had prolonged it this long; a few more days wouldn't hurt.

Chapter 36

I remember during the last few months of my senior year in high school, I was really anticipating beginning my "adult life" anew with V. I knew I wanted to spend the rest of my life with her, and I couldn't wait to begin doing just that. Little did I know I would unfortunately be drafted and inconveniently forced to fully pursue my highly anticipated dreams years later. I had to live through my real-life nightmares before I could truly begin living my dreams. Sure, I was married to V, but this was not the type of married life I had in mind. I can't see how it could be the type of married life that anybody would have in mind. Being unfairly separated from my wonderful wife, sick son and faithful family, being trained to ruthlessly kill an enemy I didn't truly hate or really even know were in no way enjoyable. In addition, being undeservedly displaced far from home, and having my young adult years stripped away were some of the many hindering obstacles of life that were placed before me, but they were not insurmountable—as I have already proved.

I can't say that I would have successfully endured these unexpected vexations if I could have prophetically been made aware of them beforehand; this would be utterly pretentious on my part. Sometimes misfortune is unpredictable and or unavoidable, and it is these two qualities of misfortune that allow one to overcome and persevere such tragedy. If someone would have told me years ago that I would have to endure the passing of my first born son, spend the first four years of my marriage away from my wife and family, and be dumped in a hostile war zone to witness more death and inhumanity than can be imagined, I honestly don't know if I would have been able to persevere through the aggravating and agonizing anticipation of what was to come without driving myself insane or taking my own life, whichever were to occur first.

When I was a young boy, probably about 6 or 7 years old, Pop would

275

Jaime Perez

have these "father to son" talks with me whenever we were alone. These talks consisted mainly of practical advice and moral adages that Pop wanted me to use as tools to help me make wise, prudent decisions in life and to guide me in becoming a just individual. One of the things I remember Pop telling me was that "…there is always going to be somebody out there who has things far worse than you do. No matter how bad things are, they can always be worse." Words like these are very difficult to accept when you feel ill fated beyond the ability to cope, but they are probably true, even though at one point in my life I didn't think my life, or anybody else's life, could be any worse.

A new year and a new decade had begun. It was 1970, and our nosy and ethnocentric country was still at war in Vietnam. The 60s were not very good to me, especially towards the latter part of the decade. I still had a little over a year of time to serve in San Antonio, and I was pretty sure that when I got out of this "military asylum/prison" men would still be needlessly losing their lives overseas. V and I hadn't really celebrated any holiday since I had arrived in San Antonio, and Valentine's Day was coming up. This year the holiday for lovers would opportunistically fall on a Saturday, which further evoked me with a newfound, celebratory desire to embark on something special. It was a new year, a new decade, and I felt an enthusiastic sensation to start living life once again now that it seemed feasible to see beyond the dissipating clouds of dismay that once impermeably clouded my ability to foresee anything remotely promising.

My hopes for a memorable evening were short lived and shattered before I could even begin planning anything special. V usually calls me on Friday evening before she gets dropped off at the bus station by my in-laws to let me know that she is on her way and to inform me of her bus' arrival time in San Antonio. I got the call; it just wasn't the familiar call I looked forward to receiving like clockwork every two weeks.

"Honey." V uttered with an ill-toned voice. I could barely hear her, for she sounded weakened and more dead than alive. She sounded like somebody who had just had her tonsils removed.

Immediately I knew something was not quite right. Just by the tone of her "Honey", I already knew she wasn't going to be able to visit this time. "What's the matter V?" I asked as I suddenly felt a shortness of breath as if somebody had unexpectedly kicked me between the legs.

"I'm afraid I won't be able to make it up there this time around. I have been feeling extremely ill. I thought it was nothing to worry about, but it comes and goes."

Through You

"What comes and goes? What are you feeling?" I limited myself to two questions even though it seemed like I had hundreds more to which I wanted answers, but I didn't want to overwhelm V, who already sounded defeated and torn.

"I feel nauseated and weak. I don't have the urge to eat, yet I still puke up colorless vomit. I was going to visit the doctor, but it went away for about two days. Then it came back again. This has been going on for the past week now. Every morning it's the same horrible feeling. I'm so sorry Honey. I wanted to do something special with you this weekend, but now I can't even see you." V said with a little more liveliness, albeit a distressed liveliness.

I knew my wife. If I didn't quickly say anything to comfort her, she would likely end up saturating the phone with her tears. I said the only thing that came to mind. "It's o.k. V. We have so many more Valentine's Days ahead of us in which we can do so many special things. I don't like the way you sound. It may be something serious like a stomach virus. Why don't you go see the doctor anyway?" I asked.

"I already called, right before I called you. I have an appointment for this Monday, the 16th at 8:00 A.M. Daddy will be taking me. I am staying with them for the weekend." She responded.

"Good", was all I could pathetically manage to spurt out.

"I don't mean to be rude, but I would like to get some more rest." V expressed as if she was pleading for permission.

"Of course V. You need your rest. It will be good for you. I want you to do me a favor though. Actually, I am demanding it of you, not asking you."

"What? Anything." V asked.

"I am going to call you at your parents' house as soon as I get the chance on Monday, probably around 1900 hours. Be expecting my call because I want to know exactly what the doctor tells you. I don't want to have to be uninformed and worried any longer than I absolutely have to. OK?" I asked her rhetorically yet with authority and sternness.

"OK, of course. I will wait by the phone for your call." She assured me.

"All right. I will let you try to get some rest." I said.

"I'm sorry Beltran." She timidly said.

"You have nothing for which to be sorry. You will just simply have to make it up to me somehow." I said flirtatiously and with a hint of playful lewdness.

277

Jaime Perez

"I will be looking forward to compensating you for any inconvenience I may have caused." V tried to utter with a sense of sensuality, but her illness commanded her tone, allowing for only a minor projection of V's usual sexiness.

"You get some rest. I love you." I said.

"You know I love you too, but I will remind you when I see you again." V said, this time with a seductively heightened and convincing tone, almost like that of an experienced, pornographic movie star.

"I can hardly wait. Good bye V."

"Good bye my soldier." V said before hanging up the phone.

Although I was really looking forward to doing something with V this weekend, spending Valentine's Day alone in San Antonio, 400 miles separating me from my wife, was far less disheartening than wasting it without her in the inferno of Vietnam, cringing every quarter second that a bullet or explosive went off. Bombs and gunfire were as constant and certain as the falling sands of an overturned hourglass, yet I never failed to instinctively cower at the sound of these failed attempts to end my life.

That whole uneventful weekend I did nothing but sleep like I was in a temporary coma. My oversleeping forced me to lose track of the day and the time, often waking up thinking that it was late for my routine duty. The only advantage of acquiescing to this uncommon lethargy was that it made the weekend seem shorter. Considering I was anxious to hear from V immediately after her Monday doctor's appointment, I welcomed the convenient acceleration of time.

Monday, the 16th, started off like any other day. I was well rested physically, but my mind was still a little uneasy. I was anticipating that my wife was well, and her illness was trivial and nothing to lose sleep over, even though I lost no sleep whatsoever.

It wasn't more than 10 minutes after arriving to my room at the end of the day that the phone rang. It could only be one person, but I still answered with relative uncertainty, not because I wondered who was calling but because I wondered what V found out from the doctor.

"V?" I answered.

"You're a psychic now?" V joked.

"Who else could it be? I was only expecting to hear from you. Well, spare me the crippling suspense, what did you find out?" I asked as I noticed V's voice sounded much more healthy and alive than the last time we spoke. I naturally extrapolated that she was better now.

"Well, I kind of hoped I could tell you this in person, but I don't know if I can hold it in any longer. Plus, it probably wouldn't be fair to you to have to wait and not be the first to know. Well, the first aside from me and the doctor." V answered.

"V, this isn't funny. Can you eliminate the unnecessary foreword and move forward to the plot?" I requested of her.

"We're pregnant again Beltran. My nausea was nothing but expected morning sickness. It is completely normal. I am a little over a month into the pregnancy."

I heard V's answer loud and clear, but it left me stunned and motionless. My mind shutdown and my ears muted everything. I suddenly began to see blurry, so I sat down and wiped away my tears. I didn't know what to say. Even if I did know what to say, I would have probably been unable to say it anyway. I felt a tightening of my stomach muscles, and I began to feel warm inside as if I was about to suffer from non-lethal fit of spontaneous combustion. I accidentally dropped the phone on my lap, and I waited for the giddiness to subside. I felt like I was riding a carousel upside down, and it wouldn't stop. I faintly heard V's voice from the phone's speaker, but I wasn't reacting to it. I simply remained motionless, in a state of momentary paralysis. As unlikely as it may sound, I don't even think my heart was beating.

"Hey!! Are you there?" V asked emphatically. I could hear her a little louder, and my senses were starting to function again.

"I'm sorry V. I…I don't know what just happened." I finally answered after what seemed like several minutes of an out-of-the-body, surreal experience. I was excited, scared and happy all at the same time.

"Did you hear any of what I said?" V asked.

"Only the first part, the part that mattered." I responded.

"Are you crying?" V asked me with her emotions pouring out from within her. I could tell the second she asked me if I was a psychic by her trembling and fragile voice that she was crying even before she called me.

I went on, without directly answering her question. "V, I had been meaning to discuss the possibility of having another child with you, but I just never got around to it. I didn't know how you would take it, and I didn't want you to think I was rushing into things. I can't explain it, but it just felt like the right thing to do—try to have another child."

"Are you serious? I wanted to talk to you about this as well, but the moment never seemed right. It's like my, I mean our pregnancy, was an accurate response to our unspoken wishes and desires to conceive once

Jaime Perez

again. The doctor said that couples who go through what we have gone through often become reluctant to discuss or act upon having another child, but he assured me that the only right time to resume with our lives is whenever we feel it's right. It's different for everybody. There is no fixed rule or law that states when one should or should not move on, or something like that."

"Well I am ready V. I want to be a father again. I want to fulfill my purpose and my longings." I assured her.

"And I want to be the mother of your child once again. I wanted to begin an attempt at motherhood, but I felt rude and inconsiderate to mention it if you hadn't done so first. I honestly didn't know if you even wanted to ever attempt having a child again, and I would understand if you were completely against the idea. I must admit that deep down inside I knew I was going to want to give this one more try. I wasn't ready to give up on a life-long desire just yet. I still have hopes for us being parents Beltran. I can see it, feel it, taste it, and now I just want to live it." V managed to tremulously utter through her pervasive yet subtle weeping.

After several more minutes of speaking to my wife, we finally hung up, even though it was a little more difficult for me to let go than I expected. I hung up feeling overly excited and rejuvenated with life. I spent the rest of the evening recalling the entire phone conversation in my head so that I could hold on to this memory as long as I could.

V was right. This news would have been better off shared in person, but something like this was impossible to prolong. At that specific moment, I felt like embracing my wife and allowing our shared tears of joy to mix and become one, part of me and part of her. Her being out of reach made me want her even more. Even though I had just heard the best news I could have possibly received, I knew this meant that V might not be able to endure driving 5 hours on a Greyhound bus every two weeks to visit me, so we were going to have to make new arrangements.

I wasn't able to ideally come home for two weeks at a time on a regular basis, but I did manage to squeeze in most weekends; and two days home with my family and pregnant wife is better than nothing. For the next 8 months, I did everything I could to accommodate my wife's needs. At times she felt like I was over-pampering her, but I knew she liked it. I didn't even allow her to tie her own shoes, so I did it for her whenever I was home. She was fragile, and I planned to treat her as if she were a delicate and crystal clear snowflake in the palm of my hand, with utmost precaution and sensitivity. Without fail, V made her regularly scheduled doctor visits, and I made sure of it when I was away, calling her to remind her a day in advance. My long distance bills quadrupled from all the calls I was making to check up on V, but this was trivial. I wanted to do everything I possibly could from 400 miles away to make V feel at ease and to eliminate the feeling that I was unable to physically be with her during these vulnerable times that can easily go from comfortably normal to perilous and volatile in less time than it takes one to blink. According to V's doctor, everything was going well, and this was a comforting sign, especially considering the heightened possibility of once again giving birth to a child with a congenital heart disease.

The following 7 to 8 months after I found out of our pregnancy were difficult because of the consistently erratic ambivalence that often managed to seep through my skull and dampen my thoughts. Optimism was difficult to attain, but I did everything I could to stop worrying about what I could do nothing about. One minute I felt hopeful; the next I felt hopeless. One minute I could picture V and I preparing our healthy child for the first day of school, celebrating birthday parties, and strolling the sands of South Padre Island barefoot, the 3 of us together, but the unhealthy envisage of burying another child always managed to pour salt on my sweet daydreams. Mentally I was as volatile as a loosely hanging pendulum being uncontrollably flailed by conflicting, fierce storm-like winds, and all I could do was wait, wait, and wait some more.

My routine at Fort Sam Houston did little to manage my self-diagnosed unsoundness, but the little that it managed to offer was probably all I needed to keep my sanity within reach. I went about my days in constant thought, often not even being cognizant to my immediate surroundings. I was a camouflaged, yet obvious wreck, walking like a zombie driven by pensiveness and the desire for normalcy, not blood.

Every encouraging conversation I had with V following a doctor's visit pushed me one short step closer to the light of stability and further away from the dark, abysmal pits of mental insalubriousness. After several doctor appointments later, V informed me that barring an unlikely premature birth, we would be expecting the delivery of our child during early to mid-September. The baby was developing and growing at a normal rate; so far V and I couldn't have asked for things to transpire any better than they were.

It was now early August, and I needed to find out if it would be possible for me to take a leave of absence to be present for our child's delivery back home in McAllen. I didn't expect to be deprived of being

Jaime Perez

allowed to leave for such a glorious occasion; I just wasn't expecting my request to be so graciously granted. Much to my surprise, my commanding officer gave me no resistance at all. I would be allowed a full two weeks! I just simply filled out a form with the specific days being requested, and that was it. My hands noticeably shook as I slowly wrote down the chosen days conscientiously selected from a US Army calendar conveniently hanging on my commanding officers wall. September 10th through September 23rd were the days I decided on. I hoped the doctor was right in his calculation for the estimated delivery date because I didn't want to miss this. I was there for Gilbert's delivery, and I had no intentions of missing this one either.

Chapter 37

Back in 1968 when we had Gilbert, V and I had decided we wanted to know our child's gender beforehand. This time, we were going to wait until our child was in our hands to find out if our child was a boy or a girl; therefore, we didn't have a name picked out beforehand. I don't know why we both chose to do things differently this time; we just did. I guess maybe knowing a child's gender is far less important and naturally becomes overshadowed by whether or not the child appears to be normal and healthy, which, judging by our telephone conversations, was obviously V's and my primary concern.

The evening of September 9th was here, and I left San Antonio for McAllen, Texas like a fugitive evading the law. I didn't pack a thing. I simply notified my commanding officer and drove off without thinking twice, still in my camouflage uniform and black Army boots. The next time I would step on Fort Sam Houston soil, I would be a father, granted everything turned out fine. I didn't even want to consider the possibility of losing a second child, but the heart-stopping thought always surfaced whenever I got overly excited about everything. Honestly, I don't think I would be able to survive another loss of a child. V would likely feel the same. A person can only take so much before he/she becomes irreparably damaged for life, whether mentally, emotionally or physically. V and I were putting ourselves at risk, but we knew going into this that anything could happen, especially the unbearable.

Last week when I last saw V, she was extremely rotund. I wasn't sure if she would now appear to be bigger than before. When I arrived home on the evening of September 9th, 1970, the first thing I saw when I walked in to my in-laws' house was V. I had never seen my wife so plump and seemingly ready to explode. It was new to everybody. Because of Gilbert's premature birth, none of us had witnessed V so full and spherical. Hugging

283

Jaime Perez

V was useless because her stomach disallowed me from actually getting a true, heartfelt embrace. Her belly kept us at least a foot away from each other, although it felt more like a yard. My father-in-law would jokingly call her Buddha because of her stomach's exaggerated protrusion, and Virginia would abashedly scold her husband reminding him that Buddhists might not like his blasphemous humor. If you ask me, V was bigger than Buddha; of course, this was only judging from drawings and sculptures I had seen of the deity in books or museums. I never joked with V during her pregnancy because I had this silly feeling that making her laugh might induce her pregnancy. As silly as this may sound, I was right.

About one week after I had arrived, the whole family was together at Mom and Pop's house. We weren't really doing anything specific, just spending time together and waiting. I was beginning to worry that I may have miscalculated the days that I chose to visit because a week had already passed, and nothing other than V's size hinted that it was time. It was already September 17th when I reluctantly cracked a joke about V that was the *coup de grace*.

V and I were watching the local news on my parents' newly purchased, Zenith television, along with Mom, Pop, Al and Virginia. They were reporting something about a fireman rescuing a little girl's Persian cat from a tree at a nearby park. V was likely feeling a little romantic and vulnerable because she started cuddling with me and brushing the back of her hand on my stubbly face as we sat next to each other on my parents' love seat. This was the most affectionate V had become in the past several months. I think all the teasing from everybody, except me, was beginning to innocuously affect V, eventually she was going to start feeling insecure and emotionally fragile.

"Would you still love me if I somehow remained this big after giving birth?" V whispered in my right ear.

"Of course V."

"No you wouldn't." Her voice went from a whisper to one level softer than normal speech.

"Yes I would." I looked her in the face as I tried to answer her convincingly but still in a sentimental manner. My next words were the inducers of labor, the water breakers. "V you are my everything. You are my world, even if your tummy and our world are almost the same size!"

V broke the silence, as well as her water, with an outbreak of laughter. I really didn't think what I had said was that amusing, or maybe my mind was just on other things to notice anything funny at that given moment.

She grabbed my right arm tightly. At this point, her laughter stopped and quickly became grunts of pain joined with winces of tenseness. No words came out of her mouth, but I knew exactly what she was trying to say.

I slowly picked up V and walked her to Al's roomy station wagon, placing her in the back seat with me. Like a pre-planned military drill, everyone grabbed their things and simultaneously proceeded to the vehicles. I rode with Al and Virginia while Mom and Pop followed in their vehicle. The McAllen General Hospital was not far away, but it sure as hell seemed days away. I did everything I could, which was really nothing, to make the drive to the hospital tolerable for my wife.

We drove up to the Emergency Room driveway, and Al called out to a nurse drinking a Coca-cola outside on a bench. Within seconds V was placed on a stretcher and being frantically rolled into the labor and delivery unit. I stayed by V's side, talking to her to try to help keep her calm. I don't recall what I was saying to her, but I was saying something. Regardless, she probably couldn't hear anything I was saying amidst the aura of panic and frenzy that probably impeded V's ability to discern my words. Mom, Pop, Virginia and Al remained in the waiting room while I confidently made my way into the delivery room and stood by my wife's side, holding her tightly clenched hand as if she was hanging on to avoid falling off a cliff.

I remember V being in labor for several hours with Gilbert before the nurses began ultimately displaying a sense of urgency. This time the sense of urgency was immediate. I didn't know if this was a good sign or something to be concerned about. I felt as if I had been here before, but some of the things were a little different. Perhaps I dreamt this but lost any recollection of the dream, until now. I began sweating and feeling warm inside, but I was not going to faint like the last time, even though a hint of vertigo was making it difficult for me to remain strong and steadfast.

Just as I felt my eyes closing in submission to unconsciousness, I thought I had heard the cries of a baby. My eyes quickly opened as I listened profoundly for another sign of new life. Once again, the piercing cries penetrated beyond the plethora of adult voices all uttering unfamiliar medical terminology to one another. With everybody talking all at once and shuffling all about, I didn't know how anything productive was getting done, but it was getting done. I felt V's hand gradually release her clutching grip; this startled me so much that my heart appeared to skip a beat. I looked at V; she was smiling as relieved from everything. The infant's cries

Jaime Perez

became louder and ever so clear. Seconds later, the doctor was holding our new born, upside down as a nurse began to cut the umbilical cord.

"It's a boy. Congratulations Mr. and Mrs. Perez! You've given birth to a healthy baby boy!" The doctor and nurses instantly began wiping the afterbirth off our son's delicate body and brought our son to V's arms. I let go of V's hand to allow her to properly hold our son at her bosom. All I could do was place both my hands over my mouth and try to contain the outpour of joy. At that point, I couldn't tell who was crying more, my son or me. Although I couldn't hear V crying, her tears were coming out just as profusely as mine. The moment was surreal, but nonetheless poignant.

I held our son for a few minutes and ended up crying all over him. I was speechless, yet I didn't feel words were relevant or necessary at a time like this.

"Jaime." V uttered as I confoundedly looked at her with teary eyes.

"What?" I asked, wiping my eyes.

"Jaime. I want to name him Jaime. I like that name. Is this all right with you?" V asked.

"Sure. Where did you pick it out from?" I wondered.

"From thin air. I told myself I was going to randomly think of name based on our child's gender immediately after giving birth. The first name I thought of was Jaime."

"Then Jaime it is. Jaime Perez." I said, concurring.

"Will you go tell our parents that they have a grandson?" V requested of me.

"Huh? Oh yeah, I forgot they are waiting outside. I'll be right back." I kissed V and carefully handed her our son.

As I slowly made my way out of the delivery room, I heard the doctor ask V for our son. He wanted to run some standard precautionary tests to make sure there are no complications or concerns. After hearing this, I suddenly felt empty and uneasy again. There was probably nothing to worry about, but I couldn't help it.

I made my way to the sitting area where Mom, Pop and my in-laws were anxiously waiting. Diana and Sarah had arrived and were now sitting next to them, and everybody got up and began walking towards me the second they saw me.

For a few seconds, I couldn't speak. It was too real, too perfect, too overwhelming. I just stood in front of my family in the middle of the hospital hallway on the 3rd floor and said nothing.

"Well son. Tell us something." Pop requested.

286

"We have officially brought Mr. Jaime Perez into the world." I said.

"It's a boy?" Sarah asked as Diana expectedly started to display her emotions before anyone else.

"Yes" I answered as I simultaneously received 6 firm hugs, leaving me pleasantly smothered from all directions. "The doctor is going to run some quick tests to make sure there are no concerns, but I am sure everything will be all right." I said as I tried to comfort everybody, including myself.

"We weren't expecting you out so soon." Mom said.

"Yes, I know. It all happened so fast." I added.

"I don't know what you told her in our living room, but, whatever it was, it worked." Al said jokingly as Diana and Sarah looked at each other with a look of slight confusion.

After a few minutes, the doctor passed by us as he was apparently making his way to the V's room. I got his attention in hopes that he could provide me with some comforting information concerning Jaime.

"Doctor. How is he?" I asked as I momentarily wished I hadn't.

"Mr. Perez. I was just on my way to talk to you and your wife, but since I have you here, I will tell you now. Everything looks good Mr. Perez. There is nothing that signifies a reason for concern. I understand the misfortune you experienced with your firstborn, and because of this, we will continue to keep a close eye on your son. I don't want you to worry yourself sick over something that isn't there. If there were reason to worry, I would be up front with you and tell you. Your son fits the medical definition of a healthy baby boy. He couldn't be any healthier if it were possible." He said with a convincing smile, placing his hand on my shoulder as a sign of assurance.

"Thank you, for everything." I said.

The doctor smiled as if thanking him was not necessary and made his way to V's room to share the news with her. I turned back to my family who had obviously heard the doctor's comments.

"When do we get to see our grandson?" Mom asked.

"I guess you can ask the doctor when he comes out of V's room. I don't exactly know where the newborns are held. Would you excuse me for a few minutes? I have to do something really quick. V is likely going to have to stay the night here and be released tomorrow morning. I will come back and stay with her so that she won't be alone."

"Where are you going? You don't have your car." Pop asked.

"I don't need a car Pop. I'll be all right." I said and set forth to do something I felt was very necessary.

Jaime Perez

I realized I had about a week left before I had to return to Fort Sam Houston, and once V was home, I was not going to want to leave her or Jaime's sight. I set off to do what I had to do in order to feel a sense of closure and contentment. This whole day had been a big blur, an unsteady, constant whirlwind of emotions and unfolding circumstances, and now I had the opportunity to put the finishing touches on this masterful accomplishment.

Valley Memorial Gardens was quite a walk away from the hospital, but I felt the walk would instill me with a much-needed therapeutic relief, a cathartic closure to conclude the chaos.

The day was beautiful. It was sunny yet invigoratingly fresh, a combination not too frequent in the Deep South. I felt good about today, and I had good reason to feel this way. A lot of the doubt that I had managed to contain for the passed several months had quickly diminished to nothing more than otiose memories unworthy of reflection.

As I approached the open black, wrought iron cemetery gate, I shamefully realized that I hadn't visited my son's gravesite since the day he was put to rest. In all honesty, I often felt the next time I would visit this cemetery would be when they would fly my body from overseas to bury me next to my son. Luckily, I was very wrong about that.

Without even thinking, I effortlessly found it. There it was: *Our Baby Son Gilberto Perez/August 22, 1968- March 30, 1969*—the imprints of his little shoes resting in the center of his headstone. The glossy headstone still shined brilliantly as if he was buried very recently. I could see my reflection on it, as I dropped to my knees.

I knew I had a lot to say to my son that I didn't get to share with him due to my being away and also to his untimely death. Without a doubt, we were denied many father-to-son discussions, the kind of priceless discussions that help shape a little boy into an honorable man. I wasn't particularly a religious or even spiritual man, but I didn't see the harm in having a few postmortem words with my dearly missed son. I didn't know where to start, so I just let my heart do the talking as the rest of me just listened.

Son, I'll never get to fully understand why things have happened the way they have. Maybe some things aren't meant to be understood, just accepted and tolerated. All I can do is remain strong through all the incomprehensible adversity that surrounds us and do everything in my power to be the man that I wished you could have had the chance to be. The world doesn't always grant us our wishes, but if I could have had just one wish granted to me in my tumultuous life, I would have wished for you to be able to grow up and live the full life that you deserved so that you could make fun of your old man, tease his funky, out-dated hairstyles, criticize his music and have a chance at the life that was stripped from you. I know I can't change anything now, but I want you to know that, as strange as this may sound, you have helped me through much of what I've been through in my life. I've learned more about life from you than I have from anybody who has ever lived. For this I thank you. No matter what happens from here on, I will always feel incomplete without you in my life, and not one day will pass that I don't think about you.

    I stayed on my knees as silent as the souls that were resting around me and wondered if there was anything else I had to say. There probably were so many other things that I had failed to mention, but I could always come back and have a chat with my son whenever I felt like it. I didn't want to leave, but dawn was beginning to set. Walking alone this late at night was not a very good idea. Before getting back on my feet, I kissed my little boy's shoe imprint and touched his headstone one more time before leaving. I reached in my back pant pocket and took out a photo I had placed there earlier in the day. It was the same family photo that V had sent me in the mail while I was away, the photo that literally helped save my life during my most difficult times. I placed it on the corner of Gilbert's headstone underneath his inscribed metal plate; this way V and I would be there with him, the way it was supposed to be.

    I began my walk back home and made it before the night reached its darkest point. I got in my car and drove back to the hospital to spend the night with V and to hopefully get to see my son, even if he was sleeping. During the short drive, I found myself smiling at nothing. Or maybe I was just happy that things were going be all right. I parked in the visitor parking lot of the hospital and looked up at the sky before entering the multilevel building. I noticed the crescent-shaped moon shining above me. The top portion of the moon was completely covered by clouds, the only part showing was the lower part. Slightly above the moon were two stars positioned approximately where two eyes would fall on a happy face. It appeared to be a gigantic smile. Apparently, I wasn't the only one smiling.

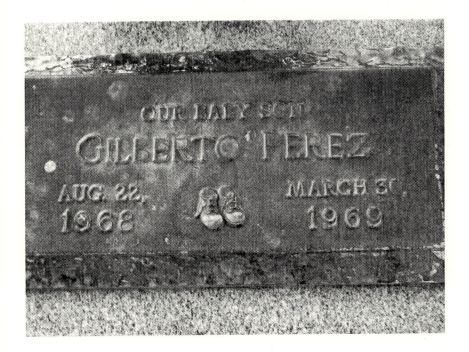

DEPARTMENT OF THE ARMY

CERTIFICATE OF APPRECIATION

In recognition of the active service of

SPECIALIST FIVE (E-5)

The United States Army presents this testimonial of esteem and gratitude for Faithful Performance of duty

13 MAY 1970
DATE

W. C. WESTMORELAND
General, United States Army
Chief of Staff